The Dissension Process

The Dissension Process

Markus James

This is a work of fiction. Names, characters, places and incidents either are the product of the author's imagination or are used fictitiously. Any resemblance to actual persons, living or dead, events, or locales is entirely coincidental.

First paperback edition February 2022

ISBN: 978-1-7397284-0-3

www.thedissensionprocess.com

You're so much more than you'll ever know.

Prologue

"How much further man?"

"Two minutes tops, Kyle. Show some fricking patience, will ya?"

"I *am* showing patience," Kyle snapped. "Just be nice to know where the hell we're going exactly."

"Lucky you, here's the entrance to the place," Dan said, stopping before a chained gate that fenced off a large industrial site before effortlessly scaling over it with a single leap.

"Coming?"

"Yeah, hang on. Some of us don't have super reflexes y'know."

"Like I wouldn't trade it in to be able to shoot ice blasts," Dan replied as he watched his reluctant friend haul himself over the gate with some difficulty.

"Where now?"

"Just there."

Kyle looked towards a large warehouse in the background, among at least a half dozen within the grounds.

"How many of us are going to be there anyway?"

"Not loads I imagine, probably just enough to get what Miles has planned done. He didn't go through every detail with me," Dan said as the two began walking towards the warehouse. "Looking forward to finding out though."

"I guess," Kyle replied as they neared the door of the building. Dan then stopped for a moment.

"You know you can trust me, don't you?" he told Kyle.

"It's not you I don't trust," Kyle meekly responded. "We don't know what's behind that door."

"Haven't you ever wondered what it'd be like to meet others like us?"

"All I've ever cared mate is improving our own crappy lives. That's why I'm here now."

"And we will, with Miles and his guys behind us. Remember, we're the real elite of society here, the rest of the big wide world just don't realise it yet."

"And if things go south in there?"

"We bail. You know you have the power to back us up too, I'm relying on you as much as you are me, man."

Kyle gave a hesitant look back.

"With me?"

".......Yeah."

Dan gave a reassuring nod back as he grabbed the handle to the door and pulled it open. Kyle followed him inside, readying himself as best he could before closing the door behind him.

Chapter 1

Idiocy...

Jamie stood poised, waiting to make her move with the usual fearful anticipation despite her disbelief at the scene that was unfolding before her eyes. The situation always brought a tense feeling that something could go badly wrong, regardless of the fact she had never failed before.

But opportunities like this didn't come by all the time.

Ignoring any further cautious thoughts, Jamie swung her arm in the usual backhanded scything motion, launching a fast-paced wave of energy towards the other side of the road. The resulting hard slam subsequently echoed across the street.

Easy part over.

Attempting to rise, the stricken target clutched at his arm while groaning in agony as the building next to him continued to burn. Before he even had a chance to compose himself, he felt someone roughly grabbing the back of his neck.

Nothing.

The disgruntled teenager then began to thrash about, attempting to swing his other uninjured arm into his assailant only for it to be caught with their other free hand. A burst of flame then erupted from his open palm without warning.

At last. Jamie held on as she felt the familiar flow of power entering her body through her left hand that was still grasping the young man's neck, a torrent of energy flooding her torso and limbs with the activation of his ability and allowing hers to take effect.

Crassly booting her 'donor' to the ground once enough of his power had been transferred, Jamie took a moment to attempt to use the newly gained ability. Within seconds, a small flame manifested within her hand, heat emanating from it though surprisingly without any accompanying burning sensation. Satisfied, she turned to leave.

She then suddenly felt a forceful blow to the square of her back that knocked her down to the pavement. A searing pain erupted from her forearm as she skidded upon the concrete before coming to a halt. Taking no time to inspect the damage, she turned around in silent anger to see the still-injured youth about to aim his unimpaired hand towards her.

Preparing himself, the vengeful teenager then hesitated as he got a closer look at his attacker underneath the black hoodie covering their head.

....That a girl?

Taking advantage of the pause, Jamie rolled backwards onto her feet and launched another kinetic energy wave, catching her opponent in the chest as he landed hard on the floor once more.

Jamie stood over him as he struggled to catch his breath, winded and barely able to deal with the pain still coming from his arm that had taken the brunt of the initial energy attack. To continue a further onslaught would just be overkill she reasoned, despite her irritation at being struck from behind.

She then looked to her own arm, her jacket sleeve very visibly torn to reveal a raw gash underneath.

Great...

"Ah, she arrives."

"Sorry, sorry, sorry..." Jamie bleated with the little breath she had within her. "Not too late I hope?"

"Just the usual ten minutes," Gabrielle jested. "Actually it might only be eight this time."

"I'm sure the road got half a mile longer or something."

"Or you just left the house late as always."

"Nah, I'm gonna go with the road."

"Yeah, yeah... So, the usual place for lunch?"

"Sure, why not?"

"Sounds good," Gabrielle replied before casting an odd look as she caught an unusual scent in the air. "Though might I ask did you walk past a bonfire on the way over?"

Jamie felt a cold sensation down her spine.

"Why do you say that?"

"Er, because you smell like you have?" Gabrielle sarcastically pointed out before noticing her friend's torn jacket sleeve. Without asking, she held Jamie's arm up, immediately viewing the wound through the tear.

"Dare I assume this isn't your average injury?"

“I…came across someone with powers like us,” Jamie blurted out, immediately seeing the worried look in Gabrielle’s eyes. “Don’t worry! He posed no serious threat to me.”

“You sure about that?”

“He could shoot fire from his hands,” Jamie answered. “Encountered him trying to burn down a jeweller’s shop window.”

“You mean *you* were the aggressor?” Gabrielle questioned with a notably incredulous tone.

“I didn’t *deliberately* engage him if that’s your main concern,” Jamie responded defensively. “It was a pre-emptive strike in case he turned his attention onto me. I managed to take him out with a kinetic energy attack. After that, he was in too much pain to stop me taking his power for myself.”

“Was it really worth the risk trying to get that power though? Especially considering your absorption ability only works when someone’s actively using their own power,” Gabrielle retorted.

“Well I didn’t have to take it but considering what I caught him doing with it in the first place and what he could’ve done to me or anyone else, it’s probably for the best he no longer has access to it for the time being.”

“And the arm scrape?”

“Believe it or not, I actually just tripped on the pavement while trying to rush over here. As you can see, it’s a gash and not a burn.”

“Always the klutz,” Gabrielle sighed in a more light-hearted voice, to Jamie’s relief. “I suppose that at least vindicates me opting to give you some of my power for self-defence on a regular basis.”

“I guess it does,” Jamie smiled. “Wanna see what I took from him?”

"What, out in the open?"

"Nah, down that alleyway."

"If you want," Gabrielle said, trying not to sound interested despite actually being somewhat intrigued.

"Alright," Jamie replied as the two walked over to the enclosed gap between the buildings. "Stand behind me."

"Ready when you are."

Jamie held her hand out as the youth had, trying to channel her absorbed power like always. Gabrielle quickly attempted to shield herself as a huge flame emerged out of nowhere from her friend's hand which then quickly dissipated as fast as it had shot out.

"Discreet much?!"

"Sorry, haven't had any time to practice with it," Jamie responded. "Pretty cool though, right?"

"I guess so," Gabrielle replied, grateful that nobody had been walking nearby. "And with that, shall we finally go grab something to eat?"

"Lead the way," Jamie answered, the duo subsequently departing the car park entrance to the supermarket where Gabrielle worked and walking down the street. Lying did not come naturally to her but Jamie acknowledged its usefulness in times of need, particularly given instances involving her powers.

But then she also didn't deny how reckless her secret activities were either, to Gabrielle's unknowing credit.

Did she have to engage with the fire-wielding miscreant in the midst of his act of vandalism? Not really. Had she actually been at any threat at all from being attacked in the first place? Probably unlikely. Did she care at all for potentially breaking the youth's arm and forcibly taking his powers against his will?

Absolutely not.

As fortuitous as she had been to gain the interesting new ability, however, the risk of exposure had been higher than her usual encounters. Most empowered individuals she came across were not foolish enough to blatantly use their abilities out in such a public space but to respond in kind herself admittedly had not been her own brightest moment, even with the thick hood on her jacket giving her a layer of disguise to her distinctive appearance underneath.

Whether or not the building that he had torched would be salvaged by the fire department on the other hand was down to someone else's intervention – she had achieved what she had set out to do and sticking around to risk further having her true nature discovered wasn't part of that.

Not to mention facing losing her best and only real friend's trust in the process too.

From a casual observer's point of view of the two girls walking side by side down the street, they couldn't have looked any more different; Gabrielle with her wavy, natural blonde hair and brown eyes while sporting her conforming work attire gave off a more conventional social appearance.

Jamie, however, with her brightly coloured purple, red and pink hair was an immediate contrast in addition to her far paler complexion and clear-green eyes. Her clothes also bordered more on the masculine side, choosing to wear a loose-fitting black t-shirt with a pair of three-quarter length, black cargo trousers. Her footwear consisted of a pair of black skater shoes woven with pink laces and topping things off was a slightly oversized black hoodie that completely obscured her slender frame.

Jamie herself had always considered their friendship an oddity, though based more on their personalities – being an introverted, self-admitted nerd growing up before finding an interest in alternative subculture in recent times, she had always been the polar opposite of the more confident and extroverted Gabrielle who blended in with the rest of 'normal' society.

For whatever reason though, the connection had always been there between them and they had experienced the best of times with each other.

And, notably, the absolute worst.

The bleak reality of what Jamie had seen her life devolve into in recent times, notably struggling to come to terms with the loss of her entire family, had been a difficult burden to bear. At times, it seemed like engaging in her incredible powers was all she had to counter the resentment and misery crippling her from the inside and even that felt as though it was barely enough to escape the constant dark cloud hovering over her.

But why did everything end up like this?

Jamie had never been oblivious to the fact she had grown up in a relatively prosperous household compared to other kids her age that had endured rougher childhoods. Being the only child of a successful scientist had afforded her the luxury and comfort of a secure home in a decent suburban neighbourhood just on the outskirts of London. Additionally she had inherited her father's intellectual prowess, with which she regularly scored the highest school grades in every subject she took, as well as being bi-lingual in both English and French courtesy of her mother's native homeland influence.

For all her capabilities, however, being adept at socialising was not one of them which had left her with very limited friends in her secondary school years, the notable exception being Gabrielle with the two becoming randomly acquainted after being seated next to each other during, ironically enough, French lessons.

The lack of an extensive friend circle failed to bother her though as she proved highly focused and dedicated towards following in her father's footsteps of curing diseases of different varieties on a genetic level – something he himself had managed to achieve to a small degree in helping to push the boundaries of gene therapy, leading to the successful treatments of some inherent genetic diseases that had previously been incurable.

Combined with Gabrielle who granted her at least a friendship with someone her own age, life was seemingly perfect.

In the middle of her final year of school just after her sixteenth birthday, Jamie found herself unexpectedly having to deal with her father's sudden hospitalisation after collapsing at work. Subsequent scans revealed an aggressive form of cancer known as small-cell carcinoma had already spread to several other organs long before the diagnosis was reached. Ironically, the man who had helped cure some of the most devastating diseases in the world was unable to save himself from his own terminal ailment, succumbing a mere fortnight after the cancer had been discovered. A grateful medical and scientific community mourned his loss, no less than by the grieving wife and child he left behind.

Despite the resulting heartache, Jamie managed to pull herself together enough to achieve her desired grades, fuelled by the determination to make her father proud and to go on and develop a cure for the wretched cancer that had taken him away so that no-one else would have to suffer what she had gone through.

After two successful years in college and mulling over where to undertake university, Jamie received a call one August day that her mother was in a critical condition in hospital, having been the victim of a hit and run collision. She arrived at the ward to be informed that her mother had already died of her injuries.

Alone, Jamie struggled to deal with the aftermath. Losing her dad had been bad enough but to lose both parents and at the mere age of eighteen no less, she all but succumbed to the resultant depression that now had her locked in its stranglehold.

Although Jamie had effectively given up on her own wellbeing, Gabrielle refused to let her close friend submit to the catatonic state she had become enveloped by, making the reluctant decision to leave her own family home to act as Jamie's care-giver in order to restore her to her normal self. What followed would be nearly half a year of mental rehabilitation and dogged perseverance but eventually Jamie began to re-establish her own personal independence from Gabrielle's round-the-clock nurturing, albeit with the trauma of the last two and a half years still weighing heavily on her mind.

Nonetheless, Gabrielle felt confident enough in Jamie's mental stability to decide to find a job to support herself, despite Jamie's inheritance leaving the pair financially stable for life, though more of a means to encourage her steadily recovering friend to regain her confidence in wanting to move on with her own life and apply for university.

Jamie, however, stubbornly resisted any attempt to move on, having effectively regressed back into adolescence with no aim of progressing into a burgeoning adult any time soon, preferring to wallow in anger and self-pity than contribute to the cruel world that had taken her beloved parents from her.

But fate could be kind as well in its own mysterious ways.

Jamie had believed firmly in science all her life. This then made catching Gabrielle accidentally smashing a vase in the living room with an invisible wave of energy from her swinging arm extremely difficult to comprehend. After all, super-human powers were science fiction and didn't exist in real life, at least so she had thought. Adding to her astonishment was the fact that Gabrielle had known about this already a month prior, having taken that time to get over the shock of it herself and attempt to learn more about it before revealing anything. All she had discovered was that it was activated with a backwards-swinging motion of either arm and that it could be charged to enable a stronger wave being launched.

Although amazed at this extraordinary discovery, Jamie couldn't help but feel a bit envious. That was, until she learned that her friend wasn't the only one who could do such a thing moments later.

Eagerly grabbing Gabrielle by her bare hand to drag her out into the garden for a proper demonstration, Jamie stopped in her tracks as she felt a strong pulsating sensation flowing through her wrist that seemed to spread throughout her body. After a few seconds, the sensation had disappeared. Jamie then dismissed it, wanting to watch Gabrielle use her ability again instead.

Outside, Gabrielle flawlessly fired another energy wave at the concrete part of the garden floor, though failing to damage the sturdy surface. In a vain attempt, Jamie tried the same backhanded swing to no effect. Out of frustration and disappointment, a second swing produced an energy wave not unlike Gabrielle's but weaker that unearthed a small turf of the lawn. Surprised but nonetheless ecstatic, she tried again several more times only to fail on each attempt before giving up.

Throughout the following day, Jamie obsessed with trying to produce another energy wave knowing she had already managed to achieve it once before. Yet, no further attempts yielded anything of the sort.

Then she considered the weird sensation she had felt momentarily the previous day, as well as the fact that she had been in direct physical contact with the person who possessed the power when it had occurred.

When Gabrielle arrived home from work later in the afternoon, Jamie tried to 'drain' the power from her again via contact with her hand while asking Gabrielle to charge a wave in her arm, more or less activating the ability without launching the wave itself. She then began to feel the same sensation as before, choosing to allow the absorption to continue longer compared to the previous attempt.

Once out in the garden, Jamie took glee in being able to produce several more energy waves than the previous day's single diminished effort. She subsequently dubbed the power as the ability to temporarily absorb and replicate other people's abilities, with the amount she absorbed dependent on how much she chose to take but of which would fully deplete upon being completely used up.

Despite the fact she technically did not possess a real ability in itself and instead needed to absorb other abilities to use as her own, Jamie considered it a welcome addition to what was her otherwise dismal and stagnant life and she proceeded to dedicate all her time towards mastering it as well as whatever other powers she could take on using it.

Two days on, Jamie unwittingly discovered a further aspect of her ability while attempting to absorb Gabrielle's power, the latter instead going on to launch an unusually powerful wave of energy that knocked the pair backwards before creating a crack in the concrete flooring. With this further development, Jamie re-assessed her overall ability as 'manipulation' – the power to augment the strength of another ability as well as also being able to absorb it for her own personal use.

As her confidence in her power grew, Jamie began to realise she could sense Gabrielle's presence whenever she had her ability in an active state. Though not a strong sensation at first, further adaption and concentration allowed her to detect Gabrielle from halfway down the street. In effect, although it could not identify the ability being sensed, it allowed Jamie to crudely track and locate other abilities around her to a limited degree, in what could prove to be an invaluable tool towards finding others like her.

*　*　*

A month on from her initial discovery, Jamie felt she had plateaued practicing with her ability as well as with Gabrielle's. She wanted more; thus she would have to go out and try and find others to absorb and utilise.

It dawned on her, however, that if she did happen to find other individuals with powers that they might not be as willing as Gabrielle to allow her to absorb them. Not that she considered herself a fighter by a long stretch when considering the option of using force but she certainly had the power to defend herself if things got out of hand.

Her first venture on an 'ability hunt', Jamie trudged around the outskirts of the city in one of her dad's old jackets with the hood completely obscuring most of her head. She felt embarrassed at wearing the oversized and ill-fitting garment but it was necessary to hide her identity in case any potential encounter ended up going awry.

An hour in, her detection capabilities managed to lead her to her first opportunity: a teenaged girl no older than herself vandalising a brick wall by carving graffiti into it with what appeared to be a rainbow-hued type of ionic energy blast.

Feeling utterly terrified but nonetheless throwing caution to the wind, Jamie snuck up from behind and grabbed both her target's wrists. Immediately, the girl began to flail about yet unable to retaliate owing to her arms being held outstretched as she felt a cold sensation passing through her body. Jamie was quickly forced to prematurely end the absorption process upon the girl opting to scream for help and flee, though she felt satisfied with having already transferred a significant amount of her ability into herself.

Moreso, she felt invigorated; the feeling of triumph as well as knowing that she had wrested back control from her depression in that moment at the very least with a brand new ability to experiment with too.

The energy reserves of the absorbed power, however, inevitably depleted as had happened with Gabrielle's powers within her after a week of practicing with it, much to her continued annoyance with the obvious and unpreventable flaw in her base power. In response, Jamie relentlessly pursued other empowered beings to gain additional powers, managing to come across several more with many of the bouts requiring the further use of aggression in order to attain them.

Jamie noted her own lack of empathic restraint in the midst of her approach, barely feeling a shred of guilt or remorse while heavy-handedly taking every power despite never being a confrontational person whatsoever, much less someone willing to be violent against other people.

In the moment though, given that every individual she had encountered had been using their abilities to cause personal mischief and criminality, all she had felt was antipathy and anger towards them – the same anger she had felt towards the trio of joyriders who had smashed into her mother's car and taken her life while out of control in their stolen vehicle. As far as she was concerned, she was doing the public a favour by taking out such dangerous and wildly unpredictable beings who posed a grave threat to everyone else's wellbeing.

Less of a concern to her though were her own increasingly ability-centric actions and state of mind; her hunts had become a borderline obsession with the desire to attain more powers as each previously absorbed one eventually faded from use.

But soon the thrill of it all had begun to wane – always eventually losing the abilities she gained was a constant disappointment in spite of what she was able to wield and control at her fingertips while she actually had them, the only saving grace being that her close friend and housemate readily allowed her to re-absorb her kinetic energy wave power whenever it ran out. Otherwise, it hardly seemed worth the monotonous effort of walking around town for hours on end trying to aimlessly detect any potential activity to begin with, especially if the ability encountered turned out to be lacklustre.

While discontent with the setback, Jamie found herself discovering another source of comfort during her time spent within her house in the form of rock music and alternative culture; she felt a kinship with the sonic vibes of the angst-ridden, guitar-orientated bands and artists within the genre complete with often dark but heartfelt lyrics that felt like they were connecting with her on a personal level, even speaking directly to her and making her feel like she wasn't alone in being plagued by such miserable thoughts and alienation during her worst moments.

Encouraged by her new interest, Jamie decided to dabble in the look of the alternative scene by purchasing several loose-fitting t-shirts with the logos of her favourite bands emblazoned upon them in addition to some simple plain black ones as well. She also bought her now-familiar black cargo trousers and black hooded jacket that, like her father's, was slightly oversized, which she had grown accustomed to the feel of after wearing it throughout her empowered miscreant hunts as opposed to a more appropriately fitting variant.

Truly mixing things up was her subsequent decision to completely dye her hair, first by bleaching the entirety of her natural brown locks and then throwing in a combination of a predominantly purple semi-permanent dye job on top with red underneath and a pair of fluorescent pink bangs. Being her first attempt, the finished look was messy but nonetheless satisfying to observe, even garnering admiration from a surprised Gabrielle over the new 'rock-chick' appearance.

Wearing the new attire out in public didn't garner much of a response owing to the conscious choice to walk about with the hood on her jacket still up over her head, negating drawing attention to her vibrant new hairstyle. Jamie had noted during her time wearing her father's loose-fitting hooded jacket obscuring her facial and bodily features that her social anxiety didn't bother her as much as it would otherwise, opting to continue doing so in addition to protecting her identity during all her enhanced human escapades.

By now, the hunts had become secondary to simply strolling about while listening to her rock and heavy metal bands through her headphones. Deep down she yearned to meet someone else from the alternative crowd so she had at least one other person she could share her musical interests with, something she was unable to do with Gabrielle as much as she loved her overall company, which in itself had been significantly diminished since she had gone back to working full-time.

That ultimately was the one thing she could not change about herself – the feeling of being so overwhelmingly lonely. It wasn't her fault she lacked the confidence and social skills to meet new people, nor was the fact she had lost her entire family before she had even entered her twenties but it didn't make an ounce of difference either way. She wanted more than what she felt her own personal limitations could actually achieve and it just wasn't realistically going to happen. The nature of her incredible powers were almost comparative to how her feelings were in regards to her deceased parents in that the ones she absorbed eventually left her no matter how much she liked having them a part of her to begin with.

And so begged the question – with every available avenue failing to give her any prospect of happiness, where did that leave her?

As suicidal as she had felt following her mother's death, Jamie had never seriously contemplated the idea of taking her own life. She still greatly appreciated Gabrielle's companionship amidst her loneliness and she also had no idea what was in store for her in the next life. Knowing her luck, probably more pain than she currently had to deal with.

The next best option was to resume pursuing university. After all, any place would happily take her on board with her intellect and grades to back it up though at the present time it only served as an unwanted reminder of the fact that her mother was killed just prior to when her first semester would have begun. The trauma associated with it was still going to take some time to get over.

Thus, the current status quo would be forced to remain. *For the time being at least.*

Jamie walked Gabrielle back to the supermarket following their lunch before she made the moderately short journey home. She often considered the notion of offering to pay her friend to simply stay at home and keep her company using her inheritance but decided to respect Gabrielle's resolve to instead earn her own living. She just considered herself lucky that Gabrielle had decided to stay with her on a permanent basis as opposed to moving back in with her family as it was.

Suddenly, she felt a sharp pulsation go off in her head, indicative of nearby ability-related activity. Whoever it was it felt quite strong, either a powerful ability or within close proximity. Jamie began powerwalking towards where her ability was detecting the source of exertion, pulling her hoodie over her head and tucking her hair underneath as she did.

As she turned the street corner, she saw what appeared to be the conclusion of a struggle between two individuals on the other side of the street next to an open alley entrance, watching as the victor of the two knocked the loser to the ground.

Assuming the one still standing had possessed the ability and had used it to attack the other, Jamie launched a kinetic energy wave in their direction. The attack, however, caught the brickwork next to her target, cleaving out a small chunk while alerting the unknown figure to Jamie's presence. She stared sheepishly back at him, having not expected the wave to miss as he ran into the alley before quickly crossing the road to pursue him as the other individual scrambled away.

The young man eyed Jamie cautiously as he stood before her with his back to the dead end of the alley. She in turn looked back at him, unable to predict what his next move would be. *Surely he could've seen that the alley led to nowhere from the entrance?*

Regardless of his apparent carelessness, Jamie knew she had him exactly where she wanted despite not knowing of the exact ability that he possessed. Oddly, he didn't seem to be preparing to defend himself or launch a counter-offensive, almost like he was willing an attack to come his way. While she had felt indifferent towards pursuing empowered beings as of late, Jamie still harboured her intense dislike of those abusing their powers to hurt innocent people and whatever he possessed couldn't be particularly dangerous enough to face down if he had felt the need to flee from her running over to him.

Jamie quickly launched a kinetic energy wave. However, the person simply blocked it with his hand.

Or what appeared to be just his hand.

Undeterred, she fired off another but was met with the same response again. This time she managed to observe what seemed to be a transparent barrier deflecting the energy wave. She took a moment to think to herself, wondering it was even worth the effort continuing the bout for a non-offensive ability, or if she could get anywhere near the person to manage skin contact to absorb it anyhow.

At the same time, the hubris within her was compelling her not to just walk away defeated. It was a stupid notion of course but as she had succeeded every time before without fail, it seemed like one heck of a streak to just toss to the side.

Jamie tried instead a flame jet attack, sending her newly acquired pyrokinetic power surging forth to try and burst through the invisible shield. Unexpectedly, the individual took to the air to avoid it, floating up onto the roof of the building of the surrounding alley wall.

What...?

Jamie looked up at the curious enhanced human staring back at her from the rooftop above. Without further hesitation, he then took to the air again, only this time appearing to blend into the sky behind a cloud of vapour the higher he ascended until he was completely out of sight.

Cloaking? Camouflaging?

Jamie was left stunned. Whoever this person was had just exhibited three different powers before her very eyes and she was at a loss to explain it. Was he just like her, able to absorb multiple abilities? Or did he possess something entirely different?

Suddenly she didn't feel so special.

But besides that, she wondered why he hadn't tried to attack her back at all despite the seemingly large array of abilities at his disposal. His reluctance didn't match up with the scuffle beforehand that drew her attention to him in the first place either. Or maybe he had actually been the victim?

One thing she did know for sure – she wasn't going to find out anything more until she managed to hunt him down once again.

Chapter 2

"Ah, the final arrivals. Welcome!"

Kyle followed Dan into the warehouse, seeing a small gathering of young men like themselves seated in the nearest left corner of the building with several portable lamps plugged into the wall surrounding them. Standing up among them he assumed was the 'Miles' person that Dan had repeatedly referred to as the ringleader of the operation. The duo took the two remaining seats in the circle.

"Good to have everyone here," Miles addressed the group, Kyle noting his friendly demeanour and clear tone of voice. "Let's get right down to business: everyone in this room has come here this evening knowing that they have some sort of super-human power, am I right?"

A few members of the circle nodded their heads in agreement.

"And I'm going to assume 'yes' on the grounds that no-one just looked at me as though I'm some sort of deranged lunatic. The fact is it's true – we all have some kind of special ability that allows us individually to do something extraordinary."

Kyle noted Miles' calm mannerisms and interactive delivery, not what he was expecting at all but it was welcomed considering it was helping to put his nerves at ease.

"And it's these very abilities that set us apart from those average human beings walking around out there. But seeing as we're the elite ones, why are we submitting to what everyone else wants or expects of us? We should be making the rules, not following them. You hear me?"

Another collective round of nods followed.

"Now you're probably thinking that this won't be an easy thing to achieve. Even with our powers, we don't exactly match up against guns, tanks or explosive devices…"

Just what does this guy have in mind? Kyle thought to himself.

"…but we *are* able to do things that can get around all that crap if we put our brains to it," Miles continued as he walked over to one of the standing lamps. "Sure, the ten of us would be heavily outgunned by the likes of the military but it's never necessarily who has the biggest arsenal, just how it's used.

"If I may reference the famous Battle of Stirling Bridge in 1297 – unlike what you probably saw in *Braveheart* with William Wallace leading his boys into a massive head on collision with the English army, the Scots simply made fine use of the terrain and used superior tactical efficiency to overcome what was probably a distinct disadvantage in terms of armament and numbers."

"Aye, ye arrogant tossers got yer comeuppance that day, didn't ya?" one of the attendees close to Kyle jested in a thick Scottish accent, leading to a chorus of laughter among the group.

"A'right, so we just need Mel Gibson and the city is ours!" another member of the ensemble yelled out, to even greater howls.

"Ah, but Mel Gibson isn't like us now, is he?" Miles cut back in. "For all we *know* anyway. But I suppose a better example would be how the Vietcong frustrated the Americans in Vietnam with guerrilla warfare until they got fed up and went home."

He then placed his hand on the cable connected to the lamp.

"Deal your enemy with a series of small but effective tactical approaches that slowly disorientate and hack away at their forces…" he stated as all the lights in the room momentarily deactivated before coming back on seconds later. "…and you will have earned a well fought victory."

Kyle took a moment to assess everything that had just occurred in the last few minutes. It felt as though everyone in the room, including himself and Dan, were being recruited for some grandiose, megalomaniacal scheme to take over London, if not the whole country. Not that he had a problem with it; he certainly didn't feel as though he had much to lose with his home life as wretched as it was – being an only child to two drug addicted parents hadn't done much for his wellbeing at all and it had shown in his social life where he had resorted to shoplifting among other small acts of criminality just to get by. Growing up in and continuing to be subject to abject poverty was no way to live a life as far as he was concerned.

He looked at Dan, seeing him fully engrossed in Miles' every word. He wasn't sure how long Dan had known Miles but he knew Dan had other friends that he saw occasionally despite spending the majority of his time in his room with Kyle playing video games. In comparison to himself, Dan had had a relatively decent upbringing but longed for independence and had struggled to attain a job to get on the ladder towards that pursuit, something that he held resentment for as well as the fact the cost of living was far too high in the capital alone. This had resulted in an extreme antipathy towards what he saw as the 'elite' of the world: the rich and powerful who seemingly held their high position in society at the detriment of the lower class, a feeling only amplified when he had discovered his powers.

Now he had someone directly telling him that he was among the *true* elite and that they were going to achieve that by their own means. Kyle couldn't blame his friend for being drawn into that mindset, considering he himself had good reason to be dissatisfied with how society was run, yet he just hoped whatever Miles had planned wasn't just some hare-brained scheme or fell short of actually achieving what he was currently hyping up so much.

"But before I go any further, I do believe it will benefit us all to do a round of introductions so we get better acquainted as well as find out what we're all packing," Miles said. "Allow me to kick things off: my name is Miles and if my demonstration wasn't obvious enough, I can disable sources of power and energy. Moving swiftly on."

"Hello all," the person to the left of Miles spoke. "My name is Bill and I can shoot laser beams from my fingers." He then looked to the next person on his left, Miles seemingly doing the introductions in a clockwise order.

"Hi, I'm Max and I generate light from my body."

"A human lighthouse, well that's a real useful ability(!)"

Everyone turned towards a smug-looking, blonde-haired teenager at the opposite side of the circle responsible for the flippant remark. Kyle then looked at Miles, his reaction quite clear that the outburst wasn't part of his plan for the night.

"Yeah, bright enough to burn your eyeballs out of your sockets," Max grinned maliciously as a luminous aura began slowly emanating around his body. Failing to be intimidated, the youth opposite quickly manifested an orb of white energy in the palm of his hand. Suddenly, both of their powers began to deactivate as Miles held out his arms in both their directions.

"Sorry for the interference gentlemen but I think it best if we save the abilities for tomorrow's part of the grand scheme, don't you think?" Miles addressed both Max and the youth. Neither responded as Miles looked towards the person seated left of Max.

"Alright, I'm Johnny and I can paralyse anyone by hand contact."

Kyle found learning about the others' powers interesting; he had only known about Dan's and his own abilities prior to this moment so to find out what variety of additional ones that existed intrigued him, although he noticed Dan scowling at the loudmouth youth who had nearly caused a full-on ruckus. He got the feeling he knew why as the bulky young man to his right introduced himself.

"I'm Liam and I have super strength."

Kyle took a quick moment to compose himself, then allowed the best introduction that he could think of on the spot to come out of his mouth.

"My name's Kyle and I can shoot ice blasts," he stated calmly and collected. Miles seemed visibly impressed as he turned to Dan, who didn't seem as confident.

"I'm Dan and I have extended jumping ability and heightened reflexes."

"Thank you very much," Miles interjected immediately after, presumably to cut off any potential second outburst from the youth with the energy orb ability in what was the only other moment of the night that Miles had appeared to lose his confident demeanour.

"T' name's Donnie and I can generate and fire off toxic sludge."

Kyle was curious as to what Donnie's ability would look like, considering it the most outlandish power he had heard so far. He was more curious though to see how the brash youth was about to introduce himself.

"I'm Alex and I can create energy spheres to blow up anything I deem worthless," he said with a degree of arrogance and venom aimed at anyone who would take offence to it.

"Well you'll get your chance tomorrow afternoon, fella," Miles responded, with a tone that appeared to appease Alex to an extent to prevent any further disruption. He glanced at the final participant, the individual with the earlier Scottish accent.

"Ah'm James and ah kin fly," he said simply.

"Good, good. So now we've all gotten to know each other, for better or worse, let us move on to how we're going to make the most of all this firepower we're packing.

"As stated earlier, we'll be approaching this slowly but effectively so I implore for you to bear patience. We will be operating in three teams and step two will begin tomorrow around 7pm immediately after the team of myself, Bill, Max and Johnny complete step one. Step one consists of completely deactivating London's electricity and power just as we head into nightfall."

"And how are you going to achieve that?" Alex scoffed aloud.

"Did you miss the bit where I told you I can deactivate energy sources?" Miles retorted. It was now becoming obvious that Miles had clearly not invited the arrogant youth himself personally, probably having tagged along with another member of the group.

"There's no way you can deactivate the whole of London's power," Alex fired back. The rest of the room looked at Miles, almost in silent agreement.

"On the contrary, I have already succeeded to a degree in that before," Miles replied. "Or has everyone forgotten the blackout in parts of East London last month?"

The room remained silent, including Alex who appeared to actually believe the claim.

"See, trying to shut down a whole house wouldn't be hard in that I would simply have to deactivate the fuse box. In the case of last month, I located a major power station of that region and deactivated the generators there before turning them back on a few minutes later. Not an easy feat but with the aid of Max, Johnny and Bill, we were able to get past security to achieve what I previously thought was unthinkable. As it is said, you never know what you're capable of until you try it.

"The country's national grid can be brought down by attacking its control centre, which I just happen to have been tipped off about by an extremely reliable source. And I should know where it is as I have already visited it and confirmed its location. It's regularly accosted by cyber-attacks as it is on a regular basis so obviously security is going to be pretty high but we're confident in our literal abilities to get to where we need to be to shut the whole place down.

Luckily the secret location just happens to be within the outskirts of London so we'll be able to take care of that and have the time to travel by car to our next location to commence our part of step two.

"Step two is simple: in our three groups, we are each going to take down a police station, either by taking out the staff or outright demolishing the building depending on your strategy. Of course I'd be slightly disappointed if at least one of them isn't completely trashed seeing as we're trying to send out a message here.

"Just to make sure there's no interference, I have, with some difficulty, managed to acquire some devices that will aid us in case our mobile phone networks go down if cell towers in London are affected by the power cut." Miles brought out a bag before the group, pulling out a pair of devices. "This first one is a Satellite Phone, capable of making calls even in remote areas owing to the fact it relies on satellites and not cell towers, hence the name. And gadget number two is a military style GPS device which offers full access to GPS and whose high level of accuracy not normally afforded to the general population will serve us well when we need to regroup in the middle of the dark. After all, if the first two phases go well then we shall be coordinating a run of anarchy on the streets, which I imagine a lot of disaffected members of society may very well help take advantage of."

Everyone in the circle appeared to have some degree of satisfied look on their face, with Kyle even noting that the scheme didn't appear to have any major flaws in it, not any that he could think of off the top of his head anyway. He would have been more sceptical had Miles not demonstrated his ability first-hand to gain assurance in the blackout part of the plan but he had delivered the whole thing in such a confident and articulated manner, as well as confidently subduing an unsavoury member of the group, that he didn't have any grievances with taking part. Above all, it was better than living in squalor for the rest of his life.

"Dan will lead his team with Kyle and Liam and Donnie will direct his group consisting of Alex and James," Miles continued. "We will co-ordinate using the phones and monitor each other's movements using the GPS devices as each one is linked to the other two. My team will head over to the control centre for six o'clock, we will have the power shut off by half six which gives us a full half an hour to be at our next location where our police station to take out will be. Whatever time you guys choose to be at your police stations is up to you but make sure you're ready to launch the offensive at bang on seven with us. If there's any delay on our part, we will notify you in advance of seven o'clock.

"And aside from that, it has been good to meet you all and I look forward to working with you come tomorrow," Miles concluded. "Everyone rest well and Dan and Donnie, just a quick word before you leave."

As Dan headed over to Miles, Kyle turned to Liam who he had briefly hung out with at Dan's house once before.

"What do you reckon mate?" he asked.

"Hey, I've got no problem with it," Liam responded. "Wouldn't mind getting even with the cops anyway, I'm pretty sure we can manage it."

"I'm sure Dan knows exactly how we're going about it anyway, just gonna follow his lead," Kyle replied as Dan made his way back over to them.

"Got the location, let's head out of here," he said as the trio left the rest of the ensemble behind. Upon jumping the fence to exit the warehouse complex, Liam split from the group to head back to his respective home, leaving Dan and Kyle to head back to Dan's on their own.

"Are you confident in tomorrow?" Kyle asked.

"Completely mate, it should be a right laugh!"

"But do you reckon it'll succeed?"

"We'll find out when we do it but it shouldn't be an issue. Why? You're not having second thoughts, are ya?"

"Like I give a toss about this city," Kyle dismissed. "I'm with you all the way but I want to know if you think this whole thing is going to work."

"Even if it doesn't, at least we gave it a try but the ten of us combined should be enough to get the job done."

"Just wonder if we're better off just creating a riot once the power's down rather than targeting those police stations."

"Remember, it's also about sending a message," Dan replied quickly. "We need the pigs to know this is a full blown attack and not a random power cut. This is only one phase in the general grand scheme of things where we position ourselves at the very top of society instead of being at the bottom of it. They've got to know we're capable of bringing London to its knees."

"True, true. Just as long as we can do some five-finger discount after we deal with them."

"Is the Pope Catholic?" Dan joked as they reached the nearest bus stop. Kyle knew the pair of them would barely be able to fall asleep in anticipation of the following day but he just hoped that things would improve for himself once it was all said and done, and with his best friend by his side in the process.

Chapter 3

Gabrielle sat at her dresser table trying to hurriedly apply her eyeliner in front of the mirror before she had to leave for work. It was eight in the morning ahead of her nine o'clock start and she preferred to arrive at least half an hour early while leaving enough time to pop into Jamie's room on the way out. Sometimes she envied her friend's confidence in being able to venture outside without make-up, one of the few things she lacked herself despite her outgoing personality though she had always considered Jamie to be a rare type of person who needed no cosmetics to improve her natural appearance anyway.

That, for the moment in time, however, appeared to be the only thing she could even remotely envy her for. There had been little improvement in Jamie's attitude in the months following her mother's death and while understandable, she just seemed to have completely given up on trying. Sharing her ability with her had appeared to perk her up a bit as had her rock and heavy metal interests, yet they had appeared short-term fixes before falling back into a slump again. Gabrielle wished for the day that she would opt to undertake university like she had originally planned instead of constantly moping around the house all day long.

Gabrielle grabbed her bag and walked out on to the landing before entering Jamie's room. As usual her clothes from the previous day were scattered on the floor instead of being put in the laundry basket against the wall. Jamie was sprawled out facedown in the double bed, sound asleep.

"Jamie," Gabrielle called out. Jamie stirred but remained otherwise motionless, leading to Gabrielle to slowly pull the duvet off the bed, much to her friend's irritation as she turned over into a starfish position in the centre of the mattress.

"Up, baby!" she exclaimed while shaking Jamie's ankles, who simply gave an annoyed moan in response. Gabrielle then raked her fingernails across Jamie's exposed abdomen, the sensation causing her to jump up with an audible yelp.

"Gabbs..." Jamie griped as she sat up. "What time is it?"

"Coming up to ten past eight."

"Urgh, really?!" she complained before falling onto her back again while hugging a pillow for warmth in absence of her duvet.

"Lemme guess – went to bed at two o'clock again?"

"One o'clock actually."

"Video games?"

"Reading through a load of articles on the risks to civilisation on Wikipedia."

"Surprised you haven't written one on the actual existence of super-powers."

"Who says I haven't?"

"Really?"

"Nah. It'd just be taken down anyway seeing as they officially 'don't exist' as far as the world's concerned."

"For all we know. Still, you know you'd get to put those researching skills to good use at university."

Jamie turned onto her side still clutching the pillow. She didn't respond.

"Never know, it might brighten things up having a structured week again," Gabrielle said, trying to avoid sounding like she was nagging.

"I know," Jamie begrudgingly replied. "I will get there eventually, you know I will."

"I just wonder when though. I worry that you'll stay stuck this way."

That hurt.

"I won't."

"I hope so," Gabrielle sighed. "I'm off to work then, I'll see you in the evening."

"Okay."

Jamie re-awoke two hours later. The sun never shined through her window until the late afternoon owing to the fact her room faced west but she could tell by the brightness outside that it was gone ten o'clock. Slowly she arose from her bed to venture to the kitchen to make breakfast.

There was never really anything on television in the mornings that she particularly looked forward to watching, normally just leaving it on the news channel to catch a repetitive cycle of the morning and previous day's events. Essentially it was background noise while she either ate or browsed random information on the internet via her laptop. Jamie was thankful in that sense that her curiosity and fondness for learning new things meant she was never truly bored per se despite how disenchanted she currently was towards her current state.

Once again, she had caught herself lying to Gabrielle. She wished she actually had been reading up on some random article regarding the potential risks to civilisation the previous night instead of simply being unable to shut her brain off and go to sleep.

The mysterious guy with the multiple powers.

Jamie couldn't shake off her fascination with him. Envy maybe, at the fact he could also wield multiple abilities? Or even just the fact he had so far been the only one to prevent her from taking any for herself?

It was possible her own proficient ability had given her an inflated ego too. Whatever it was, it annoyed her greatly. She could picture Gabrielle either yelling at her for deliberately trying to engage with an empowered being like they themselves or mocking her for getting so pent up over *some boy*.

She knew she'd rather accept the hollering.

But for the first time in a few weeks, she felt as though she had something to look forward to each morning. The only way she was going to find out more about him was to go out looking, something that no doubt would be made difficult by the fact he could fly and cover large distances in a short amount of time, not to mention his cloaking ability despite her being able to detect nearby active powers. Then again, maybe he would instead try to seek *her* out for whatever reason; maybe he had the same fascination with her as she did him. Maybe they were destined to meet again in one way or another.

Or maybe stupid teenage hormones are taking over my mind.

Jamie tried to put the thought aside. She knew her real focus was on gaining the knowledge of his abilities and not trying to get to know him personally. Above all else, she had a very distinct memory of the last time she found herself lowering her guard against someone with powers who had attempted to befriend her, who just happened to be the first person she had ever met who exhibited an ability, even before Gabrielle.

She remembered that it had nearly cost her her life.

Jamie finally left her house as noon rolled by to head into town. In addition to seeking out any empowered activity, she also had the small task of picking up special conditioner that helped counteract the brittle effect that came with bleaching her hair, which just happened to be sold in a hairdressing supply shop within London. The journey was a thirteen mile round walk which at her standard pace would probably take roughly five hours in all. Her legs would probably need an entire day to recover afterwards but she wasn't too bothered as long as she had her music in her ears the whole way.

She noted that her dark, alternative attire and hooded appearance had surprisingly not garnered any verbal abuse since she had adapted the style of clothing, being all too aware of the typical harassment members of the subculture endured for their fashion sense. Verbal insults were endurable though if it ever came her way, she accepted. Beyond that, anyone who dared to attempt a physical assault would face the wrath of a kinetic energy blast, or perhaps even mild immolation from her current fire ability.

The irony being of course that she had accosted people, albeit with powers, unprovoked herself but she had always reasoned that they had deserved retribution in some form or other for their malevolent or criminal actions while using their abilities. For simply venturing outside in a certain set of clothes certainly didn't deserve any kind of vitriol coming her way one would imagine but Jamie was all too aware, as a young woman, of attracting unwanted negative attention simply for how she looked as it was. The fact that she appeared borderline male at first glance with her loose-fitting clothes and hood covering her feminine features probably deterred any potential sexual harassment she might have endured otherwise but she would rather take a physical blow for being a 'freak' (and then winning the subsequent fight) than deal with some attempt to take advantage of her body. That was definitely not going to happen.

At least not a second time.

An hour in to her journey, Jamie had yet to detect any enhanced human activity whatsoever, though that wasn't unusual as she was lucky to sense any at all on most of her ventures outside her home with the previous day's meeting of *two* different individuals being the odd day out in the weeks she had been doing so. She was halfway to the shop and on the border of central London with the choice of going the more direct route through the streets or taking a detour through the nearby park that would add ten minutes to the trip.

The scenery of the park won out as Jamie walked through the gates. She had never explored it in detail before, having always opted to simply follow the path directly forward until she came out the other side and re-emerging onto the main road. One of the main reasons being for that was due to the sheer size of it; the four fields that she ventured through alone was only a fifth of the entire surface area on the recreational ground according to the map and she had never cared too much for exploring the rest of it. As far as she was aware, the only other notable thing there was a large lake near the furthest side and throwing bread at some ducks hardly sounded like it was worth the effort going over to it.

As she walked on listening to her MP3 player, Jamie began picturing the scene in the alley with the youth with the multiple abilities again, trying to figure out how she would approach him on the next occasion. His invisible shields alone would be hard to counter and his flight made it too easy for him to escape no matter where they were. And she had no idea whether he possessed any offensive abilities of his own to attack her first if he chose to. *Maybe it really would just be easier to try and ask instead?*

Jamie was shaken from her daydreaming by the sudden knock of someone walking into her, having not seen or heard the person approaching. Annoyed though also slightly embarrassed, she didn't bother turning around to address whoever had done so before starting to continue on with her walk.

As she did so, she felt a follow-up shove hard in the back which sent her sprawling to the floor. Jamie felt her blood boil as she got up quickly while charging an energy wave, swiftly launching it in the opposite direction without a care to see who had pushed her.

She watched as the relatively short-range attack collided directly into what appeared to be a small individual with similar but tighter dark clothes. *And green hair.*

Jamie took her headphones out of her ears as she looked down at her fallen aggressor, seeing a punk-looking girl with a black leather jacket, very short jeans bottoms with fishnet tights and a pair of industrial boots. Her anger faded as she contemplated checking on her, though also considering leaving the scene to avoid a further confrontation.

Then she noticed the electrical sparks emerging from the girl's hand…

The green-haired girl then launched a surge of electricity towards the baggy-clothed individual who had rudely shunted her and then knocked her down somehow with a backhanded blow that had managed to strike her despite being at least a metre away from her body.

Jamie quickly dived out of the way to avoid being shocked, her heartbeat racing as she realised the gravity of the situation – she had just managed to royally infuriate an empowered teenager with electrical abilities who was now on her feet and preparing to aim a second attack straight at her.

She quickly ran towards the nearest tree, the only thing remotely resembling cover as the girl moved towards her while frantically trying to figure out a counter-attack strategy in the mere seconds she had left. She had no idea how harmful or even lethal the girl's electrical discharges were; she was even more baffled by the fact the attacks themselves were not burning her hands in the process as would be expected based on science but the fact that she was even able to generate electricity through her hands alone was mind-boggling enough. Jamie knew she had to throw out what science was telling her and rely instead on instinct before she ended up being electrocuted.

The girl approached the tree, only to see her hooded opponent jump out and swing her arm in the same backhanded motion as before. Unable to react in time, she felt another hard concussive force strike her directly in the abdomen, causing her to keel over as she felt as though she was about to throw up.

As she struggled to combat the unpleasant sensation, she felt a two-handed vice grip clamp onto the back of her neck. Sparks began to emit from her body as she tried to fight back with her ability alone while her arms remained gripping her stomach but to her surprise, the grip was not being relinquished. For some reason, the individual in black wasn't being affected by the electricity.

Jamie released her hold a few seconds later and took a few steps back, allowing the girl to get back to her feet albeit still heavily winded. They stared each other down for another few seconds, waiting for the other to make the next move.

"How are you not being shocked?" the girl yelled out.

"Your power's mine now," Jamie bullishly replied.

"You're lying!"

"I took some of it for myself, you can't hurt me now!"

Feeling taunted, the girl launched another streak of electricity at Jamie who simply cancelled out the attempt with an outstretched hand.

"How do you do that?" the girl asked, her tone unexpectedly softening. Jamie dropped her guard slightly in response.

"How do I do *what*?"

"How did you take my electricity?"

"You mean just now or when I had my hands around your neck?"

"Just how did you get my power?"

"I absorbed it, through my hands. That's what my power does."

"I thought that invisible attack you hit me with *was* your power."

"That's my friend's ability. I borrowed that from her too."

"You mean there's yet another one of us out there too?" the girl reacted with more surprise.

"There's loads," Jamie replied. "You're like the tenth person I've met that has a power of some kind. Are you telling me I'm the first person you've ever met?"

"Yeah."

"Alright, where was this enquiry when you were trying to kill me with those electric blasts?" Jamie said, visibly annoyed.

"You pissed me off clattering into me and just walking off, I don't have a great temper," the girl replied. "But I honestly wasn't trying to kill you. My shocks cause pain but that's it."

"How do you know that? Can you control the voltage and amps of your charges at will?"

"Er, I don't know about any of that. I've shocked people before and none of them ever lost consciousness if that's any good?"

"And it doesn't hurt you at all to use it?"

"Nope."

Jamie felt at a loss at how this ability in particular was so blatantly defying scientific laws, more than all the others at the very least. After a moment of consideration, she approached the girl.

"Hold out your hand and activate your ability without using it."

“Why?”

“I’m giving you your power back.”

“Okay...” the girl complied, taking Jamie’s hand despite her confusion. “Does that mean you wouldn’t be able to prevent me from trying to shock you though?”

“Will you?”

“...No.”

“Even after I hit you twice with my other ability?”

“I don’t really care about that anymore, it’s just surreal to finally meet someone else who can do what I do.”

Jamie waited a moment in second thought, then decided to take the girl’s outstretched hand anyway. She then felt a surge of energy flowing out of her body until it was completely gone within a few seconds.

“That felt weird,” the girl remarked.

“Well I didn’t want to risk hurting you by transferring the electricity back into you directly so I used my own power to return the portion of your ability itself that I took from you.”

“Why give it back in the first place?”

“I don’t want an unpredictable ability that I’m not sure I’ll be able to control,” Jamie replied. “I’m actually surprised you haven’t seriously hurt someone while using it already.”

“I wouldn’t do it if I thought it could.”

“Either way, I’ve got less lethal abilities to kick people’s arses with so I don’t need it that bad.”

“You really go round doing that?”

“I only try and do it to people who either have it coming or piss me off.”

"Guessing I came under the latter," the girl said with a smirk.

"Yeah," Jamie joked back.

"How long have you known about your powers then?"

"A few months now. How about you?"

"About the same; it just came out of nowhere when I was with my ex-boyfriend and he got shocked by it. I learned how to harness it after a bit of practice, I imagine you probably would've too."

"I lose my abilities after I exhaust my supply of them anyway so I'd really just be practicing with something I'm weary of just to lose it soon after."

"That sucks."

"Pretty much why when I take one I drain as much as I can, to make them last longer. They always replenish themselves naturally anyway in whomever I absorb them from. Thankfully I normally get to grips with them easily enough by watching them being performed first to get a rough idea."

"And how did you discover it in the first place then?"

"During an incident with another person like us. I've never been certain but I would put money on it being when it activated for the first time."

"What caused it to activate?"

"I don't want to go into it," Jamie replied.

"You can tell me, I'm pretty open minded," the girl tried to appeal to her. "Girl to girl an' all."

"Appreciated but still, it stays with me for the time being."

"Is it why you dress like a guy? To make yourself come across as more imposing with your hood up?"

"I dress this way 'cause I like it," Jamie replied, trying to deflect. "Besides I doubt most guys dye their hair pink."

The girl gave an odd look before Jamie realised she still had her hood up, promptly pulling it down and removing her hair band to allow her multi-coloured locks to flow freely.

"Oh wow, that's awesome hair, man!"

"Thanks," Jamie responded, feeling jubilant at the compliment. "I like your barnet too. What's your name anyway?"

"Sissy."

"Really?"

"Well, Cecelia actually. All my friends call me Sissy though for short so I just go with it now. How 'bout you?"

"Jamie."

"Isn't that a guy's name?" Sissy joked.

"And a girl's," Jamie shot back. "My parents' names wer…*are* James and Marie, they just combined theirs to get mine."

"Well I think it's cool anyway," Sissy replied, to Jamie's delight. "What are you doing now anyway? I'm going to the skatepark at the other end of the park to meet up with mates if you wanna join?"

The invitation took Jamie back a bit, not that it wasn't something that appealed to her but she was amazed at having befriended someone immediately after having fought them. Her anxiety had quickly spiked, however, although this was the opportunity she had been looking forward to for so long – the chance to have a friend just like her, look and personality-wise.

"I'm actually on my way to pick something up but maybe another time."

Baby steps…

"No problem. Give us your number though and I'll call you next time we're out, or just to chat sometime."

"Sure," Jamie replied, giving Sissy her mobile number while pulling her phone out to receive a drop call in response.

"Whoa, is that a *dumbphone*?" Sissy asked.

"A *what*?"

"Sorry, a non-smartphone. Didn't think anyone still used those old phones."

"Does what I need it to: make calls and texts."

"Fair play. The apps on these are handy though if you ever felt like upgrading."

"I'll keep that mind. Have fun with your friends."

"I'd have more fun showing you off to them but yeah, I will."

"What makes you say that?"

"All my mates are guys so it'd be nice to actually have the one girl to hang with 'round them, on top of the fact you're drop-dead gorgeous," Sissy laughed, eliciting a smile from Jamie in response.

"I'll see you soon," Jamie said as she began walking onwards towards the city centre with Sissy walking in the opposite direction. At some point during the day she would likely rue not overcoming her social anxiety to join Sissy and her friends but at least they had logged each other's contact details to allow a future meeting.

Jamie suddenly found herself feeling happier than she could remember in a long while.

Chapter 4

"What a magnificent structure(!)" Dan jested, standing with Kyle and Liam before the police station that they had been tasked with attacking. It had just gone five o'clock in the afternoon.

"Soon to be a magnificent block of ice and pile of rubble," Liam chimed in.

"Well I sure hope we can achieve that with what we have between us," said Kyle.

"We already know the first part is doable; outright destroying it will be a bonus," Dan said.

"Will that be to Miles' satisfaction then if we can't knock it down?" Kyle asked.

"The aim of the game is to disable the thing and send a message to the pigs," Dan replied. "Freezing the entire building alone pretty much speaks volumes. Doesn't hurt to try and smash it too."

"Well I guess the hope there is that my ice powers are enough to weaken the brick walls enough for a heavy impact. You reckon you can launch a lamp post into it, Liam?"

"As Dan says, doesn't hurt to try," the burly enhanced human responded. "There'll be no problem ripping the thing out of the ground and throwing it, I've managed to do that before. The gamble is whether it will cause any structural damage but at least we get to do that bit under cover of darkness."

"And I'll be keeping an eye on the phone and GPS to make sure the others are pulling their weight in the meantime," Dan followed up, almost with a tone of disappointment that his own ability had no offensive capabilities to join in with.

"I do wonder why Miles didn't just say to us to take the power going down as the indication to start the attack," Liam said.

"Mainly because he wants all three groups synchronised," Dan replied. "It may seem overboard and pointless but he does want the police to know that we're organised and to be taken seriously."

"How do you reckon the others are going to approach their stations?"

"Beats me, all I know is how we are going to achieve our own objective. Miles just gave me the location of the place when he handed me the gear last night, how they attack their own police stations is down to them."

"Still got two hours 'til game time, mate," Kyle cut in. "What do you want to do to kill the time?"

"Let's check out the shopping centre for half an hour to see what we can pilfer after the attack and head back here. There's an alley way across the road where we can lay low for the rest of the time."

"You really want to hole up in an alley for a whole hour and a half?" Kyle exclaimed, bordering on protestation.

“No, not really but logistically it has a secondary passage that we can stay out of sight in and avoid drawing attention to ourselves while also being right next to the police station for when the call comes in to move forward,” Dan replied. “Besides, Miles will be monitoring our position as much as possible with his GPS device and the other team’s so I want to give him as much confidence as possible knowing we’re sticking where we need to be the whole time ready to launch our part of the offensive.”

“Fine then,” Kyle begrudgingly answered. “A shame we didn’t bring any playing cards.”

“Pretty sure there’s a load to steal in the shops,” Dan said.

“Not exactly low-key though if we get caught doing so.”

“Good point – better use cash for once.”

“Cash? Gonna get a bad reputation at this rate,” Kyle laughed as the trio departed for the nearby shopping centre.

Jamie continued making her way home with mixed feelings swirling around in her head. The trip to obtain her hair conditioner had been a bust – it was sold out, thereby making the journey a complete waste of time yet she marvelled how she had finally met someone with the same musical interests as herself, even if it had been a complete fluke. Now she only needed to bring herself to want to make contact with her new friend sometime in the near future, if Sissy wasn’t going to be the one to do it herself first anyway.

The attempt to locate the enigmatic multi-powered boy hadn’t gone to plan whatsoever either. Aside from the encounter with Sissy, her ability had completely failed to pick up a trace of any other power within her vicinity all day long, not that she had considered it likely in regards to the evasive nature of his powers. Chances were that she might never come face to face with him again, if she was unlucky.

Jamie checked the time on her phone. It was twenty minutes to six, later than she planned to be out for with still another half an hour walk minimum before she arrived home. Her legs were notably aching and she was beginning to wonder if it was worth simply getting a train back the rest of the journey, or even a bus. She didn't even recognise the street she was walking down, not even from the distinctive police station on the other side of the road in the distance with a large-ish looking shopping centre nearby it. She only knew she was roughly on the right path home due to the overhead signs indicating her town was in her forward direction.

She then abruptly slowed down before bringing herself to a complete halt. A weak sensation had begun to go off in her head and was staying consistent as the next few seconds passed. It felt like two small warm points had formed in the left side of her brain. *Two faint powers.* She started walking forward at a slower pace and the two small sensations began to feel like they were expanding inside her head. They were definitely nearby and on the same side of the street as her, which would almost indicate that they were both inside one of the many buildings to the left.

As she walked further down the pavement, however, Jamie noticed an opening in the line of buildings to her left.

Always an alley, she thought while removing her headphones and putting the Mp3 player with them into one of her lower zip pockets as she approached the opening. The warm feelings in her head were still present, yet she wondered why they weren't increasing any more despite her apparently close proximity. *Maybe they're further away?* She looked down the alleyway from the entrance, seeing absolutely nothing but a waste disposal unit at the dead end. Maybe she had got the location wrong after all.

Suddenly, she felt a pulse surge out of nowhere as she saw a beam of what appeared to be ice and frost connect with the side of the dumpster from an extension of the alley that she had failed to see from her current position.

"Kyle! Keep it on the low, will ya?!"

"Dude, I told you to stop trying to cheat!"

Jamie began slowly making her way down the alley, activating Gabrielle's kinetic wave ability with her arm positioned across her torso ready to launch if needed. The voices she heard seemed to confirm the two sensations in her head, yet she wondered why, aside from the brief surge, that they both felt so subdued despite literally being a few metres away from her.

With her heart pounding, she peered slightly past the corner to see three young men sitting on the floor of the alley extension apparently playing a card game.

"Snap is a rubbish game anyway; let's play Rummy or Go Fish instead."

"Can't believe this is what we're bloody doing until seven o'clock."

"Rome wasn't built in a day, Kyle."

"Dude, that's not even the right analogy."

"Well whatever, we're staying put until Miles shuts down the city's power in just under an hour. Then we can revel in taking out that cop shop."

Huh?

"I think I'll have more fun grabbing that big screen TV from that shop in the centre afterwards."

"Yeah well at least you have the super strength to be able to carry it all the way home, Liam."

"Of course that's going to have to wait until the riot's been kicked off."

"*If* it goes off; depends how your mate Miles feels once all three of our teams trash our police stations."

"Trust me Kyle, we are going home with some swag tonight whether Miles authorises it or not. But I'll almost guarantee that he'll be up for making the most of London being plunged into darkness any way possible."

"In the meantime, shuffle the dumb cards so we can get on with something to pass the time."

"Fine. Get ready for a round of Go Fish then."

Jamie took a step back away from the conversation, confident her nearby presence would be unnoticed among the trio's card game. She stood still in deep thought; whoever the three individuals were, not only were they all apparently empowered beings like herself but they were seemingly part of some grand scale plot to attack London with at least two other groups presumably just like them. She knew that one of them was a cyrokinetic judging by the ice blast a moment ago and that the large member of the group apparently had super strength which would explain why his power felt so diminished despite the close proximity, due to it being 'passively' active when he wasn't exerting himself.

More importantly, she was faced with a dilemma – she could call the police on the three but there was no evidence that had done anything and she had no idea where their co-horts were or how they planned to disable London's power. That meant that she was the only one standing in their way, even though she was outnumbered.

But not outgunned.

Jamie contemplated how she could take all three out. Clearly the biggest threat was the cyrokinetic but her fire ability could neutralise his attacks. Ultimately it was Gabrielle's ability that could deal the damage without even needing to get close to them and even if she failed, she needed only to run out onto the open street to escape. Judging by the fact their plan apparently consisted of running amok in total darkness, it seemed unlikely they would be willing to expose themselves in the open by using their abilities to pursue her.

She then realised what she was even considering doing but it wasn't just a regular attempt at garnering abilities; it was stopping a domestic terror attack on the city's streets. Moreso there was no guarantee that such unrest wouldn't spread to her neighbourhood either and there was no way anyone was vandalising the house her parents had left for her.

It was now or never.

Jamie took a sharp step sideways into the line of view of the trio and quickly launched a kinetic energy wave at the ice-powered individual to the left with his back still turned. However, her rushed attempt caused it to instead strike the alley brickwork, causing a small spray of chippings to hit the back of his head.

"What the hell?!" Kyle exclaimed while looking at the wall behind him.

"Mate, look up!" Liam yelled while pointing towards the figure standing at the open end of the alley extension. Jamie began to quickly charge another energy wave when she saw the cyrokinetic beating her to the attack, launching a sub-zero beam of energy straight at her which forced her to run out of the way. She heard the beam colliding with the dumpster and making a crackling noise, seeing the side of the unit encased in a bigger layer of ice than before.

"Get after 'em!" Dan barked as all three quickly rose to their feet to give chase. Jamie ran towards the entrance of the alley before stopping and turning around. She activated her pyrokinetic ability in her right hand while continuing to hold a charged energy wave in her left arm. As the three came into view, she could see the cyrokinetic aiming his open palm at her ready to attack again. This time she met the emerging beam at the same time with a jet of flames from her hand, the two powers colliding in the middle of the alley and producing a cloud of steam.

Feeling the stalemate, Jamie suddenly dropped her attack and allowed the weakened ice beam to continuing surging forward. She dodged while quickly launching her charged kinetic energy wave from her readied left arm, watching as the force of it slammed her opponent hard into the wall behind him.

"Kyle!" Dan yelled as he looked at his fallen friend who was completely knocked out cold while lying slumped against the rear alley wall.

"What are we going to do now, man?" Liam asked with panic in his voice.

"Whoever that is, they're going down." Dan said, seething with rage. "Distract 'em while I scale the walls."

Liam looked to the dumpster and tore off the lid before making his way slowly towards the person at the other end of the alleyway while using it as a shield. Jamie launched another series of energy waves in his direction, watching as the dumpster lid took several dents from them while the super strength individual stood sturdy.

Let's see that shield withstand fire.

Before she could react, the would-be criminal threw the makeshift shield in her direction, forcing her to sidestep out of the way. In the midst of her defensive dodge, she saw that his friend had disappeared from her line of view though she could hear his footsteps echoing around the walls of the alley.

Jamie then heard the sound of someone landing hard on the ground behind her, turning around to see the other individual quickly sprinting towards her. *Did you actually jump from wall to wall to get past me?* Caught off guard, she attempted to quickly charge an energy wave but he was too fast, snaring her in a close grip from the side while pinning her arms downs before shifting his body behind hers. Jamie struggled against the hold as she found herself being dragged against the wall with the enhanced human's body separating it from her.

"Mate, help me drag this one back to the other side of the alley!" Dan called over to Liam, acutely aware how close they were to the open street where any bystander could happen upon what was occurring.

As the larger of the duo approached her, Jamie held her right arm outwards in his direction as far as she could raise it in the midst of the pinning hold she was subject to and unleashed a small jet of fire once more, forcing him to back off.

"You need to sort that out, Dan!" Liam said aloud. "I can't get near them!"

"Don't use my fecking name, for goodness sake!"

Using the distraction, Jamie began charging a kinetic wave in her left arm to its maximum and hoped the desire effect would be achieved in the process harking back to the days of watching Gabrielle experimenting with her ability for the first time. She then used her body weight to lurch forward with her opponent still latched onto her from behind so that there was some space between them and the wall and swung her forearm as hard as she could with the overcharged attack, the resulting recoil sending them both hurtling backwards.

Dan had less than a second to react to the unexpected move before he found himself colliding with the wall hard with his quarry's body amplifying the impact. He almost immediately found his vision fading to black as his body fell helplessly towards the ground.

Jamie looked down at her defeated foe, seeing him laid out on the floor before averting her gaze back to the remaining member of the group. Now that she had time to think, she noticed one of the two sensations in her head had diminished greatly but was still noticeable.

"Stay away from me," Liam called out as he fled behind the dumpster unit. Jamie turned her attention to his fallen comrade instead, placing her hand on his neck and attempting to absorb whatever ability he had. Sure enough, she felt an inevitable surge entering her body despite the fact she didn't know exactly what power she was absorbing. She ended the drain prematurely to try and grasp any difference she felt; being a 'passive' ability, she assumed the effects of it would be constantly active and in use.

Slowly she approached the last group member.

"Stay back," Liam said once more, seeing the person taking position on the other side of the dumpster.

"So what were you up to then?" Jamie brazenly asked. "Sounded like you boys were gonna smash up the streets."

"You're a chick?" he asked incredulously upon hearing her tone of voice, only to be met with an impatient blast of fire in response being fired close by. "Yes! We were going to mess up the place!"

"Who else was involved?"

"Two other groups!"

"They have powers too?"

"Yeah."

"How many of them?"

"Seven."

"And what power does your friend down there have?"

"He has super-human reflexes."

Jamie frowned; it didn't seem like much of an ability to have.

"And you're super strength, aren't you?" she asked, recalling her eavesdropping earlier.

"Yeah."

"How are you keeping in contact with the other two groups?" Jamie interrogated further while activating a small flame in the palm of her hand.

"He has a special phone and a GPS device," Liam said in a panic, pointing to Dan slumped on the floor. Jamie went over to him and searched his pockets while simultaneously absorbing the rest of his ability with her other hand. She took both the phone and the GPS device.

"What's the point of the GPS gadget anyway?" Jamie asked.

"So we could track each other when the power went down around half six," Liam answered timidly. Jamie looked at the screen of the device, noticing two other dots surrounding the centre dot which she assumed was their current position.

"You're going to do me a favour: you're going to call up the other lot and tell them exactly what happened here."

"I don't even know their number, luv! Dan was in charge of the thing."

Jamie frowned once more. She tried the contact section of the phone regardless, noticing the relatively simple layout of the menu of it. There were only two names in the contacts section.

"I assume this is the 'Miles' guy I heard you talking about earlier. He the head honcho in this scheme?"

"Yeah."

"Here you go then," she said, tossing the phone to the terrified hulking youth. "Into that extended part of the alley and make the call."

Liam hit the call button on Miles' name in the contact book of the phone as the girl marched him into the corner of the extended alley. He was still too scared to feel humiliation over being threatened by someone who was far smaller than he was, despite how many powers they had. Jamie simply stood watching him with an outstretched palm aimed in his direction with her left arm crossed across her chest.

"*Hello, Dan?*" the voice on the other end of the receiver spoke.

"It's Liam. Listen, we've been ambushed."

"*What? Where's Dan?*"

"He's out cold, and Kyle too! Some lass with powers like us just knocked them both out. She's gonna–"

Liam suddenly found himself being hit with the same invisible attack that he had watched the girl use on both Kyle and Dan, being slammed into the nearest wall by the force of it and smacking the back of his head on the brickwork.

Jamie walked over to the unconscious street thug, hearing the voice on the other end of the receiver frantically asking for a response as she drained the super strength from the empowered being's body. She then used it to drag the unconscious bodies of his friends into the same part of the alley to hide them from view and left them with the phone on the floor next to them. She attempted to absorb the remaining group member's ice ability but found no such luck – unlike his co-horts, his ability wasn't active regardless of him being consciousness or not. She quickly gave up and began to depart the alleyway.

In her hand she held the GPS device. The two other dots on the screen were currently still. She took a moment to consider the prospects of taking on both groups at the same time but she felt such a high from not only the adrenaline rush but also the fact she had triumphed in a bout with *three* enhanced humans and gained two new powers that she didn't really care at that moment in time. It was also that same rush that was encouraging her to gain their partners' abilities too yet she knew it wasn't likely to be as easy an accomplishment as what she had just achieved.

But whatever was in store, it was going to be taking place back in the park.

Chapter 5

"How long have you lived in England anyway?" Alex asked James as they sat nearby their police station on a public bench with Donnie, who had just noticed his Satellite Phone going off in his pocket.

"Ah've lived here since ah was nine," he answered.

"So why do you still speak with that accent?"

"What's wrong with ma accent?"

"Well it's Scottish, innit? We're in England."

"Listen 'ere you wee xenophobic prick, there's no law on diff'rent accents aroond here so if yer don't like it, then piss off."

"Alright, *jocko.*"

"Will you two belt up so I can hear?" Donnie irritably exclaimed. "Right, say that again Miles."

Alex and James looked on as the expression on Donnie's face grew more concerned. He then took the GPS device out of his pocket and looked at the reading on the screen.

"Yeah, I can see it. So what do you want to do?...........Alright, we'll meet you there then."

"What was that about?" Alex asked, minus his usual cocky tone as Donnie stood up off the bench.

"Well what's happened is those clowns in the other group have been taken out and whoever did it, apparently some girl with powers like us, has run off with their GPS device."

"So? Let *them* get it back, it's not our problem."

"They can't, they've all been knocked out."

"Heh, beaten up by a girl. I knew they were no good to us," Alex quipped with arrogance.

"As much as ah'd hate t' agree with the toerag here, it ain't really our problem," James pitched in. "We kin still get this done wit'out 'em."

"As true as that may be, that device still needs to be recovered," Donnie responded.

"Why?"

"Because like the rest of them, Miles stole them from a government building that I imagine is reeeeaaally interested in getting them back as soon as and their discovery by law enforcement may very well lead to us all being jailed for nicking them in the first place."

"Big deal – we'll just chuck ours away and be free of it," Alex suggested.

"Well Dan's no doubt has his fingerprints on it and if they snag him, you think he won't grass the rest of us up to get himself off the hook?"

“Not if we get to him first,” Alex said while materialising an orb of energy in his hand.

“Shut up Alex,” Donnie replied dismissively. “If you want to attack someone, save it for when we catch up to the thief. We need to cut them off and they’re currently heading east so we’ll jump on the train and head to the nearest station within their location. Hopefully we can reach them before they get too far. Miles will try and head them off at the same time so we should be meeting up with him somewhere along the way.”

Jamie rested under a willow tree in the same field she had met Cecelia earlier in the day. It was currently 6:20pm and the sun was coming close to setting but still bright enough to visibly see everything in the field. According to the GPS device, both groups were relatively nearby, possibly five minutes away or even as close as nearing the entrance to the park although the two dots were showing a small gap between them, meaning that one was closer than the other. At least under the willow tree she wouldn’t be seen from afar.

With that in mind, she got out and placed the GPS device close to the nearest tree which was a sizeable enough distance away from her position under the willow’s branches.

She felt ecstatic at the two new additions to her ability pool; whether it was the enhanced reflexes alone or the added super strength, her legs had gone from being wearily tired to fully functional and the pace that she had gained had enabled her to make a forty minute journey in only twenty five. Still though, she knew that the nature of the two powers meant that they could run out any given moment due to the fact she was unable to deactivate them. It was a new but welcome experience for her and a flaw that she could learn to overcome with time. For the time being though, she could still feel their reserves in plentiful supply which would aid her in the forthcoming bout.

A few minutes later, she saw some figures entering the field through the pathway between the hedgerows. The sun still had not set and the surrounding buildings in the far distance had not lost their power judging by the lights in the rooms being on. Jamie felt her heart beginning to beat slightly faster once more; it was the same situation as earlier and again she had no clue as to what abilities she was up against.

Still, the two that she had already been in possession of in that situation had been enough to overpower three opponents at once and with the addition of enhanced strength and reflexes, she fancied her chances.

The group drew closer to the tree, obviously tracking the stolen GPS device. Jamie made out three of them, meaning the rest were still to come.

"Can you see it?" Donnie asked.

"No. Zoom in closer," James demanded.

"It's zoomed in as far as it goes. It has to be close, like twenty metres close or something."

"Yeah but which twenty metres?" Alex sarcastically replied.

"Hang on," James said, eyeing a patch of grass. "Ah think it's there."

Donnie walked over to the area of grass and saw the device, picking it up and looking at the screen which appeared to show that it was still functioning properly. As he stood in place, Alex and James watched as Donnie was suddenly sent flying backwards from an unknown force, landing heavily just in front of their feet.

"What happened?" James asked. "He's out cold."

"Think we've found our super-powered thief," Alex said while looking at the willow tree. He then quickly fired off an energy sphere in its direction, the attack sailing through the branches and making a concussive hit on the trunk underneath. He saw a figure emerge.

"Ah, I do believe we've got our target," Alex sneered as he prepared more energy attacks and began launching at will with both hands. Jamie simply dodged each one effortlessly with her enhanced reflexes, aided by the distance between her and her foe adding to the reaction time.

"Think y've got a problem with yer aim," James mockingly said aloud.

"I'll give *you* a problem," Alex snapped back in frustration as he moved closer to the hooded figure – presumably the girl that he was warned of – firing off more energy spheres and being met with the same avoidance despite being only a short distance away. Getting angrier still, he began producing a larger, more powerful sphere in his right hand.

"Let's see you worm your way out of this!"

Before he had a chance to throw it, he was quickly met by the same attack that had felled Donnie which knocked him to the ground hard. As he was struck, the energy sphere dropped and promptly combusted as it made contact with the earth, the resulting shockwave knocking his body across the lawn.

Jamie looked on at the downed miscreant – whether it was from her attack or the shock of his own exploding near him, he was out like his other partners in crime.

James looked nervously on. While he was fast in the air, he knew he had little chance against the power that the girl was packing, whatever it was exactly. And with sundown approaching, he would have a hard time landing a physical blow on someone who was completely clad in black and blended in with the darkness. It would just be easier to flee unscathed but that would hardly look good to Miles and the others, not to mention the fact that they were all still at risk of being shopped to the police if she were to rat them out about the GPS devices.

Whatever he was going to do, it would have to include back-up from the remaining gang members. He looked around behind him and managed to catch sight of what appeared to be a group of four people approaching in the background from the same hedgerow entrance to the field.

Miles walked quickly with Bill, Johnny and Max trying to keep up. He watched a flying individual coming directly to them, figuring it was James from Donnie's group.

"Miles, we've got a problem."

"Did you locate the GPS device?" Miles fired back.

"Yeah, but we've got trouble. The same lass who took out t' other mob has flattened Don and that wee tosser, Alex."

"What?! The hell is going on here? Is she Wonder Woman or something?"

"Ah can't even tell what she's got either, some sorta invisible blast o' energy that she fires from her arms by t' look of it."

"That her standing over there?" Miles asked, pointing at the figure in the background.

"That's her. Ah don't think we kin beat her one on one, she's too powerful and she's quick too. Alex couldn't hit her once with his energy bombs."

"Then we'll attack her as a group. If she's that confident she'll make a stand and we can take advantage of the numbers. She can attack with sheer force but we'll get her with strategy – Bill, try and nail her with your laser beams while James, you try swooping in and getting a hit on her from behind. Max, work in tandem with Johnny if you can; blind her with your light emission while Johnny gets close enough to paralyse her. I'll stand by in case things look like they're going awry before I get involved."

"What are we going to do with her after?" Johnny asked.

"We'll figure that out after we bring her down," Miles retorted. "Let's just take care of step one, then we can worry about Dan and his crew after."

With that, Bill, Johnny and Max walked over to the girl and formed a perimeter around her with James hovering behind her while maintaining his distance. Bill stared her down, being directly in her line of sight with Max and Johnny either side of her. He couldn't help but think that she didn't look so tough but considering what she had done to half the gang he wasn't about to take her lightly.

Jamie stared a hole through the person who had taken position right before her. She was brimming with adrenaline and confidence but also trying not to get ahead of herself. As thrilling as it was to have taken down five of the group thus far and with very little effort, they were appearing now to try and work together against her rather than individually.

To her benefit, the enhanced reflexes she had inherited appeared to extend to her senses too; she was aware that the member with flight was directly behind her as she could just about pick up on his air movements, aside from the fact her own sensing power could detect his flight in active use as well as hearing the approaches of the other two either side of her. If they were going to try and blindside her while she focused on the one in front of her, she needed to dissuade them of that approach straight away.

Before any of the four could make the first move, Jamie produced a large flame in her hand and quickly spun around on the spot while blasting it out in a Catherine wheel-style fashion. The gang members immediately backed off a few steps. She then watched as the one in front of her then put a foot forward while pointing two fingers at her.

Here we go.

A beam of purple light suddenly burst forth from his extended fingers. Jamie ducked down in a crouched position to avoid it while simultaneously returning fire with a quickly charged energy wave. She watched as the attack collided with the gang member's shins, knocking him down while landing flat on his face. Behind her she heard an audible moan followed by a loud thud.

Before she had a chance to look, she heard an approach from her right. She turned and dodged what appeared to be a punch being thrown, countering by using the attacker's own momentum to throw him into his adjacent partner to the left of her with her enhanced strength, the two colliding hard and collapsing in a heap.

"Urgh, watch where yer aiming those poxy laser beams, eh?!" James yelled at Bill, having taken the stray laser attack whilst hovering in mid-air.

"Then stay out the bloody way then!" Bill roared back, his shins in tremendous pain from whatever attack the girl had launched low at him. He struggled to his feet before collapsing backwards onto his rear, unable to stand from the pain radiating from both his lower legs. Undeterred, he began firing laser beams at will at his foe who simply began dodging them with lightning fast reflexes. He couldn't believe how quick she was.

Jamie was struggling to keep up with the laser blasts, noticing how fast her opponent was able to fire them and that the extra exertion of her enhanced reflexes was likely draining her reserves faster than she would like. She also noted that the stray shot that had struck the flying gang member had not pierced his skin, simply causing him great pain and were likely concussive in nature much like her energy waves.

With that, she opted to instead use the durability that came with her enhanced strength to simply swat the beams away with a mix of backhands and punches. Though she felt their impact on her skin, they were failing to deliver a great deal of pain to her hands at all but while she was able to maintain this stance for a while, she still had the other three members to concentrate on as they all slowly recovered.

She then quickly unleashed a quick jet of fire at the laser-emitting individual, causing him to cease firing his ability momentarily as he attempted to shield himself from the flame with his jacket. Seizing her opportunity, Jamie fired another energy wave, only a more powerful one that appeared to catch her foe square in the forehead. His head was thrown backwards, followed by the rest of his body as he collapsed to the floor.

One down.

She immediately turned around to dodge the quickly incoming flying enhanced human who was attempting a sneak attempt while her back was turned. Agilely, she instead turned the tables by locking his ankles in the crook of her arm and then used her strength to spin the hapless gang member around in a circle a few times before releasing him loosely in the direction of the nearest tree. She watched as he attempted to use his ability to slow himself down as he hurtled towards the oak, barely reducing the impact as his shoulder slammed into the body of the tree.

"Whad'ya reckon, Johnny?" Max asked awkwardly as the girl turned to face them.

"Just as Miles discussed," Johnny replied. "Light 'em up and I'll take care of the rest."

"Fine," Max said as he began activating his ability. High intensity light began emanating from every visible part of his skin as he aimed his palms in the girl's direction. Johnny kept his back to him the whole time.

Jamie could feel the intensity of the light, both on her eyes as well as the heat coming from it on her flesh. Unfortunately her enhanced reflexes and senses were now working against her as they multiplied the effects of the light emissions.

With her eyes closed, however, her hearing was more acutely focused and picked up the sound of a set of footsteps rapidly approaching. She turned and ran in the opposite direction in a bid to alleviate the effects of the light as well as to avoid a blindside attack from the other approaching gang member, of whom she really needed to take out quickly in order to shut down the illumination in the background.

Johnny couldn't believe what he was seeing; his sight was unaffected by the light being emitted as his back was turned to it but he could barely comprehend how the girl had managed to move so fast when running away from him, somehow covering twice the distance that he had just managed. James had said she was quick but he didn't think *that* quick. Blinding her was useless, as was his paralysis touch, if he couldn't get anywhere near her.

Max behind him had also failed to notice that the girl was running out of range of the worst effects of his ability due to it partially obscuring his own vision in his choice to go full out with it as he remained in place.

Jamie stood her ground momentarily, covering her eyes with her hand to shield them from the light. The harshness had lessened significantly, now she awaited her pursuer to take the bait.

Soon enough, she heard rapidly approaching footsteps once more and hesitated until they grew louder. She lifted her hand to see her target within five metres of her, then put her enhanced reflexes and strength fully behind an impromptu shoulder charge forward, colliding with the gang member's face right between the eyes who immediately blacked out and hit the floor.

Jamie then began firing multiple energy waves in quick succession roughly at the source of the light being emitted as far as she could see. One eventually landed a hit, causing the illuminating reprobate to deactivate his ability and drop to the floor clutching his abdomen.

Out of nowhere, she sensed the flying member of the group swoop down and grab her around the neck with both outstretched hands as she barely had the reaction time to brace him with her own hands against his shoulders while digging into the ground with her legs. If not for her enduring enhanced strength, she would have surely being knocked down by the unexpected barrage. Instead, she was just able to hold the struggle to a stalemate.

James continued his assault though was becoming incensed at the fact that he could not move the girl any further back, or that she had managed to stay on her feet in the first place. In fact it was like trying to push against a brick wall. *Where on earth is she getting all her strength from?!*

He had noticed that the rest of the group were all down but still found it hard to believe that this one person had been capable of taking everyone out.

Jamie maintained her stance. She considered moving one of her hands onto her foe's neck in order to drain the flight ability from him in order to keep him grounded. Plus out of all the abilities she had just dealt with, his seemed the most worthwhile absorbing but she was concerned that she could not hold him back with one arm alone.

Screw it.

She took a quick glance behind her to see the last remaining gang member slowly rising back to his feet while still clutching his aching stomach. She then grabbed two handfuls of the flying enhanced human's jacket via the shoulders of it and fell backwards, allowing his own momentum to launch him forward.

Max looked up as he saw a body come hurtling towards him at speed, standing no chance as the collision with James knocked him straight out with James himself landing out of control onto the ground and tumbling violently across the grassy surface. A harder surface might have result in serious injuries, the earthy texture only rendering him unconscious instead as his head and torso slammed repeatedly against it during his unplanned and chaotic descent from the air.

Jamie examined the carnage around her before averting her gaze to the one remaining person still standing, presumably the leader of the group called 'Miles'. Even from the distance between them, she could see the extremely disgruntled look on his face at the decimation of his entire gang.

Then she noticed the look turn into more of a sinister expression, and then it appeared he was no longer looking at her. She turned around to see another person emerging in the background, albeit a dishevelled-looking one. She then realised that the first gang member she had knocked out had recovered, barely, and was readying an attack.

No problem, she thought. What was one more delinquent to knock around after all?

Jamie then noticed an odd-looking substance emerging from his hand. He then suddenly launched a sizeable amount of it in her direction, only managing to land close to her feet. Whatever it was smelled odious and appeared oily in texture. All she knew about it for sure was that she did not want to be hit by it under any circumstances.

Donnie, still barely recovered from the earlier assault but able to function, began throwing a number of smaller globs of his unique excretion of toxic sludge at the girl who had blindsided him, determined to hit her with everything he had. There was hardly any force behind them but the toxicity of the substance was enough to subdue anyone if they were coated in enough of it and there was no water source to wash it off. His aim of course was to subdue the threat to the plan, but really he just wanted to make her suffer.

Jamie was having no problem avoiding the sludge balls being thrown at her. In fact, it wouldn't have been challenging even had she not still had access to her enhanced reflex ability. Whatever the gang member's intent was with his onslaught, it was largely inept. Whether the earlier blow had left his brains scrambled or his ability was just woefully out of its depth, or both, she wasn't feeling particularly threatened.

Out of curiosity, she decided to return fire, literally with a jet of flame as another toxic projectile came hurtling towards her. The substance ignited upon impact, creating a ball of flaming sludge that hit the grass.

Feeling he was being toyed with, though no less alarmed by the fact she could produce fire from her hands, Donnie opted for a more aggressive approach. He just hoped his power's reserves could keep up with him as he brought both his hands together facing towards the girl. He then unleashed a jet of his own in the form of a spray of sludge and aimed it straight at the subject of his hostility.

Jamie was taken aback momentarily, jumping backwards to avoid the jet spray of the considerably toxic substance. It was definitely a peculiar attack but also one that was becoming borderline deadly. Using the speed of her enhanced reflexes, she began racing away with the gang member following her every movement with the spray. Even with her speed, Jamie knew she couldn't outrun his arm movements and thus the spray so she resorted to quick, sudden sprints and serpentine movements while maintaining a circular path around him.

Donnie, for his trouble, was having a hard time not only keeping up with the girl but also maintaining the attack on a continuous spray, instead resorting to short bursts of concentrated efforts to conserve his power reserves. His failure to actually hit her thus far was increasing his anger; he was becoming far too obsessed in trying to achieve his revenge to notice the ring of ooze that had slowly accumulated around him.

As he prepared another spray, he saw the girl blast a stream of fire at the sludge upon the ground and realising too late what he had been duped into doing. The substance ignited once more, only this time it quickly spread throughout the enjoined lines and blotches along the ground. Donnie found himself surrounded by a ring of flames that was too high to transverse.

Worse, the burning substance was emitting toxic fumes. He began coughing heavily, trying to breathe in any clean air that he could before quickly succumbing to the gas and passing out in the middle of the inferno.

Using her enhanced reflexes and strength, Jamie jumped into the ring of fire and saw her downed opponent completely out of it. She admitted to herself in her head that the whole thing had been complete overkill and unnecessarily overboard, yet she had no regrets subjecting him to the indignity of having his own ability work against him. Then again, the smell within the circle of poisonous flames was horrific, probably just as bad on one's sense of smell as the fumes were to someone's lungs. He would slowly suffocate or be engulfed by the flames if she didn't haul his sorry backside out of there.

She grabbed his arm and popped her head under his armpit in order to hoist him onto her shoulders, the dead weight barely noticeable with her ongoing super strength. She then readied a short run up before preparing to jump back over the wall of fire.

Suddenly, his body felt overwhelmingly heavy and she was forced to drop him to the floor.

No..... no, not now!

Her enhanced strength had completely depleted. Jamie knew she was in trouble. There was no way she would be able to lift the gang member out now, lamenting her arrogance as the flames showed no signs of burning out anytime soon. Instead of finishing the fight quickly like the others, she had tried to humiliate her latest foe simply because she had grossly outclassed him in power and aptitude.

The smoke was beginning to fill her lungs, even in spite of being outside in the open air, and she opted to using her remaining enhanced reflexes to escape the circle, barely making the height needed to avoid touching the fire without the added enhanced strength in her legs. She looked on helplessly as she inhaled as much fresh air as she could before trying to hack away at the burning sludge with multiple kinetic energy blasts. While moderately effective, they were not having enough of an impact to create a large enough gap fast enough. She began to panic as she worried about the state of the empowered thug still trapped within the ring of toxic fire.

Unexpectedly, the flames began to quell and slowly dissipate. Jamie looked on in the midst of the charred outline where the fire once raged at the still body lying motionless. She rushed over and began performing CPR on his chest. Failing to get a response, she opened his airway in an attempt to breathe air into his lungs. *Gross.*

After a few attempts, the gang member came slowly to while coughing heavily, much to her relief. As she stood up, she turned her head to see the leader, Miles, standing before her.

"You could've easily taken him out like the others right from the get go," Miles spoke. "And yet you dragged it out and set him up to be caught in that predicament."

Jamie simply eyed him back.

"You nearly cost him his life. And while I'm pretty pissed at you right now for what you've done to all my boys, I have to admit I do like your style."

Jamie looked back with an unimpressed look on her face.

"I can forgive all this if you agree to join me. Together we can take over London and encourage more of our kind to come forth to help establish our dominance over the rest of society."

"For the record, I am aware of your original plan to a degree," Jamie answered. "That was one of the reasons I decided to take down your little gang."

"And the other reason?"

"Because I felt like it."

"Disappointing."

"Depends on the point of view."

"With your powers, you should be above us all. You should be running this city, not listening to *how* it's being run."

"Maybe I don't care," Jamie replied. "Maybe I don't give a toss about being on top of the world. I've got other things to worry about and none of them concern wanting to rule over London and beyond. How egomaniacal are you exactly?"

"And what *you* just did wasn't you being full of yourself?" Miles shot back. "You had no problem acting above Donnie there by stringing him about so why not on a grand scale?"

"At least I can admit that was a mistake. It was completely and utterly stupid and as you say, I nearly cost him his life. I don't want to take a life."

"You don't have to go that far to get what you rightfully deserve."

"I don't want to even *risk* killing anyone, never mind doing it outright. And you're nuts if you think unleashing anarchy on the streets is going to do any good. I'm glad I took your dumb squad of empowered bozos down, you deserve to all be locked up."

"Is that what you plan to do to us next then?"

Jamie didn't respond.

"So be it. There's no way I'm getting thrown in prison."

Before he could make a move on her, Jamie unleashed a quick energy wave attack. She looked on in shock as it failed to make any impact upon Miles at all. He gave a cocky smile at her in response, leading her to raise her right palm at him while bringing her left arm across her chest slowly charging another energy wave.

Distract with fire, knock down with kinetic energy blast. The tactic had worked all day previously; it seemed the best bet to win again now.

Jamie launched the familiar jet of fire at Miles, only to see it dissipate before her eyes much like the ring of fire had. She tried it again, seeing absolutely nothing emerge this time round. She looked at her hand in astonishment before looking back at Miles, unsure of what had happened.

"You seem so surprised. How else do you explain the fire quelling magically out of nowhere a minute ago?" he taunted. "You have your powers, but they're no match for mine. I can deactivate any energy source, that includes your little fire trick too."

Jamie's heart sank upon hearing the revelation. Her fire ability had been her main form of defence and now it was gone, permanently or not she didn't know but it was worthless using it against Miles anyway. It also explained why her kinetic energy attack had also been ineffective, yet she had been able to partially charge one just before losing her pyrokinesis. Perhaps there was a technicality to Miles' power in that it didn't shut down the source if the energy itself was no longer connected to it like her fire stream had been?

With no powers left to readily absorb and most of the gang defeated anyway, Jamie opted to flee the scene as she quickly spun round to head to the field's hedgerow exit. She instead was intercepted by the recovering Donnie who managed to haul her down to the floor by grabbing her ankle.

Jamie began trying to wrest her leg away furiously, succeeding as her shoe came loose in the process but Miles had already managed to catch up to her and applied a full nelson hold before hauling her back up. Her five foot nine inch size against his six foot three frame left her barely able to reach the ground with her toes in order to meet the height difference, giving her very little manoeuvrability and momentum to counter attack in addition to his natural body strength holding her firmly in place.

"Donnie!" Miles called. "Complete your revenge."

Donnie got up to his feet, throwing the girl's shoe at her exposed abdomen which barely elicited a response from her. Despite the fact he still seethed over his humiliation, he felt hesitation towards landing a physical blow on her which appeared to be Miles' intent for him to do but he also couldn't really risk aiming a sludge attack at her owing to Miles being in the line of fire as well.

"Go on, mate!" Miles egged him on impatiently.

Donnie reluctantly raised his hand at the girl, accepting that Miles would just have to risk being coated in sludge if he was that insistent.

"Whoa, just lump her one, bruv! I'm standing right here!" Miles protested upon realising what his friend was about to try.

Jamie could easily sense Donnie's reluctance and she didn't want to wait a minute longer to find out if he was going to do as told. She lifted her legs up and planted her soles flat onto Miles' thighs behind her before spring boarding upwards with Miles still maintaining the hold, swinging back down before aiming her weaker right foot – figuring her remaining shoe would have more of an impact than her bare left heel – straight into Miles' groin. The gang leader immediately doubled over while releasing his grip and dropped to the floor.

Seeing Donnie about to make a move with Miles down, Jamie launched a quick kinetic energy attack at him before he had the chance to do so himself, the wave doing exactly as it had done to him earlier on by knocking him down to the ground unconscious. She noted to herself that had she just done that a second time instead of dragging the fight on a few minutes prior she probably wouldn't currently smell like a rubbish tip from the sludge fumes.

As she picked up her shoe, Jamie looked at Miles once more as he struggled to get up from the low blow. This time she had nothing standing in her way from escaping but she knew most likely that this wouldn't be the end of it – Miles could easily reconvene with his gang and attempt their scheme once more some other time without her interfering which was partly the whole reason she had decided to meet them head on in the park in the first place. Really he needed to be locked away but there was virtually no evidence of any crime being committed by him whatsoever and outing them as a bunch of empowered criminals was never going to work. The best she could try was to claim they had been committing gang activities in the park and setting fire to the grass. *Better than nothing.*

But she first needed Miles out cold with the rest of his brethren. Putting her shoe back on her foot, she began charging kinetic energy waves in both her arms, with a larger concentrated effort in her left. Miles was still eyeing her angrily from his position as he slowly got back to his feet.

Jamie suddenly unleashed the energy wave in her right arm straight at Miles' head; predictably he managed to neutralise it with his outstretched hand activating his ability.

Jamie then launched the second and more powerful wave from her left arm but instead launched it directly at the ground in front of Miles, who kept his hand forward expecting to nullify the attack. The wave ducked under the attempt completely and the impact resulted in an implosion of earth and soil being sprayed directly into Miles' face.

As the gang leader recoiled in his blindness from the dirt in his eyes, Jamie seized her opportunity to strike unimpeded and launched another strong kinetic wave at Miles' upper torso from close range. Defenceless, Miles took the full brunt of the attack which knocked him off his feet and several yards across the lawn, down but not yet out.

Jamie was amazed to see him still attempting to get up, having not been rendered unconscious from what was practically a point-blank hit. She launched one final but weaker energy wave straight into the side of his head, finally succeeding in knocking him out.

Victorious, Jamie surveyed the wreckage of the gang around her, seeing no signs of consciousness. All that was left was to make the anonymous 999 call and let the police deal with them however they saw fit, if at all if she was unlucky enough.

She rummaged through Miles' coat pocket to find a phone identical to the one she had used earlier and dialed the number, requesting the police service before being given the chance to explain that gang activity was going on in a park with a large fire having been set. She then successfully asked for the call to be traced owing to not knowing the name of the park in question and then simply left the phone on the floor with the call on-going. Finally, she wiped it down with her jacket to remove her fingerprints from it.

She also remembered the GPS device she had left out on the floor near the tree, re-approaching it to wipe it clean too as she had with the other group's phone back in the alleyway. Jamie took one final look back before making her way quickly towards the exit.

The magnitude of the day's events slowly began to sink in. Meeting *eleven* enhanced humans in one day felt unreal, no more the fact that she had defeated every single one of them single-handedly including her newfound friend in Sissy earlier on. To meet a criminal gang comprised of them was just as surreal too even though they had come across as amateur-ish. It truly made her wonder just how many more of her kind were lurking out there.

Of course the one she was most interested in encountering was still at large. *If only you could have seen me today.* He was still the one blemish on her otherwise perfect success rate, though if her experiences had taught her anything that day, it was to leave her ego out of her exploits – it had very nearly cost a young man his life, even if he was a complete scumbag like all his mates.

But the unknown multi-power person still fascinated her. If not for the fact he had stood his ground against her, it was simply the desire to know how he commanded his own pool of abilities and what his own experiences were with them. It was turning into a bizarre kinship of sorts; a kinship with someone she didn't even know or might even meet again.

"Did you manage to get all that?"

"Did I ever! Sharp will be ecstatic over this!"

"Leave that for me to take care of, just blow that place before anyone else shows up."

"No worries. I'll see you in less than five minutes."

Chapter 6

"See you later, Jamie! Your breakfast is on the table, love you!"

Jamie slowly gathered her senses after Gabrielle's latest disturbing of her morning slumber. She looked at the alarm clock on the side table next to her bed.

8:09am. Again, Gabby?!

Jamie forced herself to wake up, knowing she would hate herself if she allowed the meal Gabrielle had prepared for her to go cold which of course was her friend's obvious ploy the whole time. It was a cooler morning than the previous day which she soon discovered the second she stepped onto the floor, which felt absolutely freezing. She considered putting on a pair of seldom-worn socks before just deciding to endure it instead.

Yesterday's events were still very much on her mind as she sat down to eat breakfast. There was a small lingering sense of worry that her actions may come back to haunt her somewhere down the line but she was more than ready to meet the threat if it came her way, considering the defeated gang just a bunch of wannabes. The loss of her pyrokinesis power had been an annoyance, however, seeing as she had only just acquired it but she accepted that it had probably been mostly used up over the day anyway.

Far more annoying was the fact that none of her encounters had turned out to be the mystery youth from two days ago. But the one with Sissy had opened her eyes a bit to the notion that not all of her opponents were criminals and sociopaths based on what she caught them doing. Most people upon discovering that they had powers she figured would probably want to use them for mischief or more nefarious use but Sissy appeared restrained unless it involved defending herself or, in the case of their encounter, losing her temper.

Thinking of Sissy, Jamie realised she should probably get round to texting her sometime soon. She would have attempted to do so when she got home the previous night had Gabrielle not distracted her by forcing her to strip down to her underwear by the bottom of the stairs upon realising the overwhelming odour that had just come out of nowhere was is in fact coming from her housemate. Not that she had a particular problem with her close friend and sister-figure seeing her borderline naked, more the resentment of being treated like a child. At least her half-cocked excuse of standing too close to a burning rubbish pile had been believed, much like all her other white lies.

That had become the problem of Gabrielle acting as an authoritarian mother-like figure to her when she had plunged into the depths of despair following her mother's death; it had become harder to relate to her on a friend level, even though she herself had treated her mother as a close friend ironically enough. She nonetheless hated that she felt that way with her best friend though, hoping it would wane the more she got her life back in order and Gabrielle wouldn't feel the need to be so overbearing with her.

Suddenly feeling a pang of guilt overcoming her, Jamie grabbed her phone from the pocket on her pyjama bottoms to text message Gabrielle.

> Thanks for the breakfast, it was great. Love you as always babe xx

Regardless of the topic, she had always made sure to end each text with two x characters when messaging Gabrielle, a signature trait as such that was always reciprocated. As she deposited her plate in the sink, she felt the phone vibrate in her pocket.

> No problem my sexy rock chick ;) love you always too. stay safe xx

Jamie smiled at the reply. Screw the depression – they were as strong as they ever were.

The rest of the morning went by slowly with no particular plan in mind. First she washed up with her Mp3 player blaring heavy rock and metal music aloud in its loudspeaker dock next to her, then got carried away and began dancing to the music in the adjacent living room. It didn't even bother her if anyone from the street caught sight through the lace curtains; she felt happy. That was followed by an hour of playing guitar, a more recent hobby that she had taken up following her diminished interest in experimenting with her powers. While an average player at best, the activity proved therapeutic in the challenge of trying to get better at it.

Between that and her loud music, she considered it lucky she lived in a detached house to avoid irritating the neighbours on a constant basis.

Around eleven o'clock Jamie entered the bathroom to take a twenty minute long shower, her preference to the bath seeing as she could either sing to herself in there or simply stand in deep thought while the water sprayed down onto her. When she was done, she wrapped herself in a towel and brushed her teeth in front of the mirror.

Jamie then stood examining herself for a further few minutes. Anyone observing would assume she was extremely vain, though it was simply an endless endeavour in trying to reassure herself that there was nothing wrong with the way she looked. Sissy's compliment that she looked 'gorgeous' had been nice to hear, someone other than Gabrielle offering her positive comments owing to her lack of general company. She did note that she had inherited her mother's features a lot and virtually none of her dad's with the exception of his pale green eyes.

She had, however, always felt insecure about the fact she was relatively flat-chested, to the point she could never bring herself to look at her body without clothes on (or a towel) even though she had no problem with Gabrielle doing so. Not that she had a problem with her petite breasts in itself but the fear of being judged for them had been a leading factor in shying away from being even remotely sexually active during her mid-teenage years to avoid baring herself to anyone while everyone else around her, especially in school, was seemingly experimenting at will. Her introverted personality hadn't helped in that aspect either and thus had never entertained the idea, not even with Gabrielle confiding in her own experiences which by her account had been mostly enjoyable.

Jamie then noticed that her hair dye was showing signs of fading already following the wash, only four days since she had reapplied the semi-permanent colouring. She would eventually need to buy more dyes at the rate she was using them. *And the bloody conditioner if they ever get it back in stock.*

Walking around on the streets felt like running an unnecessary risk after the previous day's events, yet Jamie found the need for walking off what seemed like a leftover adrenaline rush. During her long shower, she had contemplated just how much having her powers had been corrupting her rationality to a degree, like taking on an entire gang of empowered street thugs. Maybe it had been a good thing her interest in attaining them had decreased over time.

But what worried her more was that she was acting like she had nothing to lose in doing so when she knew she would actually be throwing a lot away, like the chance to be able to move on from her personal woes and try to make something of herself. Nobody said coping with depression would be easy, though it didn't make suffering from it any less hard.

Of course it wasn't just the depression that was affecting her mindset – her deep-lying anger was just as overbearing. She had always read anger as being a destructive emotion, if not the most alongside hatred but sometimes it felt such a release to act upon it.

Those who suffered excess levels were urged to manage it through healthier outlets like boxing or martial arts or something more practical.

Did assailing empowered wannabe criminals and vandals count as practical? Either way, she still felt no guilt for taking her frustrations out on them, especially not the gang who planned to plunge London into anarchy. Jamie didn't like the thought of it being so regardless but with so much anger remaining, there really was no other way of expressing it without turning it further inwards and becoming misanthropic instead. She wasn't impressed with how life had treated her in recent times but she would rather not hate life itself as the alternative.

She then tried to find something loud and abrasive to listen to on her Mp3 player to quell her negative emotions. And then she remembered Sissy once more.

When I get home, I'll message you this time!

Jamie then felt someone brush past her quickly, raising her guard until she realised whoever it was had run straight past her, appearing to be running for the bus stop a short distance away. She then put a single headphone in her left ear, thinking it best to have one ear available to hear anyone approaching her, especially if they turned out to be a former conquest. She curiously turned her head to see if a bus was approaching the stop ahead, assuming it was the reason the person had run past her so fast.

To her surprise, there wasn't one.

She then turned back forward. To her horror, she witnessed the hooded individual attempting to snatch a bag from an elderly looking gentleman sitting on the bench at the bus stop as he continued to run forward – except that the man had managed to cling on to the bag's strap as the robber had tried to yank it from him and was subsequently hauled to the ground as a result. The would-be thief launched a succession of kicks to the man's torso trying to get him to relinquish his hold on the bag.

Without a second thought, Jamie instinctively charged and fired a quick kinetic energy wave which struck the thief and knocked him down to the floor. Seeing him trying to get back to his feet, she followed up by running forward and planting the soles of her trainers straight into his upper torso hard and sending him back down to the concrete paving, this time with a cry of agony.

For a moment, Jamie felt stunned by her own actions – namely that she had used her powers in the open without even checking to see if anyone else had been observing her and now that the elderly man was slowly making his way back up onto his feet, she would be unable to use her ability again to defend herself if the thief got back up and decided to want revenge instead of fleeing the scene.

"Are you alright?" she asked, attempting to help the gentleman up.

"Yes, just about," he responded in a wheezing voice. "Thank you, I....look out!"

Jamie looked around to see the thief lunge forward with a crazed look of rage in his eyes as he aimed a hard right hook straight at her.

Suddenly, she felt a spike from her ability detecting an extremely close power usage.

As she felt this, the incoming fist completely missed its intended target, causing the thief to spin nearly a full 360 degrees from the force of the swing. Confused but taking full advantage, Jamie then aimed a swift kick between his legs, the impact forcing him to collapse to his knees on the verge of throwing up.

The thief attempted to get up despite the overwhelming agony flowing from his nether region all the way through his stomach to the rest of his body, barely making it to one foot while kneeling with his other leg. He took a look up and noticed in the background that a jogger of decent muscular build had just appeared from around the corner. Jamie watched as he then fled gingerly down the street before turning the corner. She followed him briefly to make sure he was gone before returning to the elderly man.

"He's gone," she said to him. "He's already halfway down the next road, he shouldn't be back."

"Well I imagine he won't be, thanks to you," the man replied in a surprisingly jovial manner for someone who had just been attacked. "Very brave of you to stand up to him, especially someone so young."

"I've had experience," she responded. "Just seem to have a knack for coming across idiots."

"Well you never know with people like that. Maybe he was just desperate enough to want to steal from me."

"Huh?"

"What I mean is, he could be destitute or living on the streets. Perhaps what he thought he was stealing from me would be worth enough to buy food or something along those lines."

"I personally wouldn't steal to get what I wanted."

"We'd never know unless we truly experience what they do and how they are. There's always people out there doing far worse than us."

"I'm guessing you've met these people then?" Jamie asked in a normal tone, though barely hiding her incredulousness at the man attempting to defend his attacker.

"Quite often," he answered. "I help run a charity that deals with a lot of homeless people as well as those who are living in poverty. You get to know them a bit and what they suffer on a daily basis in my line of work."

"Well if you ask me, that one was just an opportunistic prick."

"Luke 6:37, my dear."

"What?"

"'Judge not, and you will not be judged; condemn not, and you will not be condemned. Forgive, and you will be forgiven'."

"That a bible quote, I'm guessing?"

"Indeed. It actually means to judge mercifully; that is to not judge someone believing you are better than they are but rather with understanding and compassion. Whatever plight that young man has suffered that led him to try and mug me, I won't condemn him for it."

"Somehow I don't think he was thinking as kindly of you when he attempted that mugging," Jamie replied sceptically.

"I wouldn't hesitate to forgive him."

"Well either way, he's gone now," Jamie said, her interest in continuing the conversation wearing thin. "Will you be okay?"

"I should be fine waiting for the bus to arrive. Thank you again, Miss…?"

“Jamie”

“Well Jamie, my name is John. If you need help or guidance, feel free to drop by sometime,” he stated while offering out what appeared to be a business card. Jamie took it, more out of politeness than anything else.

“You take care,” she said, departing the scene without looking back. She put the card into her lower left pocket and reattached her left headphone in her ear before activating the randomise selection on her Mp3 player.

“I see that hooded person in the distance; gotta be them again, right?”

“Surely. Can’t be a coincidence I pick up someone using the same power they demonstrated the previous evening and they just happen to be where I locate it to. I wonder if that telekinesis ability I briefly felt too also came from them?”

“You reckon?”

“Doesn’t matter really. The main aim is to observe the absorption ability in action before we bring them to Ryan. I only managed to identify it yesterday so seeing it in active use would be nice.”

“So are we sending in Miss Dreiser then to take them on and find out?”

“Not here. We’ll tail them for a bit and see if we can catch them somewhere more secluded than an open street. If Dreiser is going to try and force whoever they are into trying to absorb her ability, then it’d be best tried somewhere where they won’t be discouraged from openly doing so.”

"They didn't seem so discouraged from using that kinetic energy attack in broad daylight."

"Well we still have an abduction to carry out afterwards regardless and I don't know about you but I'd *be discouraged from doing* that *in an open environment if we can help it."*

"Whatever you want. I'll let them get some distance and I'll start moving the van forwards."

"That's fine, just don't lose them."

Jamie continued walking aimlessly along the long street, maintaining her alertness by continuing to only listen to the single earphone which irritated her as she felt slightly disconnected from the feel of the music without both in.

She lamented the thought of possibly having to do so on a permanent basis; being able to wrap herself up in her music was an escape from her negative thoughts while walking the streets which otherwise felt like a chore without it. But if it wasn't a sneak attack from an opportunist, it could be a vengeful one from any of her past opponents and considering she had been the one to start the fights every time, they would have good reason for trying.

She did give a thought to John though. She didn't relate at all to his spirituality or the fact he could be so laidback towards his attacker. She knew she would not have let something like that go at all without putting up a fight and probably enjoy giving it back twice as hard, powers or otherwise. She certainly had had no problem doing it to the entire gang she had taken down the previous day without provocation.

She also didn't deny, however, that his words had some merit in regards to people who choose to do bad things perhaps doing so out of desperation. It felt strange that she had only been comparing her own situation moments prior to the incident in the first place; all the pent-up anger she held being a result of the tragic events that had occurred to her. Maybe the thief had indeed tried to steal from John out of a bad situation himself. At least she still had a roof over her head and enough money to live out the rest of her days despite losing her entire family.

Even though she had had no religious upbringing, she was aware of the story of Job who had been subject to immense suffering with one plight after another befalling him in spite of his good nature in what was ultimately a test of his faith, which in the end he had stayed strong in and failed to lose despite his hardship. She had compared that scenario to her own life in recent times, not believing she had done anything to deserve her suffering either but also having not lost her resolve to continue on living or trying to take her own life in despair in the face of it all.

Alas she knew she also couldn't really take the high ground while assailing other empowered beings amongst her. Maybe that was something John himself had learned some time ago in his life: that indulging in one's own anger only leads to further misery in some shape or form.

Then what the hell am I supposed to do with all of mine?

Jamie turned her thoughts to the sensation she had felt just before the thief had attempted to hit her. It was highly probable that a third party had intervened to make the punch miss its target so badly, unless the thief had been disorientated or concussed but she knew she hadn't struck him in the head with her energy wave attack. It was just too coincidental the power detection going off at the same time. Telekinesis perhaps? She certainly wouldn't mind trying that one out, if only she knew who had used it.

She then decided to get off the main road for a bit, choosing a side route that was lined with forestry either side of the path while still keeping her guard up. She could still feel a significant amount of Gabrielle's ability within her despite having not gotten a further supply of it from her in the last thirty six hours.

"Slow down, she's gone off the street."

"Yeah I can see, down that gap in the fence line. Where does it lead to?"

"According to the online map, a small recreational field that has another entrance on the other side. If we drive over to that, Dreiser can meet her halfway in. We can have the boys enter from this side and monitor from the surrounding bushes."

"For footage?"

"Don't need it. Extraction only. Floor it before we miss our chance."

Jamie walked out of the corridor to find an open field before her. She saw that it was completely enclosed with an exit visible at the other side which seemed to be a three minute walk away. Unlike the much larger park she fought the gang in though, this one lacked a tarmac path but she opted to cut through it anyway seeing as it kept her off the main street.

She then noticed someone enter from the opposite entrance; it appeared to be a teenage girl albeit younger than her and smaller. As they got closer to each other, Jamie decided to keep an eye on her with fresh memories of how her altercation with Sissy had occurred. Whoever the girl was didn't seem extremely happy, even from the distance, as though something was bothering her. She assumed she had social anxiety too.

Then, she felt a slight surge in her head which began to slowly grow bigger. She kept her gaze maintained on the girl approaching her, whom she realised was walking directly in her line of path despite having the rest of the field to walk through. *It has to be coming from you.*

As they were about to cross paths, the girl then looked up and walked around the black-clad, hooded individual approaching her head on. Jamie noted the surge peaking as she passed, yet opted to continue walking as she lacked interest in engaging someone who wasn't causing any bother with their powers.

Or perhaps John's words had affected her more than she thought.

As she walked on, she suddenly felt a strong grip around her neck from behind. She struggled to wrench herself free with her kinetic energy waves being of no use while her attacker was behind her.

Jamie then leaned forward quickly as far as she could go which caused the person hanging on to lose their grip as they fell to the floor, seeing that it was the teenager who had just walked past. Without a moment's consideration, she fired a quick energy wave with the girl managing to roll out of the way in time to avoid it. The two then stared each other down in anticipation of the other with a short gap separating them.

"What do you want?" Jamie asked, finally breaking the silence. She couldn't help but note the irony of being on the end of a sneak attack by another enhanced human instead of it being the other way round for once.

"Remember Sally, your freedom depends on how this battle goes." The girl listened through the communication piece within her ear canal.

Jamie then fired off another warning shot with the girl dodging it with lightning quick reflexes, not unlike what she had absorbed and utilised only the previous day. Her strength was also vastly disproportionate to her build based on the grip she had locked on a moment prior.

"Get angry Sally, you know it'll give you the edge."

Jamie looked on as the girl gave a look of desperation but also notably appearing incensed at the same time. The teenager then delivered a shoulder tackle that was too fast to react to, sending Jamie down to the ground before reapplying the strong grip around her throat while maintaining full control over her slightly bigger opponent.

Jamie could feel her airway becoming constricted as she battled to force herself out of the hold but she was down on her stomach with her foe on top of her which was leaving her very little room to manoeuvre. Whatever ability the girl possessed was clearly enhancing her natural strength and reflexes.

Jamie reached backwards with her arm until she felt the flesh of one of the girl's hands, then activated her absorption ability and tried to drain as much of her power into her body as quickly as possible.

In the midst of the adrenaline rush, Sally began to take notice of the surge of energy leaving her, almost feeling like pins and needles in her right hand.

"What is she doing?!" she yelled out, only to receive no response from the earpiece. Jamie noticed the grip around her neck had weakened slightly, choosing to then use all her body strength to roll over onto her side and try to pin the girl against the ground. She then began ramming her elbow into where she assumed her foe was behind her, feeling a connection with her ribcage. The jab was enough to cause the girl to release the hold around her neck.

Jamie then quickly got to her feet and aimed another energy wave at the girl, who this time was unable to avoid it, feeling it clip her right leg as she scrambled to get up.

"It's done!"

"Did she do it?"

"Yeah, she absorbed Dreiser's ability, I felt it. Take both of them."

"Don't know what your game is but you've really pissed me off," Jamie snarled at the now terrified looking teenager on the floor. "What power is that?"

"What?" Sally replied, surprised by the question being asked of her.

"Your ability!" Jamie roared. "What is it?!"

"I–it reacts with my emotions to make me stronger," Sally stammered.

"That's not really telling me much, love," Jamie responded in an irritated tone as she moved forward to launch another kinetic energy wave in anger. As the girl attempted to shield herself, she gave out a yell as Jamie noticed a dart puncturing her left leg, immediately backing off out of confusion.

"No! I did what you told me to do!" Sally called out helplessly as she yanked out the dart. Jamie watched curiously as the teenager began to succumb to what appeared to be a fast acting tranquiliser injected into her. Seconds later, she was out like a light.

Jamie looked around quickly, seeing absolutely nobody nearby but assuming there was someone watching on concealed by the surrounding bushes all around the fence line of the field. As she started to make a run for the exit, she felt a sharp pain in the side of her right thigh, looking down to see an identical dart sticking out of her upper leg just beneath her waistline and quickly yanked it out.

Panic began to set in; she had barely enough time to reach the open street and even then she had to hope someone would see her just before she collapsed. Jamie began sprinting forward as fast she could as she felt the effects begin to kick in. Her vision was quickly starting to become distorted as she neared the gate that the girl had entered through.

Then everything went black as she felt herself crashing into the lawn.

Chapter 7

"So it all went smoothly then?"

"Better than we could've imagined. It was one thing to be able to detect her use of her powers so close to our location but it was even luckier that she decided to enter a secluded area for us to make the capture."

"And how did the bout with Sally Dreiser go in the end?"

"Just as we hoped – she absorbed her emotional response enhancement ability using her own innate power. Turns out she does this via hand contact. Naturally Dreiser was the perfect choice seeing as her ability is always in active use so the fact that the subject's absorption only works when the target's power is activated was never going to be an issue in this case."

"What other powers did she demonstrate in the fight?"

"Just that kinetic energy wave ability she used yesterday. She demonstrated none of the others meaning she's either lost them or just chose not to use them. Considering that Dreiser had the upper hand for most of the bout, I would say that they no longer remain with her because she certainly would have resorted to relying on them. I did also pick up a brief use of telekinesis from an unknown party at one point but again, I doubt she was the one responsible for the aforementioned reason."

"A shame as that would've been an interesting ability. But never mind, at least we can shove her in that last remaining cell later knowing she hasn't anything useful on her to break out of it."

"Well you could always just have her comatose y'know, Ryan."

"I prefer to avoid it if I can, Dawn. Keeping that Ben kid monitored around-the-clock while he's perpetually knocked out to prevent him from using his ability to escape his confine is enough as it is as far as I'm concerned. Besides, the modified benzodiazepines we're using to constantly induce amnesia in all of them are eating into the finances."

"You're honestly that bothered about the cost of producing drugs when you own and run a company that is worth billions? Come on man!"

"Well if I was selling said drugs and making a profit on them instead of just using them for my own purposes, I wouldn't be complaining now, would I?"

"Oh, you're just a gigantic cheapskate(!). Besides, I'm sure being the world's first ever *trillionaire* will ease those money concerns when this all comes to fruition."

"That's what I've always liked about you, Dawn – you're never afraid to speak your mind."

"Hey, I'm only kidding anyway. Shall we go see your new star patient then?"

"Still in the padded room?"

"Yeah, with Mikael Alexandersson. They should both be coming to soon enough."

"I'll be heading back upstairs. Let me know when they're both ready."

Ryan Sharp made his way out of the lift directly next to his office. The 20 by 10 foot room was practically a box compared to his actual office situated in his main company building but it was nonetheless the largest room available in the facility. It was adequate enough though for the occasional visits he made to the place when not tied up in business arrangements.

He of course hoped that the facility would have served its purpose in the very near future which would allow its disintegration along with all the secrets it housed. Every day that it remained standing and in operation was a constant concern for his professional and personal life.

It had been, and continued to be, an extraordinary effort to get the place running in the first place; all the employees and scientists bound to it with their loyalty and dedication to the cause – as well as a significant amount of cash thrown around – to research the nature of super-human powers and to be able to develop the ability to integrate them into normal human beings.

Not that Sharp necessarily needed the billions that would come with the hopeful success of the scheme considering the fact he already *was* a billionaire courtesy of having inherited his late father's extremely successful pharmaceutical company. If he wanted to, he could retire at his current age of 25 and live out the rest of his days happily enough.

But he had found that money didn't buy respect. Although intelligent in his own right, he was not the genius his father had been and he did not command the same reverence from simply inheriting the great Lawrence Sharp's legacy. Not from the world, not from his employees, barely even from the few friends that he had unless they were looking for a hand-out. The fact was that Lawrence had spent most of his life helping to develop cutting edge medicines and ground-breaking technologies and procedures. Of course he had had help in that but he had long been the face behind all of it and was the person the general public connected with the *Sharp Enterprises* brand.

Not his son.

Then one day, soon after his father's death, the younger Sharp had found the most incredible thing – two seemingly regular human beings duking it out with very inhuman-like powers. He had come across the chance encounter while walking through a park in the evening and noticed the surreal battle occurring between the individuals duelling with what appeared to be jets of fire and green-hued energy coming from their respective hands in the adjacent field through a gap in the hedgerow separating them from him, choosing to film what he could using his smartphone and leaving them to continue in his absence.

Alerting the media would have been easy enough, but it had dawned on him that his footage could easily be dismissed as a hoax. After all, superhero fiction was widespread as was the availability of special effects and video editing software. What should have been instant glory could easily have turned into worldwide mockery for presenting a 'forgery' as fact, especially within the realms of the internet.

Then it occurred to him that he had the vast resources needed to investigate the phenomena and develop pioneering research into such super-human abilities, possibly even being able to replicate them.

Before he brought the footage to his late father's team of scientists, he instead presented it first to his close and most trusted friend, a young woman two years his junior by the name of Dawn to get her opinion.

Her lack of scepticism upon viewing the footage was surprising, though only half as much upon her own revelation that she herself had an ability not unlike them: the power to detect and identify other people's abilities as well as figure out how they worked. With this, Sharp not only had a confidant in his discovery but also an invaluable tool in locating other empowered beings like the two caught on camera.

Convincing his lead scientist had been a harder task. Dr Lloyd Murphy, by far the most experienced and knowledgeable person in Sharp's employment, had found the footage of the two enhanced humans displaying their powers extremely farfetched to say the least, likening it to something out of a Hollywood film scene. However, he did reluctantly agree to examine a live subject if Ryan were to bring him one, having taken into account the prospects of such a unique discovery from a science-based point of view and not believing his former boss' son capable of conjuring up such a deception.

Refusing to subject Dawn to any kind of testing or experimentation, Sharp instead partnered with his best friend to locate and capture an alternative to bring in for Murphy. For this task, he enlisted a small, off-the-books team of poachers who specialised in hunting big game for the international black market. Owing to the criminal nature of their regular activities, they could be trusted to keep quiet about their new morally dubious task of preying on human targets for a generous fee. With Dawn's powers tracking down potential desirables, it didn't take long for Sharp to bring Murphy the live subject he desired.

As shocked as he was amazed, the doctor did, however, raise his concerns in regards to the abduction of the individual Ryan had captured.

Therefore, Sharp proposed to Murphy that all subjects be administered with amnesia-inducing drugs so that none of them would recall their experiences (and more importantly, to prevent a police investigation into any of their activities) in the hope that Murphy would be willing to set his objections aside regarding testing on unwilling persons knowing nobody would suffer any lasting trauma in the process. To his surprise, the doctor would agree to the terms in the pursuit of what could be a pioneering breakthrough in something that was previously considered mere science-fiction.

Acquiring amnesia-inducing pharmaceuticals was not a major issue; his father's company had already developed such a drug that was marketed towards sufferers of Post-Traumatic Stress Disorder. It was subsequently tweaked further to erase memories that had developed within twelve hours of the effect kicking in, of which would typically occur within thirty minutes of being administered. Thus, anyone held in captivity would be given two doses a day at twelve hour intervals to prevent them remembering anything following their abductions.

Sharp also decided to only include Dr Murphy in on his scheme seeing as he was the best in his company in the field of genetics as well as to help protect the secretive nature of the project by having as little people involved as possible.

Murphy had other priorities to focus on as part of his main job though and could only be expected to dedicate a few hours a week to the clandestine project. For Sharp, this meant adapting a facility that could house captives in the short term so they were readily available for Murphy when he had the time to do so.

For that purpose, he had an abandoned building on a secluded industrial estate converted under the guise of a warehouse for his pharmaceutical supplies, only with a two-tiered basement installed with holding cells on the bottom floor and a laboratory and exhibition room on the one above. It had come at significant cost, mainly through offshore bank accounts and other methods of keeping it all off the books, as well as hiring a shady construction crew through his poacher team's contacts but within six months the facility was fully operational, complete with rooms designed to contain enhanced humans of varying abilities which would be none the wiser to the world at large.

Having put the project on hold for half a year to accommodate the facility's construction, Sharp immediately resumed his plans by having Dawn and the poacher team hunt down and bring in test subjects. Each captive would typically serve a 2-3 week stint with

Dr Murphy popping in erratically whenever his schedule would allow it to conduct his research into their abilities. Sometimes they stayed longer but were always released back onto the streets with no memory of what had happened to them. Most would probably report their own disappearances to the police but assumedly would have nothing to give them in regards to where they had been or what had happened to them and there seemed to be little investigation into what appeared to be a serial kidnapper on the loose.

In any event, Sharp saw absolutely no blowback from his scheme whatsoever. Meanwhile, Murphy was compiling valuable information that would at some point hopefully unlock the secrets behind all abilities and possibly even being able to implant them in regular human beings.

With that thought in mind, Ryan had considered maybe subjecting himself to such a process. Although her power had been crucial to his plans, he considered Dawn's ability sensing unremarkable. He had witnessed far more impressive examples and noted several as candidates for taking on as his own if the opportunity ever arose, another reason for keeping track of any released captives.

He was then brought a video from Dawn showcasing what appeared to be a brawl in a park. He soon realised it was actually a single person taking on an entire group of others with powers and that the hooded individual was using multiple abilities to not only fend them off but incapacitate them as well. Dawn regrettably had not been able to keep a trace on the subject and her sensing ability had not picked up on any base power that would explain how they had come into having so many at once. He tasked her with trying to seek out the intriguing person as a number one priority from that point on.

Being a realist, Sharp did not always expect straightforward and fast results but he had been pleasantly surprised to receive a call in the early afternoon from his good friend that the multi-powered person in the black clothes and hoodie had been found. While he felt slight disappointment in regards to the minor drawback that the base ability in question responsible for enabling this only allowed absorption of powers on a temporary and limited basis, the prospect of possessing an ability that allowed the bearer to have several more simultaneously was still an appeal to him.

And now he had her in his observation room, ready to see first-hand exactly how the absorption process worked. Or at least he would when she finally woke up.

Jamie opened her eyes groggily, looking straight into a ceiling light before the realisation of her situation quickly woke her up; she was in a room surrounded by padded walls with a windowless steel door. The first thing to mind was that it resembled something typical of a psychiatric hospital, or what she had seen depicted in cartoons anyway.

She then noticed that there was another unconscious person in the room with her, a young male who looked roughly her own age, tall with sandy blonde hair. She quickly checked her pockets, feeling relieved that all her possessions were still on her including her phone. She tried to turn it on, only to find it was completely dead despite the fact it had had plenty of battery remaining beforehand.

She could feel panic trying to set in but instead tried to quell it by scoping out the door to the room. It had no handle or keyhole and presumably could only be opened from the other side. She attempted a quick kinetic energy wave attack on it, only to find it completely ineffective against the metal surface.

"Huh?"

Jamie turned around to see that her cellmate had awoken and was very visibly disturbed by his surroundings. He then looked straight back at her.

"What's going on, who are you?"

"Abducted, just like you I'm guessing," she replied.

"Abducted? By who?"

"I don't know, I got hit with tranquiliser and I just woke up a minute ago. Didn't the same happen to you?"

"I can't remember."

"Well where were you when you got snatched?"

".......I can't remember."

"You honestly can't remember what happened to you before you got knocked out?"

"I think I recall.....yeah, I was in another room but smaller than this one. It was like a prison cell."

"Were you abducted from prison then?"

"I've never even been arrested," the youth answered, much to Jamie's confusion.

"Hello people!"

Jamie and Mikael both looked up to the ceiling as a slightly distorted voice came out of nowhere.

"Good to see you both awake. You're both probably wondering what you're doing here. Well, for you Mikael it will be the fourth time it's been relayed to you but nonetheless feel free to listen anyway."

"What do you mean 'fourth'?" he asked the voice, failing to recall having ever been previously told of his situation.

"You're here because you can both do special things. We just happen to be interested in these special aspects of you and would like to see them for ourselves up close. So what you're going to do is face each other in a quick duel using them."

"Get lost," Jamie said loudly, folding her arms in defiance.

"We can't actually hear what you say in there but in case you aren't too keen on the idea, as an incentive we are offering the winner their immediate freedom."

"What d'ya reckon?" Ryan asked Dawn as they both stood watching the large monitor in his office. "Will that be enough to coax her into it?"

"It's worked every other time, I don't see why not now," Dawn replied optimistically.

"She doesn't seem very interested."

"If she's going to be stubborn, Mikael caved in pretty fast the last few times you shoved him in there."

"True but it's not *his* power that I want to see. Guess we can only hope he brings it out of her."

* * *

Back in the room, Jamie stood firm in her refusal to comply with the demand as she turned her head to Mikael, who was facing her directly with a concerned look on his face.

"Don't be stupid," she remarked.

"I'm sorry," he replied. Jamie watched as his skin began to transmute into metal, feeling a chill go down her spine.

"They're just playing us."

"I know but I'm not staying in the room."

"You're only going to give them what they want," Jamie said, her voice almost bordering on desperation.

"Just play dead, I'll come back for you when they let me out."

"They're not letting you go anywhere, idiot."

"That's a chance I'm just going to have to take," Mikael said as he moved towards the girl before him.

"Chance *this*," Jamie replied as she fired an energy wave at him in response. Like the door, however, it had no impact on his metallic form. She began moving around the room instead to avoid him, being notably faster compared to his sluggish movements.

Perhaps the metal skin weighs him down?

Jamie realised the only way to combat Mikael was to drain his power away from him, maybe even take it for herself. But then she would be playing directly into their abductor's hands and giving them exactly what they wanted in their request for a demonstration of her ability, or at least her actual one.

Resisting that, she aimed a more powerful energy wave at her opponent. Despite dealing no damage again, the force of the attack was enough to knock Mikael backwards and off balance. Jamie followed it up with a dropkick to his chest, feeling as though she had just planted her feet into a solid structure but it was enough to knock the enhanced human into the wall.

Mikael quickly used the padded surface to springboard back forward into the girl before she had a chance to see him coming as she got up off the floor and grabbed her in a bear hug with her face facing his. He knew she would not be able to force him to release his grip in his metal form and began to lightly squeeze her.

"Seriously, just fake being knocked out so I don't have to do this," he said apologetically.

Jamie struggled to catch her breath. It appeared that Mikael was trying to compress her airway and force her into unconsciousness with his tightening grip on her torso. She knew she would soon pass out if she did nothing to counter his hold on her.

Reluctantly, she raised her arm as high as it could in the bear hug and tried to reach up under the back of his shirt. She managed to feel his metal skin with her fingertips and quickly began trying to absorb his active power.

"Ryan, this is it! She's activating her base power!"

Mikael failed to notice that his skin was slowly returning to normal flesh as he continued to hang on to the girl. Soon though, he realised that she was becoming heavier and could barely hold her up without significant effort.

Jamie began to feel the vice grip hold around her lessen in firmness as she watched Mikael's face turn back from metal to normal. Infuriated, she tried summoning his metallic power now within her, subsequently feeling her skin harden all over underneath her clothes as her sense of touch completely vanished.

Mikael reacted in surprise and horror as he saw her transform but took a steel headbutt direct to the forehead before he had a chance to react. He stumbled for a few seconds as he began seeing flashing colours, knowing he had likely just been concussed. Jamie watched on as he gradually fell to the floor in complete disorientation before closing his eyes.

Sharp looked on through the monitor as his new star subject stood tall over her fallen opponent.

"You manage to decipher how that ability works exactly?" he asked Dawn beside him.

"Yeah," she replied, in a somewhat subdued manner.

"And?" Ryan curiously responded.

"Well it's actually a multi-tiered power: what we've seen so far is the ability to absorb other powers via skin contact but it appears to also manipulate another being's powers in terms of strength from making them hopelessly weak or extremely powerful. Furthermore, it also allows her to detect the use of nearby powers within a certain range."

"But..." Ryan interjected, sensing a drawback about to be revealed.

"Unfortunately, any ability absorbed will indeed permanently dissipate upon the supply of it taken naturally running out."

Ryan couldn't help but show his obvious dismay at the unwelcome confirmation. Nonetheless, he still felt extremely content with the prospects of making use of such a power, as long as Dr Murphy was able to crack the genetic code behind it.

"Alright, think it's time we took her downstairs," he said to Dawn.

"Mikael too, I'm guessing?"

"Until we administer the next dose at least, then we could do with letting him go seeing as we've held him for over a fortnight now. I don't think we'll have much need for any of the others either soon enough."

"How so?"

"Well don't get me wrong, we're still relying on Dr Murphy's research into each individual ability to try and determine if there's a common denominator in their genetic make-up or if it's a different DNA sequence in every person. As far as garnering multiple abilities though, we can just focus on this power to achieve that."

"Even though it can't sustain them permanently?"

"If we figure it out on a genetic level, maybe we can alter it too. Then we can achieve permanence."

"Of course don't forget that the main objective is to understand all powers and not just this one, Ryan."

"Of course," he replied, reminding himself that his ultimate goal was indeed to achieve worldwide recognition for developing the ability to implant super-human powers into regular human beings. "But no harm in getting excited over this particular one though."

"Well it's an ability all the same. Just means you can charge more for it when it's ready to be marketed considering it can also acquire others."

"Uh-huh," Ryan replied, finding himself caught in two minds. He then averted his attention back to the girl on the monitor as she began attempting to tear into the padded wall in her acquired metal form. "Radio the boys and tell them to get in there with the tranquiliser darts."

"They won't work on her while she's using that ability though surely?"

"She'll either wear herself out and deactivate it or the ability will drain out of her the more she uses it. Whatever comes first, we'll be ready to strike when it's gone."

Jamie studied the room meticulously, figuring that her best bet of escaping the room would be to try and claw her way through the padded wall rather than try and dislodge the seemingly impenetrable steel door and hope the structure behind the padding was weak enough to break through with the strength and durability of her metal form.

Logically, she went straight for the wall next to the door and began raking at it with her fingers, her fingernails having converted to metal as well which gave enough of a sharp edge to slice into the padding.

As she continued to burrow her way through the thick-layered padding, she eventually reached brickwork which suffered denting upon her metal fingers scraping it. However, the metallic form soon left her fatigued owing to the increased weight with every movement, confirming her earlier theory. She quickly subdued the ability to gain a brief moment of rest, immediately feeling her entire body being considerably lighter in the process.

The door then unexpectedly burst open with two figures in black storming in with large guns at hand. Before Jamie could make a move, she felt the familiar pain of a dart piercing her leg. As she took on her metal form once more, she began to quickly feel the effects of what she assumed was a tranquiliser again as she slowly lost all sense of balance and fell to the floor in a heap.

Jamie awoke in a much smaller room, featuring a bed and a toilet with a transparent door fencing her in. She slowly rose to her feet and looked through the glass, seeing other doors of varying material along a corridor with only hers being see-through.

Attempting an immediate escape, she activated her metal form and lodged a punch directly into the door, finding it barely even scratched the surface. She deduced that she was dealing with bulletproof glass, likely composed of polycarbonate as opposed to layered acrylic plastic which, unlike the latter, was extremely unlikely to break from blunt force attacks.

Suddenly, panic fully set in; she had no way of escaping her confinement with her current powers and she had no idea where she was or how long her captors planned to keep her there. She figured Gabrielle would notice her disappearance and probably alert law enforcement but that would be to little effect in securing her release without knowing where she was. If she was even still alive by that point depending on what the overall plan was to do with her. She knew whoever 'they' were had an interest in her ability but to what extent that was worth keeping her life intact she could only guess.

She decided to shake off her fear and began analysing the room structure. Everything else apart from the door appeared to be solid steel, possibly even titanium if the cell was generally designed to contain an empowered human being and there would be little possible way of breaking through that with her available kinetic energy waves and metal form. That just left the door which, while extremely durable, had more weaknesses than the rest of the room and would virtually be her only means of escape.

As there was no door handle or lock (again) it would appear that entry to the room was controlled possibly via electronics on the other side. Jamie suddenly wished she had kept Sissy's electrical ability which, despite the lethal risk it posed using on people, would have been useful in shorting any circuitry she could access. She also felt annoyance that the gang leader from the previous evening, Miles, had deactivated her pyrokinesis.

Or was it just dormant?

Jamie reflected on Miles' use of his ability – he had easily quelled the out-of-control flames that had threatened to engulf his co-hort which had then remained extinguished but it hadn't shut down her kinetic energy wave ability, just the waves themselves.

She then recalled overhearing that his gang's plan had been to shut down London's power supply. She also remembered a part of the city suffering a power cut the prior month, not unlike what they had planned. *Was that also down to him?* The electricity had not been restored until the following morning, whether by engineering means or maybe Miles' power's effect on the source of the electricity wearing off naturally. If so, it had taken nearly half a day to restore to normal.

Jamie focused her thoughts on her pyrokinesis ability. If Miles had merely deactivated it temporarily, what would it take to reactivate it? If it restored by natural means, it had certainly been long enough in comparison to the power cut incident. Even the powers her own manipulation ability deactivated restored themselves after several hours had passed she noted.

With that, she held out her palm and concentrated hard on trying to emit a flame, feeling defeated when nothing materialised. She continued to try nonetheless in the likelihood of it going to be her only way out of her predicament. She focused even harder on trying to produce even the slightest ember, anything to show she still had the ability within her body.

Finally, a glimpse of a minor flicker emerged, quickly dissipating as soon as it had appeared.

With renewed hope, she began trying to channel her energy in trying to produce a larger flame through her hand. After a few seconds, a small ball of fire formed in her open palm and remained there with concentration. Jamie then focused on trying to expand it, slowly watching the fireball getting larger in size.

Encouraged, Jamie decided to give a go with attempting to produce a jet of fire, her previous favoured use of the ability. Only a small burst briefly emerged, nowhere near as powerful as her past uses of it but it made her all the more determined to keep trying, soon producing a slightly larger one. Eventually, the desired flame jet surged forth from her hand to her delight.

She then walked up to the bulletproof glass door. Approaching it from against the wall staring sideways into it, it appeared quite thick with varying layers. From her limited knowledge, it could be weakened by a high degree of heat but it would take a sustained effort to get through all the layers that comprised it. Ideally she would weaken it enough to be able to punch through with her metal form.

The only other problem to arise would be the oxygen level in the compact room being rapidly consumed by the flame produced. She would have to hope for a quick result before she succumbed to the air level dropping too fast for her lungs to maintain her breathing.

Jamie activated her metal form for protection against the heat and unleashed the largest flame she could produce.

Chapter 8

"Ryan, are you there?"

"What's up?" Ryan spoke into his communicator upon hearing Dawn's voice.

"Have any of the captives downstairs got a fire-producing ability?"

"Nope, the closest being Lauren Hudderson in cell 2 with her heat-emitting ability."

"Well I've just got a reading on someone very close by using such a power and I get the feeling it's that girl."

"*What?* You told me she didn't have that anymore!" Ryan exclaimed, jumping out of his chair and observing the monitor once more.

"I thought she didn't! She would've used it already against Mikael if she had it!"

"Hang on, I'm checking now," he said as he squinted at the multi-screen view of each of the six cells' security feeds. In the cell 1 screen, he caught a rear-view sight of the unnamed girl in metallic form blasting a large flame at the transparent door.

"Is it her?"

"Yeah, she's attacking the door with it," he grimaced. "Goodness sake Dawn, I would've switched her with Mikael in cell 5 with the titanium door if I'd known she had that power at her disposal still!"

"Can she melt through the glass?"

"I don't know, maybe? Bulletproof glass is only resistant to so much heat even by its durable standards and I've no idea how much of it she's putting out. Call the boys and get them ready with more tranq. Hopefully we won't have to resort to further measures."

"Like what? Shooting them?"

Ryan paused for a moment. "Let's just focus on getting the situation under control first," he said finally while keeping his gaze locked on the monitor of cell 1.

Jamie could feel the supply of her pyrokinetic ability growing weaker, opting to stop the flow from her hands to conserve it. She then slammed her metal-encased fist hard into the epicentre of where the fire had been targeted – the glass sustained some minor damage but significantly more than her first futile attempt minutes earlier. She then began hammering blows into the door one after another until she managed to cause a crack to form in the weakened polymer layering.

Retreating all the way to the back of the cell, Jamie launched herself with a running charge into the cracked glass shoulder-first. The result was a large part of the front layer shattering and revealing the outer layer that still remained intact. Jamie applied her fire ability once more at full blast, knowing it would likely be the last of the remaining energy reserve but gaining her freedom was worth it.

After putting the rest of her pyrokinesis into the effort, she then began furiously punching through the final thick layer until another crack formed and charged straight into it at full force once more, delivering a hard dropkick to the crack that caused it to resemble a spider web. With a final effort, Jamie slammed into the door and completely shattered the remaining layer, emerging onto the other side of the cell.

Feeling tired but elated, Jamie deactivated her metal form after picking herself up off the shards of bulletproof glass around her on the floor. She looked around the corridor she found herself standing in and noted five other cells – three on each side – with a heavy looking door sealing the chamber. She knew she would never be able to break through that alone and approached the cell that had been directly next to hers, reading a small whiteboard next to it with writing on it.

Lauren Hudderson - Heat Generation.

The cell featured a steel door with a keypad, presumably entry-code activated. Jamie reactivated her metal form and smashed her left fist into the keypad. She then pulled on the door handle, finding that the locking mechanism had been successfully disabled as a result as she looked inside the cell.

"Who are you?" a terrified young girl standing at the back of the cell asked.

"How long have you been here?" Jamie asked instead while dropping her metal form.

"I don't know, I can't remember. I don't even know where I am."

Just like that Mikael guy. "Come with me, we're getting out of this dump," Jamie said, trying to be as welcoming as possible to calm the girl down. Lauren slowly moved towards the doorway, feeling like she would rather take her chances with what appeared to be a rescuer than stay in the claustrophobic holding cell any longer.

"I'll smash, you open," Jamie said to Lauren as her skin turned to metal once more. She then sent her encased fist into the four remaining cells' keypads one after the other before opening the final cell door herself.

Inside she found an unconscious person lying on a medical bed in the middle of the room hooked up to what appeared to be an electrocardiogram machine among other apparatus. Jamie looked at the whiteboard next to the door.

Ben Thomas - Corrosive Touch.

"Everyone's been released," Lauren stated, walking up beside her liberator and staring into the room. "What's up with this one?"

"Says on the board that his power is something called 'Corrosive Touch'," Jamie answered. "I'm guessing they've put him in an induced coma because his ability would allow him to break out of his cell."

"Well let's just wake him up and get out of here."

"It's not that simple. The drugs currently keeping him sedated need to be eased out of his system. We could induce brain damage if we just unhook him right away. I haven't the expertise to safely bring him out of the coma."

"We can't just leave him behind," Lauren protested.

"Think we're gonna have to," Jamie replied, the reluctance obvious in her voice as the other freed captives joined them huddled around the doorway of Ben's cell. "It's annoying too in the sense that he has an ability that we badly need to get us out of here. Let's figure out what we have at our disposal in the meantime; how does yours work?"

"I generate heat from my hands," Lauren replied. Jamie grimaced as she realised what little help it would be. She then noticed Mikael and the girl she had fought in the small field standing next to Lauren.

"Well I already know what you two have," she scornfully remarked.

"It wasn't personal," Mikael rebutted.

"Just keep your distance," Jamie glared. She then looked at the last remaining captive, a young woman who appeared to be in her early twenties. "What do you have?"

"I can influence people's thoughts," she replied.

"Brilliant," Jamie sighed as her last hope of utilising a half-decent ability to forge a way through the room door at the end of the corridor was all but extinguished.

Then, she had a brainwave.

"Can you influence the thoughts of an unconscious person?" she asked the person, gesturing for her name in the process.

"My name's Tara, and I don't know about that."

"Well we've got nothing to lose by trying," Jamie replied as she grabbed the bare arm of the unconscious Ben. "How does it work?"

"I put my hand on a person and tell them what to do with my thoughts."

"Do that to him right now and tell him to activate his ability so I can absorb it."

"Are you crazy?" Mikael blurted out. "How's that going to work while he's out of it?"

"Trust me mate, I'm a strong believer in science and even I would think this would be impossible but it's a bit easy right now to throw all that out the window when you can turn your body into metal and I can throw waves of kinetic energy," Jamie snapped back before turning to Tara. "And besides, this is our only option right now. Ready when you are, love."

Tara put her fingertips on Ben's forehead and began concentrating her thoughts onto his. She was dismissive herself on how successful the attempt would be but agreed that it was better than doing nothing. Jamie started the absorption process through Ben's arm but found no surge of energy coming through her hand. It was difficult even knowing what she was trying to absorb without any knowledge of how his ability even operated and briefly paused the process. Considering his power was referred to as 'Corrosive *touch*', she fixed her gaze on his hand in hope something would happen.

"Can you smell that?" Lauren said.

"Yeah," Jamie answered, noticing the burn marks on the bed cover under Ben's fingers. She reactivated her absorption power and this time began feeling the corrosion ability flowing into her body, taking the maximum that she could before disengaging. "Right, I've got what we need. Let's head to the main door."

"And him?" Mikael asked, referring to Ben.

"He's got to come with us," Lauren chimed in.

"I know that but he can't!" Jamie snarled. "Do not guilt me about him, alright?! We can always send the police to come get him after we free ourselves but if we move him, he could die anyway. It's better to leave him alive than risk killing him in the midst of trying to liberate him."

The rest of the captives looked sheepishly back at her. As bad as they felt about the situation, they couldn't argue against her reasoning. Jamie simply walked past them towards the door, with everyone else following her.

"Your power increases your natural strength with your emotions, did you say?" Jamie asked Sally.

"Um, yeah. But it'll also weaken you if you feel scared or miserable," she meekly answered.

"I'll keep that in mind. Hold out your hand."

"Why?"

"Because I'm taking some of it for myself."

"Will it hurt?"

"I took some earlier from you, did it hurt then?"

"Uh, no."

"Then stop wasting time," Jamie replied impatiently, gesturing for Sally's hand which she eventually complied with before absorbing as much as she could. "Now I should be able to boost this corrosive ability to its full potential when I use it on the door. This may take some time so watch my back for any surprises."

In his office, Sharp was staring with increasing worry at the monitor showing the scenes in the basement dungeon. It appeared as though the nameless girl had somehow managed to extract Ben Thomas' ability from his unconscious body and was using it on the main door to the holding area. He didn't know exactly how effective the ability would be on reinforced concrete but it looked highly likely that the captives were going to escape their confinement very soon.

"I knew I was going to regret bringing that Ben kid in," he muttered aloud before addressing Dawn next to him. "I've got a plan."

"You do?"

"Yeah. But it does partially involve setting them loose."

"Would you like to expand on that?" she replied with a tone of disbelief in her voice.

"Well the problem is that even if we subdue the whole lot of them I now have no functioning holding cells to contain them and they'll soon have trashed the main door to the basement too so I'd rather not incur further unnecessary damage if I can help it."

"By letting them go and potentially sending the police to our doorstep?"

"And when exactly did we administer the modded benzodiazepines again?"

"About....twenty minutes ago," Dawn answered while checking her watch.

"They take roughly thirty minutes, maybe a bit extra, to kick in. By the time they get out of this building, they will all be close to forgetting what happened to them. No-one will remember a thing."

"But six missing youths all reappearing in one place at once may very well draw unwanted attention, Ryan. Whether they can remember what happened to them or not."

"Well here's my plan: we let them outside via the secret rear underground exit that I had installed for such an emergency which bypasses using the lift and immediately tranquilise all of them, and cattle prod the girl and Mikael if they've got that metal ability activated. Then we get the boys to dump them each near their respective residences in three different cars with fake licence plates and they can find their own way home. They'll have no idea where they came from by the time they wake up."

"And of the girl? We don't even know what her name is, let alone where she lives."

"She's still a person of interest, we can't let such a valuable ability slip away from us. We will dump her back where you picked her up earlier and we'll let her find her own way home from there while we tail her. Once we get an address, we'll be able to identify her."

"We could be waiting a while on her, it took over three hours for her to wake up both times we tranq'ed her earlier."

"Patience is a virtue, especially when it's the difference between losing and gaining critical information. Radio the guys and let them know of the plan, they have mere minutes to take their positions."

* * *

"How's it looking?" Sally anxiously asked aloud.

"You tell me, I haven't a clue how thick this thing is," Jamie snapped back. "My estimate is that I'm nearly a foot into this so we've got to be close now."

"Are we just going to leg it when we get through?" Lauren asked.

"Pretty much. Just stay behind me and Mikael, we'll shield the rest of you with our metal skin abilities."

"Sounds good," Lauren replied as she watched the girl with the colourful hair continuing to burn a large enough gap through the door. It had dawned on her to ask her for her name but didn't want to be on the end of her seemingly short fuse of a temper. Not that she blamed her; the situation was stressful for everyone but at least she was taking charge in trying to get them all out of it.

A minute later, the expectant group watched as the nameless girl finally bore through to the other side of the door.

"Alright, give me another minute and we're going," Jamie said as she furiously ploughed through trying to erode the rest of the remaining thin layer of reinforced concrete. Impatiently, she then reactivated her metal form and kicked through the last part, leading the rest of the captives through the hole and towards a set of stairs. She felt completely guilt-trodden over leaving Ben behind but she knew she was helpless to do anything about it at that moment in time, though she reckoned five abducted people suddenly reappearing and reporting the place to the police would be enough to have him safely rescued soon enough.

As they reached the top of the staircase, the group encountered a corridor with two doors either side of them and a lift at the end.

Jamie cautiously approached the transparent door to the right and examined the inside of the room that strongly resembled a laboratory.

"What is that all about?" Tara asked, peering in.

"Don't know, maybe they experiment on us in there?" Jamie speculated.

"That looks like the door from that room we were made to fight in earlier," Mikael said aloud, referring to the heavy steel door on the opposite side of the corridor.

"Seems like the lift is the only way out then," Jamie replied.

"What if it doesn't work?" Mikael asked back. "They could have disabled it."

"Let's try it out first before we come to that," Jamie responded as they all made their way over to the lift. Upon pushing the button, Jamie received the suspected lack of response from the doors.

"Guess we're busting our way in," Jamie stated, preparing to aim a metal-encased punch.

"What's this?" Sally interrupted, pointing at a slight gap in the side of the wall adjacent to the lift with light peering through it.

"Let's see," Jamie replied, sliding her fingers through the thin opening and trying to shift it sideways, feeling light movement as a result. "It's heavy. Mikael, give me a hand."

Mikael immediately activated his ability and, being the taller of the two, stood over Jamie who couched slightly to give him the needed space to manoeuvre. With their combined enhanced strength, the duo managed to pry open what appeared to be a secret corridor.

"You reckon it's a way out?" Tara asked.

"Maybe whoever captured us already used it themselves and forgot to close it fully," said Mikael.

"Well it's got to be better than trying to climb up a lift that is out of order," Lauren suggested. "I say we go for it."

Everybody then turned to the girl with the multi-coloured hair, the de facto leader. Jamie felt there was something off but relented, failing to see any alternative approach.

"Okay, I'll take the lead. We'll move cautiously 'cause it could easily be a trap."

"Ready when you are," Tara replied. Jamie then made her way through the doorway, leading the rest of the group through the secret corridor. They walked slowly for about close to a minute before a bend in the passage revealed a door that resembled a typical fire exit.

"Looks like we're out of here!" Lauren exclaimed. "Should we run when we exit?"

"We made it this far as a group, we need to stick together until we're completely in the clear," said Jamie. "Besides we don't know what's out there waiting for us so we'll need to combine all our powers if it comes to it."

"Agreed," Tara responded. "Let's go."

"Same as before – stick behind me," Jamie instructed as she pushed down the locking bar and opened the door, revealing a yard with a ring of fencing surrounded by an entire wall of trees. It was almost completely pitch-black outside with very little lighting.

"Anyone know what time it is?" Jamie asked before moving onwards.

"Haven't a clue, my phone's dead," Tara said. Everyone else checked their own phones, all of them found to be out of battery too.

"How can they all be dead? Or have we been here longer than we thought?" Sally pondered aloud.

"That's a good question," Jamie quipped, remembering the voice in the padded room commenting on Mikael's apparent extended captivity in the facility. "Let's make a move."

The group moved out and followed Jamie round the side of the building that they had just exited. Though it was completely shrouded in near-darkness, it looked to be at least three floors tall and didn't appear to cover a lot of area. Jamie squinted forward to see what appeared to be a road at the end of the yard.

"Alright, let's move towards that road," she said quietly as the rest of the group kept close to her.

"Ow!"

Everyone turned around to the source of the yell to see Lauren pulling a dart out from her arm.

"They're out here with us!" Sally screamed as Lauren slowly collapsed to the floor. Jamie brought her arm to her chest preparing to unleash a kinetic wave but was unable to see anyone nearby due to the darkness. Another dart suddenly bounced off her metal skin which she failed to feel at all.

"I'm hit!" Tara yelled as Sally was the next to fall to the floor unconscious. Mikael saw two further shots bounce off his metal form with Tara collapsing behind him. He looked towards Jamie who was still trying to scope out a target.

"They must be aiming from inside the surrounding forest," Jamie said. "I think we're going to have to make it out on our own."

"At least one of us needs to get out of here," Mikael concurred as more darts deflected off both of their metal skins. "I say we make a break for it. I'd hate to leave them behind but we need to get help."

"For once I agree with you," Jamie said, suddenly feeling a shiver down her spine as she saw two figures walking towards the pair of them with what appeared to be translucent riot shields in their arms. She fired her charged energy wave at one of them, seeing the wave weakly collide into the brandished shield.

"Just give in now!" the figure exclaimed. Jamie made them out to be wearing a pair of goggles over their eyes, most likely infrared vision allowing them to see through the darkness.

She then realised the emotional enhancement ability she had absorbed from Sally had probably just weakened her attack significantly from the fear she had felt. She tried to recall her bout with her in the field, recalling how strong and fast Sally had been when in control of her emotional state.

Jamie forced herself to dig into her anger and launched another kinetic energy wave. This time, the force of the impact against the shield sent the dark figure sprawling backwards several feet.

"Let's go now, Mikael," she muttered loudly to her ally as the two of them began sprinting forward. They quickly found though that their heavy metal forms were slowing their individual paces, Jamie gaining a slight advantage over Mikael owing to the boost from Sally's absorbed power in her forcibly angered state. As she slipped by the other assailant, she heard a loud clunking sound as Mikael was tripped over and hit the ground, still in his metal form.

She turned around and could barely make out the figure raising what appeared to be a baton in his hand while standing over the downed Mikael.

"Keep going!" Mikael yelled out to her. Suddenly, he let out a subdued scream as the assailant jammed the baton into him before going silent. Jamie figured he had most likely been attacked with a cattle prod of some variety before turning to the road and fleeing as fast as she could, desperately trying to keep her thoughts positive to maintain the beneficial effects from the emotional response enhancement ability.

As she got fifty metres down the dark road, she dropped her metal skin ability in order to gain speed from the lightened load, quickly making a tremendous amount of ground away from her attackers in the process.

"Where's the girl?" Sharp asked anxiously to the two grunts before him.

"She got away," one of them stated.

"Well that's bloody marvellous, isn't it?!" he angrily retorted. "Dawn, can you still sense her?"

"I can feel her using Dreiser's ability, probably helping her move faster. It's getting slightly weaker though so it may very well be running out and/or she's getting further away."

"Well it's been over half an hour now, the amnesia should be setting in soon enough to disorientate her. We need to get a car over to her now before she reaches town. Otherwise, trying to re-capture her will be near impossible."

"And if she's already made it?" the same grunt asked.

"Then you get out and keep an eye on her movements, especially if she decides to go home. The worst case scenario will be that she gets someone to contact the police for her on the grounds she has no idea where she is or how she got there but we'll all be out of here by then anyway and likely have dropped the rest off near their homes."

"Hope we're picking up some overtime for this," the other grunt cut in.

"You won't be if we all end up in the nick," Ryan snapped back at him. "Now make a move."

Jamie continued to run aimlessly down the road, her stamina being maintained only due to the continued effects of Sally's power but even that was barely allowing her to fight off the exhaustion and the lactic acid building in her legs. In the near distance she could see the glow of a lighted street, feeling relieved at seeing signs of civilisation and pushed on through the pain until she reached the outskirts of the nearby town.

Seconds later, she slowed down as she reached the end of the darkness-blanketed forest road and lightly jogged into what looked like a quaint-looking village immediately connecting to it.

She finally came to a walking pace while breathing heavily, moving forward before forcing herself to sit down on a low brick wall next to a public house to quickly rest her aching legs and air-depleted lungs. The lights were still on in the building; she hoped to be able to ask the owners to use their phone to call the police. The thought of causing a scene in front of everyone with the request terrified her but she knew it was no time for her social anxiety to overpower her with the others depending on her to save them.

As her fatigue slowly faded, Jamie suddenly began to feel heavily disorientated. Her head felt like it was suffering the worst migraine she had ever felt in her life. She pressed her fingers into her temples trying to make the pain go away to no avail as she began seeing colourful spots and shapes before her eyes. She cried out in anguish as she fell backwards onto the floor behind the brick wall, still holding her head.

"How's it looking, Dawn?"

"I can still detect Dreiser's ability within her, we're nearing town now."

"Good, keep your eyes peeled. I've just sent out the other two cars to drop off the rest of the group so the girl's now the only loose end. Keep in touch when you spot her."

"Will do," Dawn replied as Sharp hung up the phone call. As they arrived at the village, she could feel the emotional enhancement ability spiking in her head as it was still passively activated but as such, it would gradually diminish with every passing minute because of that fact too which would make tracking the girl nigh impossible as soon as it was completely gone, raising the need to find her ever more important before it did so.

"She near, Dawn?" one of the poacher team grunts asked while driving the car.

"Yeah. Pull over nearby so we can keep an eye out. She may be in the pub; I'll nip over and check it out. She won't know who I am anyway," she said as she exited the vehicle.

* * *

Jamie opened her eyes to see the night sky. She then sat up, only to feel a sharp ache in her head as she did so. When the pain subsided, she realised she was sitting on a grass lawn behind a shallow brick wall. An icy coldness surged through her, causing her to feel oddly weak in response as though each of her limbs weighed hundreds of pounds. Slowly, she stood up and saw the street light-lit road before her, stepping carefully over the wall and making her way to the pavement.

Where am I? And how did I get here?

The last thing she could remember doing was going to bed after having had a late shower following the battle against the gang in the park, recalling the literal dressing down she received from Gabrielle for the smell she brought in with her from it.

And then, absolutely nothing. How on earth did she end up where she was from her bed in her house?

Jamie looked at the front of the building she was currently standing beside, seeing that it was a pub. She then checked her pockets, finding her phone, door key, Mp3 player and a £20 note all on her as per always. She then felt a thin, rectangular object in her lower right pocket, pulling it out to find what appeared to be a business card. She read the text:

John Fulmer

Eastwell Charitable House

Denington Street

London

E19 6TJ

Jamie put it back in her pocket, having no clue where it came from but assumed she must have received it for a good reason, otherwise she would have already thrown it out. Her phone was completely out of battery, for some unexplained reason, which meant calling Gabrielle was out of the question and even if she had the option she couldn't even give a location for her to pick her up in her car.

That just left having to ask someone behind the bar of the pub where the nearest train station was or even what town she was in. The thought made her shudder but she really didn't have a better option.

Dawn exited the pub and immediately walked straight back to the car with the poacher grunt still waiting in the driver's seat.

"Any luck?"

"None but I can still feel her nearby. That was the only place I could think she could be in so I guess we really are just going to have to sit tight and keep our eyes out for her."

"You absolutely sure?" the grunt responded, a hint of disbelief in his voice.

"Positive. We'll give it until I can no longer track her, then we'll head back. Ryan says her memory will be gone anytime soon now so the only problem we'll have by that point is not knowing where she lives."

Jamie approached the entrance of the pub, seeing a young woman walking away from the building. Despite her anxiety, she entered it anyway to find a moderately packed room with thankfully very few customers standing at the bar. She reluctantly moved towards the waitress at the counter.

"Hi hun, sorry but do you have ID on you?" she asked.

"Uh, no I don't," Jamie replied. "I'm lost, I was wondering if you could tell me where the nearest train station is?"

"Yeah, no problem. It's literally less than a five minute walk from here. Just take a left out the door, then another and head all the way down the road and you'll come across it."

"Thanks."

"No worries, sweetie. You take care."

"Will do," Jamie replied as she headed back outside, feeling more at ease.

"Is that her?" Dawn asked the grunt as she saw a familiar figure leaving the pub entrance.

"If it isn't, whoever that is has an amazingly similar wardrobe," he responded. "How the hell did you not see her in there?"

"Must've been in the toilet while I was looking around. I think that power she absorbed from Sally Dreiser is on the verge of running out because I can barely feel it now. Let's see where she goes before following her."

"She's just turned left down that side road," the grunt pointed out.

"She must be heading to the station that's down there. If she's planning on getting home, you need to follow her on foot."

"Why not you?" he protested.

"Because she can detect powers near her and if she feels mine for whatever reason, it might give the game away. Just get after her before she escapes us again."

"She didn't feel it just now!"

"Probably because she's too busy trying to get to the station to concentrate on it! Stop arguing and make a move already!"

Jamie arrived at the London Underground station near the end of the road. She still had no idea where she was but according to the map of the network, she only needed the one train to take her ten stops to her destination with no change overs onto another line which would probably amount to a half hour journey with a subsequent ten minute walk to her house.

Walking onto the platform, the time on the announcement board stated that it was currently 7:34pm, which bizarrely was close to the time she had gotten out of the shower. *How is that even possible?* She dropped her confusion momentarily as the next train arrived, boarding it and taking a seat in the middle of the aisle.

Jamie sat despondently counting down each station as she grew nearer to her destination. It was annoying her that nothing about her current situation made any sense whatsoever; be it why she had ended up in the middle of nowhere to her phone being out of battery or even having known what the time was until the electronic board had pointed it out.

As the train stopped again for the sixth time, she noticed out of the corner of her eye that the man a little further up the aisle was staring at her. She glanced at him in response, only for him to go back to reading the newspaper in his lap.

Probably the usual moron unfamiliar with my hair and dress sense.

Ignoring him, Jamie continued sitting in wait for the train to arrive at her station.

The train then stopped at the seventh and eighth stations on her journey. Jamie gave another look at the man across the aisle who again averted his gaze from her back towards his newspaper. Another two stops and she would be rid of him.

As the penultimate stop neared, Jamie again caught the stranger down the aisle staring at her, only for him to look away in response. As the train doors opened, she began to feel more unnerved than irritated with his apparent obsession with how she looked.

Or maybe he's interested in something else...

She thought about readying a kinetic energy wave in case he tried to make a move towards her, instead deciding against it knowing she was only one stop away from getting off.

As the doors closed and the train headed on to her final destination, Jamie kept an eye on and off the man down the aisle. Now he was attempting to peep at her while holding up his newspaper just below his eye line.

To her relief, the train finally arrived at her stop. She then hesitated, keeping a watchful eye out on her apparent stalker.

As she heard the noise indicating that the doors were about to close, she leapt up out of her seat and ran through the closing doors, narrowly avoided having them shut on her as she landed on the platform. She looked back at the now closed doors, seeing that the man had also gotten up and was staring at her through the window.

She raised her arm to gesture her middle finger at him as the train continued onwards before heading to the exit.

Creep!

Arriving at her front door, Jamie slowly turned her key in the lock and crept up the staircase to her room. There, she plugged her phone into the charger and waited for the main screen to come on. When it did, she checked the date to see that it was the 23rd of March.

What?!

Jamie felt utter bewilderment. Surely it meant to say the 22nd? She then walked across the room and booted up her laptop, finding that it too was listing the date as the 23rd.

Something was definitely not right.

"Jamie?"

Jamie shook in fright as Gabrielle popped her head through her bedroom door. "When did you get home?"

"Oh, a few minutes ago," she responded.

"I didn't even hear you come in. And you didn't leave your shoes at the door like always."

"Yeah, sorry about that. I just wanted to check something online quick before I forgot. I was trying to grab some more of my hair conditioner across town and the trains were delayed by an hour on the way back."

"Did you get it?"

"Huh?"

"The conditioner?"

"Oh. No, they were sold out."

"Are you alright?"

"What do you mean?"

"Something just seems off."

"I'm fine. You just surprised me."

"Okay," Gabrielle replied, slightly miffed. "Do you want dinner? I'll put a pizza on for you."

"Yeah, if you wouldn't mind," Jamie replied as she watched Gabrielle depart downstairs to the kitchen. She shut down her laptop and laid back on her bed while kicking her shoes off. Something was seriously wrong and she didn't have a clue as to why. Did it have something to do with the person whose name was on the business card found in her pocket? If so, why would they put their name and address on it to lead her back to them?

She took the card out and put it on the desk at the end of her room. Whatever the reason, it felt as though it had enhanced human activity written all over it.

Perhaps she would pay the Eastwell Charitable House a visit the following day.

"Honestly Dawn, what do I pay these guys for?"

"Ryan, you need to keep a cool head."

"One job. One lousy job the guy had to do was tail the girl and see where she lived. Now we'll be lucky to catch her again."

"You can't blame the guy for the girl running off the train as the doors were closing."

"If that's even what happened. I tell you, if it wasn't for the fact they know too much I'd have them out of here in no time."

"Well it's just as well you have me to get the best out of them," Dawn remarked. "Here's what we're going to do: all three locations we've caught her at – the park, the street and the station she got off from – are all within two miles of each other. That helps narrow down roughly where we think she lives. We'll be focusing on her and only her for the time being seeing as it means that much that we obtain the knowledge behind her ability so you can stop worrying about everything. The most important thing right now is that all the other captives were dropped off where they needed to go and we are essentially in the clear on any abduction accusations."

"Fine," Sharp grumbled. "I'll leave it in your hands, I've got to deal with that board meeting tomorrow afternoon so you'll have to keep me updated. Also, get those idiots to contact their construction mates so we can get the basement repaired as soon as. I'll make the funds available to you for when they sort it out."

"Alright then. Just remember to be patient. Every pioneer has hit stumbling blocks on their road to success, even your dad and look at what *he* achieved."

"I know what my dad did, Dawn. I walk in the shadow of it every day," Sharp gazed back at his very visibly unimpressed friend. "Sorry."

"Just stop letting it get to you, it's all going to work out in the end," she replied as he entered the lift.

Chapter 9

Jamie sat in her bed with her laptop as she searched for the address on the business card. Apparently the location was fifty minutes away from her home on foot or half an hour with a train ride that required one changeover and at least a mile of walking either side of that train journey. She thought it hardly worth spending a fiver for a trip she could easily walk and it wasn't as though she had anything else planned at all.

Or maybe she would have if she managed to finally get round to texting Sissy. *Check this out first, then Sissy.*

She didn't even know what she would do upon finding the place. It wasn't as if anyone would openly admit to having done something to her to make her lose almost a whole day of her life, though it was still bizarre she had received a card from them (apparently) telling her exactly where to find them. Maybe she would start by asking for the John Fulmer individual who was listed at the top of the card. Even if everyone there was stonewalling her, she might still be able to detect levels of enhanced human activity within it using her own power to confirm if something was up.

On the ability front, she wasn't exactly primed for engaging in a fight with anyone; her supply of the kinetic energy wave power felt extremely weak whenever she activated it and most likely was on the verge of running out. Her measuring of it was never concrete but she believed she had enough left for one bout if it came to it, meaning the venture would most certainly strictly be of the investigative nature more than anything. She bemoaned having failed to absorb more from Gabrielle the previous night, something that would now have to wait until the evening when she returned home from work.

As she walked the open street, Jamie kept her eyes to the floor to avoid meeting anyone's gaze, still spooked by the stalker incident on the train. Whether or not it was highly unlikely that she would encounter that stranger again made no difference; she didn't like the thought of someone following her every move, particularly given the fact she was low on any offensive power to strike back. It was bad enough she felt as though she had a target on her back from having taken out the gang in the park from the previous evening.

Well, *two* evenings ago, she realised.

Smack!

Jamie shook from fright as the noise of something hitting the shop wall next to her echoed loudly, followed by the sound of water landing on the floor. She looked down to her left and saw an empty paper drink cup from a fast food restaurant.

"Hey, greebo!"

Jamie then looked to her right to see a car driving off towards a set of traffic lights, apparently the source of the missed projectile and the subsequent insult aimed at her. Fuming, she considered launching a kinetic energy wave at the rear of the vehicle despite the distance, ultimately deciding against it given the openness of the street and the few people that were currently present. Plus she needed to conserve the little amount that she still had remaining.

She walked on, getting closer to the car until the green light on the traffic signal came up. The car's tyres screeched as it zoomed away but not before the occupants of it launched another drink at a person seated on the bench next to the lights. Jamie felt even more anger at being powerless to have done anything to punish them for their malice.

Suddenly, she felt a pulse in her head indicative of an ability being used. She then saw the car swerving out of control in the distance before colliding head on with a street lamp.

As she continued walking nonchalantly towards the crash scene, several people approached the stricken vehicle. One of the few people she noticed that was not heading over to offer their help, probably for obvious reasons, was the person who had been sitting on the bench, instead getting up and walking in the complete opposite direction. Jamie gave a look at him as he walked past her with a disgruntled expression on his face, understandable given that the top half of his body was soaked from the drink being launched at him.

Was that you? Jamie thought to herself as she continued walking until she could see the damage to the left rear wheel of the car that had apparently caused it to go out of control, with the hubcap having been completely bent out of shape and shredding the tyre in the process. Telekinesis? Magnetism? Whatever it had been, it seemed most likely that the victim of the thrown drink was the culprit. She had no qualms with what he had done though, almost wishing she had been able to do it herself.

As she turned the corner away from the crash, Jamie felt another sensation, this one quite close too before dissipating. She assumed it was the same person again for a brief moment while continuing onwards.

As she let her mind wander, Jamie found herself being hauled off the street into a side alleyway and thrown to the ground.

No...

Scrambling to her feet, she felt a hand rummaging around in her jacket pocket. She instinctively pulled away and aimlessly swung a hard kick towards whoever had grabbed her. A loud groan came from the assailant who responded quickly with a hard shove, pushing Jamie back down and further into the alleyway.

"Just give me what you've got," he said to her. Without a second thought, Jamie instead swung a half-charged kinetic energy wave straight at the mugger and caught him in his midsection as he recoiled in pain from the blow.

As she went to run past him, he held out his outstretched hand with his palm facing her. A gale force wind then emerged from out of nowhere that forced her backwards. Jamie tried to steady herself but the attack was far too powerful to maintain her balance. She tried another quick kinetic energy wave but it simply dissipated into the strong wind.

Unable to think of anything else, Jamie grabbed the steel dustbin lid that was on the floor next to her and spun around several times to generate enough force before releasing it like a Frisbee in the direction of the empowered mugger.

As she fell to the ground from the recoil, the attacker simply watched as the counter force of the wind projected the steel lid straight up into the air, spinning rapidly in a circular motion and reaching the height of the rooftop before beginning its descent.

Jamie got up in time to see it falling rapidly back into the wind stream where upon bouncing off the ground, the force of the powerful gusts blew it straight into her direction. She could only watch as the metal cover flew directly into her forehead.

The thief looked on as his victim fell backwards upon the dustbin lid hitting them in the head. While a complete fluke, it had been a fortuitous occurrence as he deactivated his ability and made his way over to their prone body. He noted to himself that the hooded figure had an extremely pretty face for a guy.

Oh wait, you're a girl!

The revelation surprised him considering how masculine she was dressed, just as much at the fact she appeared to have hit him with an invisible energy attack. It mattered nothing in the end as he had out-trumped her with his more powerful ability and now he was free to claim whatever possessions she had on her.

As he prepared to bend down, a spray of water caught him in his eyes. He took a step back while trying to rub them clear for a few seconds.

Once his vision had recovered, he turned back and saw.....nothing.

No girl. Just littered debris that had scattered all over the dead end of the alleyway from his attack. He muttered angrily to himself, then made his way back onto the main road.

Jamie opened her eyes, seeing another pair looking back at her. She then rapidly came to her senses.

You...

She rolled over to the side and quickly got to her feet, staring at the youth with the flight ability standing opposite her. Without a second thought, she launched a kinetic energy blast straight at him only for it to inevitably be blocked by the same shielding power he had demonstrated previously. She tried again but she felt nothing materialise this time, the last attack having depleted her reserves.

"Are you alright?" he asked, dropping his cautious stance upon noticing that her attack had failed for whatever reason.

"Where am I?" Jamie anxiously but angrily responded, maintaining her defensive stance while examining her surroundings; it appeared they were on a rooftop somewhere.

"You're safe," he replied. "You were knocked out back there during the scrap with that guy with the wind power. I distracted him with my water manipulation ability and flew you up here."

Water manipulation?

"How long ago was that?" she asked, assuming she had been knocked out for a while.

"Well, literally thirty seconds ago."

"What?" *How is that possible?*

"Don't worry, after I flew you up I then brought you round with my healing ability."

Another one?

"Right, what the bloody hell are you?" she yelled in angry confusion.

"Well I'm human just like you," he answered. "Well, at least I think I'm human. I don't really know anymore."

"How do you have so many powers?"

"Again, I don't know exactly. I just gain them when I see someone use one and I feel like I want what they have for myself. I don't always replicate a power that a person uses though, I try not to if I don't want it or think it's dangerous."

Jamie was caught off guard by the remark, noticing that it was similar to how she herself approached absorbing powers.

"What's your story then? I assume that energy attack you've used on me the last two occasions now is what you can do?" he asked, receiving no answer in response from the cautious girl who simply stared back at him in a slightly more relaxed stance than before.

"I'd rather know how you knew I was down in that alley," Jamie broke the silence. "Were you following me?"

"Actually no. I was just flying over when I saw the car crash. I descended down onto this rooftop so I could scope it out just out of curiosity when I saw you turn the corner. Or at least I assumed it was you based on the clothes. You have quite the distinctive look among the general folk walking around."

So that was your flight ability I detected before I was attacked, Jamie thought to herself. Though she was still weary of the youth, she felt that she could accept that part of his story seeing as it appeared to add up. *You must have been too far up for me to sense you before that.*

"Then I saw that muppet haul you into the alley," he continued. "I felt like intervening but I didn't want you attacking me again if I'm honest."

"Yet you did anyway after I was knocked out?" Jamie questioned him.

"Wouldn't *you* have if the situation was reversed?" he reasoned. "Not like you could attack me while unconscious anyway."

Jamie again failed to give him a response, mostly out of stubbornness in not wanting to agree with him. The two then looked at each other in awkward silence for a moment. She observed his face again, finding him moderately attractive to her annoyance. She had waited several days for the moment to find out the secret behind his multiple abilities and now that it had unexpectedly come to fruition, she felt at a loss at how to approach it further. She had anticipated a potential second bout and had almost relished the chance to absorb his abilities.

Instead, she felt nothing in wanting to take him on again. Irritatingly, he had turned out to be a decent person, even potentially saving her life or at the very least preventing her from being mugged. Now she was clueless as what to do. Her anger had swelled with the drink thrown at her as well as the insult and it had finally peaked with the attempted robbery. Her pride had also taken a massive hit from being soundly defeated in the subsequent clash, her only real loss to date. Everything inside her was craving to release the negativity, all the hatred and frustration within demanding to be expelled in some vicious way.

But she had no desire whatsoever to take it out on the youth.

"What's your name?" he asked, breaking the silence again. Jamie looked awkwardly away, hesitant to reveal anything about herself.

"I'm Jesse," he stated, trying to get through to the reluctant girl who he noted had calmed down considerably since trying to attack him. He studied her curiously, finding her oversized-clothed appearance strange but also finding the dark attire going well against her milk-white, seemingly make-up-free skin. And her green eyes...

"Jamie," she answered belatedly, cutting off his thought process. "My name is Jamie."

"Huh," he said while looking at her with a peculiar look on his face.

"What?" she responded, confused.

"You kind of look like a 'Jamie'," he replied.

"That doesn't make any sense."

"Mind if I ask you something?"

"Depends what it's about."

"Why do you dress that way?" Jesse asked, triggering an annoyed look in the girl.

"What's wrong with it?" she snapped.

"Well nothing. I think it looks cool, it's just unusual to see a girl dress in such a guy-ish manner. And that awesome hair, I'm guessing you listen to metal then?"

"Yeah. Some."

"Makes sense. A lot of the bands I listen to dress like that."

"What bands?" she asked, taken by surprise by the admission.

"Tell you what," he said while reaching into his pocket and pulling out a device. "See for yourself."

Jamie caught it as Jesse lobbed it over to her, realising it was an Mp3 player the same make as hers albeit a different model. She scrolled through the list of artists, finding a lot of the same ones that she listened to herself among them.

"So you're into all that too," she said, giving it back to him. "You don't look very rock-ish."

"I dress a bit more reserved, I've noticed revealing myself attracts the wrong kind of attention."

Coward.

"Insults are nothing, they can't hurt you," she retorted.

"Getting punched from behind and even chased down the street is a bit more serious," he replied. She had no response to that, especially given the fact she had just had a drink thrown at her for the very same reason.

"People are pricks," she sheepishly agreed.

"Yeah. Must admit being able to fly makes escaping that crap a lot easier."

"Don't you have any offensive abilities?" Jamie queried.

"Just the one, though it's not really practical."

"What is it?"

Jesse held up his palm, which then began to emit a red hue.

"It's a heat-producing power, I don't know how hot it can get though. It was the first ability I ever absorbed but I rarely use it considering it might hurt someone."

"Why did you absorb it in the first place then?"

"I didn't intend to. The person who I replicated it from tried to use it on me, and then I used it to turn the tables on him. That was the day I discovered my ability to begin with."

Jamie stood there in bewilderment; the amount of coincidences was astounding – the similar power absorbing ability, the same reluctance to absorb other abilities that may prove overtly harmful to people.

The same discovery of his power during a traumatic event.

Jamie thought hard for a moment.

"Can you do it again?"

"What, the heat ability?"

"Yeah."

"If you insist," Jesse said, confusion in his voice as his right palm lit up again. Jamie then brought her hand up to his, feeling the heat emanating from the ability. He allowed her to place her fingertips on his wrist, then felt a slight surge through his arm before yanking it away in shock.

"What did you do?" he asked in an aggrieved manner. Instead of answering, she simply held up her own palm. He was amazed to see the same red hue suddenly appearing in her hand before dissipating just as quickly.

"I can absorb powers too," she replied at last. "I guess I didn't take enough just then, it's already gone."

"You took that from me?"

"Only a small bit."

"Can you take the rest of it too?"

"I could but it always comes back after a while."

"Really?" Jesse said, the disappointment in his voice obvious.

"Sorry."

"So you can copy powers too then, to an extent?"

"Not really. I can absorb them but only by taking the supply of it out of the person's body and into my own. I can then use it for myself until it runs out. I can also increase and decrease a person's ability and sense when they use it from a certain distance."

"That's unreal."

"I know. Bit of a drag though that they never last."

"Considering I can't get rid of one I don't even want, I think it's to your advantage."

"At least you keep the ones you *do* want."

"Swings and roundabouts, I guess."

The two looked at each other without talking again, feeling a sense of trust developing between them. Jamie could feel her bad mood subsiding too though she still remained cautious.

"How do you get all your powers?" Jesse spoke.

"I just told you how," Jamie replied.

"No, I mean how do you take them from people? I can acquire mine evidently without skin contact unlike yours; do the people you come across willingly give them over? Do you have a network of people with powers that you're friends with?"

Jamie frowned.

"Did I say something wrong there?" Jesse asked, acknowledging the sour look.

"I don't have a 'network', I just have the one friend in the world who just happens to be like us too. She lets me borrow it willingly, as you put it. Every other I've taken by force."

"Were they arseholes?"

"Nearly always," Jamie continued with an indifferent tone of voice. "But you're right if you think I'm wrong to take their powers from them without their permission."

"I didn't say that..."

"The implication was there. The fact that most of them probably had it coming doesn't really justify it in the end, I know. Truth be told, I felt gaining other powers and experimenting with them initially was one of the greatest feelings in the world, despite the fact they often confuse the hell out of me by defying the laws of science. It was a nice escape from the grim reality that was my life but it eventually lost its charm after a while. Funnily enough, *you* were the latest thing at the forefront of my thoughts in the last few days, almost obsessing with trying to find you and wanting to find out the secret behind your multiple powers. And now I've achieved that too. So I guess I'm back at square one again."

"What made your life so grim to begin with, or is it just the lack of friends?"

"You do like your questions, don't you?" Jamie said with distain.

"I find they help gain a better understanding of everything."

"I suppose you're right there."

"If it helps, I've had a pretty dire time growing up myself."

"It's not a competition."

"I'm just offering sympathy."

"I don't need pity," Jamie stubbornly responded, prompting a frustrated look from Jesse.

"I'm not saying you do, I will say though that life can get us all down at times. But we never know what tomorrow brings and we have to be grateful for the few things we do have. And chances are there's always someone out there doing even worse than us."

Jamie stared back at Jesse, feeling her irritation peaking once more. She then made her way over to him, stopping right in front of him and looked directly into his eyes, a neutral expression on her face. Jesse looked back, unsure how to react. *Did she want a hug? Was she about to hit me?*

Finally, he saw her lips part.

"My father died from cancer when I was only sixteen. Then my mother was killed in a car crash two years after that."

Jesse looked on, his eyes widening.

"I have no remaining family. I have no friends except my housemate who isn't even home half the time. All I ever do is wake up wanting to just go back to sleep because I barely have anything to look forward to."

She glared into Jesse's disheartened expression.

"My dad will never walk me down the aisle, my mother won't ever see me earn the university degree she hoped I would earn. My only friend will probably eventually meet someone, fall in love and move out which will leave me truly on my own."

She could feel her eyes welling but was determined to finish.

"And the only other thing I have in this world is this stupid, fucking power. So you might forgive me for not giving a shit about what tomorrow may bring."

Jesse simply stared back speechless. Jamie turned away and walked back to her original position, keeping her back to him with her eyes closed, hoping the tears would subside before any started falling down her cheek. As good as she felt getting it all off her chest, speaking so bluntly about her loneliness had also been bittersweet. She then heard footsteps approaching from behind.

"I'm sorry you've had to go through all that."

Jamie maintained her stance. A part of her wanted to acknowledge the gesture, another just wanted to remain apathetic. She felt completely fed up.

"And you're right when you say it's not a competition. But I know what it's like to not have my parents in my life too."

"How?" Jamie replied in a voice almost devoid of any expression.

"When I was nine, my mother abducted me and my baby sister when leaving our dad. I never saw him again."

Jamie listened with intrigue, though kept her back turned.

"She moved us in with some degenerate who never showed any care for me or my sister. We lived in fear of him for the next six years until the day after my powers developed, when I ended up taking out the person who tried to burn my face off with his power before I absorbed it and used it against him.

"When my mother's partner tried to attack me in a drunken stupor, I fought back for the first time, still feeling the rush from the previous day. I managed to kick him in the head and knock him out. While it felt great to take all those years of abuse back out on him, I was forced to leave the house with my sister while leaving my mother behind."

"Why did your mother choose to stay?" Jamie asked, still looking forward.

"She said it was to stop him from coming after me," Jesse replied. "He only wanted my mother around in the first place I suppose so I guess she stayed to placate him. Nonetheless, she managed to convince her sister, our aunt, to take us both in and we've been with her ever since. That was the last time I saw her."

"Sounds like it would've made more sense for you all to have moved in there to begin with instead of that tossbag."

"I've often thought that, but I don't know why that was never the case. I don't think my mother's completely right in the head if I'm being blunt but she always came across as looking out for her kids. And I know it's not the same as them being dead, but trust me when I say I know exactly how you feel about missing your parents and not having them around. I've lived with it in one form or another half my life and I've hated every day we've all been apart."

Jesse looked at Jamie continuing to stare forward into the skyline, unsure whether she planned to turn around to face him or not. Or if she even wanted to.

Then he saw her finally turn around, a heavy look in her eyes.

"How can you possibly feel any happiness having lived like that for so long?" she asked in a questionable and despairing tone.

"I suppose due to my anchor," he replied.

"And what's that?"

"Kayleigh; my sister. I keep going because she needs me to, and seeing her happy gives me the strength I need no matter how rubbish things are or get."

"At least you have that."

"Yeah. You know, the weird thing is she looks a bit like you."

Jamie felt overcome by surprise, cutting through her dreary demeanour.

"Well a little bit," Jesse said, getting his phone out of his jacket pocket. "What do you think?"

Jamie looked at a picture of a young girl with long, raven black hair that went past her shoulders and a smile on her face that beamed from ear to ear.

And her eyes....her beautiful blue eyes.

"She's cute," she remarked, almost feeling a slight warmth in her comment. In truth, she thought the girl shared the same appealing facial features as her brother, not that she dared say that out loud.

"I think it's the eyes."

"Huh?" she looked up from the picture.

"Your eyes; I think you both have the same brightly-coloured eyes."

"Nah, hers are more vibrant than mine," Jamie dismissively replied, though secretly liking the compliment regardless. "She seems like a happy kid."

"Yeah, it baffles me too. She just always seems so optimistic, even with all this turbulence in her life."

"Maybe because she has you," Jamie opined.

"I'd like to think so," Jesse responded. "But I believe it's more the other way round. I'd be nothing without her."

"Yeah, like me."

Jesse looked at her mournfully.

"You don't have to dress it up, we both know I'm a total negative Nancy compared to you two," Jamie grimaced.

"We've carried our pain as a team though. It's not your fault you've had to shoulder it alone."

"Maybe, I guess."

Jamie looked back at Jesse with what felt like a myriad of thoughts swirling around in her head. She had never been this frank with anyone other than Gabrielle, and even she wasn't privy to certain things in her life. Maybe because Gabrielle hadn't gone through the same trauma that she had, she didn't think her best friend could relate to that despite the overwhelming empathy she possessed.

But now there was someone before her who *had* suffered that trauma and didn't judge her harshly for acting the way she did because of it. She had never cared too much for the universe's plan for her since her mother had died but if there was ever a time to believe in that kind of thing, now seemed like that moment.

And she was so tired of carrying the burden around.

"How did it feel, to clock your stepdad?" she asked.

".....He was never my stepdad," Jesse corrected her with a resentful tone, as though the very notion filled him with disgust. It was the first break in his otherwise friendly disposition.

"Did you enjoy it though?"

"I can't say that I didn't, after all those years of abuse."

"And the guy who tried to attack you with the first ever power that you absorbed, was he just a one-off incident?"

"No, he was a high school bully who had targeted me for ages, and that was *before* I found out he had that burning ability. He probably decided to use it on me because I insulted him to someone who later turned out to be one of his mates. He chased me into the forested area beyond the school grounds and assaulted me there before I managed to use his own power against him. I believe the pain of me pushing my red-hot palms into his neck is what caused him to pass out and I just left him like that. I never saw him again and there were no witnesses to what happened but rumours started flying around that I had beat him in a fight and he was too ashamed to show his face again because of it. The general bullying I received from that day onwards just stopped, almost like I had everyone's respect at long last but no-one ever bothered to ask if it was true or not. Either way, I considered it a blessing in disguise. It got me through the last year of school with no further qualms, well except for having to move home with Kayleigh halfway through the year following me decking my mother's partner."

Jamie walked past Jesse and sat down against the doorway to the rooftop.

"Did you find some peace following all that?" she asked.

"I suppose. Well at least with the bully, seeing as I've not seen him in the three years since that went down. I guess I still feel enmity towards my mother's partner for the fact he's the reason I'm separated from her still, despite managing to lay him out. Why do you ask anyway?"

"Because *I* never got over what happened when someone with powers first tried to attack me."

Chapter 10

"When was this?" Jesse asked.

"It happened just after I got the news at the hospital that my mother had succumbed to her injuries on the operating table," Jamie answered while looking down at her shoes. "I couldn't accept what was being said to me and I did the only thing I thought I could do in response which was to run out of the building. From there, I fled to a nearby alleyway, the only place I could find that appeared to offer some solitude."

"Bit ironic considering the scraps you had with me and that idiot back there both took place in alleys," Jesse remarked as he sat down next to Jamie against the doorway.

"I sat down near the dead end of it, just crying my eyes out the whole time hoping no-one would see or hear me. I knew it was real that my mother was gone but I just sat there hoping I was going to wake up from a nightmare. And then I heard a voice from the other side of the alley."

"The person who attacked you?" Jesse cut in.

"He came to me asking if I was okay," Jamie continued on. "I didn't think I had been that loud but I was accepting of his presence because I felt so vulnerable at that moment in time even though I didn't really want anyone to see me in the state I was in. I guess the grief was affecting my mind, though I hadn't any reason to suspect any danger.

"It was then that he forced himself onto me. I tried to pull myself out from under him but he was too physically strong as he pinned both my arms down with just one of his and began feeling around underneath my shirt. I yelled out loud for help but no-one was coming. By running into somewhere so secluded, I'd almost given him the perfect opportunity to do what he wanted to me."

"Did he go further?" Jesse asked, feeling his heartbeat beginning to race.

"He reached down to try and undo the top button on my jeans but had difficulty doing it while he was leaning to one side to apply his full weight on keeping my arms pinned down with his other arm, plus I was struggling like crazy so he lifted his body up slightly to gain leverage. But he inadvertently gave me enough room to bring my knee up into his groin.

"When he released his hold on my arms, I was able to punch him in the eye. It was enough of a distraction to pull myself free and I tried to run for it, only for him to grab my ankle and haul me back down to the ground."

"And I woulda thought the low blow would have been enough to K.O. him," Jesse interjected.

"Evidently not. He tried to pull me back up but I gripped both his forearms and resisted with every ounce of energy in me until I could see an opening to attack him again.

"And that was when I felt what seemed like at the time his pulse flowing through my arms via my hands and into my body."

"Your ability manifested?" Jesse interrupted, realising how similar it was to how he had discovered his own powers.

"I didn't know what it was at the time, I was too flushed with adrenaline and busy trying to hold him off to speculate on it," Jamie answered. "Looking back on it though, it could only have been that. Eventually he managed to overpower me and dragged me back towards the far end of the alley. Then he told me he was 'going to show me something I'd never seen before'. I assumed he was arrogantly talking about his, well...thing.

"Then I saw his hand glowing green. He stood there with this evil smirk on his face seeing the terror in mine. He then said that he didn't need me alive to get inside me and he aimed his glowing hand in my direction. The last thing I remember seeing is him bringing his arm back before shooting a blast of green energy at me."

"What do you mean it was the last thing you saw?"

"I closed my eyes and instinctively held my arms out to defend myself," Jamie responded. "I honestly thought I was about to die right there and then, so much that I didn't even feel what happened next – I expected an impact of some kind but instead I found myself being knocked backwards by a heavy force that seemed to first make contact against my hands.

"As I picked myself up, I heard nothing but silence. I looked at where he had stood and saw him lying on the floor unconscious with a small, rising trail of vapour coming from his chest. I looked over him and checked his pulse to find he was still alive. In that moment though, all I cared from that point on was getting the hell out of there."

"Is that how you discovered your powers?" Jesse asked. "I guess you must have used it unknowingly to reflect his own attack back at him."

"If that's indeed what happened, it was only down to the sheer luck of having absorbed it from him in the initial struggle. Otherwise I really would've been killed there and then."

"And literally after finding out your mother had died. Piece of scum."

"I doubt he knew my mother had just died, not that it mattered. He was just an opportunist who ended up seeing his attempt to rape and murder me backfire. Who knows how many more women he's succeeded in doing the same to? He could still be doing it now if he survived the encounter and chances are he did. I should have finished him off when I had him down for the count."

"But you're not like him; you aren't a killer," Jesse argued.

"Should I be happy about that?" Jamie responded in an agitated tone. "Should I take comfort in the fact I let a vicious psychopath with a deadly ability continue living to prey on helpless people just because *I'm not a killer*? Why do I bother letting any of them walk away with their lives? All that most of them do is cause pain and misery with their stupid powers anyway."

"Because you have too much of a good heart to sink to that level."

"Oh, PLEASE!" Jamie raised her voice. "*I'm* the one who normally starts the fights with *them*! I attack them from out of nowhere just like that arsehole did to me! I even tried to attack you! And I obsessed about doing it again for several days after!"

"Do you see me coming down on you for that?" he responded. "And the more I hear what you've gone through, I can understand what drove you to do all that in the first place."

"Well whoop-de-fucking-do, pal!" Jamie yelled as she turned to face Jesse directly. "And you're so good at understanding things, can you tell me why so much shit happens to people like us?! People who have done absolutely NOTHING to deserve having their lives turned upside-down so badly in the first place?"

"I–"

"Yeah, that's right. You can't! You know absolutely nothing and yet you sit there running your mouth off pretending that you do. But it's okay because you and your sister have each other and will live happily ever after until some maniac comes by and tries to rape and kill her too!"

Jesse stared back at her, a mixed look of what appeared to be anger but mostly sadness on his face as Jamie continued to seethe back at him. He then saw her furious expression drop to one of shock as the realisation of her words set in. She then seemed caught between trying to mouth an apology and being about to burst into tears. Jamie knew she wasn't going to be able to contain her emotions this time round.

"Just leave me alone," she said as her voice broke and tears streamed down her cheeks, immediately pulling her hood over her head and covering her face with her hands with her back slumped against the doorway once more.

Jesse remained in his place, listening helplessly to her muffled cries for a few seconds before levitating into the air. Jamie felt the usual pulse in her head go off in response, dropping her hands to see that Jesse was now gone from beside her. She felt her heart sink.

"Hey."

Jamie gave a mild scream as she heard the voice from behind her, turning around to see Jesse kneeling a few inches away from her face. She immediately tried to hide her tear-soaked face behind her hands once more.

"Why are you still here?" she asked in a despondent tone.

"Because I want to be," he replied firmly. "And if I left you right now, I'd hate myself forever."

"Why though?" Jamie responded while keeping her face covered. "I just lashed out at you for no good reason at all, even after you saved me earlier. You should just go."

"I could but I don't feel like doing so. And besides, much of what you said isn't untrue anyway. That psycho *could* come across Kayleigh in the future. And I honestly can't explain why our lives have turned so upside-down despite the fact we've done nothing to deserve it."

He raised his hand and grasped the fingers on Jamie's with his own, slowly pulling her hand down from her face with her allowing him to do so. She continued to look away from him with her uncovered eye which was bloodshot from the tears.

"And you're also right about me and Kayleigh having each other."

Jesse rose to his feet while still holding Jamie's hand, who looked at him with an odd gaze in response.

"Come," he said.

"Huh?"

"We're leaving here."

"And going where?" Jamie asked, still confused.

"To have Kayleigh meet her new friend," he smiled.

Jamie was surprised by the invitation, though still felt reluctant to join Jesse as much as the idea appealed to her. She knew it was her usual stubbornness preventing her the most from opting to accept the offer as she remained sat on the floor with an unsure look on her face, something that Jesse was picking up on based on his earlier interactions with her.

"Well I have to go either way and I'd hate to leave you up here to find your own way down," he goaded in a jovial manner. Jamie gave a light-hearted smile back, using the jest as the excuse she needed to rise up at long last.

"How do you plan for us to get there?" she said, taking her hand back from Jesse's as she stood up.

"Well we can either fly there or we can get a train. And I don't really have the cash for public transport."

"Am I going to like flying there with you?"

"That depends how much you mind heights," he responded. "But even if you don't, I use my condensation ability to cloak us in the air and that makes visibility from a passenger's point of view practically impossible."

"So you don't just fly about as you are?" Jamie asked, though figuring that the condensation ability was what caused Jesse to appear to blend in with the sky upon flying away at the end of their last encounter.

"Nah, it'd be too noticeable. Not sure if the person I absorbed the power from does that but I'm not keen on drawing attention to myself."

"Is it cold?"

"It's less cold considering I don't try and fly very fast but I do recommend wearing a jacket or something warm when doing so."

Jamie still seemed hesitant.

"I tell you what – you absorb some of it first and give it a quick try so that you feel more confident."

"You want me to fly on my own without your help?"

"No, just so you have reassurance of being able to do so in case you think you'll fall off me, if that's what you're worried about."

"I'm not worried but fine, would be nice to try it out anyway," Jamie acquiesced as Jesse held out his hand. She told hold of it with her own and immediately began transferring some of the ability into herself before restoring Jesse's own reserves back to normal.

"Give it a try," he said. "Just envision yourself floating and it should happen."

Jamie began picturing the sensation in her head and tried feeling her body rising off the rooftop. After a few seconds of concentration, she managed to begin levitating slowly upwards.

"This is pretty cool," she beamed. "Wait, no, I can't stop. Help!"

"Alright, remain calm," Jesse said loudly as he grabbed one of Jamie's ankles to help anchor her to the rooftop. He then swooped up and grabbed Jamie in mid-air, using his own flight power to weigh her down while holding her closely. She wrapped her arms around his body in a panic.

"Keeping chill, we're going to descend at the same time," he said. "You can't rise any higher while I'm pulling you downwards so nothing to worry about, just focus on doing the exact opposite that you just did."

"Okay," she replied as they both lowered themselves slowly back down to the rooftop.

"It took me a bit to get the hang of it too," he said as they let go of each other. "Just try levitating inside a room starting out so you have that safety net and you'll get used to it."

"I'll keep that in mind. So how am I going to travel with you then, clinging to your back?"

"Seems the best way. I'll hover horizontally and you can hop on."

"And you won't drop me?"

"I'll hold your arms around me and fly slowly if it helps you feel safer but you should be alright just clinging on to me yourself. We'll be there in roughly twenty minutes."

"Seems slow for flying."

"Well it gets a bit windy and cooler when I go faster. For your benefit, we'll stick to that speed."

"Okay then," Jamie said as Jesse floated with the front of his body facing parallel with the rooftop floor. With some remaining reluctance, Jamie clambered onto his back and wrapped her arms and legs around his torso.

"Comfortable?"

"Enough, I suppose."

"Okay, I'll hit the vapour and we'll go up," Jesse said. Sure enough, Jamie watched as a haze began to materialise around the two of them. She then felt the ascent begin as she felt her heart rapidly beating faster. Though she could no longer see the ground, she still could envision the height they were currently rising up to and clung tighter to Jesse in response, who simply smiled to himself in amusement.

"And now off we go," he said, prompting an even tighter grip that nearly choked him slightly. He moved forward slowly before reaching a steady pace. Jamie immediately regretted not tying her hair back beforehand as it started to fly everywhere from the wind but she felt comfortable enough within the first two minutes that her heartbeat decreased back down to a moderately normal level.

The flight was relatively smooth with Jamie simply clinging on for what felt like dear life and counting down the passing minutes in her head. Jesse had been right about needing warm clothing with the wind exacerbating the mere ten degrees Celsius temperature, which was otherwise enough in regular circumstances to get away with just her hoodie. To her fortune though, Jesse's body warmth was enough to just about make up the difference except for her ankles which she could feel were slowly going numb from the cold as well as her feet within her shoes.

She noted how nice it felt simply lying across his body, albeit the back of it, wondering if it was what she missed out on by keeping herself perpetually out of a relationship. Then she forced herself to rid the thought from her mind in embarrassment.

She then felt the wind starting to decrease slowly before becoming all but non-existent barring a light breeze.

"Alright, we're here," Jesse said. "I'm going to descend slowly, it should take about two minutes."

"How can you even tell where we are through this mist anyway?" Jamie inquired.

"I just manipulated it to give me a small window in front of my eyesight. Even then it's a bit hard to see through the wind in your eyes and being so high up to make things out below but I've done the journey enough times to grasp the gist of where everything is. Of course if I ever get lost then I just use the GPS on my phone."

"That seemed quicker than expected," Jamie said, having only counted fifteen minutes in her head.

"Think I was going a bit faster than I thought, don't exactly have a speedometer. Might feel a bit more nauseating going down than it did going up."

"I've been on roller coasters before, whenever you're ready."

"Here we go then."

To her surprise, the descent did feel worse than she had expected, likely as a result of Jesse being unable to judge his speed or just being impatient. A minute and a half later he began to slow down, Jamie watching as the haze around them dissipated into thin air to reveal trees around them.

"Excuse the landing pad but it's best that no-one sees me in person touching down," he remarked.

"Well, duh," Jamie sarcastically responded. "At least you didn't whack a load of branches on the way down."

"Oh, I have gone through that before. Here's our stop if you want to jump off."

Jamie instead opted to float down using her own absorbed flight power, managing to show enough fluency in it to land safely.

"Not bad," Jesse quipped as he touched ground himself. "Follow me."

"Won't anyone that just happens to catch a descending cloud over woodland become suspicious when they see us coming out?"

"Well firstly, I'd just call them completely nuts for thinking a cloud would do something like that. And secondly, we'll just claim to have had a lovers' tryst."

"What?!" Jamie exclaimed.

"Kidding!" he laughed while turning his head towards her. "Do you normally turn that red when embarrassed, by the way?"

Jamie looked quickly away while shielding her face with her hand in further chagrin, prompting further laughs from Jesse.

"Hey, this is just the warm-up," he jested. "You'll stand no chance against Kay if you can't hold your own to *my* jokes."

"I'm sure hers won't be as embarrassing as yours(!)" Jamie growled.

"She doesn't even know you're coming which will be the fun part. From a neutral point of view, I'm going to find it interesting seeing how she reacts."

"What's she doing at home on a school day anyway?"

"Teacher strike. Our aunt is at work but I had the day off from mine so it wasn't really an issue her being home all day."

"Yet here you are."

"Unlike my aunt, I'm not as much of a worry-wart around Kayleigh. I can trust her to be responsible, probably owing to the strained childhood we both had. Besides, I'm only a phone call away and I get good reception wherever I am."

"How high up do you actually fly anyway?" Jamie said, abruptly changing the subject. "Can't be too much."

"Well I know the Shard in Central London is just over a thousand feet tall which isn't even a fifth of a mile. I flew over to it once to get a rough scope of how high I tend to go. It was pretty minuscule flying over it so I guess I go at least half a mile high on a basic guess. If I went too low, I imagine my cloud disguise wouldn't really work as well."

"I think I was kidding myself that I'd ever be able to detect you flying around just by walking the streets," Jamie replied.

"Then why did you bother in the first place?"

"My ability to sense powers has been increasing in range all the time so I thought I'd give it a go anyway. Now knowing how high up you normally are, I never had a chance it turns out. Of course, you were on the ground when I first found you so there was always the hope of coming across you again the same way."

"Well I wasn't particularly high up earlier when I saw that car crashing. In fact, I wouldn't have even seen it if I was at my usual altitude."

"And why were you flying so low, especially if it puts you at risk of being more easily seen by onlookers?"

"Because I had just spent the morning testing out how far I could travel using my flight," Jesse said as he led Jamie out of the woodland and onto the street. "I also wanted to test out how fast I could go so I put on some thermal clothes underneath my regular ones and decided to head off towards Brighton."

"With Kayleigh on her own for an extended period?" Jamie pointed out.

"As I said, I trust her and she knows how to take care of herself. I told her I was heading out for the morning and she understood knowing that I had had it planned prior to the teacher strike forcing her to stay home."

"And how did it work out?"

"The trip itself wasn't too bad, it took about an hour and a half but the air resistance made it extremely hard for me to go too fast. I've ridden a bicycle down a hill once and kept up with the cars on a thirty mile-per-hour road limit and that wasn't so bad but it did start to get a bit much going a lot faster than that up in the air. I doubt I got anywhere past forty the whole time and even then I had to slow down intermittently to allow my eyes to recover from the wind."

"Eye visors next time?"

"No doubt. Brighton beach is quite nice though, even at this time of the year. I'd love to go back in the summer when it's warmer. I left after half an hour of walking around the place and headed back to London. Even though it doesn't fatigue me to fly, the flight ability itself does end up feeling drained if I overuse it in such short time, hence why I was flying lower than usual because if I felt it about to completely deplete, I wanted to be able to land as quickly as possible lest I end up falling to my death. Then I caught sight of that crash and my curiosity got the better of me, so I took the opportunity to land on that rooftop to have a look at it."

"I guess that's why I could only briefly sense you using your flight for a few seconds if it was that low in reserves."

"Yeah, I probably would've had to wait a bit before flying us both over had you not restored it to full power again," Jesse said as he turned into the next residential street which featured terraced housing either side of the road. "Our house is halfway down the street."

"I doubt she'll like me to be honest, I look too outlandish," Jamie worried.

"Prepare to be surprised," he merely responded.

As they reached the front door, Jamie felt herself becoming a bundle of nerves; half towards making a good impression before an eleven year-old girl but also her usual distrustful nature trying to warn her that she could be walking into a trap for all she knew. And if she was, she had no way of defending herself without Gabrielle's kinetic energy wave ability within her any longer though she did now have flight at her disposal at the least. She then attempted to assert herself that it most likely was all on the level and followed Jesse inside.

"Take a seat in the living room, I'll go get her," Jesse said as he took his shoes off at the stairs and climbed the first few steps.

"Should I leave my shoes next to yours?" Jamie asked.

"Yeah, sure," he replied. "Oh, by the way – Kayleigh knows nothing about all these powers so if you wouldn't mind keeping all that to yourself while you're around her?"

"Yeah, no problem," she reassured him as he continued walking up the staircase.

She then took her shoes off and laid them next to Jesse's before walking into the living room and sitting on the end of the sofa. The house seemed small compared to her own which was an extra third wider with a bigger living room but she nonetheless found the place cosy and inviting. She then looked at her phone, realising she had missed a message sent to her from Gabrielle, deciding to open it as she waited for the siblings to come downstairs.

Just a reminder when you're feeling down that I'm always here for you xxxxxx

Jamie smiled, then remembered once again about messaging Sissy. She wondered if it was even worth attempting at that moment in time. She opened up a new message anyway and added Sissy as a recipient of it.

"Boo!"

Jamie gasped loudly, dropping her phone on the floor.

"Hmm, guess I'm not the only one who's not allowed a smartphone."

Jamie looked to her right to see a smiling young girl leaning on the edge of the couch next to her.

"Kayleigh?"

"Nah, I'm *Bart Simpson*, who the hell are you?" she smirked.

Jamie stared back in amazement, not only at the manner of her speech but also astounded at just how beautiful Kayleigh actually was in person, even more so than the earlier picture of her had indicated.

"I'm Jamie," she answered.

"Cool name," Kayleigh replied. "I was wondering when my brother was going to bring his secret girlfriend home."

"His *what*?!" Jamie blurted out, feeling her face going extremely warm again for the second time in ten minutes.

"Wow, so Jesse was right about your face turning really red," the young girl laughed again as Jesse entered the room behind her with a huge grin on his face. Jamie simply looked back at him completely mortified.

"Glad to see you've met each other," he said, prompting a crooked smile from Jamie in response as Kayleigh then clambered over the sofa arm and onto the older girl's lap.

"I love your hair," she said while running her fingers through Jamie's fringe. "Can I have mine done like hers?"

"Yeah, when you're old enough to drive(!)" Jesse responded as he walked over and lifted his sister off Jamie by her underarms and placed her on the floor next to him. "Now be a good host and go fetch the dominoes."

"Okay," she answered excitedly.

"Oh, and bring down a pair of my socks for Jamie while you're up there."

"It's fine, I don't need any," Jamie cut in.

"You sure?" he asked. "It's not too warm in here."

"Nah, I'm alright. It doesn't bother me."

"Do you want me to bring those flowers you bought for her too?" Kayleigh said mockingly.

"I'll give you flowers, you cheeky sod," Jesse replied as he shooed Kayleigh up the stairs.

"Is she for real?" an incredulous Jamie asked Jesse as he sat next to her on the sofa.

"Pretty much all the time when our aunt's not here. I ask her to tone it down when she is; I doubt she'd be appreciative of her eleven year-old niece coming out with that kind of sass."

"That's insane. I felt like I was conversing with someone our own age."

"Might be my fault a bit there. Since we moved in here three years ago, she hangs around with me in my room a lot in the evenings and I watch a lot of *The Simpsons* episodes back to back online. She could probably quote every episode by now."

"She does know that we're not actually together, right?"

"Of course, she's just winding you up," Jesse laughed. "I thought it'd be fun to tell her to play on that with you."

"Well thanks for that(!)" she replied while giving him a playful punch on the arm.

"Are you bringing those dominoes down for *today* then?!" Jesse called out to Kayleigh.

"Coming!" she called back as the sound of footsteps echoed from the staircase. "I– whoops!"

Suddenly, a loud thump rang out as if something landed hard on the floor. Jamie shot out of her seat towards the corridor with Jesse calmly following. She stood in the living room doorway at Kayleigh who was standing before her unharmed holding a small box of dominoes.

"What happened?" she asked.

"I just jumped off the third step from last." Kayleigh replied nonchalantly.

"Goodness sake kid, I thought you fell down the stairs."

"Aw, love you too," Kayleigh said warmly while reaching over to give Jamie a hug, who simply stood lost for words.

"Got the table waiting for you," Jesse said in the background.

"Come, come!" Kayleigh said to a bemused Jamie while hurriedly dragging her by the arm back over to the couch. "Played before?"

"With my dad a few times," Jamie answered. "He showed me a good technique or two."

"First to seven," Kayleigh said. "Prepare to lose!"

"You mean like *you* did 7-2 yesterday?" Jesse mocked.

"Big man, picking on a little girl," Kayleigh responded, causing Jamie to snort on a laugh as they finally got underway.

After forty minutes the score was 6-5-3 in Jamie's favour with Jesse in dead last. Everyone had two dominoes remaining as Jamie was set to make a move, having the 6-3 and 6-4 dominoes in her possession with a 6 and a 4 present on the table. She studied all the laid dominoes briefly before opting to lay the 6-4 domino down next to the 4 on the table.

"Knocking," Kayleigh said while tapping her dominoes twice on the table.

"Knocking too," Jesse said also, without tapping his.

"Hahahahaha!" Jamie said in a mock-evil laugh while placing the 6-3 domino triumphantly in the middle of the table, eliciting a groan from Kayleigh.

"How did you know we didn't have any sixes?" she asked.

"Simple math," Jamie replied. "I counted 5 sixes already down on the table and I had the last two so I knew if I left only a six at each end to play to then I would win."

"Smart," Jesse remarked.

"Yeah well, let's see how good she is at *Monopoly*," Kayleigh said as she ran back upstairs, leaving Jesse to clear the dominoes from the table.

"Ever played before?" he asked Jamie.

"Back when I was her age, I did. Not in the years since though."

"Well brace yourself because it tends to take two hours when we play with our aunt."

"Yeesh, I'll probably have to leave after that."

"Oh, really?" Jesse said, sounding disappointed.

"I need to be home for Gabby, my best friend and housemate. I agreed to do the dinner tonight and I wasn't expecting to be out this late. I've actually still got to get the food for it."

"Ah, well there'll be other times to hang out I imagine."

"Like I'd miss that chance," Jamie smiled.

"So you like us then?" Jesse smirked.

"Don't push it," she smirked back as Kayleigh came rushing down the stairs once more.

"I'm the banker!" she exclaimed.

"No cheating this time, missy," Jesse said.

"I told you, I did not stash away any £500 notes at any point last time," Kayleigh protested.

"Almost sounds like real life(!)" Jamie muttered aloud, earning a laugh from Jesse.

"Huh?" Kayleigh said with a confused look on her face.

"Oh nothing, just a left-wing joke," Jamie replied.

"Left-wing like on a plane?" Kayleigh asked.

"Nah, don't worry about it. You know when you're older," Jamie said. *So you're not too ahead of your years after all.*

The game ended up taking two hours and fifteen minutes before Jamie and Jesse faced off to decide the winner, with Kayleigh being made bankrupt just before but happy to continue doing the banking role nonetheless. Jesse held the advantage in regards to owning the more expensive properties but Jamie had more of the lower-costing ones that encompassed over half the board, requiring Jesse to avoid landing on too many squares in one round to avoid the same fate as his sister.

"Come on 3, 5, 8 or 10," Jesse said as he rolled the dice, grimacing as they totalled twelve.

"Oh, would you look at that," Jamie jested. "That will be £1,100, thank you very much."

"Lucky sod," Jesse grumbled as he handed over the money. "Guess I go again since I got a double."

"And a 2, 3 or a 5 will see me win the game, methinks."

"Not going to happen."

"Well you better hope not. Bit short-thinking blowing a load of your cash putting hotels on the two most expensive properties that barely anyone's landed on so far."

"Gotta spend money to make money," Jesse fired back. "Alright, here we go then."

He rolled the dice once more, coming to a stop on a 2 and a 3.

"Oh you're having a laugh, aren't you?!" he moaned.

"Better luck next time, Jesse," Kayleigh said as Jamie gestured an L for 'loser' with her finger and thumb at Jesse.

"Well I got further than you at least," he sniped.

"Wait 'til tomorrow," Kayleigh sneered back at him.

"And on that note," Jamie said while checking her phone to see that the time was currently ten minutes to four o'clock. "It's time for me to head off."

"Nooooooo!" Kayleigh yelled as she clambered off the couch and wrapped her arms around Jamie's body while she was still kneeling on the floor.

"Uh, Kay? No wrestling the guests," Jesse jokingly said.

"Sorry sweetness, I just have a few things to do later that I need to be back home for," Jamie said to the young girl tightly gripped around her arms and torso.

"But you'll come back, right?" Kayleigh responded quickly.

"Well that depends – are you going to hate me forever if I don't?" Jamie said in a sly tone.

"What?!" Kayleigh reacted. "Of course I wouldn't hate you! I–"

"Are you sure?" Jamie interrupted with a mischievous smile.

"Oh...yeah," Kayleigh said, finally catching on. "I'd *totally* hate you forever if you never came back."

"Oh well then, guess I better come back soon," Jamie laughed.

"Alright, Kay, if you want to get your homework done before Auntie Trish arrives and kills me for letting you get off doing it," Jesse said.

"How do you know I haven't already done it?" she fired back.

"Because it's *you*."

"Lucky guess," Kayleigh scoffed as she turned to hug Jamie again. "Catch you later, Jamie."

"See you later, little one," she replied as she watched Kayleigh scamper off upstairs.

"Verdict?" said Jesse.

"Where do I even start?"

"A loveable kid who you can relate to on a teenage level?"

"Sums it up accurately," Jamie replied. "It's so weird but satisfying at the same time."

"Do you feel slightly happier?" he asked. Jamie appeared hesitant to acknowledge the fact, opting for a slight smile while looking at the floor.

"I better head off," she said while getting to her feet. "When are you free to have me round again?"

"Sunday is when I'm off next, and obviously the nipper is home given that it's the weekend."

"Sounds like a plan," Jamie replied, walking to the front door with Jesse in pursuit.

As she slipped her shoes on, she then put her arms around Jesse and locked him in a hug, completely surprising him.

"Thank you," she said softly.

"For what?" he asked, holding her with his own arms in response.

"Everything – rescuing me in the alley, talking to me, meeting Kayleigh. It means a lot to me."

"It's alright," he said as they stood there for another few seconds in each other's arms. Jamie felt reluctant to let go, content as she felt her negative emotions from earlier completely seeping away in the warm embrace.

"Are you two going to kiss already?" a voice called out from over the bannister of the top of the stairs. Jamie, her face flushing red again, pulled away from Jesse and looked up to see Kayleigh staring at them both with a wide-eyed look and gleeful expression.

"Oit! Homework, missy!" Jesse called back.

"Aw, come on! This is better than TV!" she mocked.

"Scoot!" he said loudly as Kayleigh eventually walked off to her room.

"I'm going to miss that for the next few days," Jamie miffed.

"How are you getting back anyway?"

"I'll just get the train," she answered. "Where is the nearest one?"

"The nearest underground is a ten minute walk. You go left towards the main road and turn right, walk down it for a few minutes until you arrive at the high street and turn right again. Walk up it for two minutes and you'll be there."

"So pretty simple." Jamie said.

"You want me to walk with you?"

Jamie pondered the notion for a few seconds.

"Nah, it should be alright," she replied, opting to drown her thoughts out in her music instead throughout the way home. "Oh, drop call me by the way and I'll store your number in my contacts."

"Of course."

"You take care."

"You too," Jesse said back as he watched her walk out the door and down the street until she was out of view.

As she walked down the main road, Jamie listened to the most optimistic sounding but loud heavy metal music she could find among her collection of songs on her Mp3 player, trying to enhance the euphoria she was feeling.

It had occurred to her that she had completely missed the chance to investigate the Eastwell Charitable House regarding her memory loss but she realised she no longer cared. In fact, in that moment she didn't even seem to care about her powers either. For all the months she had been experimenting with them both in combat and for fun, they had not brought her any long-term happiness.

And now she had truly felt that, with all it taking was the company of another tortured soul with a good heart and his adorable younger sister. Between seeing them again and Gabrielle's company at home, things seemed to be looking brighter.

Gabrielle....dinner! Need to head to the shops...

Chapter 11

Jamie brushed her teeth as she hurriedly tried to get ready to leave the house by quarter to eleven, leaving her an hour before Jesse arrived at midday. She would have enough time to hang out at her usual spot in the nearby park for half an hour before returning back with fifteen minutes to spare.

She could have been forgiven for not wanting to feel any recurrence of her depression considering the happier state of mind that she had found herself in as of late; it was just unfortunate that that had led her to push anything that could trigger a negative emotion to the back of her mind, including reminiscing about her family.

One thing Jamie always found herself unable to avoid though was any intense feelings of guilt and she did not want that hanging over her while trying to enjoy both Jesse and Gabrielle's company. Rather than making herself just as glum visiting her parents' graves, however, she had decided to venture to a familiar area of the local park that she and her family had used to frequent when she was younger, thinking it better to reflect on happier times as opposed to mournful ones.

Jamie had noted the overall change in her outlook since Jesse and his sister had entered her life – whereas before she woke up struggling to find ways to keep herself amused throughout the day until Gabrielle would return home, now she had an alternative friend who she felt confident in conversing with or even visiting when available during the daytime. She had also found herself quickly coming to adore Kayleigh and was very much an important part of her life now too. In a way, she was the baby sister she never had and would always enjoy entertaining her every playful whim.

The new found optimism had also encouraged the anxiety-prone teenager to finally get round to messaging Cecelia, coming to find in the process that they shared mutual interest in a lot of bands though Sissy's overall tastes bordered more towards punk rock than the more mainstream alternative rock and heavy metal that Jamie preferred. Unlike with Jesse though, she had withheld the more troubled facts of her personal life, preferring to keep her relationship with Sissy more on the casual side. The pair had agreed to meet up at the skatepark in the large field where they had first met in two days' time, Jamie having since bothered to learn that the park's name was the bizarrely titled, *Cerulean Park*, presumably due to the large lake on the adjacent field. Even then, she considered it an odd choice.

After Sunday's visit to Jesse's house, Jamie had offered to have him round instead at hers for Tuesday, despite her own doubts of being a capable host. Luckily it had turned out that Gabrielle had the day off also and it would make the situation easier for her with her best friend's more extroverted personality bringing a more vibrant atmosphere.

She had then begun to worry that maybe Jesse would find Gabrielle more interesting than her, or even feeling attracted to one another. She hoped not, not wanting her two closest friends to become an item and leave her to be alone once more. Or maybe it was because she was unsure how she exactly felt about Jesse herself, though wasn't keen on entertaining the idea of mulling it over either, just being grateful for his company.

"I'm heading out now, Gabby!" she called out as she walked down the staircase.

"You'll be back before Jesse comes round though, right?" Gabrielle responded from the living room.

"Of course."

"Good, because I'd rather you introduce him than letting me do it for myself."

"Why? You shy about making a move on him?" Jamie half-joked, curious as to what the answer would be.

"Please girl, like I'm going to steal your guy away from you," Gabrielle replied with a sly smile.

"Told you, just *friends*," Jamie responded, half annoyed but also feeling relieved.

"I know, I know," Gabrielle relented. "I still wouldn't want to take his attention away from you though. If anything I'd thank him for finally helping you out from under that dark cloud."

"You were doing that long before he showed up," Jamie replied to her. "He and Kayleigh only finished what you started."

"Either way, I'm just glad to see you happy again. Be back soon."

"Will do," Jamie said as she exited the front door.

As she walked down the street, she could only feel serene at Gabrielle's lack of interest in pursuing Jesse. More so, she hoped that all three of them could form their own small friend group if things went well later on, even though Gabrielle had already been trying to get Jamie to join hers with her work colleagues to no avail owing to her usual social inhibitions.

In the midst of her self-reflection, Jamie unexpectedly found herself being knocked aside by another person. She turned around in irritation at the hooded individual responsible who simply kept walking on as if nothing had occurred. The usual vengeful thought in her head was the urge to unleash a kinetic energy wave in response, of which she had a full supply again courtesy of Gabrielle but opted not to, knowing better than to draw unnecessary attention to herself. Especially now that her focus was away from her powers and more on an actual social life.

"Hi, are you Gabrielle?"

"Yeah, are you Jesse?" Gabrielle asked the dark-haired stranger at the front door.

"That I am," Jesse said. "Jamie's in, I'm guessing?"

"Actually no, she's out. Have you arrived early?"

"Don't think so, she texted me yesterday to arrive at 11am."

"She told me it was midday," Gabrielle replied. *That girl!*

"Well I can come back in an hour if that helps?"

"Nah, don't be silly! Come in, I'll tell her to get her butt back here now," Gabrielle said as she ushered Jesse into the house.

"You sure?"

"Yeah, besides I want to get to know the young man who stole my Jamie's heart," she sniggered.

"Oh, we're not seeing each other," Jesse quickly responded.

"Kidding, boy," Gabrielle said as she closed the door and began texting Jamie's phone.

Jesse's here. it was for 11 and not 12. come back asap!! xx

"She should be back soon," she said.

"Where's she gone anyway?"

"Not far, she's just gone over to a small park where she used to go with her mum and dad when she was younger. I think she likes to go there to reminisce every now and then."

"She normally do that ahead of company arriving?" Jesse remarked, finding the timing strange.

"Knowing what she's like by now, she can get a bit blue out of nowhere at times and she holds a lot of fond memories there. I think it's her go-to place whenever she's feeling a bit down."

"Makes sense. Must have been pretty hard going through what happened to her."

"So you know about all that, then?" Gabrielle said, her demeanour becoming more serious than before.

"She eventually broke it to me," Jesse replied. "I think we were able to bond on that level given my separation from my own parents. Still though, to have lost them both at 18 must've been awful for her."

"It was woeful for everyone," Gabrielle sighed. "I still remember meeting her at the hospital when her mum was brought in after the car crash, not that I could ever forget that scene. The nurse told me that Jamie had fled a few minutes earlier after finding out her mum had died. Then I saw her come back; she just collapsed into my arms and we both ended up in tears."

"Did she say where she had been the whole time?" Jesse asked.

"She said she had been crying by herself in a nearby alley," Gabrielle replied, Jesse realising she was oblivious to the actual horror that had happened to her friend in the alley. "Then we both went into the room where her mum was lying dead on the operating table. I really did not want to be there but I stayed because Jamie needed me to be brave for her."

"What happened next?"

"She went over to her and just started bawling her eyes out and pleading for her to wake up. It was absolutely awful to watch, the nurse who took us in walked out soon after because I don't think she could stand being there to witness it. I went over and just gripped her from behind trying to calm her down but soon I lost it as well. It was the worst moment of my entire life."

"You did well by her," Jesse sympathised. "More than a lot other people would've."

"Well that was just the start," Gabrielle continued. "I then had to organise the funeral with my parents helping me because Jamie was virtually catatonic and the only reason that then went smoothly a week later was because she was still too out of it to really function properly. After that, I stayed at hers for a week and quit my job to be her full-time carer in effect, which I could only afford to do because she inherited the house and a sizeable amount of money that will probably last her entire life."

"Did she respond well to that then?"

"I suppose it helped her but it really took its toll on me if I'm being honest. It was like dealing with a baby, and I don't mean that in a mean way; she literally had given up the will to live. I hated seeing her like that and it went on for weeks before she eventually decided to start trying to take care of herself again. My mum swung by when she could to help, mostly because she missed me a lot but she also chipped in dealing with Jamie so I could have some respite.

"But when Jamie finally came out of her stupor, that was when the crying fits began. And they were not pleasant at all. It was just lucky this is a detached house because the neighbours would've been complaining every day about the noise."

"That bad, huh?"

"The worst moment was when she screamed so loud that the police were called in, apparently having received a call that someone was being abused in the house. I was so embarrassed but it didn't end there; they began talking about the possibility of having her sectioned against her will under the Mental Health Act if they believed her to be a danger to herself."

"Yikes."

"Yeah. But I think the incident got to Jamie too and she began to calm down after that one in particular, much to my relief. She was still heavily depressed but she would lie on the couch with me watching TV and have dinner at the table and began managing to bathe herself without me stripping her down and physically washing her in the bath all the time. Even when I finally broke down in tears one night myself from all the accumulated stress of the past few weeks, she came in and tried to comfort me, albeit in a subdued manner owing to her depression. We spent the night with me lying in *her* arms for once. It was that moment I finally felt as though I had got my friend back at last."

"One hell of a journey," Jesse commented.

"It was. And I know it hurt her a lot when I went back to work. I felt so guilty leaving her on her own half the time but we both needed to get on with our lives. I had already left my family home way ahead of any plans to do so to be her permanent housemate and keep her from being alone, I wanted a return to some normality. It does annoy me that she has so far failed to do the same and continue with her university plans but I have hope she will someday. She's way too intelligent and got far too much potential to let it go to waste."

"She will, I know of that."

"You do?" Gabrielle asked, surprised.

"Well not officially but I know she's doing everything she can to get back on her feet. When we met for the first time last week, I caught her in a pretty bad way and she even broke down to me over it. To someone she didn't even know personally at the time, I might add. And by the sounds of it, I didn't even get the worst of her depressive state compared to everything you just told me. But she's perked up in the days since and seems a lot happier."

"*Way* happier," Gabrielle interjected. "It's really nice to see her smile on a regular basis again. I owe you a lot for that."

"Please, I've done pittance compared to you. You sacrificed everything for her and she would've been nothing without you for it. You're a true friend and an example to everyone in the world."

"Oh stop," Gabrielle laughed while looking down at the floor, feeling her eyes beginning to well up. "You're gonna make me cry and I've shed enough tears to last a lifetime over all this."

"Reckon she's on her way back then?" Jesse changed the subject. Gabrielle looked at her phone.

"She hasn't responded, must be in her own world again. I'll try calling her, otherwise I'll put a film on while we wait."

Jamie leaned back into the bench she had been sitting on while gazing at the view of the skyline and surrounding areas from atop the hillside while listening to her music for the past ten minutes. Rather than anything obnoxiously loud, she had chosen a playlist of more docile songs to try and help her match the mood of the situation. It had always been peaceful and tranquil whenever she and her family had visited the spot all the years prior and it was how she preferred to remember it as.

Sometimes she wondered if it was even healthy to try and live in the past, especially for someone prone to bad spells of depressive moods. She had considered it lucky in a way that her grandparents had all died before she was even three years old so she hadn't suffered too greatly from having failed to properly know them, which otherwise would have been a nice experience for her. But she had known both her mother and father her entire life and she was very much the product of their nurturing and individual personalities. She would never forget them but she also didn't want to spend her entire life dwelling on the fact they were no longer around. It was a frustrating paradox but she could only rely on time to heal those wounds. The fact she now had a surrogate family in Gabrielle, Jesse and Kayleigh would certainly help in the future towards making progress in that.

She then felt her phone vibrating continuously in her pocket, being unable to hear it ringing due to her headphones being in her ears. She realised it was Gabrielle calling her and paused the Mp3 player.

"Hello?" she spoke with the phone on loudspeaker mode.

"*Jamie, Jesse arrived bang on eleven,*" Gabrielle said through the receiver. *"You got the times mixed up"*

"Oh, really?" Jamie replied. "Alright, I'm heading back n–"

Out of nowhere, a hand shot out and smacked the phone from her hand, thudding upon the floor with the impact knocking off the back of the phone and causing the battery to fall out.

"Jamie?" Gabrielle spoke into her mobile, receiving no answer.

"What happened?" Jesse asked.

"I don't know, there was a loud smack and then a sound of the phone hitting the floor."

"That's strange."

"Yeah. It was so weird."

"She didn't fall and hurt herself, you reckon?"

"Don't say that, I'll start to worry."

"How far away is this place anyway?"

"About a ten minute walk. I can drive us over in two minutes if you're suggesting meeting up with her."

"Might as well, it'll put our minds at ease and get her here faster. I'll hold your phone while you drive in case she tries to call back."

"Okay, let me get my car keys."

Jamie looked to her left and saw the blue-hooded figure from earlier standing next to her, jumping off the bench and staring him down.

She then realised who she was dealing with.

"I knew I recognised you back there."

The figure pulled his hood down from his head. Jamie stared back with pure hatred in her eyes.

"Looks like you've changed your appearance a lot since the last time we met," the rapist said. "I'm so glad I came across you though, seeing as we have that score to settle. And it just so happens you've led me to a completely secluded area too."

"You forget how it went down the last time?" Jamie seethed.

"Oh I've never forgotten that moment. I still have no idea how you did it but I've been waiting for the chance to even things up. I was wondering if you might answer me something though?"

"And what would that be?"

"You reckon it'd be more fun to rape you before I kill you or the other way round?"

Jamie immediately fired a kinetic energy wave in his direction, only for the attack to somehow be absorbed by a glowing green aura surrounding his body.

"Is that how you did it last time?" he sneered. "You won't be so lucky now."

"Not if I kill you first," Jamie glared at him.

"With that pathetic power? You have no idea what you're dealing with. But I'm going to enjoy every minute of watching you scream and beg for mercy before I destroy you."

Jamie held her ground, her anger overwhelming any common sense that would otherwise be commanding her to flee. Even she knew that she had won the last bout by a complete fluke but in that moment, she just didn't care; he was a monster and a threat to every girl and woman within distance of him and she needed to bring him down.

She launched a powerful energy wave at the ground in front of him, spraying chunks of soil into the malicious empowered being's upper body and face which distracted him long enough for her to deliver a dropkick straight into his midsection. Getting back up quickly, Jamie attempted to kick him hard in the head but her leg was then caught by the rapist with both arms despite him being heavily winded a moment prior.

Jamie saw his palms then light up green, yelling in pain as her exposed ankle began to burn from the heat being expelled from his grip. She then planted her free foot straight into his forehead, causing him to relinquish the hold and took a look at her lower leg to see the skin beginning to heavily blister which stung horrendously; the rapist's power was more varied than she had expected.

The enhanced brute quickly rushed to his feet, sporting a faded shoe print near the top of his forehead just below his hairline. Jamie tried another kinetic energy wave but the attack wasn't quick enough to catch her foe off guard, who simply absorbed it again with his aura.

The pain from her blistered ankle was becoming unbearable but she instead tried to focus on the adrenaline pumping through her body. Her anger was still in control but tactically she knew she was running out of options in regards to launching an offensive; her kinetic energy attacks were somehow being neutralised by his powers on contact and she had no other abilities at her disposal. The only other option would be to do as she did the first time – absorb his and use it against him.

"What's the matter, your leg hurt?" he taunted. Jamie launched another strong kinetic energy wave with her weaker right arm at the ground once more, sending more earthly debris in his direction. Having already experienced the method of attack, the rapist simply shielded his face with his arm while maintaining his aura.

Jamie then unleashed an overcharged wave from her stronger left arm, possibly the most energy she had ever put into a single attack, and shot it again into the ground. This time an explosion of large chunks of soil flew into the air and straight into the rapist who was completely taken by surprise as the barrage caused him to stumble back down to the floor. He then felt a hand grabbing the back of his neck, responding quickly by activating his body aura once more with increased intensity. He felt the hand immediately withdraw, accompanied by a loud cry of pain.

Turning around, the rapist then shot a blast of green energy straight into the back of the girl as she grasped her blistering hand, watching her fall to the floor with a burning-scented vapour emerging from the impact area.

Jamie writhed on the ground, her ankle, hand and now her back in complete agony. Before she had a chance to try and get to her feet, she felt a pair of hands reaching under her right side. She was then flipped over onto her wounded back, the resulting pain feeling absolutely excruciating.

"Ready for a good time?" he mocked while reaching down and attempting to pull his victim's cargo trousers down past her waistline. Jamie raised her left arm and attempted to swipe at his face, missing only by a short margin. She breathed heavily as she let the arm lay across her torso.

"Look love, you tried and failed miserably," the rapist sneered. "Now I suggest you just lie there and take i–"

Before he could finish his sentence, Jamie swung her crossed arm backwards with what energy she could muster and watched as the close range kinetic wave caught her attacker just above his brow. He roared as he fell backwards and thrust his hands into the afflicted area of his head trying to make the pain subside.

Jamie turned back over onto her front and began using the remainder of her strength to crawl as fast as she could towards her dismantled phone, the pain in the affected parts of her body too great to properly exert herself. She eventually reached it, all the while listening to the rapist's tortured groans in the background.

She began rapidly trying to put it back together with her undamaged right hand before attempting to turn it back on. Her heart was beating so hard she thought it was going to explode from the extreme anxiety she was feeling. She rued the fact that she hadn't had the chance to regain her borrowed flight ability from Jesse which would have made escaping in her wounded state relatively easy. Now her only hope was calling Gabrielle back and telling her to drive over to the park with Jesse to save her before her attacker managed to fully recover. If not for the overwhelming pain flowing throughout her body, she might have had the chance to further assault him to aid a retreat.

The phone then managed to come back to life undamaged as she hurriedly searched for Gabrielle's contact details.

Before she could act any further, she felt a crushing stomp square in the middle of her back. The extreme pain radiated all throughout her body, eliciting an ear-piercing scream that echoed around the surrounding woodland.

"We're here, jump out," Gabrielle said to Jesse as she pulled her car over to the side of the road and culled the engine.

"Is it through here?" he asked, pointing at a gated entrance with a forested path leading to an open field in the background.

"Yeah, she'll be on a hilltop to the left of the end of that path. Let's get over there as quickly a–"

Gabrielle paused mid-sentence as a distant but agonised feminine-sounding scream rang out from the direction of the park.

"Jamie!" she cried out hysterically, her voice breaking in the process. "Jesse, quick! We need to–"

As she reached out to grab Jesse's arm, she felt nothing but thin air. She turned around to see he had completely vanished.

The rapist flipped the heavily injured girl over onto her back once more before kneeling over her torso and struck her brow hard with his fist. Jamie suddenly felt a stream of blood pouring over her left eyelid, barely clinging to consciousness. She watched as the rapist rose up and stood over her; his brow line was beetroot red from her kinetic energy wave strike but still managed to bear a malicious smile as he studied the damage to her face.

"I'll give you your dues, you didn't just cower in fear before me," he said. "But ultimately your wimpy power was nothing compared to mine."

He pointed his open palm straight at her face.

"As I told you last time, I don't need you alive to do what I want to do to you and I'm not leaving anything else to chance. Hope you had a nice life."

Jamie watched in terror as green-hued energy began to form in the rapist's outstretched hand, tears flowing from her eyes that pooled in her eye sockets. She couldn't believe she was actually about to die. She had thought about wanting to die for weeks on end following her mother's own passing but now that it was about to become reality, she was paralysed with overwhelming fear that was masking all the physical pain she was suffering from. And worse, she had only just managed to achieve the happiness she had long craved. Images of Gabrielle, Jesse and Kayleigh passed through her mind as she closed her eyes and braced for the impact of the blast.

She then heard a loud thumping sound as she opened her eyes again, seeing that the rapist had disappeared from view.

Chapter 12

Baffled but feeling relieved, Jamie attempted to arch her head forwards and saw a figure descending from the air to the edge of the hilltop, who then turned around to face her.

"Jamie," Jesse said as he ran over to his battered friend and looked in horror at her injuries. "What happened to you?"

"He attacked me again," she whimpered.

"Again?" he mouthed as it dawned on him who the person he just flown directly into and flung down the hillside was.

"Jamie!" a familiar voice yelled out from near the bottom of the other side of the hill.

"Gabrielle, she's here!" Jesse called out to Gabrielle who was running at full speed to the hilltop, arriving a few seconds later and looked aghast at her best friend lying stricken on the floor with Jesse holding her hand.

"What happened?!" she wheezed from her exhaustion while kneeling to cradle Jamie's head in her arms.

"I think one of our kind attacked her," Jesse answered while trying to remain coy over the fact Gabrielle was unaware of the rapist's attack on Jamie the previous year.

"I can't move," Jamie cried weakly.

"We're getting you out of here, don't worry," Gabrielle said. "Jesse, get her other side."

"Hang on, I can help her," he said.

"What do you mean? Hurry and help me get her out of–"

Gabrielle watched as Jesse put a hand on Jamie's forehead and another wrapped around her uninjured right hand, her wounds slowly healing and the blood flow above her left eye coming to a halt. She then watched astounded as Jesse helped her back to her feet completely unharmed though with a large hole in the back of her hoodie and t-shirt exposing her bare skin underneath.

"How...?" she said in disbelief.

"I can heal," he replied.

"He's a guy of many talents," Jamie quipped as she gave a stern gaze towards the other side of the hilltop. Jesse and Gabrielle turned their attention to where she was looking at, seeing an angry looking individual clutching his left arm looking back at them.

"That him?" Jesse said.

"Yeah," Jamie growled.

"Gabrielle, get her out of here. I'll cover you both," he said.

"You can't take him on alone!" Jamie protested as Gabrielle grabbed her arm. They all then froze as the individual's right hand began to emit an ominous green aura.

"Get down!" Jesse yelled as he held his arm out and activated his shielding ability. Before the girls could react, a green blast of energy came shooting towards them, making direct contact with Jesse's transparent shield which began displaying a myriad of colours as it strained against the power of the energy blast.

Jesse groaned as he struggled to maintain the barrier. Jamie then ran forward and placed her open palm against the back of his neck.

"What are you doing?" he called out.

"Boosting your shield's strength," she replied, watching as Jesse slowly managed to stand firm against the energy attack still being projected into his shield. "Better?"

"Yeah, a lot," he replied. "Now I know what you went through the last time you faced this clown."

"That's an insult to clowns; this guy is just pure evil, we need to stop him before he kills all of us with that power."

"Have you any suggestions? I'm a bit occupied here."

Jamie tried brainstorming ideas in her head with the crackling of the energy blast colliding with the shield emitting in the background. She then spied the small lake at the bottom of the hill.

"Didn't you say you can manipulate water when we first met?" she said to Jesse.

"Yeah, why?"

"Use it to send the water in that lake straight into that idiot to distract him."

Jesse looked down the hill to his right side.

"That's a lot of water, Jame. I don't know if I have the power to do that."

"At least try. I'll boost that ability to its maximum too while you maintain the shield."

Jesse thought on it for a moment. “Okay, I’ll try but no guarantees.”

He then stretched out his right arm while keeping his left focused on the shield. Jamie grasped Jesse’s right wrist with her free hand and concentrated on boosting the water manipulation power.

To Jesse’s own surprise, a large ripple emanated from the centre of the water’s surface. With renewed confidence, he then focused on raising the water up from the lake. Soon a twisting spout emerged from it and began spiralling up towards the top of the hill.

The rapist, in the midst of the stalemate, caught glimpse of the tower of water that had suddenly appeared out of nowhere to his left. He immediately dropped his attack and stared at it in total horror, watching as it then came hurtling towards him. On instinct, he activated his energy-absorbing aura and held out his arms to focus his effort as the water spout slammed straight into him.

“Jamie, it’s no good. He’s just blocking it.” Jesse said, having dropped the shield and concentrating solely on commanding the water attack.

“No, he’s *absorbing* the energy from it, just like how he did with my kinetic energy waves and that’s exactly what I was hoping he’d do,” she replied with Gabrielle watching on in amazement behind her at the spectacle.

“But isn’t that going to make him more powerful?”

“I’ve got a plan. Can you give me your flight power quick?”

“It’ll definitely have to be quick if I’m to focus on maintaining this,” he replied before beginning to levitate off the ground slightly. Jamie then reapplied her hand to the back of her friend’s neck and took a small but sizeable amount of energy.

Inside the torrent of water, the rapist could feel his reserves beginning to swell as his aura rapidly absorbed the energy from the force of the water slamming into his body. A few seconds later, the attack finally dissipated. He gave out a triumphant roar while dropping the absorption aura and letting his body relax for a moment.

A split-second later, he was struck by what felt like a large object that knocked him down to the ground. He then felt an arm wrap around his neck from behind and a hand grasping the top half of his face, blocking his vision in the process. He quickly reactivated the aura in an attempt to burn the person attacking him, only to find that it was having no effect for some unknown reason.

Instead, he opted to use all his physical strength imbrued with his absorbed energy to try and wrest the individual off, managing to eventually get a grip and throwing them across the ground.

As he looked at what turned out to be the black-clad girl floating away from him instead of colliding with the floor, he was knocked back down again by an invisible force slamming into his upper torso.

"Nice shot Gabby," Jamie remarked as she dismounted next to her friend who had just launched a kinetic energy wave.

"I'm guessing that stunt over there was for a good reason?" Gabrielle responded.

"Yeah – just managed to achieve what I failed to do earlier. Now get behind Jesse."

"Huh?" Jesse said.

"He's going to launch another blast at us and you're going to block it again with me boosting your shield like before."

"What's the point in that? It achieved nothing a second ago."

"Just trust me, Jesse! I know what I'm doing."

"HEY!"

Jesse looked forward at the rapist who was emitting a green aura once more with energy building in both hands.

"Eat this!" he called out as he brought both hands together and launched a large blast of green energy at his opponents. As before, Jesse managed to block the attack with his shield ability but the force of the blast knocked both him and Jamie two feet backwards as he tried to brace himself.

"Jamie, it's a lot stronger than before," he said loudly. "I can barely hold it back."

"Just hang on," Jamie responded. The stalemate continued for another few seconds before the rapist impatiently decided to send more energy flowing forward into the blast. Jamie watched as rainbow-hued cracks began appearing in Jesse's translucent barrier.

"I can't it hold anymore, Jamie!" he yelled. "He's too powerful!"

"Perfect," she said as she then used her full body strength to shove Jesse out of the way of the blast as it completely enveloped her as a result.

"JAMIE!!" Gabrielle screamed as she watched the huge wave of green energy engulf her friend's body.

The rapist grinned with delight as he just about managed to see the end of the blast hitting the girl head on. He had no idea how she had recovered from the beating he had dealt her but it didn't matter now that she had been completely obliterated.

His glee then turned to total confusion as he began feeling his energy reserves rapidly depleting. He tried to stop the attack but he found it was no longer in his control. In stared in bewilderment as the blast continued to fire from his hands until all the energy in his body was gone and it subsequently dissipated.

At the other end, he could see the girl down on one knee with her head bowed and her hands outstretched towards him, seemingly unharmed.

Jamie raised her head, just barely able to contain the huge amount of energy she had just forcibly drained from her attacker using his own ability against him. She then stood up and aimed her hand in his direction.

The rapist began to panic in the realisation he was now powerless to launch a counter-offensive or defend himself and turned to flee. Jamie quickly shot a relatively large energy blast of her own straight at him at a low angle, watching as it came into contact with the ground just beneath his feet and caused an explosion of earth and soil, the impact sending him flying forwards and tumbling heavily down the other side of the hill.

"Jamie?" Gabrielle called out as her friend collapsed soon after.

"Are you alright?" Jesse asked while rushing over to her.

"I'm fine," she replied, deactivating the green aura from around her. "Where'd he go?"

"The blast sent him sprawling down the hill."

"I need to see!" she exclaimed while running towards the other end of the hilltop. Once there, she gazed downwards to see a lot of spattered soil among the grassy slope, yet there was no sign of the rapist at all.

No!

Jamie then swooped down to the bottom of the hill using her flight and looked in every direction around her; there was absolutely no sign of him whatsoever. She then flew into a rage as she took to the air again and zoomed straight into the nearby group of trees.

"WHERE ARE YOU?!" she yelled inside the forestry only to receive the inevitable lack of response. She then shot a blast of energy towards a bush among the ground, seeing it blown apart by the impact but revealing nobody underneath.

"Jamie!" a distance voice called. She followed it in hope that Gabrielle had located her foe outside of the trees, only to feel disappointed when she saw just Gabrielle and Jesse standing at the bottom of the hill. She then flew up high in a desperate attempt to locate the rapist from above.

"Jamie, get down before someone sees you!" Gabrielle called out to her. She eventually descended upon seeing nothing in the surrounding area.

"Jamie, it's alright. He's gone n–"

Gabrielle quickly took cover as Jamie then aimed another blast of energy at the hillside, sending more soil flying from the impact as she let out an angry yell.

"Fuck's, SAKE!!" she roared.

"Jamie!" Jesse called out. Jamie turned around with a livid expression on her face, seeing Gabrielle cowering behind Jesse. Suddenly, all her anger dissipated as she felt remorse at the sight of her terrified friend looking at her. She then dropped to her knees in despair as Gabrielle slowly approached her.

"It's okay, Jamie," she said softly as she knelt down.

"I had him, Gabby, I fucking had him!" she wailed.

"Don't worry about him now. Let's get out of here and go home."

"He's a psychopath! He'll do it again!"

"We'll deal with that another time, let's just go home for now."

Jamie looked directly into Gabrielle's eyes, knowing she wasn't going to convince her to stay and look for the rapist.

"...Okay," she begrudgingly replied as Gabrielle put her arm around her shoulders and led her around the hill towards the exit with Jesse following.

Jamie kicked her shoes off as she walked through the front door and immediately headed up the stairs to her bedroom.

"Jamie?" Gabrielle called out to no response.

"I'll go see how she's doing," Jesse said

"You sure?"

"Yeah, I don't think whatever we had planned is going to happen anymore anyway so I might as well get a word in with her before I leave."

"Okay," Gabrielle replied as Jesse headed upstairs. On the balcony, he made a guess to which room was Jamie's and headed in to see her sprawled out on her front lying on her bed, the hole in the back of her hoodie and t-shirt obvious.

"You alright?" he asked.

"Not really," she replied in a low voice.

"You want me to leave while you change your top?"

Jamie immediately got up without responding and took her hoodie off and inspected the hole in the back, grimacing as she looked at the damage.

"I liked this jacket," she lamented.

"We can get you a new one," he replied. She then took her similarly ruined t-shirt off without warning and walked over to her wardrobe to pick out an intact one. Jesse couldn't help but note her extremely lean figure as she then faced him.

"What's up?" she asked as she fiddled with the t-shirt in her hands.

"Nothing," he said sheepishly. "I just took you for the shy type."

"Only around those I don't trust," she replied while pulling the t-shirt over herself and pulling her head through the neck.

"Nice to know I'm trusted," he remarked out of lack of anything else to say in response. "Are you going to be alright?"

"Probably," she stated without any real emotion. "Just pissed that he got away again."

"How did you end up coming across him again anyway?"

"He actually found *me*, following me up to the hilltop from the street. Managed to completely ruin that spot for me now."

"Can I ask you something?"

"Go on."

"Why didn't you just run from him in the first place?"

"You know why."

"I suppose I do but that wasn't really the answer I was hoping to hear."

"Then what *were* you hoping to hear?" Jamie replied, sounding defensive.

"That you did try to escape and he overpowered you or something."

"I just didn't want him to get away with it yet again," she dismissively replied. "I mean it when I say he's a danger to society."

"I don't doubt that of course but trying to take him on nearly got you killed. And even when I rescued you, you still wouldn't let it go and got me and Gabrielle involved too."

"But together we beat him."

"That's not even the point, Jamie."

"Jesse, can we just leave it out for now?" she complained. "I really don't feel like having this discussion right now, I feel rubbish enough as it is."

"How much do I mean to you?"

Jamie found herself caught off-guard, pondering her answer for a few seconds.

"A lot I guess. I've only known you for a week though."

"Well I'll tell you what you mean to me," Jesse said in an even more serious tone. "I've only known you a week and I'll let you know now that you're one of the most important people in my life."

Jamie stared back at him with silent interest.

"You're a fun person to be around and you're also really down-to-earth; that's not an easy thing to come by every day. And I'll go as far to say that, even though I've already proved it twice now, I'd willingly risk my own safety to protect you if it came down to it."

Jamie maintained her silence but couldn't help but feel a warm feeling flow through her at that moment.

"You mean a whole lot to me and it would devastate me if you were gone from this world. And don't forget about Kayleigh – that girl absolutely loves you like her own, it would've broken her heart to find out you had died today. And also that incredible girl downstairs who you call your best friend; she's given you everything she has to help you through the worst period of your life and then some. You'll never have a greater person in your time on this earth than that."

Jesse walked over to within half a foot of Jamie and held her wrists in a soft grip with his hands as she looked directly into his eyes.

"You have a lot of good in your life and we in turn love you dearly, don't make us suffer the indignity of losing you like we nearly did today."

Jamie stared back at Jesse, almost in a trance. She didn't know how to react, not least how she *felt* like acting. In truth, she didn't want the moment to end but she knew she had to give him a response after giving her such heartfelt words.

"Okay," she said softly. He smiled back at her, then began to lightly levitate before her.

"Take it," he said, pulling his hands down to hold hers. "So I can rest easy knowing you have the means to escape in future."

Jamie brought herself back to reality, considering everything leading up to that point a gigantic wind-up as she started absorbing Jesse's flight power while simultaneously restoring his levels to normal.

"Done," she stated, nearly ten seconds after she had actually completed the process.

"Do you want to show me out then?" he said, letting go of Jamie's hands as he made a move for the bedroom door.

"W–w–where are you going?" she stammered.

"Well, I told Gabrielle I was planning on going. I just feel really worn out after everything that's happened today."

"You can stay, w–we can just, sit on the couch watching films or something," Jamie offered, bordering on pleading while feeling a massive sense of disappointment.

"I've got Thursday off so why don't we pick up where we left off today then?"

"Gabby's at work on Thursday though."

"Well, then you and me will just hang out then. We can do something with Gabrielle another time, I'll see if I can bring Kayleigh for that too."

"I guess," she glumly replied. "Oh wait, I'm meeting up with someone Thursday afternoon."

"Oh, really? Who?" Jesse replied.

"Some punk girl I met in the park last week," Jamie replied. *Did he just sound jealous?* "Thought I'd make an attempt to branch out seeing as I gelled so well with you. That's not until 4pm though."

"Well we can hook up in the early afternoon instead then before that," he replied. "Sound good?"

"Yeah, that's fine," Jamie replied, slightly miffed at now only having half a day with Jesse as opposed to the whole day. *Anything else you want to ruin, you psychopathic rapist prick?*

"Cool, Thursday it is then," he said as he again moved to head off.

"Jess," Jamie said.

"Yeah?" Jesse replied. Jamie then wordlessly approached him and locked him in a hug. He then reciprocated by holding her tightly back.

“You mean a lot to me too,” she said while leaning her head on his shoulder.

“Y’know if Kay was here right now, we’d never hear the end of it,” Jesse laughed.

Aaaannnd, it’s ruined.

“Yeah, probably,” Jamie replied, relinquishing the hold.

“By the way,” Jesse said in a more sombre tone. “I think you should tell Gabrielle about what that idiot did to you last year.”

“It’ll just upset her,” Jamie replied.

“Probably but I think she has a right to know. I do actually feel a bit bad that I know when she doesn’t, being frank.”

“I told you so I didn’t really *have* to tell Gabbs.”

“I get that. Believe me though, she obviously won’t like hearing about it but I think she’ll be grateful nonetheless that you trust her with that kind of info. That’s what best friends do, after all.”

“Fine,” Jamie replied. “But if she grounds me forever under the guise of protecting me because of it, I’m blaming you.”

“Well with my flight ability, you can just sneak out the bedroom window whenever you want so I guess that makes up the difference,” he joked back as they descended the staircase.

“Everything alright?” Gabrielle asked as the duo arrived downstairs.

“Yeah, it’s all good,” Jamie replied.

“You definitely going then?” Gabrielle asked Jesse.

“Yeah, but we are definitely all hanging out again sometime though properly.”

“Well there’s a funfair in town on Saturday in that Cerulean Park field if you have the day off. I’m free for it.”

"Sounds good, I can bring Kayleigh too."

"Unless of course you two want to go on your own and make a date of it," Gabrielle smirked at Jamie, who gave a furious glare back in response. "Oh, you know I'm just messing with you, sweetie."

"If it makes you feel any better, I'm sure to get the same treatment from Kay in a bit," Jesse said as he opened the front door. "I'll catch you Thursday, Jame."

"See you Thursday," she replied as he closed the door behind him.

"So, *Jame* huh?" Gabrielle said to Jamie with a teasing look.

"What? I call you 'Gabbs', don't I?"

"Hmm, he's already got a pet name for you."

"Oh, stop being so annoying," Jamie pouted as Gabrielle then interlocked their hands and pushed Jamie's up against the wall.

"Mwah, mwah, mwah, mwah, mwah!" Gabrielle said aloud as she pretended to fake kiss Jamie several times before giving her several real ones on the side of her neck to her friend's amusement.

"Alright, alright! Stop, it tickles," Jamie said as Gabrielle then pulled off her. She then stood awkwardly for a moment.

"You alright?" Gabrielle asked in a more concerned tone.

"Yeah," Jamie hesitated. "You got a moment?"

"Sure."

"Can we sit down in the living room?"

"Okay," Gabrielle replied, this time in a slightly confused intonation as she followed Jamie into the living room.

"I've got something to tell you and it happened a few months ago," Jamie said. "And I didn't tell you because I thought it would hurt you a lot but I think I should anyway, especially after today."

"Well I was about to make a joke about you losing your virginity but I now get the feeling it's a lot more serious."

"Well no, I haven't popped the cherry yet if you're *that* bothered to bring it up out of nowhere," Jamie said with a roll of her eyes. "But it *is* pretty serious and it does have to do with that arsehole from earlier."

"He hasn't done this before to you, has he?" Gabrielle asked with an anxious look in her eyes.

"He did," Jamie replied, preparing for the conversation to go downhill fast. "Do you remember when they told you I fled the hospital when mum died and I then came back and met you there?"

"Oh, no," Gabrielle said with a drawn out delivery as she clocked on to what Jamie was trying to tell her. "How did he do it?"

"He found me crying in an alleyway and feigned offering me sympathy. Then he tried to rape me."

Gabrielle suddenly gave the most horrified look, making Jamie extremely uncomfortable.

"But I fought him off," she quickly resumed. "Then he revealed himself to have an ability and tried to use it to kill me but my own power kicked in for the first time, which I then used to knock him out with his own attack. Then I fled back to the hospital."

Jamie sat silent as Gabrielle simply looked back at her with the same appalled expression on her face.

"Please say something," Jamie pleaded.

"Is that why you were so determined to hunt him down after you blasted him off the hill?" Gabrielle finally spoke.

"Yeah. I just didn't want him to hurt anyone else. He's evil and dangerous and I hate him."

"What would you have done to him though?"

"I don't know. Beat his face in maybe or break his legs so he couldn't try and rape anyone again with or without his powers. I dunno. But I don't think I could ever kill him though, as much as I want to."

"It makes me glad to hear you say that."

"Really? Why?" Jamie asked.

"Because you're too good a person to do that and I'm glad you know that," Gabrielle said warmly. "But it sucks that he had to try that right after your mum died though."

"Like he could've really added anything to that whole thing," Jamie replied. "Being effectively orphaned at eighteen that day was just about as bad as it got. Still hate the fact he's on the loose yet again."

"Well I tell you what – I'll take half the day off from lunch onwards tomorrow and we'll go down to the police station and report the incident."

"It happened last year though and we can't exactly tell them he has superpowers," Jamie argued.

"Well we don't have to mention his powers, just that he's a rapist piece of scum and that he's likely done it to other women."

"I don't know, Gabbs."

"Well consider it at least. I'm going to take half the day off anyway so I can spend some more time with you regardless."

"That'd be nice," Jamie said with a smile.

"Must say you're taking it all pretty well considering just how awful it all was."

"Think I let out all my negative feelings about it when Jesse got it all out of me last week."

"Jesse knew before I did?" Gabrielle blurted out.

"Oh, Gabby no, it's not like that," Jamie said, immediately seeing the hurt in her friend's eyes. "It was literally when me and Jesse first met, we didn't even know each other and he caught me at a really bad time. I just told him because I didn't think I was ever going to see him again and I just felt like getting it off my chest. That's it."

"I suppose that makes sense," Gabrielle replied, still looking downcast.

"If it makes you feel better, you'll be the only one who finds out when I finally do lose my v-plates," she joked, trying to lighten the mood.

"Well unless Jesse's the one who ends up taking them from you."

"*Gabbs!!*" Jamie yelled, turning a bright shade of crimson and causing Gabrielle to laugh out loud.

"I never get tired of seeing you turning into a tomato," she continued to laugh.

"Not funny," Jamie fumed.

"Jokes aside though, I think you've found a real good one in him."

"Meaning?"

"He seems like a really nice guy; not winding you up, I mean to just have around. You'll be better off for having people like that in your life going forward."

"I've always had that person all along," Jamie replied, lightly squeezing Gabrielle's hand. "But things do look better now. Can only see where it all goes from here, hopefully with no more idiots mucking it up either."

"Well whatever you want to do tomorrow about that one in particular, I'll be behind you every step of the way," Gabrielle replied.

"Thanks, babe." Jamie acknowledged. "Got the whole day left, wanna watch something?"

"Anything non-horror related – lived through enough of that today as it is."

Jamie stirred as she heard Gabrielle walking loudly down the stairs the following morning. She checked her phone to see that the time was 8:13am. She had slept well, having gone to bed early the previous evening owing to how worn out she had felt from the day's events and actually was in the mood to get out of bed for once.

She had decided to see how she felt when Gabrielle arrived home just after midday regarding visiting the police later on. Not that she didn't want to at least try and bring the rapist to justice but she knew from experience that the police needed concrete evidence to successfully prosecute someone, as she had found out at the start of the year when the three miscreants responsible for killing her mother in their joyride gone awry had all, in her opinion, been sentenced far too leniently with one of them already out of prison having served his time on remand.

Based on that, she knew a case against a suspected rapist with very little evidence of the crimes having been committed was far from airtight and the matter of superpowers being involved only complicated matters.

On the other hand, it couldn't hurt to at least try, she thought to herself, if it would save anyone else from going through the same plight that she had suffered twice over.

As she descended the staircase lazily using Jesse's absorbed flight, she noticed a letter just in front of the door. *The postman's been unusually early?* She bent down to pick it up, seeing that it was unmarked and didn't even have a stamp on it. Wearily, she opened it up and found a handwritten letter inside.

Hello girlie, it wasn't too smart leading me to your friend's car yesterday after you left me for dead (seem to have a big problem doing both those things I've noticed). But I assure you I am very much alive which is more than can be said for your pal Gabrielle, owner of the vehicle who's licence plate is registered to this property, if you don't follow my exact instructions.

This day at bang on 12pm you will bring yourself to the warehouse complex on Harringate Street (look it up) where you and me will end this once and for all and without your friends to help you this time. No police either. Tell absolutely no-one else or it will be everyone you love who suffers. I'll be seeing you soon.

Chapter 13

Jamie felt ill as she dropped the letter to the floor. She couldn't believe the maniac had managed to track her down to her house; she hadn't even been thinking that he could have been following her, Gabrielle and Jesse back to Gabrielle's car outside the park entrance, especially not after the final attack she had used on him.

But it was too late to dwell on it now. If she wanted proof that a psychopathic lunatic was indeed after her, the letter was all she needed, although it didn't prove exactly who wrote or sent it. The other main problem was considering the nature of his extremely destructive ability, getting the police involved (as he had instructed against) would just as likely cause more harm than good and no amount of explaining to them exactly what he was truly capable of would make them believe so. The thought of sacrificing their lives to try and spare hers and Gabrielle's did not sit well with her.

She then looked at her hand, feeling the rapist's full power still coursing through her and generating a green aura with it in her palm. And judging by the letter, he clearly held the belief that she had only beaten him on the basis of her friends being there to help her.

Jamie realised that she had been presented with an inadvertent but massive advantage if she were to indeed agree to meet him for another confrontation. The thought of doing so though in complete contradiction of everything Jesse and Gabrielle had said to her the other day made her feel absolutely awful, having vowed not to pursue anything that could jeopardise her life.

Only this time, it wasn't just *her* life on the line – it was also Gabrielle's, and even Jesse and Kayleigh's if he was able to figure out where they lived too. It still barely justified acquiescing to the rapist's demands but protecting her loved ones was a cause worth fighting for.

And this time she wasn't planning on losing.

Jamie felt nervous as she approached the chain link fencing that surrounded the industrial complex, seeing several warehouses lined up one after the other. She could think of more secluded places that the rapist could have chosen for what would be a very non-inconspicuous rematch but the abundant stacked crates lying around and the warehouses would likely block most of the general view from bystanders.

The possibility though of the whole thing being an ambush considering how many hiding places her opponent had to surprise her from was likely but Jamie knew she had gained a great deal of knowledge about how her nemesis' ability operated from the previous day's bout and the absorption shield aspect of it would nullify any sneak attack consisting of an energy blast being thrown her way. A physical attack would be far more effective but the agility of Jesse's flight would allow her to evade such an attempt with ease.

What to do with him upon being dealt yet another defeat was still a frustrating question. Cripple him? Pummel him so hard that he would be too afraid to ever bother her again? The latter would be more ideal and Jamie could still feel a plethora of underlying hatred in regards to him that would help her in that endeavour but as his determination to find out where she lived despite being blown clean off a hilltop was a clear indication of, the sadistic empowered fiend clearly didn't shrug off being slighted in any shape or form so easily, meaning it was probably going to take a lot more than a simply beating to dissuade him of further pursuit of her.

She levitated over the fence and kept to the rim of the yard. Noticing on her phone that it was only ten minutes to midday, she opted to fly up onto one of the furthest situated warehouses from the entrance and laid low on the slanted roof while peering over the edge. She had no idea whether the rapist was expecting her early or bang on time but he was now highly unlikely to get the drop on her no matter where he happened to be hiding.

At five minutes to noon, Jamie caught sight of movement close to the numerous stacks of crates back near the entrance. Whoever it was appeared to be trying to avoid being seen directly from the front of the complex by hiding behind the wall of boxes. Jamie squinted towards the person, all but convinced it was who she was expecting.

She decided to descend the rear side of the warehouse and calmly walked towards the unsuspecting individual. As she grew closer, she could easily make out that it was the rapist, who was impatiently checking past the crates every few seconds for any activity. She quietly charged a kinetic energy wave, hoping to end the fight as soon as possible but yearned to cover more ground in order to ensure the accuracy of the attack as she neared his position.

The rapist then caught sight of her in the corner of his eye, nearly jumping from the shock. Jamie unleashed the energy wave anyway, watching as it was narrowly absorbed by an extremely quick-activating aura by her foe.

"Nearly caught me out there," he said in a calm tone. "A shame for you that it didn't work, you've just lost your only chance of beating me."

"In case you haven't noticed, the score is two-nil," she replied, almost emotionlessly.

"Total luck, girl. And your friends aren't here to help you now either."

"How do you know the police don't have this place surrounded already?"

"You wouldn't have used your little power on me a moment ago if you had, I'm not stupid."

"Maybe I've told them exactly what we can do," she bluffed.

"Maybe, maybe not. Either way I don't care, I will just blast them to hell before they can do anything," he replied, confirming Jamie's worries. "It'll just be a matter of how many people I take down with you."

"Well lucky for them, it's just me," she replied. "And you won't be ending my life today or anyone else's – I'll be ending *yours*."

"Bollocks," he sneered. "You've got nothing to help you do that."

"I beat you with your own power twice, I'll use it a third time if I have to."

"Well I don't know how you gained that from me but it seems you can only do that if I use it first against you," he claimed. "I can just as easily kill you with my bare hands."

"Try me," Jamie replied. Without warning, the rapist ran over and launched a hard punch in her direction, missing as she glided backwards using her flight.

"You missed," she taunted, dodging a second fist in the same manner. The rapist looked at her in confusion, unsure how she was able to dodge so quickly and with such finesse. He tried several more times unsuccessfully before becoming tired and stopping the onslaught momentarily to catch his breath.

"How about you try fighting back, eh?" he growled. "Or maybe I should just go back to your house and play with your blonde friend instead?"

Out of nowhere, the rapist was struck directly in the chest by a flying dropkick by the girl that was too fast to react to, landing several feet backwards painfully onto the ground. As he pulled his head up, he responded by firing a ball of green energy straight back. Jamie immediately activated an aura and swiped through the attack with her hand, rather than absorb it, causing it to split and dissipate.

"You think you're in control here," she said as she aimed her open palm in the rapist's direction, who activated his own aura in preparation to absorb the anticipated energy attack. Instead, she shot a blast at the crates next to him, resulting in shards of splintered wood hitting his face and body as he barely managed to shield himself with his arm.

"You sure don't look like you're in control," Jamie taunted him further.

The rapist, now sporting several raw cuts and scratches across the left side of his face, glared back at her with a mixture of fury and fear, something that she was able to detect. She enjoyed knowing that she had turned the tables on her hated enemy but despite having the upper hand she still had to find a way to ensure he wouldn't pose a threat to Gabrielle's wellbeing.

As the rapist scrambled to get back to his feet, Jamie cut him off with a flight-enhanced shoulder barge that knocked him back down. For good measure, she then grabbed his ankle and dragged him across the concrete ground using her flight ability once more, causing him to roar in pain. She then hovered over him as he writhed on the floor.

"I hope you know your time on this mortal coil is rapidly coming to its conclusion," she said.

"Get lost, bitch," he snarled while firing another energy blast, watching as it was swiftly absorbed to no effect.

"Do I scare you more? Or is it the humiliation that annoys you the most?"

"You are nothing!" he screamed while attempting another attack, only to be cut off by a double-footed stomp to his torso.

"Then what does that make you?" she replied before floating away from him and back onto the ground. "You dragged me here threatening my friend and thinking taking me on again was going to be a walk in the park. And for the third time I've instead taken you to the cleaners. I think I've had enough of wasting my time with you."

"Waste this!" he roared while aiming both hands at her point-blank and launching simultaneous energy blasts. In response, Jamie stuck out both her hands and absorbed the twin attacks. The rapist could only look back at her with an expression of terror as he realised his powerful ability was somehow completely useless and he was now at the girl's mercy.

"How were you going to hurt my friend anyway?" Jamie said in a patronising tone. "Were you going to sneak in at night and force yourself on her? Or were you planning on busting in guns a'blazing and rape her on the spot? Well let me tell you now that you're never going to hurt anyone ever again. And you know why? Because where you lie right now is where they're going to find your body in a million pieces once I blow you to hell!"

The rapist looked back at her with a desperate gaze, then quickly scrambled to his feet and fled towards the back of the complex with Jamie watching him as he ran behind the furthest warehouse.

Wimp.

Satisfied at having intimidated the rapist though knowing he still remained a threat, Jamie activated her flight once more and soared low towards his location. Arriving behind the warehouse seconds later, she could see nothing whatsoever bar a few stacked crates against the rear of the building.

No, not again...

She moved towards the crates, seeing them as the only place the rapist could have found a place to hide. She looked at the small gap separating them from the wall, showing that the crates were fully sealed. She tried lifting the lid off the one on top of the pile, only to find it was nailed down.

She then tried to pick it up, finding it too heavy and quickly giving up assuming that aside from the fact the top of it was secured, it would have been impossible for her foe to be hiding inside it given that it was clearly already loaded with something.

In a last ditch effort, Jamie then blasted the crate that was positioned by itself on the ground, examining the remains to see that it had been completely hollow. Considering that the only others were stacked underneath the one she had already tried to lift, she concluded that wherever he had run off to, the rapist was not hiding among the crates.

She suddenly felt enraged as she levitated off the ground, both at his inconceivable escape and also at herself for once again letting her ego get the better of her and not preventing him from running away in the first place.

"I'LL FIND YOU!" she yelled out loud before speeding off towards the other side of the warehouse, the only logical place he could have possibly fled to.

Seconds later, the rapist emerged from the top crate on the pile through the hinged side of it, relieved that the girl had failed to manage to lift it up while he had been inside or consider the possibility of the crate's side wall being the opening to it as opposed to the top.

His irritation at the fact he had been forced to run and hide from her, again, however, was still present. It also confounded him how she not only was able to fly but how she had also managed to gain his ability yet again despite him not having initially used it on her this time round. It was another humiliation, on top of having been forced to hide underneath shrubbery within a mini-forest following a devastating counter-attack using his own energy against him in the previous battle. With every ounce of his strength he had managed to follow her and her friends out of the park undetected and had even managed to catch a glimpse of the licence plate of the car that they had driven off in.

Only instead, the revenge ploy had not gone according to plan. But he nonetheless still had an ace up his sleeve to combat her once more.

Checking around the corner and seeing no sign of the girl, he quickly made his way to the door on the front of the warehouse, opening it and walking inside before locking it behind himself.

"Where's the girl, Jason?"

The rapist turned around, facing the group of enhanced humans stationed within the warehouse.

"Having her way with your dad," he sarcastically replied. "She's here on the grounds."

"So why haven't you taken her down yet?" one of them fired back.

"Maybe because I'm being generous in allowing you guys to get your revenge of course."

"Yeah well right now, you'd be doing us a favour taking her out right off the bat considering she took us all down single-handedly in one go."

"Max, how about *not* pointing that out," Bill snapped.

"Gee, and I thought you guys would be eager to do the dirty on her yourselves," the rapist responded. "Or did I mistake you for a bunch of pussies?"

"Watch your mouth, man!" Alex jumped forward, seemingly ready to attack with an energy sphere before Bill cut off his approach.

"Look here, Jason, you're lucky we even agreed to this in the first place considering the fact we nearly all got busted along with Miles for being in possession of stolen government property last week. It's only because he took the rap that we're even out on the streets right now."

"I don't care about your boy rotting in jail, I'm running the show now and unlike him I'm going to make good on my plans."

"You're running nothing mate and judging by the cuts on your face, I'd say the bird messed those plans up already," Alex goaded in the background. The comment was met with a swift energy blast in retaliation, the force of the attack sending Alex slamming into another member of the gang that knocked the hood down from over his head.

"Anyone else got something to say?" the rapist remarked.

"How about you save that for the girl instead, Jason?" Bill responded as Alex's groans echoed behind him. "Thought that was the common objective we all had when I suggested you joining up with us?"

"Don't tell me what to do, you little sh–."

The rapist's attention was then caught by the sight of the youth crawling out from under Alex's prone body, his previous hood-obscured identity now obvious.

"What is *he* doing here?" he said to no-one in particular.

"Scott, you know this guy?" Donnie asked the youth.

"He's my brother," Scott replied.

"You're nothing to me," Jason snarled. "And what business do you have being here anyway?"

"I have a power just like you."

"Oh, do you now? Well I think I'd like to see that," he responded while taking a combative stance with the rest of the gang quickly moving aside.

"Can you guys sort the family squabble out later?" Bill shouted, only to have Jason aim a green-hued open palm in his direction.

"Wanna be next, junior?" he sneered before turning his attention back to his younger brother. "So what *can* you do?"

"The same as you," Scott replied.

"Then aim a blast at me," he cockily demanded while flaring up an aura around his body in anticipation of absorbing the attack.

Reluctantly, Scott unleashed what appeared to be a crimson energy whip from his hand, swinging it forward towards his older brother. The stream of energy, contrary to Jason's expectations, instead struck him directly in the chest with a concussive impact, failing to be absorbed whatsoever as he fell to the floor.

"Are you alright?" Scott meekly spoke, only to be struck with a vengeful blast of energy in response that knocked him down, leaving him moaning in pain.

"You are pathetic, you know that?" Jason mockingly said as he stood over his stricken younger brother who now had tears streaming down his face. "You were a waste of space growing up and you're a waste of space now."

Before he could fire another blast at the helpless youth, Jason found himself taking an attack from behind that felt like a hot, narrow force hitting his shoulder. He turned around quickly to see Bill holding his fingers towards him.

"Get away from him, man!" he said as his fingers glowed threateningly. Jason instead launched multiple energy blasts at the entire group who reacted by all fleeing towards the exit, the injured Alex being the last one to stumble out before Jason turned his attention back to Scott.

"I think it's time you joined your father," he menacingly stated with a ball of energy forming in his hand.

"What?" Scott weakly asked.

"Oh, you didn't know? The reason why your daddy just left two years ago and never came back? Oh yeah, I blasted him to smithereens of course!"

"That's not true!" Scott replied with a mixture of shock and upset. "He left a note saying he was leaving!"

"Yeah, some of my finest work that," Jason replied. "Killing him and making it look like he had left because he hated his family; should've seen the look on your face when our mother read that note out loud. Kind of like the expression you have right now."

Scott watched as his brother laughed at his plight, slowly feeling his emotional distress turning into extreme anger at the revelation.

"Say hello for me when you meet up with him," Jason said as he launched a powerful blast at Scott.

Instead, the youth deflected the attack away with a red-hued, aura-encased arm. Jason then watched as the red hue began slowly darkening until it was pitch black and was now surrounding his younger brother's entire body.

Before he could react, Scott unleashed a stream of dark, concussive energy straight at him and sent him flying across the room.

Jamie tried to make out where the location of the powers that her ability had picked up on were coming from, having felt two strong powers on-and-off nearby from her position in the centre of the complex among short instances of slightly weaker ones. If at least one belonged to the rapist, he was now in the company of other powers for whatever reason. Her sensing was indicating towards the furthest point of the industrial complex where he had run towards before she had lost his trail.

She then caught sight of several individuals running from the very same area of the yard. She recognised them as members of the gang in the park she had defeated previously, accounting for the numerous spikes in the power sensing aspect of her ability.

What on earth are they doing here?

Jamie then noticed one of the gang members lagging behind by quite a far distance, appearing to be jogging awkwardly as opposed to running. She flew straight towards him, cutting him off dead in his path.

"You!" Alex said as he prepared to throw an energy sphere straight at the girl, only to watch it be absorbed in a green aura nearly identical to Jason's. As he stepped back in fear, Jamie flew straight into his singed chest which was enough to send him down to the concrete in extreme pain.

"I remember getting wounded by an individual whose energy attacks blistered my skin just like yours has," Jamie stated while standing over the fallen gang member. “He wouldn’t by chance be who you’re running from now, would he?”

“Why, what are you going to do to him?” Alex spoke through the pain as the girl then knelt down close to his face.

“I’m going to kick the living daylights out of him, that’s what I’m going to do,” she replied.

“Then give him one from me; he’s inside that warehouse at the back,” he said as Jamie immediately got up and walked briskly towards the back of the complex, leaving Alex to get up and leave the vicinity with the others.

Jamie quickly contemplated what to do. Bizarrely, she was still sensing *two* abilities as opposed to just one but she didn’t seem to care; based on the gang member’s antipathy towards the rapist, chances were that whoever was currently inside the warehouse with him may very well be settling their own score with the psychopath. But her concern was still towards making sure he would not bother her or her friends again and that was business she would have to personally deal with herself.

As she approached the door, she was surprised by the sight of the rapist bursting through it and attempting to run towards the entrance of the complex like the others had. Jamie quickly launched a kinetic energy wave, striking him from the side and knocking him down before he could get any further.

“What do we have here?” she remarked as she stood before him.

“Not the time, girlie,” he responded.

“Well *I* have plenty of time,” she rebuked. “As long as you pose a threat to everyone in my life.”

Upon hearing her words, Jason quickly began formulating a new ploy in his head, one that could potentially solve both his dilemmas at the same time.

"Please, it's my brother," he then spoke. "He's lost control of his ability and is trying to destroy everything around him."

"That's *your* problem," Jamie fired back.

"It'll become everyone else's if we don't stop him now, he's even more powerful than me."

"Considering I kicked your arse a few minutes ago, that wouldn't make him very powerful," she scornfully replied. "Either way, still nothing to do with me."

"Please, it's not his fault. He's in danger too, he doesn't deserve that," Jason continued his attempted manipulation.

"Sort it out yourself."

"I'll tell you what – if you help me calm him down, you'll never see me again and I'll leave your friends alone too."

The offer struck a nerve with Jamie, who felt foolish for even considering it.

"I'm supposed to believe you'd leave me alone forever after going through all the trouble of blackmailing me to meet you here in the first place? It'd be easier for me to just put an end to your worthless existence here and now."

"Our powers combined will be enough to stop him," he continued pleading. "Family is family, girl. Surely you'd put everything aside to help out yours?"

Jamie felt herself wanting to deliver a kick straight into the rapist's head. But she couldn't ignore the prospect of guaranteeing Gabrielle's safety if he was telling the truth. And that was the problem; if he was indeed a psychopath, they had the nasty habit of lying through their teeth to get what they wanted.

On the other hand, he was no threat to her currently as long as she had his ability so any attempt at a double-cross would be easily neutralised. Annoyingly, she also knew that she would be able to nullify his brother's unruly ability using her own if it was indeed posing a threat to his own safety.

"You're going in first, pal."

Jason smirked to himself before getting to his feet and meandering back towards the warehouse door. He figured that all he would need to do was coerce both the girl and his brother into fighting each other, potentially destroying one another given the immense power they both possessed leaving him to take out whoever was still standing afterwards.

And he would be able to move on to terrorising the girl's blonde friend from then on.

"Move," Jamie impatiently ordered. Jason hesitantly opened the door, not knowing what to expect but ultimately came across silence as he walked into the warehouse. Jamie followed, hearing distant, muffled sobs in the background. She looked towards the source of them and saw a young man kneeling by one of the crates against the east wall with his face buried in his arms. Her power sensing confirmed his active ability despite the fact it currently wasn't visible.

"That him?" she asked.

"Yeah." Jason replied.

"Doesn't seem so out of control now."

"Don't underestimate him," he argued.

“Check on him so I can get out of here already,” she demanded coldly.

“He might react badly to me again.”

“That’s a risk I’m willing to take.”

Jason glared at the girl as he slowly made his way over to Scott, hoping he would still find the chance to put her in the line of fire. He began feeling slightly anxious knowing his younger brother was most likely still baying for his blood following the revelation that he had been responsible for the murder of his father.

“Hey, bro,” he spoke gently. Suddenly, Scott turned around, his pupils almost completely black as the dark aura surrounding his body re-materialised. Without warning, he shot a blast of energy straight at his brother who was sent sprawling across the floor.

Jamie watched in horror as she witnessed the youth producing a tentacle-like stream of dark energy and attempted to plunge the spiked end straight into the rapist’s prone body on the ground. On instinct, she blasted the tentacle with a shot of green energy despite the effort saving the rapist’s life.

“You have the same power as him?!” Scott raged at the black-clad, hooded figure. “So you’re on his side!”

“I’m on no-one’s side, kid,” Jamie shouted back.

“Did you help him kill my father?!” he roared back.

“He did *what?*” Jamie responded while shooting an evil look towards the downed rapist.

“Leave him to me!” Scott yelled while producing two more tentacle-like streams from both hands.

“For your sake, I can’t let you kill him,” Jamie replied.

"Then you will die with him!" the youth shouted back as he attempted to stab his downed brother with both streams, only for them both to be blasted away again by the girl. He instead launched a dark energy sphere at her which she managed to avoid by diving out of the way, leaving the attack to blow apart several more crates stacked against the west wall.

Seeing his opportunity, Jason shot a two-handed blast of energy at Scott which connected and then combusted against his torso.

"You scum!" Jamie uttered aloud, believing the rapist had just murdered his own brother.

However, the youth instead stood undamaged, his aura having shielded him from the effect of the blast.

"You're on your own, girl!" Jason remarked as he fled towards the exit and disappeared straight out the door.

Not wanting to face the younger brother's wrath herself, Jamie immediately followed as Scott began screaming aloud with shards of dark energy scattering from his body. As she closed the door behind her, she could hear the energy shards impacting against the walls of the warehouse while failing to pierce through them.

She then turned back towards the rapist who was already halfway across the yard towards the front fence of the complex. Taking to the air once more, Jamie rammed her body at high speed straight into his back to cut him off, resulting in him bouncing off the concrete floor before slamming against another stack of crates.

"Y'know I'm not surprised you lied to me," Jamie said as she stood over the irredeemable fiend. "But to murder your own father is unreal."

"Please, I murdered *his* father," Jason grinned. "We only share the same mother and he should consider himself lucky I left her unharmed too."

"It just gets better and better," Jamie disgustedly replied. "Guess you must be proud?"

"This is just a fundamental rule of how the world works, girl – the strongest dominate society and I'm just living up to what I was made to do!"

"Well I sure dominated your weak arse(!)"

Before he had a chance to react, the girl quickly whipped her arm backwards and Jason felt a strong force hitting his right arm, hearing a snapping sound as an immensely painful sensation surged into the limb. He yelled out in agony as she approached his side.

"Here's how it is: I'm going back in there to rectify the mess you've created and you are going to stay away from my house and my friends. For if I ever come across you again, I will break all your other limbs before emasculating you in front of your very eyes while leaving you to live the rest of your life in that state."

"He'll kill you before you get a chance, you know that," Jason arrogantly responded despite being in a vulnerable position.

"Not if I can help it," Jamie defiantly replied before flying straight back to the warehouse.

Chapter 14

Jamie stood before the door to the warehouse, rapidly planning her approach to dealing with the rapist's younger brother. His ability appeared to be the same as his sibling's except for the fact he chose to manipulate it into physical forms to attack with instead of pure energy. She did not know if the streams were absorbable using the aura shielding though but it wouldn't matter as long as she could drain away and ultimately deactivate his power in order to try and reason with him.

For a moment she wondered why she was even bothering. The matter really did not concern her beyond forcing the rapist to leave her alone by intimidating him with his own ability, breaking his arm and threatening to castrate him which she hoped had driven the message home that she wasn't someone to mess around with. But she couldn't help but feel some degree of sympathy for the younger brother, particularly in regards to the fact he had lost his father in such appalling circumstances.

Disabling his ability though probably wouldn't be as simple as all the previous times she had done so to every other enhanced human out there but it still remained possible.

She entered the warehouse interior, seeing the youth already glaring towards her from the east wall side.

"I'm not here to fight," Jamie spoke to him in a calm manner. "I know what that scumbag brother of yours did to you but you need to rein in your powers, they're going to get someone killed."

"You've got that right," Scott responded as he unleashed two dark streams of energy in the girl's direction. Jamie managed to avoid them both by flying quickly in-between the pair of them and soaring over her opponent before grappling him from behind.

She quickly began attempting to absorb some of his ability while simultaneously deactivating it. The youth's ability proved too overpowering, however, as he generated a shockwave of physical energy emanating from his body to knock her off before attempting again to strike her with an energy stream.

Jamie utilised the speed of her flight to avoid the attacks coming her way before finally taking a blow from one of them, feeling the equivalent to being hit with a lead pipe across her back. She swiftly retaliated with a kinetic energy wave but was cancelled out by the same stream of energy whipping into it.

Knowing she had absorbed some of the youth's ability, Jamie attempted to manifest the same energy tentacles from her hands, managing to succeed though noticed that they were red-hued as opposed to the same black colour as his.

Nonetheless, she sent them lunging towards the youth in an attempt to restrain him in order to deactivate his powers further, only for him to resist by pushing them back with his own and leading to a stalemate in both sets of energy streams pushing against one another trying to gain the advantage.

Scott felt aware of all his negative emotions surging forth and enhancing his ability's power, to the point it almost seemed as though *it* was actually the one in control of the situation. He knew his anger belonged to him alone though; all the pain and hatred he could feel as a result of his wretched older brother's evil actions and unleashing it all on everything around him was of little bother to him now. Whoever the girl was, just also happening to bear Jason's ability, she deserved all that she got for trying to manipulate and destroy him just as Jason had tried to do. If his ability was simply responding to that desire, then as far as he was concerned it could indulge itself all the way.

Jamie noticed she was struggling to match up to the sheer strength of the younger brother's powers and even despite having drained some of it away. The only way to stop him truly was going to be by completely nullifying his power with her own but getting close enough to him again to do so was proving a hurdle.

Repeating the earlier tactic, Jamie dropped her energy streams and flew straight at the youth again while dodging his own as they came slamming down where she had just been standing and managing to tackle him down to the ground.

"Doing this for your own good," she said as she wrestled the young man down onto his front and applied a full nelson hold with her hands interlocked on top of his bare neck which allowed her to also begin draining away his power.

“Get off!” Scott yelled, helpless to move with his arms pinned back and the girl’s full weight on top of him. Even in his enraged state, he still had the common sense to know that another shockwave would probably dislocate his shoulders in the process of forcing the girl off. Likewise, trying to attack her with an energy stream blindly posed the risk of striking himself.

He could feel his energy growing weaker for some reason despite the fact his increasingly agitated state should have been increasing it. He began to feel despair in the midst of his rage; first, his brother had killed his father and made it look like he had left the family out of disinterest, then he had humiliated him in front of the rest of the gang.

And now some random girl who shared Jason’s powers was trying to put him down even further.

Jamie continued to forcibly decrease the boy’s ability, feeling from her sensing power that it was definitely having an effect. Suddenly, she felt him beginning to forcibly wrench himself free from her grip as she struggled to keep her hands locked together.

Impossible...

She held on for several more seconds until her hands were pulled forcibly apart and the youth managed with ease to lift her body off with the sheer strength of his own. She had no idea where he was summoning the power from considering she had just significantly weakened it.

Jamie quickly flew a safe distance away towards the other side of the warehouse and gazed at the younger brother, whose eyes now looked as though he hadn’t slept in days and was breathing heavily; he looked absolutely awful and Jamie could only assume it was the strain of his ability negatively affecting him if he was delving into it to forcibly increase his strength and power.

Scott felt exhausted but nonetheless encouraged by his enduring powers that were allowing him to continue the bout. He then unleashed another spraying energy shard attack which was quickly blocked by Jamie manipulating her share of the ability into a makeshift energy shield.

Without even checking to see if he had managed to successfully hit the girl or not, Scott materialised another pair of energy streams and used them to grip and hurl two nearby crates straight at her. Jamie re-engaged her flight to avoid being struck by the projectiles though fell back down to the floor soon after against her will.

"No, not now!" she spoke aloud as she realised her absorbed flight ability had been completely used up, having been too focused on her counter-attack to notice its levels had been steadily decreasing. She quickly blasted apart two more crates as they hurtled towards her, starting to feel a sense of dread with her speed advantage now gone and unsure if her current power reserves were enough to match up to the youth's unpredictable and increasingly unstable ability.

Growing in determination, Scott sent his energy streams straight in the direction of the girl who held them back with two of her own in another test of strength. Jamie knew she could only resist them for so long, quickly trying to figure out a way to escape the situation the first chance she got. As much as she sympathised with the boy's treatment at the hands of his brother, she wasn't about to risk losing her life over trying to calm him down and her only real method of doing so had twice failed to quell his ability.

* * *

Jason peered through the gap between the warehouse door and the frame, seeing his brother and the girl locked in a stalemate with duelling solid streams of red and black energy. The sight was surreal but he knew he wouldn't get a better opportunity to strike if he didn't act now. He opened the door and began charging the most powerful energy attack he could with his unbroken left arm.

Jamie grew worried as the youth's energy streams began steadily pushing her own back towards her. A sudden powerful surge of her remaining power would probably be enough to force the opposing streams away and give her enough time to flee the warehouse in hope that he wouldn't follow her out.

Then she felt a second power spike go off in her head. She looked towards the source to her right; the rapist was at the door and his left hand was glowing green as he brought it back to launch an attack.

"No!" she yelled out loud as he unleashed a powerful looking blast aimed at his younger brother.

Scott, in reaction to the girl's outburst, turned to the direction she was looking in and saw a green-hued blast of energy heading his way. He quickly dropped the energy streams and focused his energy into producing a barrier that just barely managed to deflect the blast up towards the ceiling, the impact causing chunks of roofing to fall down in front of Jason's position who was momentarily distracted by the collapsing debris before him.

"No, don't do it!" Jamie cried in vain as she saw the youth quickly respond to the botched sneak attack with a single stream of dark energy unleashed from his right arm, watching as it pierced through his brother's chest.

Jason simply stood in both physical and mental shock as he felt the tentacle-like energy attack puncturing his torso, barely even registering the loud scream from the girl that subsequently rang out in the background. Scott then yanked the energy stream angrily out of his brother, the force of which pulled Jason down heavily onto the floor with a sickening sound of his skull impacting upon the concrete surface.

"What have you done?" Jamie said softly, completely shaken from what she had just witnessed.

Giving an angry yell in response, Scott attempted to blast the girl with a concussive energy attack. Jamie reacted quickly, forming an energy shield and blocking the attempt, pouring every last bit of energy she still had into the barrier to hold off the ongoing attack. As she felt her own reserves dwindling, she also felt the pressure against the energy shield easing off too.

Mercifully, she then felt it completely disappear as the last of her own energy finally ran out.

Falling to her knees from exhaustion, Jamie looked up at the youth who was similarly down on one knee trying to catch his breath. She noticed his black aura had completely disappeared and she could no longer sense his ability in active use.

He then looked back at her, still looking worn out from the effort.

"Are you okay?" Jamie asked.

"Will you shut up?" Scott aggressively responded.

"Will you calm down for once and talk to me in a normal manner?" she fired back. Scott attempted to aim an energy attack in her direction though failed to bring forth any power at all. In his frustration, he yelled angrily into the air.

"You don't have to keep acting out now," Jamie said "I'm not trying to wind you up or anything but you need to control yourself. Or is killing people really what you want to do?"

"Stop pretending to care!" he roared. "You're not tricking me like he did!"

"I'm nothing like that prick, I was trying to help you the whole time whether you believe it or not. Your power was going to destroy everything around you, including yourself."

"Stop lying to me!"

"I'm not! I know exactly what you're going through."

"How the hell do *you* have any idea what I've gone through?!" Scott argued loudly.

"I lost my dad too," she mournfully replied, noticing the boy's demeanour soften slightly in response.

"Was he murdered like mine?" he asked, still with an aggrieved tone to his voice.

"No, he died of cancer."

"Then you're not the same as me," he stubbornly replied.

"If we're going to play it like that, is your mother still around?" Jamie asked.

"Yeah."

"Mine was killed in a car crash, by three arseholes who stole a car and took it for a joyride," she followed up. "Should I start trying to blast everything around me?"

"I'd kill them," he replied.

"What?"

"Your mum's killers; I'd destroy them for that."

"Well I haven't, as much as I've felt like it over the past few months. I even wanted to kill your brother but I didn't because I'm not that kind of person, unlike him."

Jamie then grimaced at the sight of the rapist's lifeless body. "Is that something you're honestly proud of?"

"He was pure evil, he brought it on himself," Scott bullishly responded.

"Are you really just as bad as him? Or are you just saying this crap to make yourself feel better about killing him?"

Scott took a look at his brother's corpse. The anger suddenly began to fade at long last.

"I will never be as bad as he was," he said. "But no, I'm not glad that I killed him."

"Good," Jamie remarked.

"What do I do about him?" he asked. "Will I go to prison?"

"I don't know," Jamie said, realising the grave situation of trying to explain away her involvement in the fact there was a dead body lying on the floor in a warehouse. "I'd hate to sound insensitive but I should never have been here in the first place. It's only because he threatened my friend's life that I agreed to meet him in the hope of getting him to leave her alone."

"So he screwed you over too?" Scott asked.

"You're right; he was pure evil. But I can't honestly say this is what I wanted of him, as much as I thought of it."

They both stood in silence for a brief moment. Jamie began to feel like she really didn't want to be around the rapist's body any longer.

"If anything, his cauterised wound will barely be explainable to law enforcement," Jamie stated uneasily. "I can only suggest leaving his body here to be found. The hole in the roof will probably look like he broke in or something."

"Just leave him with me," Scott said, showing some signs of emotion towards his fallen family member. "I'll use my powers to carry him away once they recharge and after the sun goes down to bury him nearby."

"Are you okay with that?"

"Not really but at the same time, I doubt he'll be missed that much. Only my mother would care if she knew he was dead but he walked away from both of us a while ago anyway. If we're lucky, he knew no-one who would be looking for him."

"Okay," Jamie simply replied, feeling some relief that she may not end up under police investigation after all. "I'll leave you alone now. Hope you'll be alright in the long term."

"Are *you*? After losing both your parents?" he asked curiously.

"I'm getting there. I think you will too eventually about your dad," she answered, sharing a comforting smile with the youth as she made her way to the door.

As Jamie was about to make her way through the door frame, she suddenly heard a thud behind her. She turned around to see the boy slumped over on the floor.

"You alright?" she called out, receiving no response. She then approached him, noticing that he wasn't breathing as he lay prone upon the floor. She put her ear to the left side of his chest and felt no heartbeat whatsoever.

Jamie felt a cold rush. Somehow in the few seconds between speaking to him and trying to leave, he had seemingly collapsed and died on the spot.

The icy sensation was followed quickly by an anxiety attack. She tried to calm herself but instead ran straight towards the door and bolted from the warehouse.

After a few feet, she dropped to her knees and put her hands to the floor with her head facing down. Her anxiety then turned to sorrow and she saw tears dripping down and staining the concrete before her. She felt like bawling her eyes out but managed to prevent herself from completely losing control of her emotional state.

After several minutes of trying to regain her composure, Jamie chose to roll onto her back and stare up at the sky while lying on the ground. For all her hatred of the rapist, it had shocked her to the core to witness him being killed in the manner that he had, no less by his own younger brother who she couldn't believe was now dead too after everything they had gone through beforehand. If it was the over-exertion of his ability that had taken his life, she was glad to now be rid of it herself but she couldn't help but consider the fact that he wouldn't have put such a strain on his body if she hadn't drained the power from him in the first place, forcing him to push his reserves to beyond their limits.

She didn't want to dwell on something that ultimately ended up being an unfortunate occurrence but it was hard not to feel some degree of responsibility. She had seen both her parents die before her eyes and the pain had been overwhelming; the emotions she was feeling now were notably different but it was still witnessing death all the same and it bore the familiar catharsis that she had hoped never to have to deal with again.

At the very least though, she took comfort in the fact that the rapist could never bother her again in any way.

Jamie sat upright in response to the sound of tyres screeching in the distance, calming herself upon realising nobody was nearby. She then looked towards the open door of the warehouse, noticing that the rapist's body wasn't visible lying on the floor through the doorway despite being slain close to it.

Alarmed, Jamie got up and slowly approached the warehouse. Looking through the door, she stared in disbelief upon seeing that the brothers' bodies were no longer there.

Completely dumbfounded, it then came to her attention that there was another door at the rear of the building, albeit closed. But how in the world had anyone even known about the bodies within the last few minutes, let alone steal them in that small window of opportunity?

In the midst of her confusion, she quickly realised that the problem of being caught with a pair of corpses was now effectively eliminated. Already weary as it was, Jamie decided to leave the complex at long last, quickly walking all the way to the entrance and mounting the fence in the absence of her now-depleted flight. Once she noted the street was completely devoid of company, she headed in the direction of her home.

* * *

It had felt like an eternity walking the twenty minutes back to her house and Jamie had barely managed to hold it together the whole journey, shedding more tears on two occasions which her hood covering her bowed head had barely concealed.

She rubbed her eyes dry as she approached the gate, noticing Gabrielle's car was parked outside which wasn't surprising considering it was now 12:45 in the afternoon. She didn't have a clue what she was going to say in regards to the matter, if she even wanted to at all. The easiest thing to do would be to simply go along with the plan to visit the police station which would solve the issue of ever worrying about any mention of the rapist being brought up again in the future beyond an interview seeing as he was dead and his body mysteriously missing.

The negative of that would be technically lying to law enforcement if they were ever to connect her to all that had happened at the warehouse complex, especially considering that she had interacted with the gang member at one point who could act as a witness against her.

Maybe not.

She walked up to the front door and took out her keys. Gabrielle would probably be disappointed in her for not reporting the previous day's incident but hiding behind the excuse of being too traumatised to deal with the police would hopefully be enough to have her letting the issue go.

"I was about to call you," Gabrielle said from the front room upon hearing Jamie opening the front door. "Where have you been?"

"I was just having a stroll," Jamie meekly replied, taking her hoodie off and hanging it on the coatrack.

"So have you decided whether you want to report it t–"

Gabrielle stopped in her tracks as she stared at her friend's face from the doorway of the living room.

"What's wrong?" Jamie asked.

"You've been crying," Gabrielle replied, looking at the redness around Jamie's eyes. "What happened? Did that scumbag come back?"

So much for the easy way out.

"No, I just got bummed out by what went down yesterday while out on my walk," Jamie tried lying her way out of the situation.

"Jamie, look at me," Gabrielle approached Jamie while placing her hands on her friend's shoulders. "You don't have to hide anything from me."

Jamie looked back at Gabrielle, not wanting to lie to her any further but also afraid of the consequences of telling the truth. But maybe she would understand she had been caught between a rock and a hard place?

"He left a letter for me this morning," she stated. "If I didn't meet him or I called the police, he would come for you."

"H-how did he find out where we live?" Gabrielle stammered out of shock.

"He somehow managed to follow us out the park and caught sight of your licence plate, which he used to track us down."

"And what happened when you met him? I'm guessing you won seeing as you're unscathed this time."

"Yeah, I did. Initially anyway. Turned out the arsehole had a younger brother whose life he had also made a living hell and he ended up being killed by him in a fit of rage."

"He *what*?" Gabrielle said in an exasperated tone. "You're saying he's dead?"

"Yeah," Jamie replied. "Weirdly I didn't feel any glee when I saw him being killed on the spot. Then the brother died as well I assume from over-using his ability."

"So somewhere out there, there are currently two bodies lying around?" Gabrielle pointed out, in a tone that bordered on worry and irritation.

"No actually, they had both been snatched away when I went back to check."

"How do two bodies just disappear into thin air?"

"I don't know. But at least they're not just lying around for someone to find them now."

"Oh, Jamie..." Gabrielle said, now sounding more displeased than anything else.

"Gabby, I didn't ask for any of this," Jamie replied out of frustration.

"I know, it's just so annoying that you keep ending up in the middle of these things."

"That's not fair on me though, I didn't want to have to face down that prick after everything we went through yesterday."

"I don't mean to sound like I'm coming down on you," Gabrielle responded. "I just worry about you getting hurt or worse."

"You don't have to worry about that, I can handle myself well enough."

"That's not what I saw the end result of yesterday when me and Jesse found you battered on the hilltop."

"That was a one-off – I've beaten tons of other idiots like him before without picking up a serious injury."

"What do you mean?" Gabrielle replied, giving back an intrigued but stern look.

"Nothing," Jamie dismissively answered, realising her huge slip-up.

"No, I want you to elaborate," Gabrielle fired back. "What other idiots?"

Jamie knew she had dug herself into a hole that she wouldn't be able to climb out of without divulging the truth.

"I used my powers to take theirs for myself; random others who I came across on the streets."

"You've actually been interacting with these lunatics the whole time, just to have more powers? And using my ability in the process, I'm guessing?"

Jamie sheepishly looked away without answering.

"Oh, that's great. Just great!" Gabrielle angrily said as she walked towards the staircase before stopping and turning back towards Jamie. "You know, it wasn't easy for me taking care of you for weeks on end when I moved in here after your mother died but I put in that effort in the hope it would help you get some semblance of a life back eventually. And then you decide to repay me by deliberately and repeatedly putting yourself in danger. Thanks, Jamie(!)"

"I was just trying to do something to get rid of the depression," Jamie attempted a defence.

"There are better ways of doing that, Jamie!" Gabrielle turned back around, her voice elevated. "How about going to university or going out and getting a job? I know we didn't ask for these powers but that doesn't mean we have to indulge in them by stupidly trying them out on others like us! Try growing the hell up at long last!"

With that, Gabrielle stormed up the stairs and slammed her bedroom door behind her, leaving a devastated Jamie standing forlorn at the bottom of the staircase. Of all the times she had let her pride get the better of her, this was by far the worst and she knew it was going to take a lot to fix the situation.

She slinked into the living room and threw herself onto the sofa, grabbing the nearest cushion and pressing her face into it as she began crying uncontrollably.

Chapter 15

Jamie awoke to the morning sun coming through her bedroom window. She didn't feel like getting out of bed at all, still hopelessly miserable following the falling-out with Gabrielle the previous evening. She had never seen her friend so angry towards her before and it was a sight that she couldn't erase from her mind.

She saw that the time was half past eight, meaning that Gabrielle had already left for work. The fact she had spent the rest of yesterday inside of her bedroom, only coming out to make her own dinner in the evening, was a testament to just how furious she was. Jamie couldn't disagree with what she had said either in response to her antics, even though it had still hurt regardless.

Now she was fraught with worry that her best friend would abandon her and go back to living with her mother which just made her feel only worse. She couldn't stand the thought of being alone again. She needed to sort the mess out but it felt too early to attempt to speak to her or even text an apology.

Whatever the solution was, she wasn't going to stay inside the house by herself all day dwelling on it.

Jesse walked to his front door upon hearing a knock. He opened it to see Jamie standing on his doorstep.

"You're early," he said.

"I know," Jamie replied in a low voice.

"What's wrong?" Jesse asked, immediately noticing that something was amiss.

"I screwed up. Can I come in?"

"Of course," he answered, stepping aside as Jamie walked in, slipping out of her shoes and leaving them by the wall. "So what happened?"

"The rapist is dead," she nonchalantly blurted out.

"How?" Jesse reacted with surprise but also concern. "Wasn't you, was it?"

"No, it was someone else. He tried to lure me out into some remote area by threatening to hurt Gabrielle but I ended up dominating him with his own powers again. Then he pissed off the wrong person who killed him right in front of me."

"And what about the other person?"

"He died from what I assume was heart failure, I don't know. I think his ability took his life to be honest, he used it way beyond his natural limits."

"That's mad," Jesse commented in a neutral tone.

"Not as mad as Gabrielle," Jamie mournfully said. "I let it slip that I had been fighting people like us the whole time."

"Oh really? Didn't go down well then?"

"Nope, she threw a fit and hasn't spoken to me since."

“How are you feeling?”

Jamie shook her head slowly while looking down at the floor. “I don’t want her to go.”

“She’s not going to leave you,” Jesse attempted to reassure her.

“You didn’t see her yesterday, Jesse. She’s never been that angry before.”

“It’ll be alright,” he responded, walking over to Jamie and hugging her as it became obvious she was heavily resisting getting upset in front of him. She comforted herself against the warmth of his body, trying desperately to rid her thoughts of any further sadness.

“I’ll tell you what – you go upstairs to my room and pick out a DVD to put on down here. Anything you want.”

“Thought everyone just *streamed* films nowadays,” Jamie said.

“Meh, I’m a dinosaur,” he smiled.

“I’m not going to come across any rude magazines, am I?” she half-jested.

“Please,” Jesse gave her a dry but amused look. “People can find that on the ‘net for free.”

“Good to know(!)” Jamie gave the same look back but with an added smile as she climbed the stairs.

“Last door on the right at the end of the corridor, the box room,” he called out as he pulled his phone out.

On the upstairs landing, Jamie walked towards Jesse’s room and opened the door. Even the smallest room in her own house didn’t compare to the lack of space in his; the single bed took up half the floor alone with a flat screen television set mounted to the wall and a wardrobe in the far left corner. A small shelving unit that occupied some of the remaining space adjacent to the bed housed a number of DVDs. She had a skim through and opted to pick one of the horror films.

Then she noticed Jesse's wallet lying on top of his bed, deciding to have a look inside. She found a provisional driver's licence, ignoring everything else in order to not *completely* invade his privacy. His full name read 'Jesse James Webster'.

Jesse James. Jamie couldn't help but laugh to herself at the coincidence, though also finding it curious his middle name was the same as her late father's. She put the licence back in the wallet and took the DVD back downstairs with her.

"Back," she said as she walked into the living room.

"What'd you get?" Jesse replied, seemingly finishing writing a text message before putting his phone away. Jamie showed him the DVD cover. "Nice, you'll love this one."

"Why, is it really good?"

"No, because of how *bad* it is," he laughed.

"Oh, should I go get another then?"

"Nah, you'll like it. It makes for good comedy," Jesse said, taking the DVD and putting the disc into the player underneath the television set. He then sat back down as Jamie looked awkwardly at him. She couldn't resist.

"So...." she said. "Robbed any banks lately?"

"Huh?" Jesse replied, the reference going completely over his head.

"Don't be mad but I did sneak a peek at your driving licence while I was in your room, Jesse *James*."

"Oh, no!" Jesse cringed as he buried his head in his hands.

"Oh, it's not that bad," she laughed.

"Yeah, try telling me that back in secondary school when some of the kids in my class snuck a look at the register and found out my full name. The jokes went on for nearly six months."

"And there I thought kids worshipped criminals," Jamie continued to jest.

"Alright then, where's *your* ID then?" Jesse countered. Jamie went wide-eyed.

"Don't carry any," she replied with a smug look.

"Well what's your full name anyway? Come on, it's only fair."

Jamie mulled it over before opting to get her phone out and texting Jesse's her full name. She grimaced as he then felt his phone go off and looked at the message that had just come through, giving an odd look as he attempted to read it aloud.

"Jamie Avo-*noit*?"

"AH-von-*wah,*" Jamie corrected him with a slightly irritated look.

"How come it sounds nothing like how it's spelt?"

"It's only the last syllable, you plonker. It's a French name."

"How'd you end up with that?"

"My mother was from France and my dad took her name when he married her."

"Unusual," Jesse remarked.

"Guess he just liked her name that much."

"Well I think it's cool."

"Well I'm glad *you* do, bloody nobody else thought that back in school. Every teacher always pronounced it wrong like you just did and I had to correct them each time in front of everyone laughing. I was Jamie *Avo-noit* from that point on."

"Kids are cruel."

"Gabby even called me it occasionally but she did it in more of a friendly ironic manner after we became friends. I did grow to laugh along with it in the end rather than get annoyed at it. Think that was the earliest I learned to not let petty insults wind me up as much."

"If your mother was French, does that mean you can speak it?"

"Oui," Jamie replied.

"Oh even I know what *that* means," Jesse scoffed.

"Et maintenant? Tu comprends ce que je dis?" Jamie responded.

"Uuuuhh," Jesse attempted to fruitlessly guess.

"I asked if you understood me now," Jamie replied.

"How did you pick it all up anyway?"

"I just grew up around my mother speaking it to me and I guess I acquired it the same way you learned English from your parents and everyone else around you."

"You must have been a star in French class then."

"Well funnily enough that's how me and Gabrielle became good friends because she was clueless with the language and I helped her out with it all the time. Then we got to know each other better from there."

"You are a fascinating person, you know that?" Jesse smiled, to Jamie's embarrassment. "Oh, the film's starting."

The film went on for an hour and a half and Jamie soon came to agree with Jesse in that it really was bad but the fact it was terrible was what made it so entertaining, with Jesse practically doing a running commentary the whole time pointing out all the flaws, something that Jamie began to join in with as it progressed, much to her fun.

"Well that was trash," Jamie stated.

"Yeah, that's what I thought the first time out of the twenty occasions I've watched it," Jesse replied.

"How on earth can you watch something that bad twenty times?"

"Dunno, I just like the familiarity of watching something that I already know what happens in."

"Well at least it's good for a laugh," Jamie said, finding herself actually agreeing with Jesse on his point.

"It's only midday, shall I pick this time?"

"Have you actually got any band shirts like mine?" Jamie asked off-topic, motioning towards her black Nirvana shirt.

"Only about five. Didn't you check my wardrobe too?" he sarcastically replied.

"No, but I want to see you in one," she smiled.

"Why?"

"Just wondered what you look like when you actually dress in the style you want."

"If you insist," Jesse replied as he led them back upstairs and into his room. He looked through the hanging up t-shirts and pulled one out that had a logo on it representing a band called 'Alice in Chains'.

"Ah, good taste," Jamie said, being aware of the band's music.

"A real Grunge connection we have."

"Now put it on," Jamie said.

"What, right now?" Jesse asked.

"Not shy, are you?"

"My body's just not as attractive looking as yours," he blurted out, almost without thinking.

"I don't care what you look like, you muppet," Jamie replied, desperately trying to quell her face flushing red again in front of Jesse from the unexpected compliment.

"Fine," he said as he tried to make the changeover as quickly as possible. Jamie stared curiously as Jesse managed to get his current top off and stood briefly bare-chested as he fumbled with the band t-shirt, noting that like herself he was quite lean and with no obvious muscular build in his upper torso.

"Satisfied?" he asked upon putting the t-shirt on.

"Looks good on you," Jamie stated. "Surprised you don't have any body hair though."

"Mostly confined to my legs," Jesse replied. "And even that doesn't account for much. My dad didn't have much either when we went swimming in my youth."

"Must be your genetics then, or your skin follicles have a stronger tolerance for testosterone that prevents body hair growth."

"That why women don't have much either then?"

"Well we do produce testosterone but obviously not to the extent of you blokes. But yeah, pretty much."

"But you still have to shave your legs though?"

"No, actually."

"What, you don't grow leg hair?" Jesse asked in surprise.

"Nope," Jamie replied simply. "Don't really grow any body hair at all if I'm honest."

"What, literally none at all?"

"Erm...." Jamie hesitated to answer.

"Just winding you up," Jesse smirked as he pulled out a DVD from the shelving unit. "Shall we head back down then?"

"Alright. What have you got us watching this time then?"

"Slightly better horror film, bit more gory though."

"I've probably seen gorier in real life," Jamie replied, making a subtle reference to the rapist's demise and even her own mother following the car accident.

"After this one, we'll go pick up the little one from school," Jesse said, in regards to Kayleigh. "Are you heading off to your other thing after?"

"Yeah, I'll probably make my way over to the park from there," Jamie answered as Jesse placed the next DVD in the player and put the previous one in its case before sitting back down on the sofa.

The second film proved gorier than she had been expecting and not completely to her liking but Jamie nonetheless could tolerate it. Around halfway through, she chose to lie across the entire sofa with her head lying on Jesse's lap; he didn't appear to object.

"Do you think Gabrielle will leave me?" she sombrely asked out loud at random.

"I highly doubt that," Jesse replied.

"I think she will."

"Gabrielle loves you with everything she has; she won't abandon you over all this."

"I hope," Jamie quietly replied. She could have very easily fallen asleep where she was lying but forced herself to stay awake.

She thought to herself just how complex her bond with Jesse was becoming; he presented himself as a down-to-earth and sometimes playful person but she couldn't really tell if he was more comfortable with her acting so physically close to him, certainly greater than more experienced friends of opposite genders probably behaved. Or maybe it was just because of his similar relationship with his younger sister that he was so relaxed about such closeness.

"Jesse, have you ever been with a girl before?" she bluntly asked.

"Now who's getting personal with the questions?" he awkwardly replied without any of his usual jokey-ness.

"Was just curious, don't mean to pry."

"Well what do you mean? Like romantically or physically?"

"Either I suppose."

"I only ever had the one girlfriend like 2 years ago which ended after just two months. Don't think I was prepared for a relationship really, plus she had a problem with Kayleigh hanging around us when she stayed over and I didn't like it. It's not like we were going at it all the time and needed the privacy for crying out loud."

"You do it much with her in that time?"

"Only five times. I wasn't her first but she *was* mine and the first time went pretty much as you'd expect."

"Fifteen seconds followed by fifty minutes of crying?" Jamie joked.

"Bit longer than that, minus the crying," Jesse joked back. "We both laughed it off and tried again a few minutes later. It was never really going to be great though because of my lack of experience and also I don't think she knew what she wanted to do either."

"How could you tell?"

"She pretty much just lied still on the bed most of the time and let me lead, despite me being a noob at it. I never bothered to ask how good I was but at least she didn't throw it in my face when she stormed out of my house and broke up with me when I snapped at her trying to shoo Kay out of my room."

"How'd you even meet her to begin with?"

"She was an ex-colleague at my workplace. We flirted all the time but it was against company policy to hook up with each other, but once she got another job we decided to take the plunge."

"Does it feel weird telling me all this stuff?" Jamie enquired.

"Strangely, no." he replied. "I wouldn't normally be the kind to kiss-and-tell but she has no connection to me anymore so doubtful anything I ever say will get back to her."

"I always found there to be too much pressure to have sex during school."

"Well I was the perennial virgin of my place, but they would've said that about me anyway even if I wasn't owing to my massive unpopularity. I find it over-rated anyway now that I've actually done it."

"Really?"

"Well not based on the five times I've done it anyway. There are probably some out there that take great pride in being good at it including one or two other friends of mine but I don't care too much for it. If I want to get better at it, I'd ask people I know how they do it."

"Gabrielle once told me she fakes a lot of noise half the time just to make it more interesting."

"You sure she wanted you telling me that?"

"You never heard it from me," Jamie backpedalled. "Does make sense in a way though if it makes it more enjoyable for the other person."

"Suppose so. How's it been for you if you don't mind me asking?"

"Well it hasn't," Jamie miffed. "Never even had a boyfriend let alone had sex with anyone."

"I'd have thought you'd have at least half the male population trying to hook up with you, and probably even some of the female side."

"Why would that be?"

"Well, try taking a look," Jesse said as he held his phone in front of Jamie's face with the selfie mode of the camera activated.

"What am I looking at?" she asked as she stared back her own face with a neutral expression.

"Try the naturally gorgeous face that doesn't even need any make-up, you pleb," Jesse replied.

"I've had tons of guys want me for my looks, that's generally how I know not to bother with them."

"You get to know each other after the initial attraction."

"Well excuse my jaded outlook but the school environment I grew up in generally gave the impression that every full-bloodied guy was simply looking to get in my pants."

"People mature as they get older, you might find it different now."

"After my experience with that arsehole rapist, it'll be a while before I trust a guy to attempt it with," Jamie replied, putting an abrupt end to the conversation. She then began wondering how she had even managed to have such an in-depth personal discussion of that nature to begin with, as interesting as it turned out to be.

The film came to its end forty minutes later, Jamie barely having paid attention to half of it but had enjoyed lying quietly pretending to do so next to Jesse nonetheless. She still felt unease over the Gabrielle situation but hoped to make the most of her time with Sissy later on in spite of it, which in itself made her extremely nervous meeting the rest of her friends.

"Shall we head off then?" Jesse asked.

"Can't, too comfy," Jamie playfully replied.

"Uppppp," he responded as he lifted her head up while getting to his feet.

"Can you lift me up?" she continued.

"I'm probably not that strong enough."

"You calling me fat?" Jamie joking responded.

"Course not!"

"Then try. Besides you do it with Kayleigh."

"She's half your size. But if I must," he finally complied, initially struggling to lift the dead weight of Jamie's body in his arms but finally managing to do so with the aid of his flight ability.

"That's cheating," Jamie said.

"It worked, didn't it?"

"Alright, to the door," she mockingly ordered as Jesse complied, though managing to accidentally smack Jamie's foot against the doorframe in the process which caused her to yell in pain and wriggle free from his grip to inspect the damage.

"Well done(!)" she sarcastically said to Jesse, seeing a large piece of skin loose with a small, raw wound exposed.

"Just as well I'm good for this too," he replied as he put his fingertips around the injury on Jamie's foot, healing it in seconds.

"I'll never get used to seeing that," she said as she carefully peeled off the remaining torn skin still hanging off. "Better get my shoes on before you stand on my toes next, you klutz."

"What, you mean like this?" Jesse said while pretending to step on Jamie's feet as she hurried over to her shoes.

The journey to Kayleigh's primary school was relatively short at only ten minutes, Jamie noticing just how many parents were arriving along with herself and Jesse. It reminded her just how unfortunate Kayleigh was to not have either of her parents in her life at such a young age, both of which she felt were missing out doting on such a loveable child. It made her feel lucky that she at least had had that luxury growing up despite everything that had happened since.

"When will she be coming out?" Jamie asked as she and Jesse entered the playground, everyone around them notably staring at Jamie's exotic hair colouring.

"She'll be out soon, it's gone three o'clock," Jesse replied.

"Hope sooner than later, don't like all these people staring at me."

"Probably just the gorgeousness," he joked back.

"Ha ha, funny guy," Jamie responded. Suddenly, she heard a high-pitched noise in the background calling her name out loud. Everyone else in the yard turned their attention to the source of the commotion as Kayleigh ran to Jamie and jumped up at her as the older girl caught her in her arms.

"What are you doing here?" she gleefully exclaimed.

"Been hanging out with your brother," Jamie replied, happy to see the youngster.

"Oh, so *that's* what you've been up to," Kayleigh slyly replied with a cheeky smile.

"Kay!" Jamie just about managed to dampen an embarrassed shout with several surrounding parents watching on sniggering.

"Time to go home, Kayleigh," Jesse cut in, trying to rescue Jamie from further public humiliation.

"They're only looking at you because they're well *jel*," Kayleigh said aloud to more quiet laughter from the crowd as Jamie carried her towards the exit with Jesse.

"So are you coming back to ours?" Kayleigh asked as she held a hand each from Jesse and Jamie while they walked down the street.

"I wish but I'm meeting up with someone else in a bit," Jamie replied.

"What's his name so I can beat him up?" she responded with a frown.

"It's a girl actually; she invited me to hang out with her in the park later."

"Are we still going to the funfair on Saturday?"

"Of course we are," Jesse replied, sensing Jamie's hesitation based on the conflict with Gabrielle.

"Hope you like rollercoasters!" Kayleigh said to Jamie.

"Probably won't be loads of those at the park but there'll be other fast rides I'll go on with you," Jamie replied.

"Well make sure you don't eat too much beforehand, I'll be holding you to that," she said with a smile. Jamie returned the warm expression, just feeling slightly happier to be in good company to get her mind off Gabrielle being mad with her.

That situation would still have to be dealt with later she knew but for the time being, she looked forward to getting to know Sissy better and hoping she would turn out to be as receptive to her as Jesse and Kayleigh had been.

Chapter 16

Jamie began making her way to the underground station from Jesse and Kayleigh's house in order to journey towards Cerulean Park. Walking back on herself with the siblings had worked out in her favour as it would be 3:30pm before she caught the train and the remainder of the travel would probably take a further half hour, making her bang on time to meet Sissy near the skatepark.

She wondered if she should attempt to bring any alcohol with her along the way, not that she drank any herself but she was aware everyone her age was always trying to do so at the first opportunity.

It dawned on her though that she lacked any form of identification and most likely wouldn't get served but opted to draw some money from the nearest cashpoint in case Sissy wanted some anyway and knew someone old enough to buy it. Maybe she was over-thinking things but she was hoping to make a good impression. After all, it wasn't every day she came across someone exactly like her and there may not be another chance if she was unlucky enough.

Jamie approached the entrance to Cerulean Park and began walking in the direction of the field with the skatepark in it. She was slowly becoming a bundle of nerves with every step she took. All her insecurities were bubbling up all at once, though determined not to flake out at the last minute.

As she approached the skatepark, she saw a group of youths congregating in the centre with several skateboarders using the ramps and rails around them. In the midst of them, she spotted a green-haired girl who no doubt had to be Sissy, the only female member of the crowd. *No wonder she wants another girl around her.*

She began nervously walking towards Sissy, her heart rate steadily increasing the closer she got. One of the larger guys then turned to see her approaching, tapping Sissy on the shoulder presumably to alert her to that fact. Everyone else then turned around with her with several wolf whistles ringing out, much to her annoyance even if it was in a joking sense.

Sensing Jamie's discomfort, Sissy then walked over to meet her halfway.

"Hey, babe!" She excitedly greeted Jamie who could only muster a slight smile out of her nervous disposition. "Don't worry, the guys are just being friendly in their own warped way. I've told them you're completely off limits."

"Don't worry about it," Jamie replied.

"I just want to introduce you quickly and we'll go off and hang by ourselves for a bit."

"You sure?" Jamie asked, hoping the answer would be in the affirmative.

“Yeah, c’mon over,” Sissy said, taking Jamie’s hand and leading her over to the rest of the group. Jamie worried she would be able to feel the sweat from her hand.

“Everyone, this is Jamie,” Sissy proudly introduced her new friend, with the group giving an over-the-top response. Jamie felt her anxiety spiking but at the same time loving the positive attention she was receiving, the complete opposite of what she was normally used to getting.

“So this is the gal who knocked you flat on your arse, eh Sissy?” one of the punks said out loud in a jovial manner, Jamie being surprised that Sissy had told anyone else about that. “Well you’re definitely right about her being stunning.”

“And remember, she’s under my protection,” Sissy replied just as humorously.

“Well make sure to bring her over when you’re finished breaking her in, she can check us out on the ‘boards.”

“Yeah, she can watch Rob break his other leg trying to *ollie*,” another of the group yelled out to everyone’s laughter.

“Come on, we’ll go chill by the swings in the playpark,” Sissy said to Jamie.

“Before we do, does anyone want to get drinks?” Jamie asked, holding out five ten pound notes.

“This is fifty quid,” said a bewildered Sissy. “Can’t let you spend that much on them, girl.”

“Nah, it’s fine. I can afford it.”

“As long as you’re alright with it?”

“Yeah, go for it,” Jamie insisted as Sissy turned back to the group.

"Hey, Ryan!" she called over to the larger boy who had brought up the girls' previous scuffle.

"What's up?" he asked.

"Can you get a load of beer for everyone?" Sissy said, holding out the money.

"Where'd you get all this?" Ryan asked before looking at Jamie. "Is this yours?"

"Yeah," Jamie replied.

"Aw Jamie, you don't have to spend all this on us," he replied. "We're just happy to meet you."

"No, it's fine. I got a bit of money passed down to me, it's not a problem."

"Alright but just this time, we don't want you thinking we're taking advantage of you."

"Not an issue," Jamie replied.

"What are you having anyway?"

"I don't really drink," she answered.

"Well what better time to start?" Sissy jumped in. "Get her the same as me."

"Too right, spending this much on us," Ryan said.

"Hey Ryan! Stop trying to chat the new girl up!" one of the group called out in the background.

"She just gave us a round of drinks, you prats! Show your appreciation!" he called out while holding up the money, leading to the entire group giving a round of applause in response. Jamie could barely contain her embarrassment.

"We're heading over to the play bit, go grab the drinks with the others and meet us back here," Sissy said to Ryan, who obliged and took the rest of the group with him to the nearest off-licence.

"Actually, seeing as they'll be gone for a bit, we can just sit and chat on top of the skate ramp."

"We just walk up that second ramp?" Jamie asked, pointing to the lesser-angled ramp attached to the large, half-pipe structure.

"If you want but it's quicker to just run and jump up the other side," Sissy replied as she walked over to the half-pipe, running from one end and straight up the other side onto the top of it. Jamie was surprised by her athleticism, quickly following her up by the same method.

"Doesn't surprise me that you found that easy," Sissy said.

"I'm amazed you could do that in those boots," Jamie replied.

"Not easy but it's just about pushing through."

"Are they comfortable to wear?"

"You tell me," Sissy said. "What size are you?"

"I'm a six."

"Just as well I accidentally got the next size up then," Sissy said, slipping out of her shoes. "I'm a four but you should still be able to get into them as they're size five. Just undo all the laces."

"Okay," Jamie replied as she loosened the laces and put both boots on. They felt slightly uncomfortable due to being undersized for her, opting not to do them up or walk about in them.

"They really go well with your cargo trousers," Sissy said.

"You think?" Jamie said, wishing she had a mirror to look into.

"Hang on," Sissy said while taking a photo with her smartphone. "Have a look."

Jamie took the boots off and looked at the picture, agreeing that they matched the rest of her attire before slipping back into her own shoes and passing the phone back.

"Reckon you'd get your own?"

"Maybe. I'd need to try a pair my own size."

"So you're a fan of Nirvana then?" Sissy moved on.

"Oh, yeah," Jamie replied, realising she was referring to her t-shirt.

"I started off on them originally, they were my gateway to the punk music I listen to mostly now."

"So what do you like?"

"The Ramones, The Clash, Rancid, Sex Pistols, Bad Brains, Black Flag, just to name a few off the top of my head. The guys favour a lot of hardcore punk too, my stuff is a bit lighter compared to that but I listen to it all the same when they blare it out."

"I mostly listen to grunge and alt-rock but also metal," Jamie replied.

"Aside from Nirvana I don't listen to much of the Seattle bands but many of them did take a lot of influence from punk bands when they were starting out. We all do listen to general rock and metal too though as the club we go to on Fridays from time to time is always playing the usual floor fillers and well-known songs."

"Where's that?"

"It's actually in the suburbs believe it or not. It's run in a venue that also houses band rehearsal spaces, which is how we found out about it. Some of the guys are in bands and they practice there when they can afford it. You can enter if you're over 16 years of age but you can only drink if you're 18."

"How can they tell who's underage once you're inside?"

"They give everyone who's legal to drink a disposable wristband to wear and they change the colour of it each time to stop people trying it on the following week."

"Seems like a smart idea on their part."

"You'd think but we've gone so much in the last year that I've now got one of every colour under the sun from everyone else and I just put on the one I need when one of the others enter first and tips us off what colour we need."

"So, do many of you need to do that?"

"Just me and two others, everyone else is over 18. Ryan is the oldest at 21 and he generally organises us, he's quite outgoing and friendly which is what you probably noticed when he tried to stop you buying us all that beer."

"I didn't mind," Jamie refuted.

"Yeah but most others would've just taken that cash without a second thought. We're quite a tight-knit group; if someone turns out to be an arsehole we just boot them out and tell them not to bother with us anymore. And trust me, we've known people like that. You're better off without them."

"Well I'm aware of people who try to appear friendly and then reveal themselves to not be," Jamie said, the rapist being the first person to come to mind.

"You got any friends like you then?" Sissy asked.

"Just the one who likes the same music as me," Jamie replied. "He's only been in my life for a week but he's a good friend."

"More than a 'friend'?" Sissy smiled.

“Oh, don’t you start too!” Jamie laughed while cringing simultaneously. “I get enough of it from his little sister and my best friend.”

“No worries, I’m just mucking around,” Sissy said. “You’ll have to bring him out sometime.”

“Yeah, maybe,” Jamie replied. “You get that a lot around all those guy mates of yours, then?”

“They all know where I stand with them. Some have tried it on but I always let them down gently and they accept that. It’d be weird anyway, I see most of them as my brothers by this point now and if I were to date any of them and it went bad, it would sour the group relations so it’s better off like that. And besides they don’t want to drive away the only person preventing it from being a total sausage fest.”

“Where’d you meet your ex that you mentioned last time then?”

“At that club. We’re chummy with most people there but we have our own individual groups outside of it, sometimes meeting up to hang out. My ex came from his own group and when we got together, we sometimes combined both but that fell apart when we broke up. Still though, we occasionally have some of them come over and vice versa despite that. Ryan’s band’s bassist comes from their mob and he hangs out with us from time to time.”

“What does Ryan play?”

“He does vocals and guitar. He’s not a great singer but he couldn’t find anyone willing to do it so he stepped up himself, though he doesn’t need to sound too melodic when he’s screaming out words to hardcore punk anyway.”

“People watch his band?”

"Yeah, we all go and support him and all our mates' ones too at the club or wherever they find to play. Last place they played at was in someone's basement, which was alright until the police came by after a noise complaint. Just lucky for us they never bothered to come inside or they might've found the weed lying on the kitchen table that everyone was using to roll up some joints."

"Can you play anything?" Jamie asked.

"I could sing if nothing else, I don't have too bad a voice for it but I can't play an instrument."

"Why didn't you front Ryan's band?"

"Because I didn't have the bottle to stand up and be the centre of attention," Sissy laughed. "Besides, his stuff is a lot more abrasive compared to my singing voice, I can't produce the same yells and screams that he does. Do you play anything?"

"Tried teaching myself guitar, I don't think I'm too bad," Jamie answered.

"Good enough to play live?"

"Don't know about that."

"Well you get better and I'll get Rob from the group to teach me bass and we can join up to form our own band," Sissy eagerly offered. "Give those boys a run for their money."

"Sounds like a laugh," Jamie replied, finding the idea intriguing. "Took me a week to get the hang of guitar, might take you around the same time on bass."

"Well I need to be able to afford my own bass and amp first. I can jam on Rob's whenever I'm round his but he'll need it for his own band. Guess I'll have to get a part-time job in addition to doing college."

"I could buy one for you," Jamie offered.

"Don't be silly, I'll pay for my own," Sissy politely declined. "I need a job to pay for my nights out anyway. Used to just scrimp together my remaining allowance from being a college student but the government recently scrapped that because of course they did(!)"

"Guessing you won't be voting when you come of age, being punk and all that?"

"Undecided. A lot of the guys align themselves with that train of thought but overall we're not too bothered about politics, it's rarely brought up in conversation. Losing that support allowance was a bit of an eye-opener for me though. Do you bother with all that?"

"I voted in the local elections last year with my mum after I turned 18 but I just voted for someone who wasn't really in with a good chance of winning."

"Then why bother voting for them if they couldn't win?"

"Well every vote counts in the end, I just thought his policies were the least stupid. And not to sound like a raging feminist but I feel the need to exercise the right to vote as a woman seeing as we originally didn't have that right and what we went through to get it."

"Nah, I respect that," Sissy replied. "You really don't have your say if you don't take part in the process either I guess. What would you do if all the candidates sucked?"

"Probably write 'F-You' next to every name on the ballot and hand it in like that," Jamie joked, Sissy reacting with a laugh.

Several minutes later, Sissy pointed out the return of Ryan and the rest of the group carrying several shopping bags filled with alcohol.

"About time!" Sissy called out.

"Calm your tits, love! We got everything you wanted," Ryan called back. Jamie began to feel a slight sense of dread at the prospect of being involved with the whole group despite how well conversing with Sissy had gone.

"C'mon girl, let's head down," Sissy said to her as she descended the angled ramp with Jamie slowly meandering behind.

"Here you go," Ryan said passing a four-pack of beer to Sissy.

"Merci beaucoup," Sissy replied, handing one of the cans to Jamie.

"Oh trop sympa!" Jamie replied, to the confusion of Sissy. "Sorry, 'you are too kind'. Thought I'd join in the French talk."

"Check out the linguistics on Jamie," the punk known as Rob said as everyone else kept sorting the alcohol out.

"Guess you paid attention in French a lot better than I did," Sissy said.

"Something like that," Jamie replied as she opened her can. She had absolutely no idea what it was going to taste like but she took a small sip anyway. Immediately, she spat it back out on instinct soon after.

"You alright there, Jamie?" another of the punks asked.

"Jamie doesn't drink much," Sissy replied. "Does take getting used to though, sweetie."

"See if you can finish the whole can at least," Rob chimed in.

"I don't know if I can manage that," Jamie said.

"Come on. Jamie! Jamie! Jamie!" Rob led a chorus of everyone trying to coax Jamie into drinking the beer.

"Alright, alright, no peer pressuring Jamie," Sissy jested, "Show us your skateboarding skills before you get too plastered."

With that, the rest of the group put their beers down and headed with their skateboards over to the ramps. Jamie watched with interest, considering it a risky activity but finding it fascinating to witness nonetheless. She looked at Rob taking the first go, recalling earlier that he had broken his leg previously presumably doing the very thing he was currently attempting with a prominent scar on his left leg. However, he subsequently managed to manoeuvre across the half-pipe from one side to the other flawlessly, repeating the feat several times without fail.

"Look at that bloody show-off," another of the group said aloud before downing an entire can of beer and riding his skateboard towards a low railing embedded in the ground.

"Go get 'em, Jez," Sissy yelled out as they watched him grind the railing with the edge of his skateboard. Jamie then watched the other five punks minus Ryan take to their skateboards and all began exhibiting their skills at once. She marvelled at their talent and their ability to execute what seemed like complicated moves, all the while trying to gently sip down her can of beer. The taste of it was not improving at all but she wanted to at least prove she could drink the entire can.

"Hey Jamie, you should have a quick go," Sissy suggested.

"I can't ride those," Jamie replied.

“Nah, we’ll help you. Come on,” Sissy responded, grabbing her hand and pulling her over to the middle of the skatepark with Jamie reluctantly allowing her to do so. “Guys, chuck us a board.”

“Jamie having a go?” Rob asked while offering his skateboard over. “Here you go.”

“I really can’t...”

“It’s easy,” Sissy cut in. “Just put one foot on and push away with the other. Me and Rob will walk with you.”

“I’ll try,” Jamie acquiesced as she stood on the skateboard with Sissy and Rob each holding one of her hands. She then pushed away with her other leg gently and allowed Rob and Sissy to lead her around the skatepark, which she found enjoyable enough after the threat of falling off had effectively been removed.

“See, it wasn’t that bad, was it?” Sissy remarked.

“Not when I can’t injure myself doing it,” Jamie quipped.

“Was still fun though. How far down that can have you got?”

“About half way.”

“Well finish that and try one more.”

“Aw Sissy, one’s bad enough as it is!”

“Come on, you need to get used to it if I’m going to be dragging you out every other Friday night to the rock club.”

“I can get by without drinking a load round there.”

“True, as long as you can mosh with me. I’ll settle for that.”

“Fair play,” Jamie replied, all too aware of what that involved from watching videos of live gigs online and never having considered being caught up in it, though believed she could hold her own if she was able to take enhanced humans on single-handed.

* * *

For the next hour, Jamie sat with Sissy and everyone else on top of the same ramp she had conversed with Sissy on earlier with everyone steadily consuming the available alcohol. She found herself a spectator in the various conversations that sprung up, mostly because she had no clue to the personal situations that the others had been involved in and were discussing, though content on simply listening and being a part of the crowd.

She had also been nursing the second can of beer throughout the conversation to the point it was beginning to taste flat in addition to the less than desirable flavour, noting she really was going to have to get used to drinking it for the future.

She checked her phone and noticed that the time was nearing six o'clock. As much as she had enjoyed her time with everyone, she knew she still had to try and make peace with Gabrielle rather than letting things drag on. At least Sissy wanted to get her back out again in the future and she actually looked forward to the prospect of forming a band with her new friend which would give her more incentive to practice playing guitar more.

"Yo Jamie, can you show us how you rock out?" Rob said out loud.

"Huh?" Jamie responded.

"You know," he replied, banging his head while holding up the 'devil horns' gesture with his outstretched hand.

"Yeah, come on. Show us what you've got," Sissy added while playing some obscure heavy metal song out loud from her phone. Jamie froze on the spot where she sat, not wanting to humiliate herself in front of everyone. As she looked at everyone's expectant gazes towards her, she realised they were all behind her as opposed to trying to make her feel small.

Screw it.

Jamie then stood up to a chorus of everyone giving her encourage. She then started banging her head and letting her hair fly everywhere to even more appraise and even attempted to perform a circular windmill movement with her head before giving up after a few seconds as dizziness started to set in. She rested an arm against the railing bordering the top of the ramp for balance as Sissy led a round of applause. She smiled in response through her hair completely covering her face before moving it aside.

"I'd hate to say it but I think I need to head off," she then said out of nowhere, much to the chagrin of the group.

"You're really going now?" Sissy asked in a disappointed tone.

"I had planned to leave around six and I need to sort out a situation at home, have enjoyed meeting you all though."

"Hey, thank *you* for buying all this beer," Ryan responded. "Come join us anytime you want, you're fun to have around."

"I'll walk with you to the front of the park," Sissy said as she got up, followed by everyone else who proceeded to give Jamie each a hug goodbye, who felt enamoured by the warm reception she was receiving. Eventually they allowed her to descend the ramp with Sissy in tow as she made her way out of the skatepark.

"You did well," Sissy said to Jamie as they walked. "I could tell you were nervous around them."

"They did make me feel safe, I'll admit," Jamie replied.

"They're a great bunch of guys, I'm lucky to have them as friends. I'm just wondering though if you've had any bad experiences that might have made you cautious being around a load of blokes."

"Just shyness," Jamie insisted. "I'm not really good with meeting or talking to new people."

"That's alright. But if you feel like opening up, you can confide in me. I won't tell anyone."

"I will," Jamie replied, suddenly remembering their conversation from the previous week where she had withheld from Sissy the incident that had caused her powers to activate and was assuming correctly that it was a sexual assault, albeit an unsuccessful one.

"I don't suppose I can interest you in coming out tomorrow for a night round the club for the first time?"

"I can't, I've got somewhere to be the next morning and I think I need to develop a taste for alcohol before I make the most of that kind of thing. Plus, I need to send off for my provisional licence so I actually have ID to buy said drinks."

"Well you won't need ID just to get in of course."

"Yeah but I'd need to get one anyway so I can at least buy it myself seeing as I'm actually legal to do so but got no way to prove it."

"True. I'll get you out soon though for it. In the meantime, I'll be learning bass and getting a job to afford my own."

"And I'll be getting my guitar skills up to scratch."

The pair continued walking until they reached the entrance, Jamie almost beginning to feel the dread of making the journey home.

"I'll message you later, tell me when you get home," Sissy said as she hugged Jamie goodbye.

"Will do," she replied before making her way down the street towards the nearest tube station.

Jamie had found herself fretting the entire time as she had made her way home. Now that she was in front of her front gate, the anticipation felt even worse than when she had approached Sissy and her friends earlier on. She really did not want to go in and face Gabrielle's wrath but she also couldn't keep on tip-toeing around her amidst a tension-filled household. It was just one of those difficult situations that had to be addressed whether she wanted to or not.

She tried to quietly sneak in through the front door, still barely having the courage to approach her best friend but knowing she had to be the one to step up. She walked into the living room and realised Gabrielle was sitting down on the couch looking at her phone with the television off in the background, feeling her heart nearly missing a beat.

"You want to sit?" Gabrielle said to her, her tone of voice almost indescribable. Jamie sat down next to her, unsure how to act next but it seemed as though she wasn't going to be the one leading the proceedings.

"Hey," she weakly said as she stared back at Gabrielle worriedly as though she could feel something bad about to happen.

"I've been thinking a lot about you today," Gabrielle said. "And even though I made my point pretty clear yesterday, I do feel the need to reiterate that I feel really let down by you. I mean you really have made me feel stupid after everything I've done to help you through what happened the last few months–"

"Please don't leave me," Jamie blurted out unexpectedly.

"Huh?" Gabrielle said in surprise.

"Please, please, I can't be here without you," Jamie pleaded on the verge of tears. "You mean everything to me, I won't do anything to betray your trust again."

"Oh Jamie," Gabrielle sighed, almost in annoyance. "This is what's been bugging me all day long. I want to be mad at you but I don't want to upset you thinking I'm going to walk out on you. I'm staying here."

"Really?" Jamie replied, to her immense relief.

"I'm not going to be giving you my ability anymore though, at least not until I feel I can trust you with it again. These powers were interesting to begin with but it seems to me you've let having them go to your head."

"I really don't care about having powers, I just want you around," Jamie maintained the apologetic tone.

"Well I'm glad to hear," Gabrielle replied. "And I don't want to come across as your mother but I really think you need to re-consider going to university or at least getting a part-time job or something to give you more structure in your life. It's not healthy for you sitting around here by yourself all the time, especially if it leads you to do reckless stuff like looking for trouble all the time."

"I don't think I'll be doing that again anytime soon," Jamie said in a more relaxed voice as she lied down and rested her head on Gabrielle's lap. "Besides I've got more things to focus on now, actual company at long last."

"Visit Jesse earlier then?"

"Yeah, probably would've gone mad with worry had it not been for him this morning."

"I know, he texted me earlier when you were round his telling me you were about to have a breakdown," Gabrielle smirked as Jamie's eyes widened.

"That bastard!" she yelled while bolting upright, causing a laughing Gabrielle to catch her in her arms.

"Chill sweetie, he only told me you were worrying about me leaving you," she said. "And I'm glad he did because it helped mellow me out a bit from that angry mood I'd been in since yesterday. Goodness knows I can be as stubborn as you sometimes in not letting something go but I couldn't help but feel a bit guilty making you fret like that all day."

"I'll be fine as long as I always have you," Jamie replied, allowing Gabrielle to continue holding her.

"Don't know about you but I just want to relax so do you want to cook something from scratch or shall I just order a takeaway?"

Jamie gave a faux-guilty but insinuating look back.

"Thought so. What do you feel like having?"

"Pizza sounds good."

"Cool, you're buying."

"So doc, how is progress?"

"Ryan, please. *Lloyd* will suffice," Dr Murphy replied. "There's not much to update you on so far other than how the two young men both came to be deceased. And might I repeat my disappointment in the fact you absconded with their bodies rather than allowing the law to notify their parents."

“It’s not something I enjoyed doing, Lloyd,” Sharp rebutted. “But you don’t just pass up on an opportunity like that to bring in dead specimens that can’t resist our attempts to properly research their biology to figure out the nature of their powers. Luckily Dawn managed to track the girl using her ability while in the company of them, otherwise we might’ve missed out.”

“Seeing as you didn’t bring her in too, I’m guessing she’s no longer of interest?”

“No, she’s very much still of interest. I just don’t have an available cell ready yet to contain her in but hopefully that problem will be resolved by tomorrow. I’ll give credit to those knucklehead poachers who managed to grab the boys without her even noticing they were gone, or so they say anyway.”

“And what do you plan to do with them once we’re finished here?”

“A van with fake licence plates dropping them off in some remote location with an anonymous tip-off using a burner phone always sounds good. A post-mortem will of course uncover foul play on our part but good luck to them being able to trace it all back to us.”

“Well I think the nature of the elder boy’s injury will baffle them enough as it is.”

“Feel free to elaborate just for the sake of it.”

“Well whatever spiked him through the chest managed to cause catastrophic damage to his aorta that quickly led to death. The fact the wound is completely cauterised is astounding though, like he was pierced with something extremely hot.”

“Kind of reminds me of what a lightsaber does to people’s limbs in those *Star Wars* films.”

"For a lack of a better comparison, I agree. The younger boy seems to have died from heart failure with signs of significant cardiomyopathy and damage to the heart muscle. For someone so young to suffer this, I'd suggest he was born with a congenital defect."

"Or maybe some of these powers are more trouble than they're worth."

"Are you suggesting his ability caused a huge strain on his heart and subsequent death?" Murphy asked.

"That's something we may or may not find out during the examination," Ryan replied while checking his phone upon feeling it vibrate in his pocket. "You'll have to excuse me, Lloyd. It seems Dawn has an urgent e-mail I need to read up on in my office."

"And what's that?"

"The background check on the girl after the boys managed to track her down to her address after her bout with the brothers. Not really essential seeing as we now know where she lives but it doesn't hurt to have all the facts. I'll leave you to your work."

"I'll let you know if I discover anything," Murphy responded as Ryan left the laboratory, making the short trip upstairs via the lift and coming across Dawn in his office still sitting at the computer desk.

"So Dawnie, what do we have?"

"Well she's nineteen years of age, born on the 13th of February," Dawn read off the screen aloud. "Parents both deceased as well as all other members of kin. Quite a bright kid though with impressive GCSE and college exam results. Surprising she isn't in university already."

"Has she got a name?"

"Yeah, bit of a weird one mind."

"Lay it on me."

"'Jamie Avo-*noit*'," she pronounced.

"That *is* a weird name," Ryan remarked before something appeared to come to his mind. "Wait, say that last name again."

"'Avo-noit'?" Dawn attempted again to Ryan's apparent dissatisfaction as he walked over to look at the screen himself.

"No..." he said aloud, sounding shocked. "Surely *not*."

"What's the matter?" Dawn asked, confused.

"We had someone who worked at Sharp Enterprises by the same last name before he died three years ago, he was really something else; helped dad develop the company into a major brand and pushed the envelope when it came to furthering the success of gene therapy. He was content on letting the business take all the credit for his work but he was rewarded well for his contributions. His name was James Avon-*wah*."

"'Avon-*wah*'? Weird way to pronounce it."

"What info do you have on the parents?"

"Roughly the same basic stuff as we have on the girl; her mother was Marie Avonoit, an immigrant from France – I guess she's the source of the unusual surname – and she died just last year from injuries sustained in a traffic collision. And her father was *James Avonoit* who died *three years ago* from cancer."

"I don't believe it," Ryan commented. "The girl with the extraordinary ability we've been preying on this whole time is none other than the great James Avonoit's daughter."

"One hell of a coincidence," Dawn replied.

"Well her dad helped make Sharp Enterprises the juggernaut it is today, I guess we'll come full circle when his offspring helps take it to the next level."

Chapter 17

"Gabrielle, I'd never thought I'd say this but are you nearly ready yet?!" Jamie yelled down the corridor from her bedroom towards her friend's.

"I'll be good in a few minutes!" she yelled back.

"What on earth are you doing?" Jamie muttered to herself as she walked over into Gabrielle's room, seeing her gazing into a full-length mirror in just her underwear.

"Hey!" she yelled out while attempting to cover her stomach area. "Do you mind?"

"What? I see you naked all the time, what's the big deal if I see you in your bra and knickers?"

"It's not that. Just don't think I should've had that pizza the other night."

"Are you seriously suggesting that you've gotten fat from one lousy pizza, Gabbs? Please."

"Err, have you checked out this gut?" Gabrielle replied, pinching her stomach outwards.

"You wouldn't still be bloated from eating that a day and half ago. You're just coming off your period so it'll probably go down to normal soon. Look at my stomach," Jamie said as she lifted her t-shirt up and rubbed her abdominal area. "I ate the same amount as you did and absolutely nothing."

"I want your belly!" Gabrielle replied jokingly.

"Yeah well I wouldn't mind your boobs but unlike your stomach, they're not going to grow bigger depending on whether I'm on or not. Now choose something to wear, Jesse and Kayleigh will be here soon."

"Bollocks to it, I'm going for something loose fitting."

"Such a girl," Jamie mocked as she walked downstairs and sat down on the couch in wait of the siblings to arrive. She was glad to have made up with Gabrielle ahead of the funfair trip, considering it to be less fun if they would have had to visit it without her. Or they would at least if she could ever sort her wardrobe out.

Out of the corner of her eye, Jamie spotted Jesse approaching through the window with the top of Kayleigh's head showing above the fence line. She decided to quietly open the door to them as they approached.

"Jamie!" Kayleigh said aloud.

"Sssh!" Jamie whispered back, while ushering them both in.

"What's going on?" Jesse quietly asked.

"Just wait," Jamie said before turning to the stairs. "Hey, Gabby! Are you nearly ready now?"

"I'm just picking out a top, be patient!"

"Can you come out here quickly? I just want to check something!"

"Oh Jamie, no," Jesse disapprovingly said as Jamie stifled a laugh.

"What's up?" Gabrielle said as she came into view at the top of stairs, still not having chosen something to wear over her torso aside from her bra. She froze as she realised Jesse and Kayleigh were looking at her.

"Oh wow!" Kayleigh said aloud as Jesse attempted to cover her eyes, though equally amazed at the sight.

Gabrielle let out a scream before running back into her room.

"JAMIE!!" she yelled as Jamie laughed out loud.

"You're so awful," Jesse said to her.

"Oh, you've seen her embarrass me before," Jamie replied. "You ready for the rides, kiddo?"

"Do bears take a dump in the woods?" Kayleigh responded with her usual sass.

"Come on, Gabbs! Kayleigh wants you to take her on the rollercoaster!" Jamie called back up the stairs. After two minutes, Gabrielle finally emerged wearing a loose blouse with a leather jacket on top and an unimpressed look on her face.

"See, was that so hard?" Jamie said.

"Hey, Jesse," Gabrielle said, completely ignoring Jamie before bending down to Kayleigh. "And you must be the munchkin I'm going to be going on a scary ride with, apparently."

"You betcha," Kayleigh responded. "Anyone ever tell you how *fit* you look?"

"Well I don't know where you picked up that language but I'll take it as a compliment," she smiled while picking Kayleigh up and rubbing her face affectionately against the young girl's.

"Yeah, seriously Gabby, have you thought about being a model?" Jesse chimed in politely.

"Well I apologise for my friend's little joke," she said while giving a glare at Jamie.

"You're welcome by the way," Jamie sarcastically replied. "Ready to go?"

"Yeah, bring the car keys," Gabrielle replied while carrying Kayleigh out to the car with Jesse and Jamie in pursuit.

"So how long have you been driving?" Jesse asked Gabrielle from the back seat as the group drove towards Cerulean Park.

"Not long," Gabrielle responded. "I only passed my test less than a year ago."

"Yeah, the clever clogs managed to pass both the written and practical on the first attempts," Jamie said from the front passenger seat.

"Well it makes getting the shopping easier and cuts down my travel time to work but the insurance was an absolute bitch for a first year driver, like nearly two grand!"

"Whoa," Jesse replied.

"Managed to get it down to £1700 by agreeing to drive around with a black box attached for the first three months, although after that period they decided I wasn't entitled to a bonus owing to some of my driving habits. Apparently I don't leave enough stopping distance when braking at lights or in general."

"Well the idea is to cause less risk of smashing into the back of another car," Jamie argued.

"Thank you, Miss back seat driver(!)" Gabrielle snapped.

"I'm in the front!"

"You know what I mean," Gabrielle replied as she pulled up at a set of traffic lights. "See? Nothing wrong with my stopping distance."

"Not what the insurance folk think," Jamie playfully quipped back. Kayleigh sat in the rear left seat in silent amusement at the two older girls' antics.

"Keep an eye out for when the traffic to the left looks like it's about to come to a halt," Gabrielle asked while looking out to her right side.

"Why?" Jamie replied.

"Just do it," she insisted while unrolling her window. Jamie and the siblings looked out to the right to see three topless men working in the front yard of a house with scaffolding on.

"They're hot," Kayleigh remarked.

"The traffic's slowing down," Jamie said. Gabrielle then put her fingers to her lips and a loud wolf whistle erupted from her mouth, drawing the attention of the workers.

"Put those smoking hot bodies away, you're distracting everyone!" Gabrielle yelled out, eliciting a round of smiles from the trio as well as drawing loud laughter from Jesse, Jamie and Kayleigh. She then floored the accelerator pedal and the car zoomed through the traffic lights as the amber light was turning to green.

"Where the hell did that come from?" Jamie said in amazement.

"Hey, it's not just you I enjoy trying to wind up," Gabrielle replied with a grin on her face.

"How long do we have to park?" Jamie asked.

“I just paid via the app,” Gabrielle replied. “I can leave the car here for three hours.”

“Should be long enough for the Miss to go on every fast ride available,” Jesse remarked.

“Well was hoping to do them all twice,” Kayleigh retorted.

“Well you have until I run out of cash.”

“I’ve got it covered,” Jamie said.

“Oh I don’t know about that,” Jesse replied.

“Listen to the wise girl, Jesse,” Kayleigh said as she clambered up onto Jamie’s back. “Lead the way!”

“A bit over-excited, are we?” Jamie remarked. “Alright, let’s make our way over.”

The group walked through the park gates and towards the funfair in the near distance. Having chosen to arrive at eleven o’clock in the morning, it didn’t appear too crowded as planned. Jamie was actually curious to see how well Kayleigh would hold up on some of the more scary rides, as well as seeing how much money she would end up burning through in the process.

Within seconds of entering, Kayleigh had already made a beeline to the nearest ride. To Jamie’s surprise, it merely featured giant spinning teacups that rotated on a giant platform.

“What, you want to start on this?” Jamie asked incredulously.

“It’s only the warm up,” Kayleigh replied. “Come on, everyone climb in!”

“Are we all going to fit in there?” Gabrielle asked.

“Only one way to find out,” Jamie said, taking Gabrielle’s arm and pulling her towards the cup with Jesse following.

"Looks like we spin it by turning the wheel in the middle," Jamie said.

"Do *not* spin it too fast," Gabrielle said. "I don't want to feel like throwing up."

"Well let's find out how much you can take," Jamie smirked as she began rotating the centre wheel.

"Jamie, no!" Gabrielle yelled, trying to hold the wheel in place only for Kayleigh to join in trying to move it too. Eventually Gabrielle relinquished her hold and simply covered her face with her hands in defeat as the cup began to spin around. Jamie then began to slow it down as the ride activated, wanting to give Gabrielle half a chance at lasting the whole duration.

In the end, the force of the rotation wasn't enough to make her feel overly queasy, completing the ride dizzy but without feeling the need to vomit. Kayleigh simply jumped out unaffected.

"Excuse me if I don't join you for the next few rides," Gabrielle said.

"Better be ready for the rollercoaster later," Jamie taunted.

"Can't forget about that!" Jesse joined in as Kayleigh led them around the rest of the fair.

Jesse and Jamie took alternating turns in joining Kayleigh on any two-seater rides while all sharing a ride that would permit three of them at once. Gradually, Kayleigh began deliberately screaming on each one, leading Jamie to absorb the adrenaline rush of the rides and join in. Jesse simply remained quiet, enjoying his time with the girls while Gabrielle was happy to stand and watch from below, occasionally taking a video with her phone.

Eventually, Kayleigh insisted on going on a rollercoaster ride, albeit the smaller of the two in the whole funfair.

"It's your big moment, Gabbs," Jamie mockingly said.

"At least it's not the larger one," Gabrielle grimaced. "Are you sure, Kay?"

"No chickening out now," Kayleigh replied.

"It's alright, we've got you covered," Jesse said, taking Gabrielle's bag and handing it to Jamie. Gabrielle then gave off a mild scream as Jesse then surprisingly picked her up in his arms.

"Lead the way, Kayleigh!" he said as the younger girl gleefully skipped towards the rollercoaster.

"Jamie, help!" Gabrielle called out amidst her loud and exaggerated giggles. Jamie simply looked on, feeling a slight sense of deflation as she watched her two best friends playfully interact.

"What do you make of it, Dawn?"

"I can't detect her using any powers but she's got to be in there, the car was pulled up close to the entrance of the park so they all must have gone into the funfair."

"Why are we bothering monitoring her now anyway when we've got no chance of nabbing her?"

"Over-excitement on Ryan's part," Dawn responded to the poacher team member. "Dr Murphy rang him up yesterday night to confirm that he had isolated the gene sequence within the two dead brothers responsible for giving them their powers and now he's eager to try and replicate the girl's DNA too seeing as she can absorb everyone else's abilities."

"So he's actually managed to figure out how to transfer powers into ordinary people? Hmm, maybe I should accept x-ray vision as my next payment."

"Make it sound so simple, don't you?" Dawn replied. "But whether the foreign DNA can be implanted without causing harm to the new host has yet to be tested. I just hope Ryan's not stupid enough to put himself forth as patient zero."

"Nah, a rich guy like that? Too much to lose."

"I hope you're right."

"This is what we've been reduced to, man? Pickpocketing at the fair?" Johnny bemoaned.

"Stop whining like a little bitch," Bill replied as he tried to eye up any likely victims.

"This isn't even worthy of our time."

"You think Miles is going to be out of prison anytime soon to help formulate another great plan for us?"

"Hey, *I'll* come up with something if it means not degrading ourselves with this rubbish. Max, you wanna chip in here?"

"Better than nothing, I suppose," Max answered with indifference.

"Well stop complaining that my idea's crap and come up with a better one then!" Bill argued before looking forward and seeing a man in the near distance looking at his phone. "Alright Max, you bump into him and I'll yank that wallet out of his pocket. Let's do this."

"Following your lead," Max said as he walked forward with Bill, leaving Johnny standing by himself. He began scanning the surroundings in his boredom, trying to think of something, *anything* that would be a better alternate to the current ploy being undertaken.

He then took a double take of the rollercoaster in the background, specifically the area before it – it appeared to be a figure clad in black clothes that were eerily familiar.

Her.

Johnny stared hard at the individual, all but convinced it was the girl who had twice defeated him and his gang members. He hadn't seen her without her hood down before but the purple and red hair could easily belong to her.

"Ten lousy pounds! I should've just put the bloody thing back in his pocket," Bill griped as he and Max returned to Johnny.

"Bill, check out over there," Johnny said.

"What are we looking at?" Bill turned his head with Max.

"Person in black clothes near the rollercoaster. Look familiar?"

"You're kidding," Bill said aloud. "That *her*?"

"Sure looks like," Max commented. "Nice hair though."

"Do you really have to compliment the bitch who kicked our arses?" Johnny replied.

"Just sayin'" Max said.

"Well I say some payback is in order," said Johnny.

"Too right," Bill added while looking at the person standing beside the girl. "You reckon that's her fella next to her?"

"Who cares? He gets in the way, he goes down with her," Johnny rebutted.

"We can't do it here, there's too many witnesses," Bill argued. "We need to wait until she leaves, then we'll batter them both."

"How do we know how long she's going to be here for anyway?" Johnny replied.

"Well that's what *you're* going to find out for us while we continue doing what we came here to do," Bill answered, to Johnny's annoyance. "Don't give that look, it doesn't take all of us to keep an eye on her and you didn't want to pickpocket in the first place. Might as well make some cash before laying down a beating."

Johnny simply stared back, unimpressed.

"We'll catch you in a bit. Drop us a text when you catch her leaving," Bill said as he and Max departed.

"So Gabby, how was the rollercoaster?" Jesse said to a clearly nauseous-looking Gabrielle as she walked with the ever-excitable Kayleigh from the ride.

"Yeah, how was it?" Jamie taunted.

"I'm skipping lunch," Gabrielle replied, taking slow breaths.

"That one next," Kayleigh said while pointing to a ride with pods on crane arms that elevated into the air and spun round clockwise.

"Jamie's go," Gabrielle groggily said.

"Come, come!" Kayleigh said as she dragged Jamie forward by the hand.

"Come on, you'll be alright," Jesse said to Gabrielle as he put his arm comfortingly around her shoulders while walking her forward.

Jamie took a look backwards, feeling uncomfortable upon seeing her two friends bonding so closely. Out of nowhere, she felt her power sensing go off in her head, which was indicating an active power very nearby to where she was standing.

She then noticed that Kayleigh was no longer trying to pull her forward and was just standing still, looking at Jesse and Gabrielle as she was. The sensation in her head then disappeared.

"Is everything alright?" Kayleigh asked in a confused but concerned tone.

"Yeah, everything's fine," Jamie smiled. "Shall we go on the ride?"

"Is the Pope a Catholic?" the young girl cheekily answered as they both continued walking forward.

"Jamie, don't you dare!" Jesse said aloud as he saw Jamie about to pay for Kayleigh and herself to the ride conductor.

"Toooo late, Jess," Jamie replied as she and Kayleigh boarded one of the pods.

"Will you scream like Gabrielle?" Kayleigh asked with an intent look.

"On this? Good luck with that," Jamie scoffed.

"Guess I'll wait until we take on the big rollercoaster then," Kayleigh replied gleefully as the ride began to move, taking Jamie's hand and interlocking their fingers together. Jamie smiled at her as the ride began to pick up speed, Kayleigh soon yelling at the top lungs to encourage her to join in.

"Come on, Jamie!" she said after receiving no response. Jamie relented, letting out a scream to appease her young friend who screamed in unison to the amusement of Gabrielle and Jesse back down on the ground.

"Look at those two," Gabrielle beamed. "They're like two peas in a pod."

“Practically sisters,” Jesse replied, though immediately dropped his happy expression upon noticing Gabrielle trying to hold back tears. “What’s the matter?”

“Nothing,” Gabrielle answered, wiping away a tear. “It’s just so nice to finally see her enjoying herself after everything she’s gone through.”

“She’s got close friends who will always be there for her,” Jesse said, giving Gabrielle a consoling hug. “We’ll all be making sure she’s never miserable again.”

“Yeah,” she replied, reciprocating the gesture.

From the ride, Jamie looked worryingly at the sight of what appeared to be Jesse and Gabrielle embracing. Then she felt her power sensing going off again, only to disappear seconds later. She felt Kayleigh take back her hand, looking to her as the young girl then reached over and gave her a side hug from her position in the pod.

“You alright?” Jamie asked Kayleigh.

“Yeah, just thought you might want a hug,” Kayleigh replied, to Jamie’s confusion but nonetheless wrapped her left arm around her in response.

After the ride concluded, the foursome made their way out of the funfair area and into the adjacent field where they found themselves practically alone, the fair attracting every other visitor away from the vicinity.

“Are we going back in?” Kayleigh asked as she joined Jamie sitting down on the nearby picnic bench.

“We will, we’re just going to go and get something to eat for all of us,” Gabrielle replied.

"Will you two be okay sitting here while we head off for ten minutes?" Jesse asked.

"What are you getting?" Jamie responded quickly, a look of concern on her face.

"Just fish and chips – saw a vendor as we came out so should be even less than ten mins if there's no line," Jesse answered as he and Gabrielle began walking back to the funfair. Jamie looked enviously on as she felt Kayleigh's head fall into her lap.

"Boo!" she said playfully while taking Jamie's hand once again. Jamie smiled and brushed her hair with her free hand before sinking into deep thought. She didn't even know why seeing Jesse being so chummy with Gabrielle bothered her so much, especially with Gabrielle having already said that she wouldn't make a move on him. Still, they did look good together.

But maybe she was in complete denial that she didn't have feelings for Jesse herself; she liked how it felt to receive a hug from him, even just to make some kind of physical contact like holding his hand. He was kind and thoughtful and always there for her when she needed it the most and just made her feel so warm and loved, something no other boy had ever done.

Maybe I do....

Once again her power sensing sprang to life, telling her that enhanced human activity was right near her for the third time that morning and just as quickly dissipated. Jamie wondered what was going on, that maybe her powers were being sent out of control by her emotional state of mind.

"Jamie, are you sure you're alright?" Kayleigh asked, looking straight up at Jamie.

"Yeah, I'm fine babe," Jamie replied.

"Y'know Gabby and Jesse seem to get on well," she followed up.

"Yeah..." Jamie thought aloud, triggering more uncomfortable feelings.

"Do you love him?"

"What?" Jamie quickly responded, surprised by the question.

"Jesse," Kayleigh said in a curious tone. "Do you have feelings for him?"

Jamie felt flustered, not knowing how to answer the question and being too embarrassed anyway to even comprehend a logical response.

What?

Again, her power sensing kicked in and quickly faded. Was it really her emotional response causing it?

"It's okay, Jamie," Kayleigh said. "You don't have to admit it. I just thought it would help to discuss."

"What makes you think I like your brother anyway?" Jamie asked defensively.

"Because I can feel your conflict over it," Kayleigh replied.

"What so you mean?"

"I mean I can literally feel your conflict over it. When I hold your hand; I felt what you were feeling."

Jamie froze.

It's Kayleigh!

Chapter 18

"How are you able to do that?" Jamie asked Kayleigh, though while pretending to be completely oblivious to the nature of super-human abilities as a whole.

"It just started happening recently," Kayleigh replied. "It's only when I want to normally but sometimes it happens without me trying. I first found out when Jesse told me off for talking to someone I didn't know at the front door. He gave me a hug afterwards because he felt bad but when his hand was on the back of my neck, I could feel exactly how he felt – remorse for scolding me but also nearly being on the verge of tears out of fear of losing me."

"He loves you with all his heart," Jamie mused, almost in amazement at how far Jesse's fraternal instincts and empathy extended.

"And what of you?" Kayleigh asked Jamie. "I won't tell anyone but, is it true? Do you love him?"

"Kayleigh..." Jamie said, the usual hot, tingling sensation flushing her cheeks being dowsed by her own confused feelings.

"You don't have to worry about Jesse," Kayleigh eagerly cut in, sitting up and looking Jamie straight in the eye while grasping her hoodie sleeve-covered hand with both of her own. "He is the kindest, most generous person you'll ever meet. I know he will treat you well, and he will love you exactly how you deserve to be loved."

"So you weren't completely joking about that all the time," Jamie smiled as she looked back at Kayleigh's awed gaze.

"Please tell me that you love him," she said, bordering on pleading. "You'll be so good for him too. He needs someone to take care of him like he takes care of everyone else. What do you say, Jamie?"

"Got lucky with the line, eh?" Gabrielle remarked with her and Jesse finding themselves only fifth in the queue for the fish and chips vendor.

"Yeah, which is good because we can get back to Kayleigh quicker," Jesse replied.

"You know she's in safe hands," Gabrielle replied regarding Jamie.

"I know," Jesse reassured her. "But I never stop worrying about that child."

"It's admirable," Gabrielle said with a sly smile on her face. "But while we're on the topic of caring about people, how do you feel about Jamie?"

"What do you mean?" Jesse played dumb, suddenly feeling that the line couldn't move fast enough.

"No need to be coy with me, Jess, you can completely confide in me. Jamie may be my sister from another mister but I'm not going to go blabbing to her what you tell me here."

"There's nothing really to talk about," Jesse replied in a deadpan voice.

"I had to ask," Gabrielle said. "I've known that girl for a while and she has never found anyone, never mind a *guy*, that she trusts as much as you. Come on, she didn't even trust me enough to tell me about the attempted rape or the fact she was fighting all those lunatics out there, but she had no qualms telling you."

"I think I was just a convenience," he deflected. "Someone who she barely knew who she couldn't really hurt with such revelations."

"Jesse, are you telling me that you don't have a single feeling towards Jamie at all?" Gabrielle relented, refusing to drop the matter.

"And I thought Kayleigh banged on about this a lot," Jesse said aloud. "Are you sure you're not looking into this way too much?"

"Not hearing an answer, buster," Gabrielle smiled with folded arms. Jesse could tell she was being serious enough to warrant a proper response.

"Jamie is one of the most interesting individuals I've ever met in my life," he began. "She is so quirky, likeable and Kayleigh absolutely adores her. I'm lucky to have her as a friend."

"But that's all she is to you..." Gabrielle interjected, the bitter disappointment in her voice unmistakable.

"I'm not going to tell a blatant lie and say there isn't a bit of an attraction there," Jesse continued. "But I don't think I'm the right person for her anyway even if I did have a desire to be with her, which I can't say I do. Kayleigh always comes first in my life and it was my devotion to her that all but destroyed my only real attempt at a relationship."

"You do realise that Jamie loves Kayleigh as much as you do?" Gabrielle argued, feeling her hopes rise once more. "Any relationship you had would flourish regardless of that matter."

"Gabby, I know you want this – it's obvious," Jesse replied. "But I know my place in this world; I love to see people happy and I will always do what I can to make Jamie happy but I believe that that's better served the way it currently is. And I'm far too damaged anyway, I will end up hurting that girl with all the baggage I have and I'm not prepared to do that to her. She's suffered enough in her life."

"As much as I want to smack you right now for being a stubborn prat, I really don't want to rock the boat to the point of capsizing it by accident," Gabrielle backed off. "But I will say that you put yourself down far too easily. You are more of a responsible human being than most people out there and Jamie's heart would not be in any safer hands than yours. I hope you realise that some day before you miss out on something good."

"Do you believe Jamie feels that way towards me then, is that why you're asking?" he asked, unsure of what he wanted the answer to be.

"Honestly, I have no idea how she feels about you but I get the feeling she's not telling me to avoid admitting it to herself."

"Maybe it's just what you want it to be."

"Maybe, but I want her to be loved by someone who will treat her right. She'll never meet a better person than you."

"That I can probably agree on. And I assure you, I'm always going to be there for her, even if it's not in the sense that you and Kayleigh yearn for, you pair of hopeless romantics(!)"

"You win for now," Gabrielle joked. "I'll be watching you though!"

"All you like," Jesse accepted. "Oh and we're next in the line."

"Nothing like love to pass the time," Gabrielle smiled.

Jamie looked into Kayleigh's eyes, seeing such a desperation that she couldn't help but feel bemused though also touched by the young girl's sincerity.

"You really are the sweetest kid ever," she spoke.

"You don't, do you?" Kayleigh said, almost sounding angry.

"I don't know, Kay" Jamie replied.

"But do you feel anything for him at all?"

"I really don't know," Jamie responded in an ambiguous tone. "And it's really been confusing the hell out of me lately."

"Just tell me how you feel about him," Kayleigh pleaded, squeezing Jamie's hand tighter.

"Can't you already tell with your psychic powers?" Jamie half-joked.

"Your jacket sleeve is blocking skin contact so it's not working," she replied. "But I want to know from you directly; tell me what you feel in your heart, Jamie."

"I feel affection for your brother that I haven't felt in my whole life," Jamie replied. "Emotions I've probably not felt towards any boy. I feel completely safe around him, I feel like he's courageous in every sense of the word and that he has one of the biggest hearts in the whole world. And I can't deny that I like how he makes me feel when he holds me close and vice versa."

Kayleigh looked back as if she was about to explode with glee.

"Kay, I know you probably want this more than anything in the world but it's not something that you can force to happen."

"I know but I can always hope," Kayleigh replied. "But you're saying that you at least *think* you like him."

"Maybe, maybe not. Guess you'll be the first one I tell but until then, please don't try to make it happen against our will. I don't know exactly how I feel towards Jesse but there's no guarantee he even feels anything towards me anyway so it's best to just leave things the way they are. If the universe wants it to happen, then you have to let things naturally occur."

"I guess that's how true love really works," Kayleigh bemoaned.

"Sure was an interesting chat," Jamie joked.

"Well *I* love you anyway," Kayleigh said, giving Jamie a hug.

"Love you too, kiddo," Jamie reciprocated, the two girls holding each other for several seconds.

Kayleigh then suddenly backed off Jamie and had a fearful expression on her face. Jamie turned around, recognising the three figures standing behind her.

"Don't mind us," Bill said with an extended finger pointing right at the source of his and his friends' recent humiliation, Johnny and Max flanking him either side. "If you wouldn't mind telling the pre-schooler to bugger off, we've got some unfinished business with you."

Jamie scrambled out from the bench and guarded Kayleigh on top of the table.

"What's going on, Jamie? Who are these guys?" she asked in a frightened voice.

"Everything's going to be alright sweetie," Jamie replied. "You're going to run away as fast as you can and leave these idiots to me."

"Are you mad?" she cried. "There's three of them!"

Without warning, Bill aimed a laser beam straight at Jamie who ducked to avoid it while pushing Kayleigh underneath the table, partially protected from a stray shot. She then rolled onto the other side.

"Stay down, Kay," Jamie said aloud, though aware she was at a disadvantage considering she had barely any of Gabrielle's ability still remaining within her so each use of it would have to count. She quickly launched one straight at the gang member who could shoot laser beams, judging him to be the most threatening.

The wave narrowly missed as Bill ducked before shooting an array of laser beams back in return. Jamie commando-rolled to the side and whipped a quick kinetic energy wave back at him, watching it connect and knocking him into the hedgerow.

"Approach her from either side," Johnny said to Max as they ran around the table in a pincer movement. Jamie took a few jumps backwards, happy for them to approach her in order to drive them away from Kayleigh still underneath the table.

She attempted to aim a kinetic energy wave at the gang member approaching from her left, only to see him jump over the invisible attack. However, it left him in mid-air just long enough for Jamie to hit his legs with a dropkick as he descended, smashing him hard into the ground that left him downed.

This allowed her to quickly launch another energy wave at the remaining individual coming at her from the right, who she recalled as having the ability to emit high intensity light from the previous bout. The attack struck Max directly in the abdomen, severely winding him and sending him down to the floor too.

"Hey, girl!"

Jamie turned around to see the laser beam gang member had Kayleigh by the arm while still under the table. She froze as she tried to think what to do to assure her safety while neutralising the threat he posed.

"Better back off her, pal," she menacingly called out.

"Approach slowly and I'll let her go," Bill called back. "Otherwise I'll shoot her at point blank range.

Jamie reluctantly walked over slowly, too afraid of endangering Kayleigh with any rash action.

"He's lying, Jamie!"

Jamie stopped in her tracks in response to Kayleigh calling out to her.

"I can feel him, he doesn't want to hurt me!"

"Shut up, you little sh–"

Before Bill could finish his sentence, he found himself being knocked down by a second concussive projectile attack from the girl, leaving him sprawled out on the grass in pain beside the bench. Jamie felt thankful that Kayleigh had let her know of her power beforehand as well as the fact the gang member had been unlucky enough to have grabbed her bare arm, necessitating the required skin contact to enable her to read his emotions.

She was suddenly knocked down from behind though by the light-emitting gang member who then proceeded to grapple with her on the floor. To her surprise, her level of physical strength was not too far off from his own, able to hold his arms back enough to place her soles onto his chest and subsequently push him away with her feet and down to the grass.

As Jamie got up, she heard a piercing scream as the remaining gang member began pulling Kayleigh out by the ankle from underneath the table. She attempted to launch another kinetic energy wave, only to find that her supply had completely run dry.

With no other option, she ran to physically attack the gang member as he brought Kayleigh up to her feet.

"Stop right there," Johnny called out to the girl as she halted her approach only five feet from his position. "I won't hurt her but I will paralyse her with my power so that she'll be unable to move until I deactivate it, which will be never if you don't submit yourself to us now."

Jamie hesitated and then looked to Kayleigh. Seeing as the gang member had his bare palm on the back of her neck, she would be able to confirm the truth of his statement. To her dismay, the young girl simply looked back with an affirmative look.

"Do what you want," Jamie replied, staying where she was. She watched as the laser beam gang member got back to his feet.

"You heard her, Bill," Johnny said aloud. Jamie tensed up as she watched 'Bill' shoot a laser from his fingers directly into her shoulder. The concussive blow sent a wave of pain shooting down her right arm and the right side of her upper torso as she yelled out while falling to her knees.

"Jamie!" Kayleigh wailed, close to tears.

Jamie gripped her right shoulder as she was booted down to the ground from behind by the light-emitting gang member who followed it up with a hard kick to the ribcage.

"You reckon we should get involved, like maybe tranquilise those idiots so they don't take out Ryan's pet project?" Dawn asked the grunt at the wheel of the van from her position along the fence line of the field that she was currently watching the girl receiving a beating from long distance.

"We can if you want, as long as we don't get caught in the process," he replied. *"It may just be better to let them have their way with her and continue monitoring her afterwards."*

"While I'd otherwise agree with you, we don't know if they plan to kill her or not. She did embarrass them only a week and a half back."

"Up to you, Dawn. We get paid either way."

"Hang on," Dawn said abruptly. "I'm picking up someone else using an ability, rapidly approaching. *Flight.*"

Jamie struggled to bear the pain of her aching ribs but was otherwise powerless to prevent any further blows lest Kayleigh be indefinitely paralysed. She wondered how far the gang's retribution against her was going to go. Until she was knocked unconscious? She still fretted over what would happen to Kayleigh though even after that.

"Max, back off for a moment, I've got a few beams ready to let off," Bill called out.

A second later, the revenge-obsessed gang member was struck from behind by a heavy concussive strike and hit the ground in considerable pain. As Johnny looked to his right in response to the commotion, he found himself being tackled by something that dragged him through the air before throwing him across the lawn.

"Gabby!" Kayleigh yelled, running towards Gabrielle who received her with a tight hug. Jesse stared down the remaining gang member standing over the fallen Jamie.

"Better leave her alone while you can, pal," Jesse warned in an aggressive tone.

"We're not finished yet," Max replied, immediately activating his illumination ability which caught Jesse completely off guard, shielding his eyes to block the intense light.

In response, Jamie aimed a double-footed stomp from on the ground straight at the enhanced human's knee. Distracted, Max's ability subsided briefly as he clutched his knee joint, allowing Jesse to take advantage by slamming into him with his flight ability.

"Jesse!" Jamie called out as she spotted the individual named Bill aiming his fingers straight at Jesse from the floor, who then blocked the subsequent laser beam with his shielding ability.

"What?" Bill exclaimed, aiming several more but finding all of them being nullified by seemingly his opponent's open hand, or something invisible extending from it.

"Not worth it, mate," Johnny said as he quickly got up and began to run away from the scene.

"Are you kidding?!" Bill shouted back.

"Did you not just see all that?!" Johnny yelled back at him. "First her and now this tosser! It's not revenge if we get our arses handed to us instead!"

Groggily, Max hauled himself to his feet and ran over towards Johnny as they both departed the field, leaving Bill to face down Jesse by himself.

"Want to try your chances?" Jesse threateningly held up his hand as it began glowing red from his burning ability. The emergence of yet another power from him was enough to convince the isolated Bill to finally call the attack off as he too fled to join Johnny and Max already far in the distance, shooting off a parting laser beam as he did which was easily blocked by Jesse's shielding ability.

"Jamie," Jesse said as he knelt down beside his fallen friend and quickly activated his healing ability while gripping her arm.

"Is she okay?" Gabrielle approached with Kayleigh piggybacking her.

"I'll be fine," Jamie replied herself as she stood up rejuvenated.

"Old friends?" Jesse asked, Jamie responding with a weak, affirming nod.

"Are you guys super-heroes?" Kayleigh asked. Jamie, Jesse and Gabrielle all awkwardly looked at each other.

"No," Jamie finally answered. "But we can all do extraordinary things for whatever reason and it's best that we keep it to ourselves for our own safety. I'll keep your secrets if you keep mine," she smiled at Kayleigh who realised Jamie was referring to her own newly discovered power and smiled back.

"On that note, shall we go back to mine?" Jesse said.

"Home already?" Kayleigh disappointingly replied.

"Babe, it's best we head off," Jamie sympathetically spoke. "We don't know if those idiots that attacked us plan on coming back." Kayleigh still looked despondent.

"We can play games back at our house, Kay," Jesse said to his sister.

"Are you coming round too?" Kayleigh asked Jamie, who looked at Gabrielle in response.

"Better than rollercoasters," Gabrielle said, much to Jamie and Kayleigh's delight. "Shall we head to the car?"

"Sounds like an idea," Jesse answered as they all began to walk back towards the funfair. Suddenly, Jamie stopped in her tracks.

"What is it, Jame?" Jesse asked.

"Somebody with an ability in active use," Jamie replied, looking towards the outer boundary of the park in the distance. "Coming from over there."

"Crap," Dawn muttered to herself as she noticed Jamie looking straight in her direction through the railings from the distance, the girl's base power having detected her use of her own ability identification power. "Warm up the van, I think she's seen me."

Jamie then saw a figure move away from the railings surrounding the field, followed by the sight of a large, black vehicle driving off in the opposite direction until it faded from sight.

"Can you still feel something?" Jesse asked.

"No, it's gone," Jamie replied. "Let's just get out of here."

It was only half one in the afternoon when the group arrived at Jesse and Kayleigh's house, though the rounds of board games made the rest of the day virtually fly by. Despite only joining in to appease a traumatised young girl, Gabrielle found herself being quickly endeared by Kayleigh's charm and playfulness, much like Jamie before her. It also amazed her how much older she appeared to act too, using slang and popular culture references that she wouldn't expect from an eleven year-old but figured it was probably down to her unstable childhood, the same reasoning behind her older brother's advanced maturity for his own age.

Jamie couldn't have felt happier herself; despite the day out being ruined by the remnants of the ability-based gang she had previously defeated, she was where she wanted to be – having fun with all her closest friends. She had never imagined having such a group to call her own, even including the pre-adolescent Kayleigh but she was grateful for all that she got, as well as Sissy and her punk skater friends.

Still bothering her though was what the person on the other side of the railings was doing spying on her. Whoever it was had definitely been an enhanced human, it was no coincidence that her power sensing had detected them and immediately dissipated the second they had been rumbled. Had they sent the gang after her? Or was their presence there just random? She had far too many questions than answers and little way of finding out.

Then she remembered the missing day in her life from the previous week. Maybe the reason for her lost memory was more sinister than she had previously thought, especially if it was to do with her abilities.

She then had a radical notion towards trying to regain her memories, if it was even achievable but she had seen more bizarre things occur as of late and it was worth a try.

At around five o'clock, Gabrielle announced her intention to return home, feeling worn out from the day's events and wanting to have dinner. She turned to Jamie as she got up.

"Ready to go?" Gabrielle asked.

"Erm, not that I've asked them yet," Jamie replied, turning to Jesse. "But I was wondering if I could stay the night round here?"

"YES!" Kayleigh exclaimed. "We can have a pyjama party!"

"Don't see why not," Jesse said, intrigued but nonetheless happy to entertain the idea.

"You alright with that, Gabbs?" Jamie asked.

"Yeah, it's fine," Gabrielle replied. "I might actually have dinner round my family house if you're staying out anyway. Will you be alright getting home in the morning?"

"Not a problem," Jamie replied.

"Alright, I guess I'll see you all again soon I hope," Gabrielle said to Jesse and Kayleigh.

"Safe journey, Gabby," Jesse said.

"Bye, Gabbs!" Kayleigh yelled, mimicking Jamie's mannerisms.

"Bye, sweetness," Gabrielle smiled, also kissing Jamie on the forehead as she departed.

"Guessing I'm on the couch then," Jamie remarked.

"You can sleep in Jesse's bed," Kayleigh mischievously said.

"Well then where do *I* sleep?" Jesse argued.

"Well in the same bed, *duh*!" Kayleigh replied, Jamie laughing in response instead of her usual embarrassed reaction.

"Jamie can sleep in your room, there's plenty of space compared to my shoebox," Jesse affirmed.

"You can give Jamie some of your pyjamas," said Kayleigh.

"You have pyjamas?" Jamie asked Jesse, surprised.

"Only bottoms," Jesse quickly responded. "I'll give you a large t-shirt to go with them."

"Sounds good to me."

Eventually, Jesse and Kayleigh's aunt, Tricia, arrived home from work at half six, surprised by her unexpected guest but welcoming of her nonetheless under the assumption of Jamie being her nephew's girlfriend, prompting an immediate correction by Jesse. Since her earlier talk with Kayleigh, Jamie almost felt more at ease with the running joke of her and Jesse being a couple but was still openly dismissive of it all the same.

Yet she couldn't help wonder what his actual feelings towards her were, if he had any at all in that sense. While she seemingly didn't like the idea of another girl taking his attention away, she still didn't feel completely confident in her own feelings towards him to make a move.

Following dinner, Tricia sat down with her nephew and his friend for half an hour with Jamie managing to avoid revealing the more awkward details of her home life as she described herself to Jesse's aunt. All the while, Kayleigh kept popping her head into the living room in hope of the conversation's conclusion in order to claim Jamie for herself. Tricia eventually got the hint, allowing her niece to have her wish with Jesse and Jamie both heading upstairs with her.

"Go get Jamie's pyjamas, Jesse," Kayleigh said upon reaching the balcony.

"Yes, oh tiny mistress," Jesse jested as he headed into his room with Jamie following Kayleigh into hers. It was moderately big with a single bed occupying the corner of the room, Jamie assuming she would be sleeping in the middle of the floor. She also believed Tricia probably wouldn't allow her to stay in Jesse's room anyway, laughing to herself at the thought seeing as nothing would happen between them anyway. *I would think.*

"Nice room," Jamie remarked.

"I like to think so," Kayleigh replied. "Oh look, your wardrobe's here."

Jamie turned around, seeing Jesse holding out a pair of folded pyjama bottoms and a black band t-shirt.

"Can change in the bathroom if you want," Jesse said.

"She can get changed in here, you doughnut!" Kayleigh rebuked her brother while approaching the door to close it. "Girls only, I'm afraid."

"Honestly, Kay," Jamie smiled as she removed her t-shirt.

"Wow, and I thought Gabrielle looked good," Kayleigh said as she stared at Jamie's slender, topless frame.

"Gabby's got more shape than I do," Jamie replied. "I'm more of a stick compared to her."

"What size bra are you anyway?" Kayleigh asked curiously.

"34A," Jamie answered.

"Is that small?"

"It's considered the second smallest cup size. I've never had a large bust."

"I did think Gabby was a bit bigger earlier," Kayleigh said.

"She's size DD, way more than me. I actually don't bother wearing a bra half the time anyway."

"Do you reckon I'll be small too? I don't seem to be developing much and I'm eleven already."

"I wasn't developed much at your age either but that doesn't mean you'll be this flat-chested," Jamie blunted stated.

"Does it bother you?" Kayleigh asked, feeling resentment in Jamie's tone.

"It used to. I was nervous about it while getting changed for P.E. but my mother bought me a sports bra to wear for that and later got me a padded bra for general use. Nobody ever realised I was a lot smaller than I came across but now that I'm out of that peer-pressure environment, I don't really care about it."

"But why do you wear loose fitting clothes then?"

"It's just the style I like. Besides, there's no requirement for girls or women to wear clothes that show off their figure anyway – we can wear whatever we want and I like it like this."

"You're so cool," Kayleigh beamed.

"I know," Jamie smiled back as she finished putting on Jesse's shirt and removed her cargo trousers. His pyjama bottoms just happened to mostly fit her waistline, though were slightly longer than she had expected as she stood up in them.

"I think my feet have disappeared," Jamie said.

"Nah, I can still see your toes," Kayleigh replied. "Ever had your nails done?"

"Just my fingers. Not for a while though."

"Ever had them done by *me*?" Kayleigh smiled.

"Only the fingernails," Jamie relented. "I'm not walking about like a weirdo while the other ones dry. Are you going to get into your pyjamas then or is this a solo party?"

"You go join Jesse, I'll be over in a minute," Kayleigh replied, rushing to her dresser drawer.

"We hanging in his room then?"

"He has the TV."

"Won't it be cramped in there?"

"Nah, it's cosy."

"Soon find out," Jamie muttered as she exited the room and walked into Jesse's next door to find him already sitting on his bed in his own pyjamas.

"Have fun?" Jesse asked.

"Yeah, changing into nightwear is certainly a laugh riot(!)" Jamie sarcastically responded. "Where are we all going to sit?"

"Kay will bring in her pillows and you and me will rest on them against the wall while little Miss lies on me, or you in this case if she wants."

"Cool, what are we watching?"

"Still got Season 8 to finish of *The Simpsons* if that's alright with you?"

"That's fine, though I think I've already seen them all by now."

"Here's my pillows," Kayleigh said, popping into the room now in her pyjamas.

"Thanks, babe," Jamie replied, taking them and crawling over to the top of the bed.

“I’ll be back, just grabbing my nail polish,” Kayleigh said as she returned to her room. Jesse propped up his own pillows and sat back on them next to Jamie.

“You really agree to let her do that to you?” Jesse smirked.

“Nothing wrong with letting a kid express herself,” Jamie scoffed.

“I should know – she did mine last week.”

“Oh really?” Jamie reacted with surprise.

“Yeah, though I scrubbed it off the second she fell asleep.”

“Ah, not as feminine as I thought.”

“Only removed it because it felt uncomfortable, like my fingernails couldn’t breathe.”

“Yeah, don’t do it myself too often for that reason,” Jamie replied, hoping Kayleigh would come back in as soon as possible to ease the tension she felt from sitting next to Jesse in just their night time clothes.

“Got it,” Kayleigh announced as she returned, jumping straight onto the bed and nestling herself between Jamie’s legs facing towards the television set. “Hand please.”

“Sure,” Jamie obeyed, giving Kayleigh her left hand. The trio went on to watch at least six episodes with Kayleigh eventually managing to coax Jamie into letting her paint her toenails as well, much to her chagrin despite the fact she loved appeasing the young girl. The day’s events finally caught up on Kayleigh though with Jesse noticing she had fallen asleep towards the end of the sixth episode.

“Think it’s bedtime for Kay,” Jesse said to Jamie.

"Looks like it, I'm surprised the poor thing wasn't more traumatised from earlier."

"I reckon she just doesn't want to acknowledge it, lest it threaten to disrupt the evening."

"Well I'm pretty wiped out too so guess I'll be hitting the hay with her. Where am I going to sleep?"

"There's a blue sleeping bag and a blanket in the cupboard in her room. Are you alright sleeping like that?"

"It'll be fine," Jamie replied, easing Kayleigh to the edge of the bed where Jesse picked her up in his arms.

"I'm not asleep," she briefly woke up.

"Yeah you were," Jesse replied. "Come along, Jamie's going to sleep with you."

"Can I have a quick word when you put her to bed?" Jamie asked.

"Yeah, sure," Jesse replied as he left the room with Kayleigh, returning a minute later. "What's up?"

"Can you close the door?" Jamie asked, with Jesse obliging.

"So what's on your mind?"

"What are the limits of your healing ability?"

"Er, I don't know," Jesse replied with mild confusion. "I haven't actually used it too often. You're one of only two people I've ever used it on with your injuries at the hands of that maniac on the hilltop being the worst I've healed."

"Where did you get it from anyway?"

"A friend from work, who moved away to Birmingham last year to live with a girl he met online. When a box fell on top of me in the stock room and left me paralysed, he happened to be the one to find me and immediately healed me with his ability. I then revealed to him that I was like him too and we formed a friendship over it. Did hurt when he left because he was my closest friend but I suppose the heart wants what it wants. If not for him, I probably would've never walked again."

"Well I'm not going anywhere," Jamie said sympathetically.

"I'm glad," Jesse replied. "He was the only other person I've ever healed; I absorbed his ability at some point and I used it to heal a pulled calf muscle he had suffered."

"Do you think it could heal the mind?" Jamie asked.

"Why do you ask?" Jesse replied.

"Last week, I lost an entire day of my life and I cannot remember anything at all. It was the day before we met. I was curious at the time but I let it go after I started hanging out with you and Kayleigh and generally felt happier with myself to not bother caring about it. The gang that attacked us earlier was my fault because I had previously taken them on and won but the person who was watching us as we left, I'm certain they had an ability. I could sense it coming from their direction and it felt off that they were spying on us."

"I suppose it would've been odd to see a whole load of super-powers being used right before their eyes, maybe they were curious seeing as they had an ability of their own."

"You may be right, but I still want to know what happened to my memory. Maybe they were involved in that and it was the reason why they were there. Do you think you could target my mind with your healing ability?"

"There's no harm trying I guess," Jesse said as he brought his hand up and placed it on Jamie's forehead. "Tell me if you remember anything after."

"Go for it," Jamie replied as Jesse activated his healing power, allowing it to work for nearly half a minute owing to the fact he had no way to tell if it was having an effect compared to a more obvious flesh wound. Jamie simply closed her eyes and tried to remember anything from that missing day.

Then slowly, images began to fill her mind from what had happened during that twenty-four hour period. As Jesse deactivated his ability, she opened her eyes with a weary expression on her face.

"Did it work?" he asked.

"Yeah," Jamie replied gravely. "I remember exactly what happened now – I was abducted and imprisoned in a facility."

"You were *what*?" Jesse exclaimed in disbelief.

"I was made to fight a guy with metal skin and then I was placed in a cell with several others with powers. I broke out and freed the rest of them. They were all recaptured but I managed to escape to the nearest town where I made my way home via the trains. And I remember someone tailing me on the train but I managed to lose them."

"So there's someone out there abducting super-powered human beings for whatever reason?"

"Apparently so," Jamie replied. "Maybe that person who I caught watching us earlier is part of them and were tracking me."

"What do we do about it?" said Jesse. "Alert the police?"

"Ideally, yeah. But what evidence do I have? That building I escaped from will likely be fronted by something else, if only I can get photographic proof of the holding cell area where I was held. That would be enough to prove that there are nefarious activities going on in there,"

"This is sounding pretty risky, Jamie," Jesse said.

"Risky would be letting them get away with doing it even further," Jamie argued. "All I need is proof that they're abducting people and those cells are more than enough. I can remember some of the names too of the others they captured. It'll be all I need."

"Don't you mean *we*," Jesse replied.

"What do you mean?" Jamie asked.

"I'm with you on this. Two of us trying to get the evidence will be more effective than just you. We'll have each other's backs."

"Jesse, it's alright. You don't need to put yourself in danger, I can handle it myself," Jamie said.

"Like I could live with myself if something happened to you in the process," Jesse replied. "You're not going to change my mind on this. If you insist on doing it, then I'll be with you all the way and get those guys shut down."

"Thank you," Jamie remarked after a slight pause. "I guess we should meet up tomorrow in the morning or so."

"What's your plan of approach?"

"We use flight to get in via the upper floors and see if we can work our way down to the basement area. My only worry is that they had a goon squad armed with tranquilisers last time which I only avoided due to having the ability to turn my skin metal. Your shielding power may offer us protection this time round and I'll see if I can convince Gabrielle to let me borrow her ability again after what happened earlier to defend ourselves if we run into trouble."

"Are you going to let Gabby know?"

"No. Not after everything else that has happened, I don't want to worry her with this or get her involved unless I have to."

"I suppose it's for the best. Let's get some sleep then if you plan to head off early to meet Gabrielle beforehand tomorrow."

"Yeah. Going to be one heck of an outing," Jamie said with a hint of worry in her voice.

"I'll see you in the morning then."

"Goodnight, Jess," Jamie said as she walked out the room and into Kayleigh's. The light was still on with the youngster drifting in and out of sleep in her bed.

"Jamie...?" Kayleigh stirred.

"Hey," Jamie said as she got the sleeping bag and blanket out from the cupboard. "You're knackered girl, get some sleep."

"Do you know where all our powers came from?" Kayleigh asked.

"I've honestly no idea," Jamie replied. "Maybe we'll find out sometime, it's just easier keeping them to ourselves for now though."

"I don't want to be alone, will you sleep with me?"

"What, in your bed? It's only a single."

"Please?"

Jamie took a moment to mull it over, deciding it wouldn't hurt her to share the bed and climbed in with Kayleigh. As she laid back, Kayleigh rested her body on top with Jamie wrapping her arms around her.

"Comfy?" Jamie asked.

"Yeah. Love you, Jamie," Kayleigh said.

"Love you too," she replied, knowing she would barely sleep herself with her plans to deal with the facility on her mind but she knew it would have to be done if she was going to be free from what happened to her occurring again. She just hoped the whole thing would go as smoothly and straightforward as she planned.

Chapter 19

Jamie arrived back at her house early, just managing to catch Gabrielle on the way out who reluctantly agreed to give her more of her ability on the grounds of self-defence following the ambush the previous day. That was the easier part of the overall plan taken care of, if only the main task would be as simple.

The meeting point with Jesse was at the tube station in the small town that Jamie had found herself just prior to losing her memory. From there, they would use flight and air vapour cloaking to approach the warehouse that contained the underground facility. Owing to what she was aware of the people running it were capable of, it was important to get what they needed as soon as possible and get away from the place. Then an anonymous tip to the police while sending over all photographic evidence to spark an investigation would hopefully be enough to put an end to the operation for good.

"Are you feeling as nervous as me?" Jesse asked Jamie upon meeting outside the station at around quarter past ten.

"Of course, but it shouldn't take too long to get what we need," Jamie replied as they began walking towards the end of the street. "We alright to use your phone to photograph what we need?"

"That's not a problem, more hi-def than that burner phone of yours."

"I'll admit that smartphones have their uses."

"If we get out of this alive, reckon you'll finally get one of your own?"

"Melodramatic much?" Jamie gave a crooked smile.

"I kid," Jesse said. "I just hope it's as straightforward as it sounds."

"I'm personally amazed you believed me in the first place."

"You haven't given me a reason to doubt you yet, and it's not too farfetched to believe some shadow outfit would want to capture people with powers. My only worry is that it's linked to the government or something."

"It didn't really feel like a government operation, more like some megalomaniacal vanity project. Whatever it was, I doubt it's on the level at all."

"Then it'll be easier to get it shut down if we're lucky. But let's not worry too much about garnering proof if it looks too dodgy; we'll just shop them in with what limited info we already have including the names of the others that they abducted with you. Maybe it'll be enough in itself to get the old bill involved."

"Okay then, nothing risky. I do owe it to Gabby to stay away from that crap now anyway. I doubt she would've handed her power over to me had yesterday not occurred. How is Kayleigh feeling anyway?"

"Surprisingly okay, considering what actually went down."

"I am sorry about that by the way."

"Sins of the past, and all that. It's not like I've never done anything reckless in my life but what happened happened. You're not actually going out of your way to fight people with powers anymore so you've proven to me you're moving on from that. It's all you can do."

"It'll be one less thing to worry about when we take care of this too," Jamie said as the duo reached the end of the road and turned right, continuing until they reached the beginning of the forest route.

"You know where we're heading then?" Jesse asked.

"Yeah, let's do this," Jamie replied as she took Jesse's hands and absorbed both flight and the cloaking abilities. "Can you give me some of your healing ability too?"

"Yeah, that makes sense," Jesse said as he began to activate his healing power, allowing Jamie to absorb that too. "I'll fly us both over while you direct me. Are you confident enough to fly solo once we get there?"

"I've gotten good at flying now, I'll only have to worry about focusing on using the haze at the same time but I won't really need it until we flee the scene."

"Hop on then, we'll head over," Jesse said with Jamie clambering onto his back. The two then took to the air as the vapour cloaking kicked in, rendering them all but invisible to everyone back on the ground.

It didn't take long for Jesse himself to spot the warehouse from the altitude they were at with Jamie confirming that it was the same building that she had previously escaped from. As they descended slightly, Jamie opted to disembark and take to the air of her own accord, while activating her own vapour cloaking.

"What do you reckon?" Jesse asked.

"We approach from the rear but stay in the air," Jamie replied as they descended further towards the back of the warehouse. "I'll try and spot an open window or attempt pulling on the outer frames to see if any are unlocked."

"And if there aren't any?"

"Then I guess we'll just settle for the anonymous tip to the police without any photographs and hope for the best regardless," Jamie replied. "Watch my back and have your shielding ready to use if you see anything."

Jesse kept his eyes on the surrounding area below as Jamie began pulling on the frames of the windows. One by one they all failed to budge, causing Jamie to feel despair. *Guess the tip-off will have to suffice at this rate.*

"Ow!" Jesse yelled.

"What's up?" Jamie asked, noticing that Jesse had inadvertently deactivated his vapour cloaking power. She then felt her blood going cold as she realised a dart was sticking out of her friend's torso.

"Get out of here!" Jesse said while removing the tranquiliser, though quickly began to succumb to the effects and started falling through the air. Jamie flew down to grab her helpless friend and attempted to lift him away to safety, only to feel a sharp prick in her leg as she did. Without even looking, she knew she had been shot too and it was only a matter of seconds before she would completely pass out as well.

How did you know we were here?

Jamie attempted to fly away into the surrounding forest while clinging on to the unconscious Jesse but it was too late; she descended rapidly as the tranquiliser took effect before collapsing onto the floor. She saw two pairs of boots approaching her from the distance as her vision faded to black.

Jamie slowly opened her eyes, finding herself looking straight up at a familiar ceiling. Her heart sank as she realised she was back in the same cell she previously occupied before turning to worry over what had become of Jesse. She discovered that she was completely unable to move any of her limbs minus her eyes and eyelids.

The sound of a heavy door opening rang out in the background before closing again, followed by light footsteps.

"Hello, Jamie."

Jamie recognised the voice; it was the same one that had spoken through the PA system to her during her battle with Mikael in the padded room. Unable to turn her head around to see who it was or open her mouth to respond, she simply waited to see what the next words to come from them would be.

"My apologies for the pre-caution of paralysing your nervous system in advance of my visit but you left a lasting impression on this place the last time you were here. Wouldn't want that happening again."

Jamie tried moving her body again but to no avail. Out of desperation, she then activated her borrowed flight power, managing to levitate her limp body in mid-air before turning 180 degrees to face where the voice was coming from. Though unable to lift her head, she could just about make out a man in a dark suit standing behind a pane of bullet-proof glass.

"You really are extraordinary," Ryan remarked, surprised at Jamie's tenacity. "Seeing as this will be a one-way conversation, allow me to introduce myself – my name is Ryan Sharp and I am the owner of Sharp Enterprises which was previously run by my father. I believe he knew *your* dad, James, rather well."

Though her facial expression remained numb, Jamie's eyes lit up upon hearing her father's name.

"Once I realised who you were, I just had to come down and meet you personally," Ryan continued. "The daughter of the great James Avonoit. It was his contributions to the company that helped make it a global force, although he always seemed content to stay in the shadows rather than accept the glory his efforts deserved. Maybe he was thinking of you, wanting to keep his family out of the limelight. It seems a coincidence that both our fathers helped turn the page in treating genetic diseases, whereas both their children will help pioneer transplanting special abilities into regular human beings.

"I suppose you somehow managed to remember your last visit down here, the reason behind your return. The only problem with that my dear is that we detected you coming in advance and were well prepared to neutralise you upon your arrival in spite of your use of that vapour manipulation ability you were using to try and disguise yourselves with. You see I have a friend with her own special power that lets her know not only the location of an ability being used but also what it does."

Jamie wondered if the person Ryan referred to was the same one who she had caught monitoring her the previous day in the park.

"When she informed me what your ability could do, I was fascinated – the ability to absorb other powers, even if it was only temporary. That certainly would've pushed our agenda forward, except that you managed to trash my holding cells and free the rest of the subjects but we were lucky enough to be able to track you down and discover your identity. From that point on, it was just a matter of waiting for the right moment to re-capture you. Well, until this morning when you decided to stop right at my doorstep and make the whole thing easier for us.

"But you also gifted us something else yesterday; in the midst of the scrap you had with that gang, my friend managed to detect another individual with multiple powers like you and who just happened to be fighting by your side."

Jesse!

"My friend had difficulty determining what he could do initially aside from the individual powers he possessed. But then you brought him here with you and she was able to fine-tune her ability to determine exactly what *he* could do – the ability to absorb another power based on his desire to acquire it. And unlike yours, the powers remain infinite."

Jamie could only feel total guilt for having allowed Jesse to get involved in the first place.

"Right now, he is being examined by our resident scientist who is going to replicate the DNA sequence within his body that will allow us to transplant it into normal human beings, thereby giving them the same ability to absorb other powers too. It'll probably earn us a Nobel prize among many other awards," Ryan chuckled to himself to the continued irritation seen in Jamie's eyes.

"You might be wondering right now why I'm bothering to tell you this, or why I've kept you down here when I already have the ideal test subject. Simply put, I plan to also market your capable and versatile ability too and it helps to have a backup if your friend fails to survive the procedure."

Jamie felt a stream of anxiety flow through her, no less by the crass way the comment was delivered by Sharp at the thought of Jesse being killed.

"And by the time those drugs begin to leave your system, we'll be ready to place you in an artificial coma while loading you with memory erasing drugs again with the intent that you won't recover your memories this time round or your friend's if he lives to see tomorrow. And if you think I'm sounding harsh here, do keep in mind that you did wreck my facility and let loose all my captured subjects so you might forgive me for holding a small grudge against you."

Jamie glared back at Sharp.

"And now you'll have to excuse me as I await the good news from the lab. The next time you see me will probably be on the cover of magazines worldwide on the development of transplantation of super-human abilities," Ryan egotistically remarked as he opened the heavy steel door and exited the room, closing it back up behind him.

Jamie slowly lowered herself to the floor, still unable to move but able to position her body lying down using her flight. All she could think about was Jesse and what could be happening to him. She hated being so helpless in his time of need, after everything he had done to help her. She needed to escape again and save him, if only she actually had a way of doing that.

"How's it going, Lloyd?" Ryan asked via the intercom to the laboratory. Dr Murphy approached the transparent doors.

"I've managed to isolate the genetic material within this young man responsible for his ability," he stated. "It's a matter now of reproducing the DNA sequence ready for insertion into another human being."

"Finally, this is all starting to come together," Ryan said.

"Well the matter of patient zero to implant it into is still an ethical dilemma," Murphy replied.

"I'll make sure whoever volunteers is very well compensated, doctor," Ryan reassured. "I'll let you continue with your work."

"Very well," Murphy said as he turned away while Ryan exited the laboratory area. He then bumped into Dawn in the corridor.

"So how's it going, we got everything at long last?" she eagerly asked.

"Have we ever," Ryan enthusiastically answered. "The end goal is nearly in sight."

"Glad all this has been worth it," Dawn said. "What of the girl downstairs?"

"I actually managed to get a word in with her," Ryan replied. "It was of course one-sided but it was interesting to see her up close knowing now who she is. Might've been a touch mean letting her think her friend might die though."

"Ryan, honestly," Dawn scolded him.

“Hey, her breakout set us back time and money. I thought some emotional manipulation wasn’t too out of line.”

“Still a crappy thing to do though. You’d do the same if you were imprisoned against your will.”

“It’s alright, once the amnesia-inducing drugs have had a chance to erase her memories again we’ll let her go along with her friend seeing as we have everything we need now. I’ll always know where she is if I need to use her again but I think it’ll be unnecessary at this point.”

“What happens to this place once it becomes obsolete?”

“Exactly as planned,” Ryan replied. “Can’t leave any loose ends regarding what occurred down here. A shame the place has to go considering how much work was put into constructing it and everything it has achieved but it’s not worth the risk being investigated by the police for it.”

“I doubt you will need it again, Ryan. Just fill it with concrete and revel in the fame you’ll enjoy from bringing this all to the public’s attention. It’s what you strived for all this time.”

“Yeah. Shall we grab some celebratory drinks in my office?”

“I hope it’s some *decent* champagne this time.”

“Gotcha, no cheaping out this time.”

“Fine, I’ll meet you in your office in a bit.”

Jamie tried to raise her arms again, barely managing to move either. She had no idea what time it was or how long she had been imprisoned since the morning but despair was really starting to set in. She couldn’t just lie there while her close friend’s life was hanging in the balance, not while she was still alive and within distance of saving him.

But with what powers? Or even mobility to execute them for that matter. Having the rapist's powers back would have been useful in the current situation, maybe even his younger brother's even though it did kill him in the end.

The worry and anxiety was driving her mad. She so desperately wanted to help Jesse and be free of her captivity. She imagined blowing the cell door into a million pieces and tearing the entire complex to shreds. She could feel her heartbeat increasing rapidly from inside her paralysed body, presumably from the stress she was causing herself.

Then it wasn't just her chest she was feeling a surge of activity in – it was also her arms and legs. All four limbs were starting to swell with feeling until she found she was able to move them.

The drugs wearing off?

Even she knew that the effects of the drugs in her system would not simply just stop working in an instant. She rose from the floor using her flight and stood on her feet, able to weakly stand of her own accord.

Jamie noticed that throughout her entire body she could feel a tingling sensation, almost like pins and needles but without any unpleasantness. Additionally, she felt herself swelling with overwhelming power of some variety.

Jamie looked at her hand and saw a familiar black aura emerging around it.

The rapist's brother's ability...

Jamie's thought process subsequently became heavily confounded by destructive impulses, almost as though she wasn't in control of what she was thinking. The thoughts were compelling her to attack the bullet-proof door with everything she had, even though logic was informing her that it would be near impossible to achieve anything.

Slowly though, the logic began to erode in favour of the irrationality building inside her. She chose to give in to the craving for mayhem and took aim at the transparent door.

To her surprise, a huge flow of energy began surging through to the palms of her hands. With reckless abandon, Jamie propelled a huge blast of black-hued energy straight at the door, barely having any reaction time to block the resulting impact.

"Ryan," Dawn said aloud while attempting a sip from her champagne glass.

"What's up?" Ryan responded, sitting up in his chair and alarmed by his friend's tone of voice.

"Just got a reading on an extremely powerful ability; it's the same one that dead kid had."

"You mean the one we brought in with his equally dead brother? You telling me he's come back to life?"

"I don't think so," Dawn said, looking towards the monitors with a concerned look on her face. Ryan turned his head to the screens as well.

"No..." he mouthed as he caught glimpse of Jamie Avonoit standing before her cell door with her arms raised. They then witnessed her launching a large energy attack that completely shattered the bullet-proof glass. "How is that even possible?!"

"What? The fact that the paralysis drugs are suddenly not working properly or that she somehow has that kid's power?"

"Both!" Ryan yelled in annoyance, regretting not putting the girl in a coma the second she was brought in owing to his own arrogant decision to taunt her directly. "I'm calling the poacher mob to stand by, get to Dr Murphy and evacuate him and everything he has accumulated on that girl's friend's ability."

"You want me to go down there now?" Dawn asked with a slightly scared tone.

"Don't worry, that mob will be down there soon after with their tranquilisers to put her back out. In case they fail, we need to get everything of importance out of here."

"You better be right," Dawn said as she accessed the lift, leaving Ryan trying desperately to get through to the team of poachers.

Jamie slowly stood up amongst the wreckage of the cell door littered all around the floor. The shock from the attack had snapped her from her aggressive stupor as the dark hue surrounding her body began to subside.

She then took a moment to comprehend what had just occurred – somehow she was in possession of the rapist's brother's ability once more, despite having seemingly exhausted it in the fight with him.

The only explanation she could amass was that a remnant of it must still have remained within her the whole time, having only felt completely depleted. It also made sense in that she had not even considered attempting to re-use it after witnessing it cause the brother's death, not wanting to be in possession of such a risky and dangerous ability.

Now, she could feel it taking over her mind and driving her thoughts in a manner not unlike what the youth had probably felt when it had overwhelmed him too. It was amplifying itself based on her need for it and she could feel the exhausting effect it was having on her body to allow it to do so but the alternative was to remain trapped in the dungeon while Jesse's life hung in the balance.

Jamie felt the surge of power building in her again and she approached the large steel door at the entrance of the holding room. She stood well back and prepared an even stronger attack to launch, just hoping her body could handle the strain being placed upon it.

She then expelled a huge energy blast at the sturdy door, witnessing a similar but larger explosion like the previous cell door impact. When she looked again, she could see a large enough gap in the destruction to be able to fit her body through to escape.

Physically weakened but still standing, Jamie hurriedly made her way towards the ruined steel door and through the hole to the adjacent staircase leading to the upper corridor in hope of finding Jesse before it was too late.

Dawn quickly exited the lift and ran to the laboratory entrance, hammering on the doors.

"Lloyd!" she called out to the disgruntled Dr Murphy, irritated at being interrupted yet again as he made his way over.

"Dawn, this process works a lot easier when I'm left in peace."

“There’s been a breach downstairs, you need to collect everything relative to your research regarding the girl’s friend and be prepared to evacuate right now!”

“How serious is it?” Dr Murphy asked.

“Very. She could be on her way up any second so grab what you can and let’s get out of here. Ryan’s squad will be down soon to try and hold her off and hopefully stop her.”

With that, Murphy headed back over to the other side of the laboratory, leaving Dawn anxiously waiting by the doors. A loud explosive noise then rang out from the corridor that startled the pair of them.

“Was that her?!” he called back.

“I imagine so,” Dawn responded as she saw the poacher team finally coming down from the lift and making their way towards the end of the corridor.

“Got a situation, we hear?” one of the grunts asked.

“Yeah, sounds like she’s broken through the main door,” Dawn replied. “She’s probably pissed as hell and looking for her friend so try and tranq her the first shot you get.”

“Like you even need to ask,” the grunt said as he and the team pushed towards the basement staircase with Dawn standing by the laboratory doors. She watched on as all four of them began taking shots with their tranquiliser guns, though appearing to fail with every single attempt as they all reloaded for another go.

Out of nowhere, several dark-hued energy tentacles surged forth and slammed the poachers backwards across the hallway, displacing their guns in the process.

Terrified, Dawn screamed as she fled past them towards the lift, frantically pressing the buttons to open the doors. Looking backwards, she caught view of the girl climbing up the staircase and knocking all four of the poachers against the walls with the same energy tentacles.

Jamie looked forward at the young woman at the end of the corridor running into the lift as the doors opened. Reacting quickly, two of her tentacles forced the doors to remain open while the remaining two wrapped around the screaming woman's body and hauled her back out.

"Who are you?" Jamie growled.

"D-Dawn. My name is Dawn," Dawn stammered.

"Ryan's friend by chance?"

Dawn shook her head, only for Jamie to tighten the tentacles' grip on her in response.

"YES! I AM!" she yelled.

"The same friend who detects our powers?" Jamie asked.

"Yes..."

"Show me."

Confused but scared, Dawn complied and began to activate her power detection ability. Jamie, sensing it in active use, quickly brought her open hand forward and grabbed Dawn by the neck, immediately absorbing the ability through the use of her own and taking the maximum possible.

"Now take me to Jesse," she demanded.

"He's in there," Dawn motioned towards the laboratory. Jamie made her way over with her captive still ensnared in her energy tentacles while smashing the doors down. Upon entering the room, she noticed a man in a white coat cowering by the furthest wall and an unconscious body on the table close to him.

Jesse!

Jamie yanked Dawn over to the table as she looked at Jesse lying motionless upon it.

"What've you done to him?" she menacingly asked the apparent scientist trying to maintain his distance against the wall.

"He's fine," Dr Murphy responded in a panicky voice. "He's just under sedation."

Jamie then noticed a figure at the laboratory entrance out of the corner of her eye who was aiming a handheld gun at her. Defensively, she pulled Dawn in front of her using her energy tentacles.

"Seems you like to put my friend's life at risk, how does it feel when one of yours is in the same position?" Jamie spoke to Sharp.

"Believe me when I say that this gun isn't packing any tranquilisers," Ryan responded, maintaining his stance. "You've got your boy back, now let her and the good doctor go."

"You're not the one in control here, friend," Jamie replied.

"Neither are you. That ability is no doubt rapidly draining your health just by using it so what I'd suggest is that you let everyone go and I'll allow you and your friend to leave."

Jamie glared back at Sharp, feeling confident in the fact she knew he had no other recourse but to barter for his friend's life. However, he wasn't wrong about her use of the rapist's brother's ability – it was placing a tremendous amount of stress on her body to maintain using it and she realistically needed to escape with Jesse before it completely overwhelmed her.

She attempted to calm her mind and rationally plot a way out of the situation; taking out Sharp would not be hard at all with her powers and escaping with Jesse in tow. The overall problem was that the whole complex would still exist beyond doing so and it would continue to put her and everyone like her at risk in the future.

Unless I put an end to that problem now.

She looked up at the corner of the ceiling, believing it to be the furthest point of the layout of the underground structure beneath the warehouse. Taking aim with a single open hand while placing the other on Dawn's shoulder to discourage Sharp from firing at her in response, Jamie unleashed a piercing wave of dark energy straight into the ceiling.

Dawn screamed with Dr Murphy diving to the floor on instinct as an avalanche of debris came crashing down into the laboratory. Jamie saw light shining through the hole in the ceiling and blasted it one further time to enlarge it.

Ryan looked on in a mixture of horror and anger at the destruction of his facility but could not bring himself to shoot his gun with Dawn's life still at stake. He reluctantly looked on as the Avonoit girl moved over to her unconscious friend lying on the table while still propping her captive in front of her as a human shield.

Jamie knew she was now in serious trouble with the further energy manipulation ability use having left her experiencing severe chest pains and exhaustion, something that Sharp no doubt could tell just by looking at her. She desperately grabbed a hold of Jesse's arm and realised she was going to have to dig into the depths of her remaining energy one last time in order to be able to lift his dead weight.

With everything she had, she hauled Jesse from the table and pulled his torso into hers in a bear hug before slowly levitating into the air.

As Dawn ran away from her, Jamie heard the noise of a gunshot go off as she rose up to the hole in the ceiling, feeling a terrible piercing pain in her ankle at the same time. Maintaining her determination though and fighting through the agony in her lower leg, she pulled Jesse out of the laboratory and into daylight.

Finally outside of the complex, Jamie continued to fly upwards with Jesse in tow without bothering to activate her borrowed hazing ability and headed a hundred feet away from the warehouse into the forest area surrounding it. Finding a gap in the trees, she descended while lowering Jesse to the floor before collapsing next to him.

Bordering on delirium, Jamie grabbed Jesse's bare arm and began hurriedly trying to restore him to consciousness with her borrowed healing powers knowing she was about to pass out herself any moment.

"Jesse, please...." Jamie pleaded aloud as she began to see her friend stirring at last. She continued the healing process until the pain in her leg from the gunshot wound began to send her body into shock.

As she saw Jesse's eyelids beginning to flutter, she found her own vision going dark.

* * *

Jesse looked up at the sky, feeling oddly peaceful with the noise of birds tweeting in the background. He then realised he was lying in the middle of a forest for some unknown reason and sat up.

It was then he noticed Jamie's unconscious body lying beside him with what appeared to be a gunshot wound to her left ankle accompanied by a pool of blood rapidly forming around it.

"No. JAMIE!" Jesse screamed as he immediately flipped his unmoving friend onto her back while grabbing her leg and hand on her left side while activating his healing ability. He stared into her lifeless face as tried to revive her with every bit of power he had.

Jesse then saw the bullet emerge from Jamie's ankle and the wound seal itself up. However, the healing attempt was still failing to bring her back to consciousness.

"Jamie, please....think of Kayleigh, think of Gabrielle. They're going to miss you so much," Jesse pleaded as tears began to stream down his face with the situation looking absolutely hopeless. He then took his hand off her leg and placed it just above her chest, hoping the direct placement near her heart would help rejuvenate her.

More seconds passed by with no response at all.

As Jesse began to despair, he finally saw movement from his friend's eyelids. Jamie then opened them to see a relived and red-eyed Jesse staring back at her.

"What happened?" she exclaimed while bolting upright. Jesse simply collapsed to the floor in response, happy to see her alive and awake.

"Was kind of hoping you'd tell me," he replied while wiping his eyes.

"Were you crying?" Jamie asked with a humorous tone.

"Just some dirt in my eyes," Jesse joked back as Jamie laid her body over his. He wrapped his arms around her in response as they absorbed each other's warmth. "I so thought you were dead."

"I thought *you* were dead!"

"Thank goodness for healing powers."

"Yeah," Jamie said as she then moved her head over in front of Jesse's and stared into his eyes. After a moment's thought, she brought her mouth to the side of his face and kissed him once on the cheek.

"What was that for?" Jesse smiled.

"Just 'cause," she replied warmly before lying on the ground beside him.

"So what actually happened while I was out then?"

"Well we were both captured and you were apparently experimented on while I was thrown back into the cell I was in last time," Jamie answered. "I then somehow managed to regain an extremely powerful ability that I had once absorbed and thought I'd lost and used that to blow the place apart and fly you out."

"And all without breaking a sweat?" Jesse joked.

"More than a sweat, I'll tell you that. Using that power felt like it was taking years off my life. Now I understand how it killed that kid – I drained so much from him that he had to overuse the small amount he still had which pushed his body far beyond its limits."

"And you were doing the same?"

"Maybe even worse. I thought I had used up all of his ability to the point I couldn't even feel it within me anymore. I guess the tiny amount I still had reacted to my desperation and amplified it to the same inhuman levels that his did when he found out his own brother killed his father."

"You think it's gone for good now?"

"I hope so, don't want that kind of power within me. I've no intentions of dying any time soon, not anymore."

"I'd hope so," Jesse replied as the two shared a smile. "What now then regarding that place?"

"Think I've got a phone call to make," Jamie replied.

"Did you get any photos of the inside of the place?"

"No but don't need them now, the police can see the inside of it just by looking," Jamie smirked.

"You know exactly what you're going to say?"

"Yeah; tell them there's been an explosion at that exact location while also dropping the names I can remember of the captives I shared the basement with to give them an idea of what's been going on over there the whole time. And from there, just hope we get no more trouble."

"Reckon we'll find out in the days to come?"

"Guess we'll just have to keep an eye on the news. The head of a multi-billion pound company caught abducting citizens and locking them in an underground dungeon for experimentation? Might be hard to keep that out of the papers."

"Not worried about our kind being exposed in the process though?"

"I don't care," Jamie replied. "If the whole world wants to know about the existence of abilities, so be it. I've got more important things than powers now to worry about," she said while taking Jesse's hand and squeezing it lightly.

"Shall we go do this then?"

"Yeah," Jamie said as they both got up. "Going to need to buy a disposable burner phone first though."

Chapter 20

Jamie sat with Gabrielle on the sofa watching the morning news in their pyjamas with a bowl of cereal held right up against her chin to prevent the milk within from dripping down her front. It had been the first time in nearly a week that Gabrielle had had a day off from work and the two had been determined to enjoy each other's company during it, although as always Jamie had no idea what to plan around it.

Worn out from her recent unusually heavy work schedule, however, Gabrielle had been more than accepting of simply lying around the house for once.

It was no coincidence of Jamie's interest in watching the news though – it had been eight days since it had been widely reported that a certain Mr Ryan Sharp of one *Sharp Enterprises* had been connected to a series of abductions of youths and young adults following the discovery of a hidden dungeon and laboratory under an isolated supply warehouse. It had also been mentioned that Sharp had since become a wanted fugitive after his own hired poacher goons had co-operated with police in exchange for leniency for their part in the whole scheme.

Although it was still very much a viable company, Sharp Enterprises' share price on the stock market had dramatically fallen overnight and its reputation had been seriously dented by the scandal. Jamie had monitored the story as it developed and had been relieved to find no mention of super-human abilities being behind Sharp's motives for having done so, which was baffling considering that all of his many victims shared that trait and could have been tempted to bring it up but apparently not.

Mostly, she was satisfied that her anonymous call to the police which had sparked the investigation to begin with had not been tracked back to her, leaving her to live her life as she wanted fear-free.

And life had been going pretty well since then.

Aside from Gabrielle at home, she had hung out with Cecilia and her group of punks and even managed to attend the night club with them that Sissy had spoken of. It had been an interesting but terrifying new experience owing to the overwhelming social anxiety she had felt that not even being tipsy from alcohol had quelled but she somewhat enjoyed the looks she had gotten from half of the male attendance in the room. At least the kind that made her feel more confident in her appearance and not the one overzealous person who had tried to force her onto the dancefloor too eagerly which had led to a protective Sissy and her friends to threaten him into backing off, nearly causing a fight in the process.

The incident hadn't deterred her from future visits though; on the contrary, she looked forward to it as well as meeting up with Sissy to work on developing their musical endeavours.

Of course she had made plenty of time to invade Jesse and Kayleigh's space too, not that the latter in particular ever minded. It was always tempting to have a more adult conversation with her but Jamie was always mindful to treat her as the eleven year-old child she actually was, seeing as she had a lifetime of being an adult still to come. She still allowed the typical boy talk to commence though, albeit with Kayleigh's teasing of any potential relationship between Jamie and Jesse having diminished greatly since their more serious talk during the fun fair.

Her actual bond with Jesse was still a major conflict to her. The prospect of ever being up front with him about how she felt to a degree were still slim and she still didn't know if it was what she even wanted from him. She know she liked being held by him and making any kind of physical bodily contact in general, as well as listening to anything he had to say without losing interest.

But ultimately it came down to whether making a move would potentially ruin a perfectly good platonic friendship in the process. It always seemed to come down to that factor and she would rather have him in her life as a friend than not at all.

And other times, she wished she had just kissed him on the lips rather than his cheek the week prior when the moment felt right.

"You heard any more news about that serial abductor who ran the company your dad worked for?" Gabrielle asked.

"Nah, he must still be on the run," Jamie replied. Though she had withheld the details of her involvement in trying to bring Sharp to justice, she had allowed Gabrielle to at least know that her father had been in his company's employment.

Learning from Sharp himself no less that the same company was responsible for the abduction, imprisonment and experimentation of enhanced humans had been a profound shock to her too, lamenting that her father's work had eventually led to that activity. Not that he would have seen that occurring but it wouldn't have been the first time in history that someone had taken something designed for good use and utilised it for nefarious purposes.

From that point on though, Ryan Sharp was no longer her problem and she didn't want him to be. She just wanted to get on with her new lease on life.

"Do you want to have those re-done?" Gabrielle asked Jamie, referring to her worn nail polish which she had actually ended up keeping, not wanting to disappoint Kayleigh in the process of removing it despite how uncomfortable it had felt for the first two days.

"Wouldn't mind removing it all now to be honest," she replied.

"You should let me do them next time."

"What was wrong with how Kayleigh did them?"

"Nothing, I'm just saying you never let *me* do them," Gabrielle gave a hinting smile.

"If it'll make you happy," Jamie replied.

"Cool, and then you're going to let me do your make-up after."

"But I don't wear make-up!"

"Might as well see what it looks like too seeing as you gave your nails a go."

“Get the feeling you’re enjoying the prospect of doing all this way more than me,” Jamie replied with a laugh.

“Go on, be a girly-girl for once in your life!” Gabrielle said excitedly.

“Fine but I’m still having a shower afterwards,” Jamie relented as Gabrielle ran upstairs to get her make-up supplies and nail varnish.

While she was gone, Jamie noticed a breaking news report coming on the television set. She watched in astonishment as it detailed an apparent terrorist attack on a double-decker bus that appeared to have been completely twisted by some extraordinary but unknown method as opposed to having been blown up.

Although she had tried to put any thoughts aside regarding enhanced human activity since her escape from Ryan Sharp’s facility, the damage to the bus almost appeared to have been inflicted by such. It wasn’t unlikely, especially considering she had actually witnessed someone performing magnetism mere moments before she had met Jesse on the rooftop over a fortnight ago. *But why showcase it out in the open like that?*

As Gabrielle made her way back down the stairs, Jamie hurriedly grabbed the remote and changed the channel.

“Back!” Gabrielle said carrying her cosmetic equipment. “Felt like learning to make some meals?”

“Huh?” Jamie replied before realising she had switched to a cookery show. “Oh, just channel hopping. The news was getting boring.”

“Glad I’m not the only one who was thinking that. Alright, give me a hand. Whichever one first.”

"Here," Jamie replied, giving over her left hand before flicking through the channels again to find something else. She decided she would read up on the report later in her own time, wanting to keep Gabrielle from worrying about enhanced human activity in the capital but the incident was nonetheless concerning. She knew she would have to monitor the situation if a rogue empowered street thug was causing serious trouble such as that in broad daylight.

Jamie opted to take her shower just after eleven o'clock, completely removing the make-up job Gabrielle had performed in the process. While she didn't dislike the resultant look, she concluded that it really wasn't how she preferred to be seen but complimented Gabrielle on her efforts anyway to appease her. It felt nice to have tried it though with her best friend, just something fun for them to do with each other.

As soon as she was finished, she headed over to her room and booted up her laptop to find the online report on the bus incident. She had decided to take the plunge and purchase a smartphone two days prior but still preferred to use the computer to do her internet browsing.

She did, however, enjoy using the option on her new phone to download and send memes back and forth with Jesse, in which they were both relentless but she found it was just a good excuse to communicate with him on a regular basis even in a jokey manner.

The online version of the story featured no real additional information that the news channel had reported on but did feature additional close-up photographs of the wreckage. Jamie looked at how the metal was twisted and deformed with no sign of any explosive burns at all. It surely had to be the handiwork of someone with an ability. It was such a brazen act of destruction though and to have done so was clearly to be issuing a statement. She wondered if the ability-based gang had reformed yet again with a member who possessed magnetism.

Then she realised she now had the power to specifically target certain abilities courtesy of Ryan Sharp's friend, Dawn. She hadn't actually made use of her absorbed power since she had acquired it, not having had a reason to do so but for curiosity's sake she began to activate it, seeking out any use of magnetism anywhere nearby.

After a few seconds, Jamie decided to give up after failing to detect anything. Perhaps it worked in the same manner as her own innate power in that it required an ability to be in active use, she wondered. Either way, she wasn't going to let it play on her mind too much while she wanted to focus on spending her time with Gabrielle instead.

For the rest of the day, the duo simply watched numerous films while talking to each other. It was a simplistic approach to their free time together though it felt like a day well spent nonetheless with Jamie even preparing dinner, a seldom-performed task by her own accord.

Having rarely been subject to it as such, Gabrielle was pleasantly surprised to find the meal up to high standards, considering the possibility that perhaps the earlier cookery show on the TV hadn't been a random channel hop after all and maybe Jamie actually watched them during the daytime while she was at work. She hoped her friend would get more into the habit of doing so seeing how well it turned out when she did.

Gabrielle eventually decided to go to bed early at 9pm with Jamie staying up for a further hour to finish her film before climbing into Gabrielle's double bed with her and ending up hogging more than half of her own side. A mock-nudging battle commenced for the next few minutes before both girls decided to fall completely asleep.

Jamie awoke to the sight of Gabrielle sitting at her mirror applying her make-up, assuming it was around eight in the morning considering she was yet to leave for work. She checked her phone on the side cabinet to find it was even earlier than that at 7:45am.

"You've taken all the warmth with you!" Jamie jokingly moaned.

"Sorry babe, duty calls," Gabrielle jested back while remaining fixated on her reflection.

"I think you should go in without wearing all that cosmetic stuff."

"Absolutely no chance!" Gabrielle laughed.

"Are you really going to deny the whole world what that gorgeous face looks like under all that gunk?"

"This 'gorgeous face' is only so because of said 'gunk', unlike you Miss Cheekbones."

"Please, girl. I'll come over and wipe it all off if I need to!"

"You dare!"

"You do owe me, seeing as I let you do my make-up yesterday," Jamie replied slyly. Gabrielle pondered for a few seconds.

"Maybe tomorrow."

"Yes!" Jamie exclaimed.

"But I'm faking being ill and coming straight home if I get too many weird looks."

"That'll be from all your admirers, Gabbs."

"Yeah, yeah. Right, I'm done. How about you fix us up breakfast before I have to leave seeing as you did such a good job of dinner?"

"Man, I've literally just woke up!"

"Oh, don't be such a baby. Or do your ribs feel like a visit from my fingernails?"

"I'll kill you if you do."

"Thought so. I'll get the frying pan out for you," Gabrielle said as she made her way downstairs with Jamie reluctantly levitating out from under the covers and down the staircase behind her, sending another meme to Jesse on her phone as she did.

Despite asking Jamie to prepare breakfast, Gabrielle ended up joining in to accommodate for the limited time window she had before having to set off for work. Between them, they managed to create a spread of bacon, beans, fried toast and scrambled egg, which Gabrielle swiftly wolfed down in less than five minutes owing to running behind schedule, much to Jamie's amusement.

"You are going to have such a bad case of indigestion all morning," Jamie said as Gabrielle quickly grabbed her car keys and handbag.

"Which is why I'm glad I'll be at the till all morning," Gabrielle called back out from the corridor as she opened the front door. "See you later!"

"Bye!" Jamie called back as the door slammed shut. Before clearing the table to do the washing up, she replied to Jesse's recent response on her phone with another meme. She wondered how long they would keep up the back and forth before getting bored and simply texting each other like normal.

Eventually after an hour, Jamie decided to end the sparring and resort to texting Jesse instead, which in itself became an endless exchange of jokes and sarcasm among the actual serious parts of the conversation. She was finding herself eagerly awaiting every response to the point she failed to do anything else but lie on the sofa with the television on in the background until they came through.

She had generally talked to Jesse over the phone for a few minutes at a time since meeting him but having a jokey text and meme battle with him was a new development, one that she found herself enjoying a lot. In her logic-based mind, it didn't make a lot of sense talking about nothing of substance but it was nonetheless fun and enthralling.

After another hour, Jamie was left waiting several minutes for Jesse's latest reply. Gradually, she became impatient, noticing it had been over ten minutes since he had last responded. After another fifteen minutes, Jamie decided to take her morning shower while expecting a new text to have been received by the time she came out.

Twenty minutes later, Jamie exited the bathroom and laid out on her bed in her towel, finding that Jesse still had not replied to her. *Maybe he's gone out without his phone?* Although she felt silly doing so, she decided to call him. After nearly half a minute of endless ringing, she gave up the attempt and settled for the fact he was most likely busy with something.

Then the phone immediately started ringing. Jamie saw that it was Jesse returning her call as she pressed the 'receive call' option.

"Hey," she said warmly.

"......Hello, Jamie."

Jamie paused in confusion upon hearing the voice speaking to her who clearly wasn't Jesse despite it being his phone.

Then she froze as she realised who it was.

Ryan Sharp.

"Surprised?" Sharp spoke again, breaking the silence. *"Don't worry, your friend is perfectly fine. Okay, maybe a little beat up but he's here with me right now. He's hoping you can join us."*

"Where are you?" Jamie angrily responded, trying to disguise her angst.

"You're the one who can detect powers, why don't you figure it out?"

"Don't mess me around, what the hell have you done to Jesse?!"

"Alright, I'll text you a massive hint but I'd best hurry – I'm only giving you an hour before I finish the job here. See you in a bit."

"Ryan!" Jamie yelled as the line went dead. Seconds later she received an address which she quickly checked online; it showed an industrial complex with two warehouses, one of which Sharp was presumably holding Jesse in. She couldn't believe she was in the exact same position that the rapist had previous put her in, except that this time one of her friends would most certainly die if she didn't show compared to just being threatened with harm.

Jamie thought for a moment, trying to figure out the negatives of simply agreeing to make an appearance – Sharp definitely would have something planned considering how powerful he knew she was based on their last confrontation alone. Maybe he had recruited some enhanced humans of his own to combat her? And maybe the attack on the bus was indeed a message from him. She had no idea but she knew she couldn't approach the situation without an arsenal at her disposal.

The only problem was that she had no readily-available offensive powers to absorb. Sissy was always an option but her electrical ability was still considerably unpredictable and she really did not want to end up taking a life in the process of using it against someone, even if it *was* a lowlife such as Sharp and whatever goons he had hired.

Jamie then saw the calling card on her bedside table, the one she had received from the man she had saved from an attempted mugging in the street over a fortnight ago by the name of John.

She gave it a thought for a moment; it would only take her ten minutes to fly there while using the sat nav on her phone to direct her while using her borrowed hazing ability, leaving her enough time to travel to Sharp's location afterwards. It would be a long shot but it was an option that in the current situation would prove invaluable if successful.

Wasting no further time, Jamie left the window in Gabrielle's room at the rear of the house unlocked and left without her keys, money or any source of metal on her person besides her phone after closing the front door behind her.

Jamie stood before the Eastwell Charitable House on Denington Street, comparing it to a borderline-dilapidated building but choosing to go inside anyway. According to her phone, she had exactly 42 minutes to meet Sharp.

Within the small foyer area, Jamie walked down a small corridor until she came across a room that was labelled 'John Fulmer's Office'. Hesitantly, she knocked on the door.

"Ah, hello there, Miss Jamie," John said upon opening the door. "What an unexpected surprise."

"Hello, John," Jamie replied. "Can I have a word?"

"Certainly, if you'd like. What does it concern?"

"It's best if I sit down and explain it."

"Okay, well I'll do my very best to listen," John said as he walked back behind his desk and sat down with Jamie sitting opposite him. "So how can I be of help?"

"Do you remember the mugging attempt that I intervened in before?" she asked.

"Yes, it was hard to forget. Not the most pleasant of experiences."

"Well I knocked the guy down initially with something you'll either believe or be surprised by, but I'm guessing the former."

"What do you mean?"

"Watch my arm," Jamie said as she fired a weak kinetic energy wave at the floor. John heard a loud thud ring out upon the invisible force striking the floor, not enough to damage it but enough to cause the noise.

"How did you do that?" John asked, not appearing as shocked as Jamie would have expected from someone witnessing such a thing for the first time.

"Believe it or not, I have the ability to project kinetic energy by swinging my arm," she replied. "I can actually absorb abilities from others who have them and use them for myself. The energy ability belongs to my friend as it was what I used to defend you from the mugger."

"I would have had to see it to believe it," John remarked.

"The reason I came by was because I believe you have your own talents," Jamie quickly moved on.

"I'm not sure I follow," John responded, looking uneasy.

"When he aimed a punch at me, it impossibly missed. My ability also detects the active use of other powers and that sprung to life at that exact moment. I can't confirm it of course but I believe someone telekinetically diverted his punch away from my face. And I believe that person to be you."

"Miss Jamie, I'm afraid I can't entertain these absurd accusations," John sat up, visibly irritated. "I do thank you for your help on that day but I do have a lot of work to do so maybe it's best that you take your leave."

"John, this is your one chance to be open about who you are, what you have," Jamie attempted to reason, hoping she was right. "You don't have to be afraid, I won't judge you for it. I completely understand what it feels like to have something like this that isn't fully understood and can't be shared with the world at large for fear of repercussion. You can confide in me."

John stood hesitantly at the desk for several seconds before looking downwards.

"It's been a great test of my resolve to come to terms with this thing," he stated. "As a man of faith, it is almost incompatible having a psychic ability when it is the thing of evil."

"You are not a person of evil though, John."

"I'm afraid that is beside the point," he argued. "This unnatural thing that I possess, for whatever reason, it has long felt a curse. Ever since I discovered it all those decades ago, I have fought the temptation to ever use it or even acknowledge it within me. And as I realised yet again the other day, I cannot help myself."

"You saved me from serious harm; an evil person would not have done that."

"Again, beside the point."

"I am not a Christian person, John. But whatever your belief in your powers, you do not use them selfishly nor in vanity. At least not in my presence anyway."

"We could go back on forth on this endlessly, my child," John responded. "But I get the feeling you didn't come all the way to see me just to convince me this power of mine is benevolent."

"You're right, I didn't."

"Then what is actually on your mind?"

Jamie gave him a hard but weary look.

"What's on my mind, is that someone very close to me is currently on the verge of being seriously harmed or worse, at the hands of some maniac who abducted people like you and me for experimentation in order to understand and utilise our special abilities. And he is expecting me to meet him in less than 40 minutes to face whatever onslaught he has in store for when I arrive."

"Are you asking for my help?" John interrupted. "Because I'm afraid I cannot be a party to that with my powers."

"I'm not asking that of you," Jamie replied. "What I'm asking is to allow me to absorb your telekinesis so I can use it to save my friend and bring this individual to justice."

John stared back at her in concentration.

"You should call the police and let them deal with it," he responded.

"I could be sending them to their deaths," Jamie rebutted. "In case you haven't seen the news lately, someone with seemingly magnetic powers or otherwise completely managed to mangle a double decker bus. I can't risk putting unprepared and probably disbelieving police officers in that line of fire. And to do so would be to put my friend in further jeopardy. With your powers at my disposal, I can catch the culprit and whoever he has working for him off guard and save my friend with little bloodshed or injury to anyone. Surely you agree with that?"

"I don't disagree with your approach at all, but for whatever reason I was given these powers, they are mine to bear the burden of alone. I will not allow them to corrupt anyone else."

"They won't corrupt me! You can trust me with them, John!"

"I thought the same in my younger years, Miss Jamie," John spoke in a lower tone. "But I let them get the better of me and I ended up doing stupid and, at times, horrible things with them. I have spent nearly 30 years fighting against the temptation to use them, even for good because I know they are truly a negative force in this world. Using them to prevent you being harmed last time we met was one thing but I can't let you have them, they will try to destroy you like they did me."

Jamie felt complete disappointment in the decision, getting up from her seat and preparing to storm off. Then she had another thought pass through her head.

"If the powers are a burden to you, then why don't I simply remove them?"

"What do you mean?" John asked, surprised that Jamie had decided to turn and speak to him further.

"I don't just absorb powers – I can also deactivate them. I can remove the temptation to use them completely from you."

John looked sceptically back at her.

"You don't believe me, do you?"

"Forgive me, I just don't know why you are only offering that now after I refused to give you what you wanted."

"Because I'm not heartless," Jamie responded. "If your powers have taken such a toll on your life, let me allow you to live it without further worry."

John still looked hesitantly back at her.

"It's only an offer, John. Yes, I am a bit bummed that you won't let me have it to help my friend but if it'll make you happier with yourself, I don't mind helping you."

Jamie stared back into John's eyes, sensing a lot of reluctance but hoping he would accept.

"What would I need to do?" he finally replied.

"Hold your hand out and activate your powers," Jamie said, trying to contain her glee. "I'll take hold and deactivate it. It should be turned off once I'm done."

"Will I feel anything?"

“Maybe a tingling sensation or a rush of energy but you’ll know when you try to use them again and nothing works.”

“Okay then,” John said, holding his hand out. Jamie felt absolutely awful but she knew it was for the greater good. She took John’s outstretched hand and began absorbing his telekinesis, feeling it surging into her body rapidly until she could no longer feel any more of it draining into her.

“It’s done,” she said. “Try it.”

John attempted to levitate a pen sitting on his desk, finding that he was unable to do so.

“You did it,” he said, though notably without as much relief as Jamie expected. “Is it gone forever?”

“I can’t guarantee that,” Jamie half-lied while making it sound like the truth. “But I can always return to do it again if it doesn’t.”

“I urge you to get the police involved in your matter, Jamie. It’s better than nothing.”

“I suppose I will,” she replied as she turned to leave. “I’ll let you know how it all goes though.”

“Please forgive me for not being more help to you.”

“Don’t worry – I already have.”

Chapter 21

Jamie arrived at the yard where the two small warehouses were situated. She attempted to detect any ability nearby but came up with nothing.

Her concentration was then broken by the sound of a rusty door swinging open, noticing that it came from the warehouse to her right. She was definitely getting a déjà vu vibe about the whole thing but just like the experience with the rapist, she had no intentions of losing whatever fight she was about to walk into, particularly not with her new secret weapon. And she couldn't forget that Jesse's life was very much on the line too.

She then put her phone down by the nearest bush, the only thing she had on her that contained metal, and slowly approached the open door.

"Miss Avonoit. Good of you to join us!"

Jamie looked aghast at the sight beholden to her at the other end of the warehouse – next to Ryan Sharp was Jesse with his hands impaled by long nails to the wall as well as sporting a bloodied face.

"You managed to arrive even faster than I thought," Sharp continued. "Guess your boyfriend really means a lot to you."

"Where's your goons?" Jamie said, seething but confused at the lack of hired hands on standby to attack as she assumed.

"I don't have any," Sharp replied. "I don't have anything anymore. You saw to that, when you sent the police after me. All my accounts are frozen and I'm currently being subjected to a manhunt. But thankfully they didn't think to track me down at one of my unlisted properties."

"If you don't have anyone helping you, how the hell did you kidnap Jesse?"

"Well funny story; it turns out he's actually partly responsible for his own abduction," Sharp sneered while grabbing Jesse's hair forcefully. "Me, Dawn and Dr Murphy managed to escape my facility soon after the two of you fled, managing to get as far as Derbyshire and with all of our accumulated research into abilities. That also included that of your pal here."

Jamie suddenly felt as though she knew where the conversation was going.

"Luckily I had a laboratory up in the midlands as a back-up in case of emergencies like this and it was there that the good doctor finally managed to achieve what we had been striving for since we began this operation – being able to implant a replicated ability into regular human beings. I'll give you a clue as to who the successful guinea pig was."

"So you're the one who trashed that bus?" Jamie responded.

"Wasn't too hard when you have the power of magnetism at your disposal," he answered, confirming Jamie's suspicions. "Of course I couldn't have gained that power without Jesse's ability here being the base power that I had implanted into me. It even came with all his absorbed abilities too, a real package deal if I do say so. And with Dawn's power sensing ability absorbed, I can track anyone I want and gain their powers."

"A monumental achievement(!)" Jamie replied with contempt. "So is this just a massive temper tantrum then?"

"You really shouldn't be trying to piss me off right now."

"What do you plan to do? Torture Jesse in front of me?"

"You took my life away from me," Sharp said as his expression turned darker. "I had everything and was soon to become even more than that until you ruined everything. So no, I didn't summon you here to torture your friend in front of you. What I brought you here for is to witness me destroying something that means the world to you instead!"

As Sharp raised his hand towards Jesse, Jamie quickly used her absorbed telekinesis to fling him away towards the other side of the room. As she then rushed to Jesse, Sharp commanded a barrage of nails magnetically, sending them flying in her direction.

Acting instinctively, Jamie used telekinesis to divert the nails into the wall beside Jesse where they became embedded. Sharp then attempted to use his magnetism on Jamie, only to find it having no effect.

"No metal on you then?" he said.

"Not when you were stupid enough to broadcast the fact you had such an ability on the news," Jamie fired back.

“Well that’s the fun of luring you to an environment where there’s tons of the stuff just lying around,” Sharp responded as he launched a discarded crowbar straight at Jamie who was forced to block its trajectory to prevent it hitting the defenceless Jesse behind her. She soon found that Sharp’s power of magnetism was relatively even matched against her telekinesis, the only problem being that she only had a finite supply compared to his so dragging the bout on was not in her best interest.

With that in mind, Jamie exerted an extra amount of force into the crowbar to divert it into the wall just above Jesse’s head. She then hurled Sharp with telekinesis towards the open door before launching herself at him with her flight, tackling him mid-air and out into the yard.

Jesse, noticing that the spikes through his hands pinning him to the wall lacked rounded ends, slowly attempted to free himself by bringing his arms forward slowly. As his punctured hands moved half an inch along the nails, the resulting horrendously painful sensation he felt doing so forced him to stop. However, he knew he was completely useless remaining where he was and tried once more to summon the courage to bear the agony.

Outside, Jamie stared down Sharp as they both landed on their feet using their respective flight abilities after freeing themselves from the mid-air grapple.

“Not as much metal out here,” she taunted.

“More than you’d expect,” Sharp replied, causing several embedded metal objects from the ground to come forth and attack Jamie, who was forced to take to the air to avoid them all.

Undeterred, Sharp simply directed the dozens of objects to give chase. Jamie could only look back upon realisation that trying to outfly the barrage was nearly impossible and swooped low near her adversary, hoping to catch him with his own missiles.

Sharp, however, simply used flight himself to dodge to the side and avoided Jamie completely before commanding the swarm of objects to surround her mid-air until she was practically encased within a sphere of them.

Jamie hovered as she tried to telekinetically move a large amount of the shrapnel out of her way to enable an escape but was suddenly struck in the shoulder from a piece of metal from behind which broke her concentration.

She then focused her telekinesis on pushing back the entirety of the sphere of objects as Sharp directed them to envelop her. Jamie knew she would have to find a way to break through the 360 degree barrage quickly before her limited supply of John's ability gave out, which was being heavily drained by the force of the magnetically-powered onslaught.

As Ryan looked on with maniacal glee, he was unexpectedly barged into from behind. As he fell to the floor, his concentration broke on controlling his magnetism ability and the swarm of metal objects trying to close in on Jamie immediately fell to the floor.

Sharp turned around and saw Jesse standing before him, blood dripping from the holes in his hands having managed to agonisingly free himself from the wall. As he attempted to use his magnetic ability again, he found himself being flung across the yard again telekinetically by Jamie, managing to prevent himself from being slammed into the steel wall of the warehouse by pushing back against it with magnetism.

While maintaining the telekinetic hold on Sharp, Jamie descended to Jesse and placed her hand on the back of his neck, activating the healing ability that was still within her from the previous absorption of it just before infiltrating Sharp's underground facility. Soon, all Jesse's injuries including the holes in his hands were completely restored to normal.

"How long can you keep this up, Jamie?" Jesse asked while Jamie continued to fight against Sharp resisting her telekinetic hold with his magnetic push against the steel wall.

"Not long as this rate, my telekinesis will be drained," she replied. "Have you tried absorbing his magnetism? It might prove useful against him."

"I've been trying since he abducted me, for some reason I can't despite how much I want it a part of me."

"How can that be?"

"I don't know. Maybe my base power won't allow me to absorb replicated powers."

"Guess that means you can't absorb my telekinesis either. At least *he* can't too if that's the case, I don't want to be making him even more powerful while my abilities slowly drain."

"You can always drain his powers too."

"Getting close enough to do so is the problem."

"Right. Get ready to grab hold of him," Jesse said, immediately flying towards Sharp.

Too distracted to sense the approaching flight ability in use with Dawn's absorbed power, Sharp was quickly grappled by Jesse who attempted to choke him out with an arm hold around his throat.

Jamie relinquished her telekinesis and flew quickly over to the two, placing a hand on Sharp's face and attempting to absorb his magnetism ability. Having anticipated the absorption attempt, however, Sharp had already deactivated his magnetism in response.

"I'm not getting anything, Jesse," Jamie said aloud, who was then completely caught off guard by Sharp flying straight into the air and slamming Jesse's still-attached body hard against the warehouse wall to force him to release the choke hold. Sharp then ascended higher as Jesse remained hovering where he was with Jamie watching on from the ground.

"Here's another new one for you!" Sharp called out while holding his palm out towards the sky. Jamie's power sensing immediately picked up on a spike in activity and activated Dawn's absorbed ability to decipher what Sharp was attempting to do.

"Jesse, look out!" she yelled out loud as Sharp aimed a blast of dazzlingly bright energy towards Jesse. Reacting to the warning, Jesse quickly swooped out of the way rather than attempt to block with his shielding ability as the attack crashed straight into the wall of the warehouse.

Jamie and Jesse both looked at the area of impact, seeing a large, scorched imprint on the metal surface.

"What was that?" Jesse asked Jamie as he descended down right beside her.

"Solar energy manipulation," she replied. "How he got his hands on such an ability I can't imagine but it looks pretty deadly."

"Wasn't strong enough to obliterate that structure though, maybe I can block it and we'll have some form of defence against it."

"I think we're going to need something more effective to win this," Jamie replied as she saw Sharp preparing another attack from high in the sky.

"Got any ideas? Because I don't really have much else at my disposal."

"Neither do I. But I know of a power that could probably shut him down without as much effort as trying to get up close to him to deactivate his abilities, which he knows to thwart my attempts to do so."

"And what would that be?"

"Hold on!" Jamie replied as she telekinetically forced Sharp's arm to aim the subsequent follow up blast of solar energy straight into the side of the warehouse once more. "It's an ability that I faced off against once before and it's extremely effective. It's just a matter of locating the individual who has it."

"Can the power sensing ability you took from Sharp's friend help do that?"

"Probably easily enough but I'd need them to be using it."

"Wanna try?"

"I'll need a distraction."

"I can give him something to aim at," Jesse suggested as the pair both saw Sharp summoning a nearby discarded, dilapidated car with magnetism, appearing to be putting extra concentration into the effort owing to its heavier weight than the smaller objects he had been typically conjuring throughout the bout.

"Jesse, he'll kill you."

“Only if you don’t have a follow-up to attack him on his blind side while he’s focused on me.”

“Okay then, give it a go,” Jamie replied as the car came hurtling towards them, narrowly missing them both as they flew in opposite directions to dodge it.

Jesse then levitated right in front of Sharp’s view. The mere sight of Jesse was enough to encourage Sharp to charge another solar energy blast, hoping to take him out right in front of his own friend, the girl who he hated so much for ruining his life.

Out of nowhere, he felt an overwhelmingly painful sensation emanating from his left thigh, looking down to see a sharp, metal rod protruding through his upper leg. Completely overcome with agony, Sharp began slowly descending to the ground, Jesse floating down to Jamie’s position several feet away.

“Pretty brutal, Jame,” Jesse said.

“Yeah, well now he knows how *you* felt. But crippling his body isn’t the problem; it’s his pesky abilities and my telekinesis has already been pushed too hard, there’s not much left already. Soon I won’t be able to fight him head on so I need to use the time I have now to try and locate that ability I need.”

“And if you can’t?”

“Dunno but he knows where we live so it needs to end here or he’ll simply keep coming after us. Give me a moment but keep an eye on him in the background.”

Jamie began concentrating fully on what she wanted to sense using Dawn’s ability while Jesse looked towards Ryan Sharp, who was struggling to draw the courage to remove the steel rod impaled through his thigh near the warehouse. He then saw Jamie open her eyes.

"I can feel it," she said.

"Can you get it?"

"If I hunt it down now, goodness knows how long it'll be in active use for though."

"I'll stick around, make sure he doesn't leave the area."

"Don't do anything stupid, Jesse," Jamie warned. "I'm going to fly as fast as I can, I should be back in ten minutes if I'm quick enough. The source doesn't feel massively far away."

"Head off now then while you still can," Jesse replied.

"Back soon," Jamie said, taking to the sky while activating her sustained hazing power.

Back on the ground, Jesse kept a close monitor on Sharp as he attempted to extract the rod from his leg with magnetism, managing only a slight movement but causing so much pain in the process that he was forced to hold off attempting it further. Jesse simply hoped that he would continue to struggle with his predicament until Jamie would return with her apparent problem-solving power.

Jamie landed atop a high-rise block of flats and attempted to sense out the ability again; she could feel it being activated constantly on and off but enough to be able to get a reading on it. It was close and she could see from where she was currently positioned to where it was likely located.

She took to the air once more while reactivating her haze ability and flew for half a minute until she found herself hovering over a prison yard.

Descending but maintaining the haze, Jamie began moving from window to window, checking each one as she did. Eventually, she stopped outside one in particular and used her telekinesis to forcibly extract the glass window from the frame, leaving just the bars on the inside. She then approached the open hole and looked inside the cell.

Jesse watched nervously as Ryan Sharp continued in his attempts to remove the metal rod from his leg, having managed to get it almost out with a few inches remaining.

What Sharp would try and do after it was fully removed he could only guess; it would be far too painful surely to continue his efforts but he appeared to have very little to lose and that made him an extremely unpredictable foe. His magnetism, flight and solar energy manipulation abilities also did not rely on being able to physically engage anyone, probably the main reason Jamie had prioritised gaining her apparent game-changing power.

After two more gruelling minutes, Sharp finally succeeded in pulling out the rod. Jesse watched as he hovered lightly above the ground before descending once more from the pain of the air breezing through the hole in his thigh.

Desperately, he removed his jacket and pulled off his t-shirt in order to wrap it around the wound. The makeshift bandage immediately became blood-stained but appeared to allow Sharp to take to the air without causing as much discomfort. Jesse knew he would have to get involved soon enough to prevent him from leaving.

Ryan looked around the yard as the pain continued to radiate around his thigh, seeing no sign of the duo still being around. He attempted to detect any nearby abilities with Dawn's power, sensing someone using flight in the distance.

"Prepare to suffer a fate worse than death," he muttered to himself angrily as he steadily ascended into the air. He then felt another flight power being used very close to his current location, looking around and seeing Jesse perched upon the roof of the warehouse.

"Are you just a glutton for punishment?" Sharp called out.

"Are *you*?" Jesse flippantly replied, hoping to be able to handle himself for at least another five minutes if Jamie's estimation was accurate.

Without further hesitation, Sharp quickly charged a solar energy attack and fired it straight at Jesse. The lag of the charge up period though was enough for Jesse to avoid the blast easily as it tore into the metal roof of the building. He then flew directly at Sharp who was caught off guard by the sudden counter attack, attempting a barely-charged beam of energy but was grappled by Jesse and locked in a bear hug.

"Think I owe you for the abduction and beating from earlier," he stated while driving a hard fist directly into Sharp's wounded thigh and immediately flying away as the maniac screamed in pain. While a worthwhile tactic, Jesse knew it was only going to make him angrier and he was far outclassed in terms of offensive capabilities but while Sharp's attention was fully on him, he would hopefully not be picking up on Jamie's return.

Still in pain, Ryan summoned his magnetic ability to direct the same bloodied metal rod that had gravely injured him straight at Jesse, hoping to enact the same punishment. Jesse began dodging it as it attempted to spike him right through his torso, immediately coming back towards him.

As it quickly rebounded to try again, Jesse blocked it with his shielding ability, holding it at bay as it tried to break through the barrier.

Jesse then found himself being grabbed from behind and his arms pinned down by his sides, having completely neglected to maintain any awareness on Sharp himself while focusing on his shielding ability. The barrier dissipated with the break in concentration, allowing Sharp to direct the metal rod straight into the front of Jesse's left shoulder, though not deep enough to inadvertently impale himself in the process. Jesse yelled in agony as he felt the sharp object driving slowly into his upper body.

"Thought your shoulder might like to feel exactly how my leg does!" Sharp maliciously said as he drove the rod in by another inch.

"I can heal you!" Jesse exclaimed through the pain.

"Liar!"

"Check your power sensing ability, you know I can do it," Jesse pleaded in desperation. "It's the only way your wound will heal if you refuse to go to the hospital as a wanted fugitive. I can fix it in seconds."

"And why would you do that?" Sharp growled, though curious at the offer considering the fact he indeed could not submit himself to medical aid without risking the threat of arrest.

"Remove the spike and I'll do it."

"You try anything and it goes through your head," Sharp replied, quickly removing the rod with his magnetism ability to Jesse's pain but overall relief.

Ignoring the gaping wound in his shoulder, Jesse slid down the makeshift bandage on Sharp's thigh and began activating his healing ability, albeit as slowly as he could.

Sharp, detecting the use of the power with Dawn's sensing ability to verify Jesse's claim, slowly began to feel the pain in his leg beginning to dissipate. Jesse continued to draw the process out for at least a minute compared to the usual few seconds it would've otherwise normally taken, still in the hope that Jamie would return soon to save him.

After another half-minute, Sharp could feel the pain having completely gone.

"Thank you," he stated before magnetically commanding the metal rod to fly horizontally towards Jesse's throat, pressing up against it with Sharp grabbing both ends while pressing his knees into Jesse's back. Jesse attempted to push back against the bar with his hands but his weakened shoulder was hampering his efforts in combination of the advantageous positioning of Sharp.

"Believe me when I say I'm going to enjoy choking you to death and dismembering your corpse for your little girlfriend to discover," Sharp gleefully stated.

Jesse attempted a last ditch effort to activate his burning ability to force Sharp to release his hold on the bar but the power would not activate with his quickly fading state of consciousness. As extreme panic began to set in believing it to be the end, Jesse found himself passing out from the lack of oxygen.

Sharp could no longer feel resistance, though continued to apply pressure to make sure Jesse was truly dead.

Suddenly, he felt his arms being forced out into a crucifix position as his power sensing ability sprang into life, detecting the use of telekinesis as well as flight and took a heavy blow from between his shoulder blades that nearly dislocated them in the process.

Jamie watched both Sharp and Jesse rapidly falling through the air, rushing forward to catch her unconscious friend and lowering him to the ground. As she turned to face Sharp once more, she was struck by the metal rod along its length straight in the stomach and pinned down to the ground by it as it bent around her waist and the ends lodged themselves into the concrete surface.

Sharp looked angrily down at his now defenceless nemesis, beginning to charge another solar energy blast in his hands. Though he had hoped to draw out Avonoit's agony, he had grown weary of all the sneak attacks against him and had settled for simply killing her as swiftly as possible.

Jamie looked on and aimed her palm towards Sharp, only for the metal rod restraining her to tighten with magnetism, the pain causing her to drop her attempt at a counter attack. She felt extreme anxiety as the glowing aura in Sharp's hands began to peak.

"Enjoy hell, you pair of arseholes!" Sharp yelled as he unleashed the energy blast straight at Jamie and the unconscious Jesse lying on the ground.

As she saw the beam of energy surging towards her head-on, Jamie raised her hands once more and put every last bit of effort into activating her newly-acquired ability and hoped for the best.

Just as the blast looked as though it was about to make contact, it suddenly began to rapidly dissipate into nothing.

Sharp looked on in disbelief, attempting to conjure another attack but finding himself unable to with Jamie maintaining her outstretched hands from below. He then attempted to tighten the metal rod restraining her again with magnetism but found that that was no longer activating either.

Jamie then used some of her remaining telekinesis to force the bent rod off from round her waist and then immediately used her borrowed healing ability on Jesse lying next to her. To her relief, he eventually came round with a large gasp of air.

"What happened?" he asked in a disorientated state.

"I'm about to make Sharp my bitch," Jamie gave a confident smirk as she used her flight to quickly ascend towards the confused Ryan Sharp still hovering in mid-air. He attempted to charge another solar energy attack, managing to succeed only for it to quickly fail once more as Jamie approached with a single hand thrust up towards him.

Trying again in a last ditch effort to launch an offensive, Sharp instead was grabbed by the throat by Jamie who immediately began deactivating the solar energy manipulation ability with her own innate power and locking on her grip with continued telekinesis, preventing her foe from trying to wrench her off.

With the deactivation complete, Jamie then began draining the flight ability from Sharp and into her own body while he remained powerless to stop her.

After nearly a minute, Jamie relinquished her telekinetic hold and allowed Sharp to plummet helplessly through the air before stopping him from hitting the ground with John's borrowed ability once more before descending herself.

"What do you think I'm going to do with you now?" she taunted Sharp in a threatening tone as he remained held in place by telekinesis.

"How did you turn off my powers?" Sharp begrudgingly asked, a hint of fear in his voice.

"I went and visited an old friend and he allowed me to absorb his energy disruption ability," Jamie replied with a smug look on her face. "Once I neutralised your magnetism and prevented your solar energy attacks with that, I just had to take out your other ones with my own ability. Maybe if you hadn't been so deranged in trying to kill me, you might've thought to detect what I did yourself."

Sharp gave a sullen look, refusing to respond.

"You taunting me in my cell that day knowing I was supposed to forget it all anyway due to your memory-erasing drugs was your biggest mistake; in that one act of pointless arrogance, I knew you would apply that same attitude to your newly-gained powers and you didn't disappoint. Gaining that energy disrupting ability was indeed luck but you made it possible for me to get it in the first place with your carelessness. And in a way, I don't blame you – I was once like that too with my ability but unlike you I had people around me to steer me away from that reckless and self-absorbed attitude."

"Whoop-de-f'ing-do," Sharp scornfully remarked. In response, Jamie telekinetically ripped out a part of the chain link fence surrounding the yard area and wrapped it around Sharp's body, completely immobilising him.

"Let's see how *you* enjoy being thrown in a cell to rot," Jamie said as she used telekinesis to summon her phone from where she had left it lying prior to the bout before levitating the helpless Sharp into the air, flying up into the sky with him in tow.

Tom sat at the main desk carefully eyeing the clock up on the wall. The junior police officer had had more interesting days, the highlight so far having been to deal with a stolen bicycle report which he knew would be near impossible to investigate anyway owing to a lack of available security camera footage. The end of his shift couldn't come soon enough.

A loud banging noise erupted from the front door, as though someone had smacked into the glass window. Tom got out of his seat to investigate, being completely surprised to find a conscious person lying on the other side of the door completely encased in a layer of metal fencing.

"Are you alright?" he said as he approached the trussed up individual. He then realised who he was talking to upon seeing the unfortunate person's face before reaching for the communicator mounted on his vest.

"I need immediate back-up outside the front of the station now," he spoke.

Epilogue

Jesse rested on the floor of the rooftop, feeling content as he saw a familiar cloud descending down towards him from high in the sky. The haze then quickly faded as Jamie touched down next to him.

"All go according to plan?" he said, levitating to his feet.

"Yeah," Jamie replied. "Still a bit weary of having left him with the police considering his powers will restore to normal function eventually. Didn't really know what else to do with him though."

"Maybe they'll just end up shooting him if he tries anything stupid."

"Or he'll kill them."

"Might be possible they're actually aware of us now and know how to deal with him."

"Do you really believe that?"

"You never know."

"Maybe," Jamie said, walking over to the edge of the rooftop and resting against the boundary wall with her arms. "Of course that does mean that they could start trying to hunt down and imprison the rest of us if that were the case."

"True," Jesse replied. "Not that we've done anything wrong."

"Well, *you* haven't."

"What, your scuffles from before you met me? Doubt anyone will come after you for that."

"It's probably what I did to gain that energy-disrupting ability that would see me in hot water."

"I was actually going to ask where you ended up acquiring that," Jesse said, walking up to Jamie.

"The 'donor' was a guy I previously defeated, the reason why that trio came after me at the funfair," Jamie said. "They were part of his gang who were plotting to turn London into a cesspit of anarchy using their powers, until I interfered. I found him in prison when I located his power, which he was using to wind up the guards by constantly disrupting the electricity. I don't know exactly what he got sent down for seeing as I anonymously grassed him up on gang-related activity that could barely be proven but I guess he had done other things that warranted his arrest when they found him.

"I then offered him a deal – his power for his freedom."

"You broke him out of jail?" Jesse asked, shocked at the revelation.

"The alternative was a rampaging Ryan Sharp with the ability to twist metal structures and destroy things with the power of the sun at his disposal," Jamie replied. "I chose the lesser evil."

"Were you seen?"

"Cloaked by your hazing power the whole time; nobody would've picked me up on camera or anything."

"Guess you're off scot-free then," Jesse remarked in relief.

"I hope," Jamie replied. "I'd be a fool to think this is all really over though. Looking back on it, I do have myself to blame. I mean, drawing attention to myself combating others like us to gain their powers the whole time in the first place. I probably never would've been on Sharp's radar had I not made myself a target."

"Had all that not occurred, he might still be abducting people and experimenting on them and ultimately getting away with it."

"Or he might not have ever succeeded in discovering how to transplant abilities into other people like himself, especially not with me leading you to him."

"As much as we can argue about it, I don't really care," Jesse said. "Had you not gone about your hunts for powers, I would've never met you to begin with. And I would be far less happy without you in my life."

Jamie bowed her head, trying not to show any emotion but couldn't help but feeling touched by the kind words. Instead, she approached Jesse and locked him in a hug.

"You are the soppiest git in the world, you know that?" she jokingly remarked.

"Love you too, Jame," Jesse joked back. Jamie enjoyed the warmth of the embrace, still frustrated with her seemingly unrequited feelings but nonetheless happy to have such a wonderful friend in her life, and that was better than nothing at all.

"What do you wanna do now?" Jesse asked.

"Watching films round yours until Kayleigh comes home from school, then Monopoly?" Jamie replied, relinquishing the hug.

"Sounds like fun as always, especially after the morning we've had."

"And we're ordering in pizza too."

"That goes without saying," Jesse smiled as he began levitating off the rooftop, with Jamie doing the same.

"Race you to yours," she said as they both activated their hazing powers.

"See you there," Jesse replied as they both flew off into the sky.

Acknowledgements

To think if you had told me back in 2011 when I started writing this novel that I would ever see it being made into a physical book or e-book format, I probably would've liked to believe it but deep down would've known it would never happen owing to my laziness and lack of general ambitions. And I suppose that's where my first, not so humble, thanks goes to – myself for eventually realising that things require hard work, dedication and realistic expectations in order to succeed (which I somehow did not grasp the concept of even in the midst of labouring over thousands of words worth of dissertations during my university years a decade prior when earning my degree!).

On a more serious round of acknowledgements, it goes without saying that I owe a lot to my family and friends, without whom I would never have managed to find the opportunities and gain the experiences to even think of bringing this novel to fruition, and even after I succeeded in getting it published. And of course, helping to keep me grounded enough to not want to give up all hope in the midst of the years of chronic depression that have plagued my adult life (and which you all continue to help me through to this very day when it tries to rear it's ugly head once more).

Then there's certain people and things in life that I suppose warrant an acknowledgement (not to be confused with thanks) for influencing my novel despite my outright dislike and even loathing towards them but then, you have to take the good with the bad and vice versa.

Thus, I would include mentions to the likes of unscrupulous politicians who regularly plunge the lesser off into poverty and despair normally while gaining something for their own benefit in the process; sexual predators who strike terror into the hearts of women (and men) while turning their lives upside down with their abhorrent actions and attitudes; greedy business owners who take in record profits while failing to pass it on to their employees when the cost of living is increasingly hard enough as it is in the face of price and tax hikes; manipulative sociopaths who haven't an ounce of shame towards taking advantage of people, vulnerable or otherwise, for their own gratification; and finally, the wretched depression that sees thousands of lives lost every year of people who feel the only escape from it is to depart this physical realm no matter how much they're leaving behind.

And why acknowledge such detestable aspects of society? Well I've often found that trying to ignore such things and problems can be even more detrimental than if you were to openly point them out. I've learned more things than I ever would've thought possible from people talking out loud about such grievances and I hope that this book will be another contribution to the overall discussion.

But most of all, let us be there for one another and check in on those you know, even if nothing seems obviously wrong. You never know just how much of a difference you'll be making.